SPINE DAMAGE

SPINE DAMAGE

SHARON ST. GEORGE

W🌐RLDWIDE®

TORONTO • NEW YORK • LONDON
AMSTERDAM • PARIS • SYDNEY • HAMBURG
STOCKHOLM • ATHENS • TOKYO • MILAN
MADRID • WARSAW • BUDAPEST • AUCKLAND

Recycling programs for this product may not exist in your area.

Spine Damage

A Worldwide Mystery/November 2019

First published in 2017 by Camel Press,
an imprint of Epicenter Press Inc.
This edition published in 2019 with revised text.

ISBN-13: 978-1-335-45563-5

Printed in U.S.A.

ACKNOWLEDGMENTS

With thanks to my dependable and talented critique members Chloe Winston, Laura Hernandez, Ellen Jellison, and Vickie Linnet for spotting the bloopers in my early drafts. Thanks to fellow members of Sisters in Crime and Guppies for their constant support and encouragement and to the Crime Scene Writers Group for help with forensic details. To Eric and Susan Feamster for answering questions about medical interpreters and for describing the reality of caring for coma patients. My deepest appreciation goes to Jennifer McCord and Catherine Treadgold for their masterful editing skills, and for their professional and caring approach to making my work the best it can be.

ONE

JARED QUINN BURST into the Timbergate Medical Center Library minutes after I arrived for work on a sunny Thursday morning, dashing my hopes for a tranquil June day.

"Machado, are your parents still here?"

The administrator knew that my parents were visiting from the Azores, but I was puzzled by his question and his demeanor. He stood across from my desk, shoulders stiff and jaw clenched, waiting for my answer.

"Yes. They're at the waffle place down the block right now, having breakfast with my brother. After that, they're coming by the library—"

Quinn cut me off. "Call them, Aimee. See how fast they can get here."

"Why? What's going on?"

"A gunshot victim just arrived in the Emergency Room. He doesn't speak English and has no ID and no phone. Dr. Preston can't communicate with him, other than a word or two that resembles Spanish. He thinks the man's speaking Portuguese."

"None of our medical interpreters speak it?"

"There's only one on the list who's fluent in Portuguese. He's out of town. Some family thing. Wedding, funeral… I'm not sure." He tapped a finger on my desk. "Has your mother kept up her credentials?"

I understood why he was asking. My parents had retired two years earlier and were living in the Azores, where Dad had inherited property in the port city of Horta on the island of Faial. Before retiring, Mom had been on TMC's list of medical interpreters. Though my father is Portuguese and my mother is Chinese, it was my mother's help that Quinn needed.

I answered with my phone in my hand. "Yes, she's current. She's been interpreting for a hospital in Horta. How much time do we have?"

"Not much." Quinn glanced at his watch. "The neurosurgeon is fifteen minutes out. They're trying to stabilize the patient in the ED, but he'll be transported to an operating room as soon as possible." My usually well groomed boss was obviously stressed. His dark, wavy hair looked a little wild, and his tie had flipped back-side out. "Ask them to hurry," he said. "A couple of policemen are hoping to question the patient before he goes into surgery."

Mom answered right away. I explained the situation, and she agreed to come immediately. I hung up and told Quinn my parents were on their way.

He backpedaled toward the exit. "Tell them thanks. I'll take care of the paperwork. Come over to the ED as soon as you can." He hurried out with his phone to his ear.

I admired Quinn for coming to the library in person to explain the situation. A bachelor with a memorable smile, he was easy on the eyes and nice to be around, but it was his compassion for patients over concern for revenue that made working for him rewarding. His rugged good looks and muscular build belied the stereotype of the soft-bodied, heartless hospital administrator.

I closed the library and headed across the hospital complex to the Emergency Department. When my mom and dad arrived, Quinn introduced them to Dr. Preston. I appreciated the care Quinn took to pronounce our family name, *Ma-SHAW-doe*, correctly.

My mother and the doctor entered the trauma room, where the patient still awaited transfer to surgery. Two police officers went in with them, while Dad stood by just outside the door, along with Quinn and me.

I raised my eyebrows at Quinn. *Do I stay or go back to the library?*

He shrugged his answer, which I interpreted as, *Suit yourself.*

If there was anything to learn from the patient, my mother would be able to help. Opting to go back to work, I invited Dad to come with me to the library, but he chose to wait for Mom.

I asked the nurse at the ED desk to send my parents to the library when my mother was finished. Back across the hospital complex, in the building that housed the library, I began my usual morning routine by checking email. Most of the messages were requests for resources in the form of articles from the medical journals in our database. I spotted a terse email from Cleo Cominoli, Director of Medical Staff Services, a close friend as well as my most trusted colleague. *Call me.*

Cleo was at least ten years my senior, a full-figured and feisty Italian who grew up in Brooklyn but found her way to Timbergate, my hometown of ninety thousand residents, in rural Northern California. She had lost her accent, but not the spirit and toughness that kept more than three hundred doctors on our medical staff in line. When she wanted to talk, it was wise to find out what was on her mind. I punched the number I kept on speed dial.

"What took you so long?" she said.

"Sorry, something came up." I explained about the gunshot patient.

"I just heard a few minutes ago. Didn't realize you and your parents were involved."

"They're still in the ED, but they'll be coming by the library when they're finished. Why did you ask me to call?"

"I wanted to give you a heads-up about Dr. Carver. He's probably going to show up in your library. If not today, then soon."

"Dr. Carver? That would be a first. Why?" Dr. Godfrey Carver was a gifted neurosurgeon, known for enjoying fast cars and fast women in spite of being married and approaching sixty. He liked to tell new acquaintances, "*Just call me God.*" Carver might have been an attractive man once, but time had not been kind, leaving him balding and jowly, with dark, bushy eyebrows.

"His medical staff membership is up for renewal this month," Cleo said, "but there's a problem."

"Really? What's the problem, and why does it involve me?"

"The obstacle is his continuing medical education credits. He's fallen short of the fifty credits he needs for renewal."

"How short?" I asked.

"He wouldn't say. I took that to mean he's seriously in arrears."

"I get it," I said. "Carver hasn't been doing his homework. TMC's bylaws say he can't renew his medical staff membership if his CME credits are deficient."

"Exactly right," Cleo said. "You've learned well."

"How much time does he have?"

"Until the end of the month, but that's only two

weeks from today. It may not be long enough, depending on how many credits he has to make up."

"If it's the full fifty, he's going to be a busy boy," I said, "even if he's doing most of it online."

"He has a demanding solo practice to maintain at the same time," Cleo said. "Carver isn't a gracious fellow at his best, so be prepared. And make sure he understands that we have to handle this by the book."

On my first day as an employee, Cleo met with me to explain how continuing medical education was tied in with the privilege of medical staff membership. The renewal of membership and privileges coincides with the renewal of state medical licenses, which happens every other year, in the physician's birthday month.

Cleo requests license confirmations from the medical board. If the state board has renewed the medical license, the physician's TMC membership renewal request goes to the TMC Credentials Committee and works its way up the chain of appropriate medical staff committees until it reaches the governing board. It's an exacting process, and most patients have no clue that it is going on behind the scenes.

A dilemma arises at times because the Medical Board of California accepts the physician's certified, signed statement that he or she has completed the required continuing education credits, but the TMC Medical Staff Organization isn't so trusting. If Carver didn't show proof of his CME credits, his medical staff membership would be suspended as of midnight on his birthday.

"Are you saying the state board went ahead with his license renewal?"

"Apparently so. He's paid his renewal fee and passed their scrutiny. He's had no disciplinary actions by a government agency or other disciplinary body, and he hasn't been convicted of any crime in any state."

"So, according to the state board, his license has been renewed, but TMC's medical staff still won't renew his membership or privileges?"

"That's what I'm saying. Even if the doctors on our medical staff sign the certification of completed CME hours on the state's renewal application, our credentials committee wants proof. Apparently, TMC has had some cheaters in the past who put the hospital's accreditation standing in jeopardy."

"They claimed they'd done the work when they hadn't?"

"Right. And when they were audited by the state after the fact, the truth came out that they'd been practicing without a license in good standing. No one here wants to see that happen again."

"Of course not. This situation hasn't come up since I was hired," I said. "Any advice?"

I heard Cleo's heavy sigh. "You can imagine how steamed Carver is. Knowing him, he'll try to get you to dummy up some CME credits. He tried to convince me that he's already earned the necessary fifty, but I told him he was barking up the wrong tree." She made a derisive noise that sounded a little like a snort. "I told him you're in charge of TMC's continuing education program."

I had to laugh. Cleo wasn't intimidated by doctors. She had probably used those exact words. *Barking up the wrong tree.*

"Sorry, I didn't realize this was his year to renew, or I'd have been looking more closely at his total credits. I didn't see him on the list of pending renewals you usually provide."

"Don't apologize. A new trainee prepared the list

from our database, and she somehow missed his name. The buck stops with me on medical staff renewals and I should have checked her work. Besides, you only have stats on the credits Carver's earned through TMC's education programs. He claims he's done most of his continuing education through other sources."

"If that's true, he shouldn't have any trouble providing proof."

"That's what I said, but by that time, he was so angry he stormed out of my office muttering about incompetence and threatening to raise hell—blah, blah, blah." Cleo laughed. "Sorry, it's not funny, but his comb-over flopped down off the top of his head as he stomped out of my office. It looked so funny, hanging there alongside his ear." She snickered. "Wish you could have seen that."

"Glad I didn't," I said, "but thanks for the heads-up. He's in for another disappointment if he comes to me."

"Even so, I wanted you to be prepared." Cleo had recovered from her giggles. "He mentioned he'll be tied up in surgeries all day today, so he might not get to you until tomorrow. When he does, he'll try everything to get you to cave."

"His timing isn't good. I'm taking tomorrow off and Nick and I are flying my parents home to the Azores this weekend. We're going to be vacationing there all of next week. If Carver's problem isn't resolved while I'm gone, I'll do what I can to make this work out for him and the hospital when I get back."

"I'll see what I can do in the meantime," Cleo said. "I feel somewhat responsible for not catching this sooner. If Carver raises too much of a stink while you're gone, I'll get Dr. Poole to step in."

Dr. Phyllis Poole was the medical supervisor of our

continuing education program and chair of the hospital's CME Committee. An exceptional urologic surgeon, she was fearless in the OR and in the conference room. Carver wouldn't have any better luck with her than he had with Cleo. Both women were impervious to sweet talk or intimidation.

With the emails and Cleo's call out of the way, I was about to walk back to the ED for a progress report when Mom and Dad entered the library, holding hands. To my proud eyes, they're still an attractive couple who look young for their years. Dad is strong and muscled, with sun-bronzed skin and a thick shock of salt-and-pepper hair. Mom has delicate Asian features and a petite figure. Their combined genes resulted in my black hair, and dark brown eyes. I owe my physical strength to years of my father's coaching in jujitsu, and my height of five four to my mother. Thanks to her, a subtle hint of Asian ancestry in my eyes and cheekbones sometimes prompts people to ask if I'm Hawaiian.

"How did it go?" I guided them over to a reading area where we could sit around a table.

Compassion etched my mother's brow. "His name is Paulo Ferrera. He's definitely Portuguese. From the Azores."

"Which island?"

Dad answered, giving Mom's hand a comforting squeeze. "He's from Pico, our nearest neighbor. How about that?"

Faial, where my parents live, and Pico are the two islands situated closest in the nine-island Atlantic archipelago. Only a thirty-minute ferry ride separates them. Pico takes its name from the volcanic Mt. Pico, one of the highest Atlantic mountains.

"Were you able to help the police?" I asked.

"I'm not sure." Mom's forehead creased. "I was able to interpret what the patient was mumbling, but it was mostly anxiety about his sister. In spite of his dismal prognosis, he was only concerned about her. If he survives, he could end up permanently paralyzed by the bullet in his spine. He kept begging to be taken home to Pico if he dies. He's very young, barely twenty-one." Mom paused to take a deep breath. "He reminded me of Harry."

Dad glanced at my mother. "This was hard for her."

My brother, Harry, is two years younger than I am, and since there are just the two of us, he's still Mom's baby at twenty-seven.

She took a breath and continued, "The poor young man kept saying he didn't want to live if he's paralyzed. In spite of that, he repeatedly begged the police to find his sister."

"What happened to his sister?"

Mom glanced down at a small notepad in her hand. "It was hard to follow, but best as I can tell, she took the ferry from Pico to Faial to go to a yacht party at the Horta Marina. She hasn't been heard from since. That was almost two weeks ago. Her name is Liliana. She's barely fifteen, and her family's been frantic. Her brother set out a week ago to search for her."

Dad looked around the room, as if searching for the girl himself. "Somehow he ended up in Timbergate with a bullet in his spine."

"Mom, were you able to help the police find out who shot him? Or why his search for his sister led him from the Azores to Timbergate?"

"I'm afraid not," she said. "There wasn't enough time before they rushed him into surgery."

TWO

THAT AFTERNOON IN the library seemed endless, probably because it was my last workday before starting my vacation. My boyfriend, Nick Alexander, and I had been set to fly my parents back to the Azores on Friday morning, starting with a flight to Boston. From there, a five-hour Atlantic flight would take us to the island of Faial.

Now, with my mother acting as interpreter, our departure plans were temporarily on hold. For Nick, a corporate pilot for a billionaire philanthropist, the trip would combine business and pleasure. His boss, Buck Sawyer, had business interests in Boston and had already agreed to arrange his meetings so he could be dropped off there while Nick and I continued on to the Azores with my parents.

The Cessna Citation we were using was one of Buck's fleet. It seated eight passengers, in addition to the two seats in the cockpit, so there was room for everyone. I hoped we wouldn't be delayed for long. Nick and I had our hearts set on spending some quality time together. After a prolonged breakup followed by an on-again off-again reconciliation, Nick and I had finally gotten back together. That was almost three months ago. Since his job kept him away so often, we rarely had more than a few days at a time together.

We first met on a gun range, where Nick was a volunteer instructor. I fell for his smiling blue eyes and fair hair the color of summer wheat, but more than that, I loved his hands. I still get a rush thinking about that first lesson, when he taught me how to squeeze a trigger. Slowly and gently. It's a wonder I remembered anything he tried to teach me that day.

I reluctantly dragged my thoughts back to the present and how much I looked forward to spending an entire week in the Azores with Nick. I could almost taste the *Vinho Verde*, a tender and delectable green wine, and the buttery and spicy cheeses, made from the milk of the world's most beautiful and pampered cows. Together with the mild, temperate climate and the passionate sounds of Portuguese Fado music, it promised to be the perfect romantic getaway.

I had expected to finish packing after work, but my last update from Quinn changed everyone's plans. The gunshot victim was out of surgery, in the ICU, and in a coma. The coma was an unexpected complication, but every effort was being made to discover its cause.

That news led to a hastily convened meeting around a wrought-iron, glass-topped table in Amah and Jack's rustic, open-beamed family room. Dinner was courtesy of Colonel Sanders. Six of us gathered there at the Highland Ranch in Coyote Creek, a ranching community a few short miles from Timbergate. The group consisted of Mom and Dad, Amah and Jack, and Nick and me.

With my grandparents' consent, Nick's two-year-old Chesapeake Bay retriever, Ginger, rested on the floor next to her master's chair. This doggy intrusion had caused Amah's peevish Maine Coon cat, Fanny, to retreat to the highest shelf on their wall of bookcases. Ginger lived with Nick and me in a recently expanded and modernized apartment above my grandparents' llama barn. Our cozy home sat just far enough down the lane from the main house to allow us privacy, but close enough for us to be there for my grandparents if we were needed.

I had lived there alone for several months, rent-free, doing chores involving the llama herd and occasionally ranch-sitting. When Nick moved in with me, we insisted on paying rent. Amah and Jack liked having us close, so they reluctantly agreed, rather than see us move to an apartment in Timbergate. Although tall, lanky Jack and petite, energetic Amah were more active than most people in their mid-seventies, we did our best to relieve them of the physically demanding chores the ranch required.

Just as we were finishing our fried chicken, biscuits, and corn on the cob, Harry showed up with his girlfriend, Rella Olstad. The woman had caused a breach in my relationship with Nick in the past, but that misunderstanding had been sorted out by the time she began dating Harry. Rella and I weren't close, but we got along okay, despite her being a statuesque blonde and a former fighter pilot who currently worked alongside Nick on a somewhat regular basis.

"Who wants the last drumstick?" Harry asked.

We all knew he wanted it, so no one spoke up. Between his day job as a busy architect and his volunteer work three times a week teaching jujitsu at our local dojo, Harry managed to turn a lot of calories into muscle. People sometimes assume Asian men are shorter than average, with slender builds. Not Harry. He passed six feet at seventeen and kept going for a couple more inches. As far back as high school, women found his striking Asian and Portuguese features captivating. Rella was no exception.

Nick and I both spent a lot of our spare time at the dojo, but we always seemed to be a degree or two behind Harry when it came time to test for a higher black belt rank. We were both at third degree. Harry had been one of the youngest in our national organization to reach fourth. Dating Harry had apparently prompted Rella's renewed interest in the gentle art. I'd seen her at the dojo a few times. A first-degree black, she wasn't bad, if a little rusty.

While Harry and Rella were eating, Dad mentioned that he and Mom had been asked to postpone their return to the Azores until the return of the hospital's interpreter, who was fluent in Portuguese. The hospital needed someone who could communicate with Paulo Ferrera's parents in the Azores.

"We were assured it wouldn't take more than a day," Mom said, glancing at my father.

I hoped that was true. The trip to the Azores was to be my first vacation since starting the job at TMC last August. Only ten months ago, but so much had happened during that time, it felt like years.

"Mom had a great idea," I told Harry. "We're going to see if we can work out a visit with Paulo Ferrera's parents while we're in the Azores."

"It won't be a big deal to revise my flight plan." Nick turned to me. "Aimee and I were already planning to spend time on Pico, so we're okay with that, right?"

"Of course. We can't pass up an opportunity to offer them our sympathy and support."

"I wish we could do more," Mom said.

"You know, there might be something more." Nick excused himself from the table, pulled out his cellphone and walked outside to make a call. Ginger padded along with him.

Harry glanced at Rella. "Do you know what he's up to?"

"He's probably calling Buck."

"Rella, will you be going along to the Azores as co-pilot?" Amah asked. As Buck Sawyer's second pilot, Rella was affected by any plans that involved Nick and/or Buck. She and Nick sometimes flew together if the flight was extraordinarily long and complicated. Other times, they took turns.

"Not this trip." Rella smiled at Harry.

Which meant Rella was catching a full week of time off. Her romance with Harry was still blooming, so I imagined the two of them would make the most of it.

Likewise, Nick and I had hoped to enjoy our first romantic island vacation together after returning my parents to their home in Horta. That was before the shooting incident involving the young Portuguese man with the missing sister. We had planned to enjoy an entire week of everything the islands had to offer. Romance and relaxation were foremost, but also on my list was the opportunity to visit the Horta Public Library and Regional Archive. I was eager to learn more of the history of my father's side of the family.

Nick was looking forward to sailing, fishing, and a day hike on Mt. Pico, which I'd agreed would be a shame to miss. I'd heard all my life about the generations of Machados who had made the nearly eight-thousand-foot climb a family tradition. On my last visit, more than a year ago, there hadn't been time to fit it in.

Nick stepped back inside with Ginger heeling near his left leg. He sat and signaled to her. She dropped down, resting her snout between her paws.

"Okay, folks, here's the plan," he said, giving the dog an approving scratch behind her ears. "I just spoke with Buck. If the Ferreras are able to make the trip, we can offer to bring them back to the States with us on our return flight."

"Then they can be here with their son." Mom clasped her hands together. "That's a wonderful idea. If I can get their contact information from the hospital or the police, I'll call them right away. We want to give them as much time as possible to make arrangements. I hope they have passports."

Jack broke in to ask one of his, as always, practical questions. "Nick, do you want Rosa and me to watch your dog while you're gone?"

"Thanks for the offer," Nick said, "but Ginger will be in boarding school while we're gone."

Hearing Nick say her name, the dog raised her head from her paws and looked at him expectantly. He reached down and stroked her fur, quietly saying, "Ginger, stay." With that, she emitted a sigh and lowered her head again.

Jack raised an eyebrow. "That dog spends a lot of time at school. She ought to have a PhD by now."

My father came to her defense. "Hey, she's a bird dog breed, but from what I hear, she doesn't chase your turkeys. Or your llamas, for that matter. I'd say that's two points in her favor."

"That's right, Lucas." Amah turned to Nick. "But you know, Jack has a point. By now, your pretty dog should have acquired lots of skills. What sort of things is she learning?"

Nick's face took on a trace of color. "Nothing special, really. Obedience. How to retrieve, of course." He seemed evasive about his dog. Knowing him, I figured there was a reason. I made a mental note to ask him later, and then shifted the conversation back to the business at hand.

"Mom, did Quinn say he'd contact you as soon as the interpreter gets back?"

"Yes, honey. They have my cell number and I gave them yours, too. And Jack and Rosa's landline here."

Jack glanced at Amah. "Too bad you never learned to speak the language."

"I agree, but back when I was a child, my parents were first-generation Americans. They saw the difficulties my grandparents had learning English as immigrants. All they wanted was to fit in and for their children to be considered American in every way."

"I hate to break up the evening," I said, "but Nick and I should go out to the barn and finish packing. Mom, will you and Dad be ready if we're able to take off early Saturday morning?"

Dad answered for her. "We're ready right now. I want to get back home to Horta before I have to start canceling next week's classes." He taught jujitsu at a dojo in Horta several times a week.

"And I promised the Horta Hospital I'd be home on Tuesday." Fluent in English, Portuguese, French, and Hindi, Mom was a huge help as an interpreter at Hospital da Horta, where tourists and the yachting set contributed to the diverse population of patients.

"Wish I was going with you," Harry said. He glanced at Rella, who had barely spoken during the entire conversation. In our family of talkers, Nick had learned to jump in when he had a chance. Rella, not a big talker to begin with, wasn't often heard from at our table.

Harry realized too late that he hadn't included her in his wish to go with us. An awkward moment, but they were still in a new relationship. Maybe he thought it was too soon to invite her to visit the home of his ancestors.

"Wendi, how soon will you try to contact the Ferreras?" Amah asked Mom.

"As soon as I get a phone number from the hospital or the police."

Harry held up his phone. "You might not need to wait for that." Harry could use the Internet in ways that were beyond my comprehension. As a teenager, he'd dreamed of working cyber-security for the CIA, but he'd left that career path behind when he became an architect. At least, that's what everyone in the family thought. I wouldn't put it past him to be living some sort of double life.

"Try some of these numbers, Mom." Harry handed her his phone.

"They're six hours ahead of our time here in California," Mom said. "It's nine o'clock here; that's three in the morning there. I'll wait until at least midnight our time."

"How did you do that?" Jack asked Harry.

"Took a minute to find a phone directory for Madalena. It's the main city on the island of Pico. There are several Ferreras, but one of them is bound to be the right family."

"I'll be damned," Jack said.

Harry blushed. "Anyone could do it."

Sure, Harry. Anyone working for the CIA.

THREE

NICK AND I walked hand in hand down the lane to our apartment over the barn with Ginger close at Nick's side. The air was balmy for early June and carried the soft, lemon-candy scent of evening primrose. Faint light from a half-moon cast elusive shadows across the pasture where the llamas kushed for the night in woolly mounds.

"You seemed a little uncomfortable being questioned about Ginger's schooling back there." I spoke quietly to avoid disturbing the snoozing livestock. "Isn't it working out? She seems like a pretty smart girl."

"She's doing fine." Nick reached down to touch the dog's head. "Truth is, I signed her up for an advanced class so your grandparents wouldn't have to watch her while we're gone."

"What kind of advanced class?"

"Macramé." He chuckled softly. "She'll probably flunk out. No thumbs."

We reached the steps to our abode over the barn. Ginger ran up ahead of us and stood at the door, tail wagging. Nick and I stopped at the bottom step.

"Smart ass." I poked his chest. "You know, if you don't want to tell me, you can just say so."

"I don't want to tell you."

"Why not?"

"You're not going to let this go, are you?"

"Not yet."

Ginger looked down at us from the top of the steps, whining her impatience.

"Let's go up," Nick said.

Inside, we each checked our cellphones and found no new messages. I spotted the message light blinking on the old landline Jack insisted we keep in the apartment. The only call there was from Cleo, reporting that Dr. Godfrey Carver had confirmed her hunch by looking for me in the library at the end of the workday. He found me gone and the library locked, so he caught up with Cleo as she was closing her office.

"He tried to wheedle your private phone number out of me," Cleo's recorded voice said. Nick stood next to me and listened while the rest of her message played. "I refused, of course. I told him you'd be out of the country for at least a week. He thinks you're already gone, so it looks like you caught a break. *Bon voyage*, girl. Hope you and your hottie have a glorious time. Don't think about work. Dr. Poole and I will deal with Carver."

"What's that about?" Nick asked.

"Nothing important. It can wait."

"That's what she calls me? Your *hottie*?"

"You weren't supposed to hear that." I couldn't suppress the flush that heated my cheeks. "Let's get back to Ginger's macramé class. Care to explain?"

Nick busied himself setting up the coffeepot for morning. "Don't you have more packing to do?"

"I can finish tomorrow," I said, "now that we've delayed the flight until Saturday." His evasive tactics aroused my curiosity. I waited while he poured in the water and ground the beans. The rich aroma of French Roast filled the small kitchen.

Nick set the timer and turned to me. "It's late. We should get to bed."

I plopped down at the dinette table in our kitchen. "That's not going to work." He knew I'd be at a disadvantage if he got me into bed. My neocortex would shut down and my lizard brain would take over.

With a reluctant sigh, Nick sat across from me. "You need to understand that what I'm going to tell you is confidential."

"If you say so, of course." A lot of my work at the hospital was confidential, so I was used to keeping secrets. Nick knew that.

"All right." He frowned, still hesitant. "You know about Buck's private foundation?"

"I know he donates a lot of money to drug rehab programs."

"That's part of it."

"What else?"

"It goes a lot deeper with Buck. The flow of illicit drugs coming into this country and others around the world is staggering. Most people have no idea."

"You're probably right, but what's that got to do with Ginger.... Wait, are you saying she's being trained to sniff for drugs?"

"Among other things." Nick looked over at Ginger, who was settled on her sleep cushion next to the kitchen door. "A few months ago, I talked to one of the trainers at her obedience school in Timbergate. He thought she'd be a good candidate for law enforcement training."

"That's why she's been spending so much time in that training program down in Southern California?"

"Right. It's an academy that trains dogs for work in law enforcement. She started with a four-week patrol school to learn the basics. Next was three weeks in drug detection, but that got interrupted after the first two weeks by some high-priority emergency. That's been resolved now, so Ginger's going to finish her final week of narcotics training while we're in the Azores."

"Will her schooling be finished then?"

"There's more, but I haven't decided about the rest."

I glanced at Ginger, asleep on her mat, hind legs twitching as if she were dreaming of some exceptional feat of doggy valor.

"There's more, isn't there, Nick?"

"More what?"

"More to explain about Ginger's training. More to explain about the work you do for Buck."

Nick leaned back, arms crossed. Blew out a breath. "I knew this was coming. Hoped to put it off a little longer."

The aroma of fresh ground coffee beans still lingered in the air, tempting me to go ahead and push the *brew* button. I resisted. Bedtime was near, and I suspected I wasn't going to drop off to sleep easily.

"Nick, does Rella know about these things you obviously aren't comfortable telling me?"

Nick avoided my eyes. That meant the answer was *yes*. "She works for Buck, Aimee. She has to know."

I paused. "Does Harry know?"

This time Nick met my gaze. "He knows enough."

Hurt, I tried to make sense of what I was hearing. "Then I don't understand. It sounds like I'm the only one you don't trust."

"Don't put it that way, Aimee." Nick seemed to weigh his words. "It isn't about trust. It's about timing. Back when you and I weren't solid, it wasn't necessary to pull you into the deep end." He reached across the table, touched the back of my hand. "We're on firm ground now. There are some things you need to know before we reach the Azores. But I was hoping not to have to share that burden with you."

"It's better to know than to wonder." I tried to lighten the moment. "At least fill me in on what your dog knows."

That earned me a smile. "I can do better than that," Nick said, clasping my hand in his. "For starters, Buck is doing more than funding drug rehab programs. He's been using every business trip, no matter where he goes in the world, to keep eyes and ears open for any hint of drug trafficking. He knows people in government agencies who can give him some leads, and because he's a civilian, a private citizen going about his legitimate business, he's managed to avoid being identified as an informant."

My pulse ticked up several beats, and I disengaged my hand. "But you're there, almost everywhere he goes. What part do you play in this arrangement?"

He leaned back again. "I'm the typical bored corporate pilot, hanging out in coffee shops or bars, killing time, and occasionally observing or overhearing something worth a second look."

"Cripes, you're a spy for the DEA?" I couldn't help the elevation in volume.

He raised a palm in protest. "Whoa, Nellie. Spying is way above my pay grade."

I threw up my hands. "What, then? What are you planning to do when we get to the Azores?"

Despite my raised voice, he kept his tone casual. "The same thing I do at any destination. Keep my eyes and ears open. I'm particularly interested in the Horta Marina. That's the last place the missing girl was seen. I did some checking. Turns out that's the fourth most visited marina in the world. Imagine what might pass through there."

"They must have some sort of oversight or surveillance in place," I protested.

"Granted, but think about it. During peak season, it would be impossible to keep eyes on every vessel at all times. I have to wonder how vigorously those docks are patrolled."

"Or how often a naïve teenager goes missing," I said, calmer now. "There must have been hundreds of sailboats and yachts in that harbor last time I was there."

"It'll probably be no different this time."

"Sounds like our island getaway is going to be more about crime solving than about romance." I couldn't help the slight bitterness that had crept into my voice.

Nick got up, walked around the table and pulled me into his arms. "I hope not, but just in case, let's get a head start on the romance."

FOUR

I woke up Friday morning to the rattle of kibble being poured into Ginger's bowl. I caught the aroma of coffee brewing and maybe a whiff of bacon frying. The remodel Harry's crew had done a few months earlier had enlarged my barn-top home from a studio to a two-bedroom apartment. It was quaint and comfortable, but still small enough that any activity going on in the kitchen was bound to rouse a late sleeper.

The bedside clock read seven fifteen. Normally anything after six thirty was considered sleeping in. I pulled on jeans and a T-shirt. On this last day before our trip, I wanted to do my routine chores. It was silly to think the llamas would miss me—that they could possibly care who tossed their hay twice a day—but I liked to think so.

I ran a brush through my hair and wandered into the kitchen. Nick stood at the stove in faded Levi's and a navy T-shirt, keeping an eye on the bacon.

"Chores first…or breakfast?"

"Chores." I yawned. "I feel guilty if I eat before I feed the livestock."

"Work on that." Nick pointed his spatula at me. "You do realize they don't know the difference?"

"I know. But I noticed you always feed your dog before you eat."

"That's because she *does* know the difference. If I eat first, she's right there, watching."

"Good point, but I'm still going out. Back in a few."

Outside, I tossed hay to the herd. While the llamas munched, I surveyed the pasture. All was well. Jack's dozen turkeys were down from their roost, pecking and scratching. Native songbirds flitted from one majestic blue oak to another, competing for most melodious greeting of the day.

Back in the apartment, Nick had breakfast ready. Bacon, biscuits, scrambled eggs. I dug in, loving that he liked to cook. And that he didn't distinguish between men's and women's work. Especially important when it came to his career. With a former fighter pilot like Rella as his co-pilot, he'd be in trouble if he had workplace gender issues. The thought of flying brought me around to our impending trip.

"Nick, I'm going to go up to the main house after breakfast to see if they've had any news about Paulo Ferrera's medical status. We need to know if the hospital's interpreter is back in town."

"While you're at it, ask if your mom got through to his parents about returning to the States with us."

"That, too." I crunched a bite of perfectly fried bacon.

"While you're doing that, I'll run Ginger into Timbergate. Her local trainer here is going to transport her down south to the academy, along with a few other canine students. Maybe you'll know something by the time I get back."

"I hope so. Did you already file a new flight plan?"

"Not yet, but I need to get that done as soon as we know for sure we're leaving tomorrow." Nick downed the last of his coffee and started to leave the table.

"Wait…sit for a moment. Okay?"

I saw misgiving in his eyes, but he sat. "What's up?"

"I've been thinking about what you said last night. The spy thing. I have a question."

"Go ahead."

"In the past, you've come home from some of your flights looking as if you'd gone ten rounds in a boxing ring. You always came up with a sketchy explanation. A hostile drunk in a bar, or a mugging on some dark street. Now I'm wondering if your secret agent work had something to do with the scrapes and bruises."

"This is why I haven't been more forthcoming before now." Nick glanced at Ginger for a moment before he met my gaze. "You're going to worry, and you're going to ask a lot of questions I'd rather not answer."

"For now, just answer one question, okay?"

"Maybe." He leaned back with his arms crossed.

Not the response I'd hoped for, but I went ahead. "Are we a team?"

"That isn't a yes or no question."

"We're either together, or we aren't. Yes, or no?"

"You're not playing fair," he said.

"Yes, or no?"

Nick reached over and took my hand. He turned it up and kissed my palm, sending tingles rippling throughout my body. "Of course we're together, but I'm not quite ready to involve you in something you didn't sign up for. It could be dangerous."

"Then promise you'll fill me in when there's something I need to know."

"I promise," he said. I wasn't convinced his definition of *need to know* matched mine.

Nick loaded Ginger into his pickup and headed off to Timbergate. I walked up the lane to the main house, where Mom and Dad were having breakfast with Amah and Jack. I accepted a cup of coffee and the offer of a small helping of *linguiça*. Even on a full stomach, I couldn't resist a few bites of the highly spiced Portuguese garlic sausage. It had been one of my favorite foods for as long as I could remember.

"Any news from the police or the hospital?" I asked.

"Some good news," Mom said. "The interpreter is back, so we can start for home tomorrow as early as Nick wants to take off."

"Good, he can file a new flight plan right away."

"Where is he?" Dad asked.

"Taking his dog to town to catch her ride to school."

Jack chuckled. "I hope I didn't offend him with my teasing last night."

"Nick's not that sensitive. I doubt he gave it a second thought." I stopped myself before I blurted out what Nick had told me about Ginger's training and the dicey side of his work.

"Will you still be making an overnight stop in Boston?" Amah asked.

"We'll drop Buck Sawyer off there and stay overnight. Nick's flying solo, so we want him to be rested for the Boston to Horta leg of the flight. That'll be almost another five hours."

Mom and Dad exchanged glances. "That might work out just right," Mom said. "Did you know Tony and Tanya are appearing in a play in Boston?" She was referring to my Grandfather Machado and his wife. They lived in New York City, but their flourishing post-retirement careers as character actors took them to professional theater companies throughout the Northeast.

"Amah mentioned it a few weeks ago. *Bus Stop*, isn't it?"

"Yes. Our commercial flight from the Azores had a layover in Boston, so we were able to catch it while we were there." Mom smiled, remembering. "Tanya's role is the waitress, and Tony is the bus driver who flirts with her."

"It would be cute to see them in those roles, but we

won't be able to catch it tomorrow. It'll take around five hours to get to Boston. With the different time zones, we wouldn't be there in time for the Saturday matinee."

"Maybe you can go on the way back," Amah said. "I know Tony and Tanya would love to see you."

"That might work. I'll talk to Nick about it."

Grandpa Machado and Amah had gone their separate ways in an amicable divorce before I was born. They had each remarried, and the two couples remained good friends—something I had always admired. Grandpa and Tanya thrived in New York City. They loved city life as much as Amah and Jack loved country life. It gave the rest of the family wonderful opportunities to experience both worlds.

Mom and Amah cleared away breakfast while Jack and I went over the list of barnyard chores Nick and I usually covered for him. It made us feel less guilty about the disgracefully low rent we were paying. Those tasks would need to be done while Nick and I were gone. Between the small llama herd and the turkey flock, there always seemed to be something needing food or water. Or cages to clean or droppings to shovel and haul away. I suggested Harry be commissioned to take care of that task. Occasionally Jack had trouble with his back, and he didn't need to risk throwing it out.

By the time we had that sorted out, I spotted Nick's pickup driving down the lane toward the barn. Home from Timbergate without his sniffer dog. I was about to head to the barn myself when Mom's cellphone chirped. Dad and Jack and I listened to her end of the conversation, which was brief.

"I see." She nodded. "That's good. We'll keep him in our thoughts. Thank you." She ended the call. "That was your boss calling from the hospital, Aimee."

"Did he say how the patient is doing?" I asked.

"Still in a coma. The poor young man." She met my father's eyes. "We'll have to visit his family when we get home, Lucas."

"Of course. Their daughter is missing and their son is critically injured. Imagine how devastating that must be." Dad glanced at me, as if to confirm I was safe and whole.

"Mom, I thought you were going to ask if they want to come back to the States with us," I said.

"Thanks to Harry's phone numbers, we did make contact, but the parents are distraught, as you can imagine. They were unable to decide about coming back with you and Nick. They're still hoping their daughter will turn up there in the Azores."

"Maybe a face-to-face visit will help them decide," Amah said. Her next words were directed to all of us. "Once you reach Faial, please keep us informed here at home whenever you have news."

"I promise," I said. Mom and Dad nodded in agreement.

Jack emptied the last of the coffee into his cup. "Rosa and I will follow up on this end and reach you by cellphone if we hear any news about the patient."

Back in the apartment, I filled Nick in on everything I'd heard at the main house.

He looked up from packing his duffel bag. "That boy's still unconscious? Damn shame."

"I know. Mom and Dad definitely want to visit his parents when we get to the Azores."

"Should we go with them?" Nick closed his duffel and placed it near the door.

"I think so. It might ease the Ferreras' minds to meet you if it turns out they want to come with us on our return flight."

FRIDAY EVENING, WITH Nick's flight plan filed and our packing done, we shared a simple dinner of tomato soup and crab salad. We took our glasses of wine out onto the newly expanded deck overlooking the llama pasture. After a long day, it felt good to sit in patio chairs and unwind for a few peaceful moments watching the sun's nightly glide path. It slowly disappeared, leaving the western horizon blazing a fire-tinged shade of pink and turning the mountains to the west into a deep purple silhouette. I must have sighed, because Nick asked if there was something wrong.

"I can't stop thinking about the missing girl," I said. "There are so many terrible scenarios running through my mind."

He reached over to touch my shoulder. "We can't control that right now, Aimee. Try to keep hoping for the best."

"I'm trying, but a fifteen-year-old could be—"

Through an open window, I heard my cellphone ring, interrupting me mid-sentence. I headed inside and found a message from Cleo. Rare that she would call on a Friday night. We were the best of friends at work, but we seldom spent personal time together. She and her husband, Sig, had married only months ago, and they loved spending their leisure time with each other.

I answered with misgivings. "Hi. What's up?"

"Can you talk?" Cleo and I sometimes had to discuss confidential hospital matters outside the workplace, so we were careful to keep those conversations private.

"I can. Nick's outside on the deck. We just confirmed we're flying out tomorrow morning. Is there something I need to know before we go?"

FIVE

"NOTHING URGENT," CLEO SAID. "The opposite, actually. I feel bad that I got you involved in Godfrey Carver's medical staff membership renewal just when you and Nick are heading off on vacation. You two shouldn't be thinking about anything but each other. I have news that'll take Carver's problem off your mind."

"You mean his CME credits?" Carver was already the last thing on my mind, but I didn't say so, since Cleo the Romantic was doing something thoughtful. At least she thought so. I realized she wasn't up to speed on our trip to the Azores—how it had taken on a new purpose. I filled her in on our plans to visit Paulo Ferrera's parents, and the possibility that we would bring them back to the States with us.

"Does Quinn know about this?" Cleo asked.

"He will, if it's certain we're bringing the parents back, but that's still up in the air at this point."

"When will you know?"

"Maybe not until we get to the Azores and meet the Ferreras. But we're getting off topic. What were you going to tell me about Carver?"

"That's not exactly off topic." She paused just long enough for me to wonder if we'd lost our connection.

"Cleo? Are you still there?"

"I'm here. Thinking of the best way to explain this. Carver has taken over as Paulo Ferrera's primary physician."

"What? Wait. How did this happen?" I was confused. "Yesterday, Carver was scrabbling for a way to keep his medical staff membership from expiring."

"It looks like he found a way." Cleo's exasperated sigh told me she wasn't happy about what had transpired. "I'd have called you sooner, but I didn't hear about this until almost quitting time today. Dr. Prine called Quinn yesterday afternoon with an emergency. His teenage daughter, who lives somewhere in Florida, was rear-ended on a highway and suffered an injury to her upper spine. Prine was desperate to be with her and to consult with the doctors on her case."

Dr. Oliver Prine was Paulo's neurosurgeon, and one of only two in town board-certified in the specialty. "I don't blame Dr. Prine, but how can Carver take over the case if his privileges are about to be suspended?"

"It's already a done deal," Cleo said. "Quinn said Prine turned the case over to Carver yesterday afternoon, right after he got the call about his daughter's accident. Quinn explained immediately about the pending suspension of Carver's privileges."

"And that goes into effect two weeks from yesterday?"

"Yes, Quinn made that clear, but Dr. Prine wasn't concerned. He insisted on leaving for Florida immediately, and he recommended Carver be assigned to the Ferrera case."

"How long will Prine be gone?"

"He expects to be back in just a few days."

"And if he isn't?"

"That's why I'm calling," Cleo said. "Quinn and I wanted to be sure you knew what's going on."

"I appreciate that. Let's stay in touch by phone while I'm in the Azores next week. I'd like to know right away if Carver makes up the deficient CME credits or better yet, submits proof of the credits he claims he's earned."

"You sound skeptical," Cleo said, "and I don't blame you, but at this point, we have to give Carver the benefit of the doubt. If he doesn't come through, the best we can hope for is Prine's early return. Odds are Carver will only be on the case for a few days, mostly just watching and waiting. Dr. Prine assured us he'll return from Florida as soon as he's confident his daughter's in good hands."

"Let's hope his daughter's case isn't too serious. What have you heard?"

"Not much. It may be nothing worse than severe whiplash, and maybe a concussion, but of course Prine is going to want to see for himself." She hesitated for a moment. "I'm sorry to dump this on you. I debated with myself about whether I should fill you in now or wait until after you got back from your vacation."

"You did the right thing," I assured her. "I'd rather be forewarned, even though this will probably be sorted out before I get back."

"I hope so," she said. "Try not to give it another thought."

I was not about to let Cleo's news spoil my vacation. Dr. Prine would most likely be back from Florida before I got home from the Azores. And Godfrey Carver's lack of attention to continuing education was the last thing I intended to lose sleep over while Nick and I tried to claim a few days of our island trip for ourselves. There would be time to deal with that problem when I got back.

MOM AND DAD had returned their rental car on Friday, so they rode with Nick and me to the Timbergate Municipal Airport Saturday morning. Buck was already at the hangar waiting when we arrived for our early-morning flight. With neatly cropped white hair and his slender frame dressed in khaki pants and a plaid shirt, he looked more like a Walmart greeter than a sharp-witted billionaire entrepreneur. From what Nick had told me, Buck could clearly morph into any image he wanted to project.

I enjoyed watching my parents' eyes widen when Buck's Cessna Citation rolled out of the hangar.

"Oh, my goodness," Mom said.

"Son of a…" Dad caught himself, coughed and cleared his throat. "That's some ride."

Nick smiled, and we traded glances. I knew he was enjoying the moment and looking forward to their re-action when they saw the luxury of the interior. The soft, ergonomically designed leather seats and carpet-ing were the color of champagne. The cabin had plenty of leg room and adjustable ambient lighting. There was Wi-Fi, standard power outlets, even a refreshment cen-ter with a microwave.

After Nick did the usual preflight walk-around in-specting the exterior, we all boarded the plane. He performed the cabin and cockpit inspection while my parents got settled in their seats. I had to struggle not to laugh at Mom and Dad's excitement about flying home in such grand style. They'd be ruined forever for flying economy class on a commercial airliner.

THE CITATION TOOK us across the country in just over five hours. Buck hung out in the cockpit with Nick during most of the flight, while my parents and I passed the time relaxing in the main cabin. Mom and Dad eventu-ally ran out of steam and napped the last two hours. The time change put us at Hanscom Field, a general aviation airport near Boston, around five in the evening. Nick had arranged overnight parking there for the Citation. The two rental cars he had reserved were waiting. One was for Buck, who headed to the hotel where he was to connect with his business associates. The other car was for Nick and me and my parents.

We were soon on the road toward our planned dinner with Grandpa Machado and Tanya at a five-star seafood restaurant close to Boston's theater district. They had less than two hours between the end of their matinee and their six-thirty call for the evening performance. While Nick drove, Mom called Amah to let her know we'd had a safe flight. I put in a call to Cleo to ask about Paulo Ferrera's condition.

"Basically unchanged," she said. "The interpreter has agreed to be on hand as needed. I'll let you know if anything new develops."

"Good. I'll check in again on Sunday when we land at the airport in Horta." I put my phone away, trying to keep my hopes up for Paulo's recovery and for the safe return of his missing sister.

Grandpa Machado's face lit up when we arrived at the restaurant. Handsome as ever, he was an older version of my father, but with more silver in his hair, more years etched in creases and laugh lines, and—most unusual but not unheard of in people of Portuguese lineage—his eyes were startlingly blue instead of deep brown like my father's. He stood and waved us over to the table he'd reserved for our party. When we reached him, he wrapped me in a bear hug.

"How's our baby girl?" He turned to Tanya. "Look at her. She's as beautiful as ever, right?"

Tanya caught my eye with a conspiratorial wink. "Of course she is, Tony. She's your granddaughter, isn't she?" I had long ago accepted that I would always be his baby girl.

We settled around the table and studied the menu while we sampled the wine Grandpa had ordered. As soon as we'd told the waiter our choices, Tanya turned to me.

"We're hoping you'll be able to catch a performance when you return from the Azores. Do you know yet when that will be?" Tanya could play any sort of character a script called for. Her usually dark-blonde hair was streaked with gray, no doubt in keeping with her role in the play. She had once described her figure as matronly, laughing that in today's terms, it simply meant she could afford to lose ten or fifteen pounds. But on her, it looked comfortable and just right.

I left it to Nick to decide about the play. "What do you think?"

"Unless something unexpected comes up, we'll be back in Boston on Thursday afternoon and fly back to Timbergate Friday morning."

"That's perfect," Grandpa said. "You can come to our closing night performance and join us for the cast party."

"Why are you closing on a Thursday night instead of a Saturday?" I knew enough about theater to realize that was unusual.

"Our run was supposed to end last night," Tanya said, "but due to popular demand, we were held over."

"Only until Thursday," Grandpa said. "One of our cast members has a commitment in New York on Friday." He nodded toward Tanya. We all looked to her for an explanation. "Tell 'em, honey," Grandpa urged her.

"I've been offered a small part in a daytime drama." Tanya blushed. "Tony's more excited about it than I am. It's only a two-month contract. The character I'll play is a grandmother with a broken hip." She laughed. "What is it they say? Don't buy any green bananas."

"You're going to be great," Grandpa said. "Just you wait. They'll want to keep you on."

"We'll see," Tanya said.

Our dinners arrived, and conversation took a backseat to the extraordinary seafood dishes placed before us. We gave ourselves over to enjoying fine cuisine in the stylish comfort of the dining room while live piano music drifted in from the lounge area.

"Hear that?" Grandpa said. "'I Could Have Danced All Night.' Audrey Hepburn. She was a class act." He leaned toward Tanya. "Remember her in *My Fair Lady*? Well, of course, she didn't sing it herself, but she acted the heck out of it. None of the new crop can hold a candle to Audrey. Tattoos. Drugs. What are they thinking?"

Mom and Dad had been letting the elders carry the conversation until dessert arrived.

"Lucas," Grandpa said, "fill us in on island life. How are you and Wendi adapting?"

Dad had inherited a house from my Great Uncle Jorge, Grandpa's older brother. Over dessert, Grandpa and Tanya were filled in on life in the Azores. Dad divided his time among his favorite pastimes, teaching martial arts a few times a week, sailing, and learning to cook traditional Portuguese dishes. Mom's work as a medical interpreter kept her active.

The conversation lulled me into a warm and happy place, but fatigue from the long day finally set in. I was running out of steam and suspected everyone else felt the same. No one objected when I said Nick needed to get a good night's sleep before flying out to the Azores the next morning. We hugged all around, promising to try our best to return in time for the play Thursday night. Grandpa and Tanya insisted on staying behind to pay for the dinner, so the rest of us made our way back to the hotel in our rental car.

SIX

I CALLED CLEO Sunday morning just before our flight
and was told Paulo was still in a coma. With the help
of the interpreter, TMC's social worker had contacted
his parents with his current health status. After I filled
Mom in on Cleo's update, she called the Ferreras to ask
if they'd be willing to have us visit them in their home.
They agreed, but Mom said Paulo's mother was barely
keeping it together. No wonder. A missing daughter and
a son who hovered between life and death.

Flying across the Atlantic, Dad rode shotgun in the
cockpit with Nick while Mom and I had the spacious
cabin to ourselves. We passed the time by discussing
the mystery surrounding Paulo and his sister, and making plans to meet with the Ferreras on Pico.

"Do you think they'll want to return to the States
with us?" I asked Mom.

"They're still uncertain. They keep thinking their
daughter is going to turn up, either on Faial or on Pico.
They don't want to be away from their home if that
should happen."

"Not much chance of that after she's been gone for
more than two weeks, but I'm sure you didn't want to
say that to the mother."

"Of course not." Mom glanced out the plane's window at the ocean below. "It's heartbreaking to think
about, but she has to be wondering if she'll ever see her

daughter again. The police in the Azores haven't come up with any substantial leads so far."

"Didn't you say the brother mentioned a yacht party at the Horta Marina? Seems like that would yield something."

"Honey, do you remember how many yachts were docked at that marina when you were there last year during peak season?"

"Hundreds." My hopes for that young girl sank. She could be anywhere in the world.

Our flight neared its end as Nick circled above mist-shrouded Mt. Pico. The mountain makes up most of the land mass on Pico Island, Faial's closest neighbor. While Nick made his way toward final approach to the Horta Airport on Faial, Mom and I fell silent. Most frequent flyers know that take-offs and landings are the highest-risk moments in any flight. We both knew touching down on the Horta Airport runway was way trickier than the average landing.

The single runway requires a leap of faith on the part of any pilot or passenger, whether flying commercial or private. It is situated on a scrap of peninsula, where it begins at one end of the land mass and ends at the other. There is no margin for error. If the pilot doesn't time the landing precisely right, the airplane will continue beyond the runway's end and drop into the sea. With Nick at the controls of the Citation, I wasn't worried, but still, there is always that moment of relief when the landing gear touches down and the plane comes to a halt.

Nick took care of arrangements for the Citation while Mom and Dad lined up a taxi to take us to their home. On the way, I calculated how to change the time on my watch. Our five-hour flight had begun in Boston at eight o'clock in the morning, but the time difference put us in Horta at four in the afternoon, island time. We were six hours later than California, where it was ten in the morning.

We soon reached Mom and Dad's sweet little cottage. I called Cleo while Nick began unpacking our luggage in the guestroom.

"Glad you called," Cleo said. "I take it the hottie got you there safe and sound."

"Of course, but you need to stop calling him that. He knows."

"How?"

"He overheard a message you left on my phone."

"Oops, sorry." She didn't sound sorry; she sounded amused. "I'd rather refer to him as your husband, but the two of you won't cooperate. However, we have more important things to discuss, don't we? I'm guessing you called for an update on our Azorean patient."

"That first. What's the latest?"

"No change. Carver is on the case now and seems to be devoting an appropriate amount of time and attention to the patient."

"Is Paulo still in a coma?"

"Afraid so."

"What about his mother and father? Has the interpreter been in touch with them again?"

"He has. They've been told to expect to hear from you and your parents."

"Mom's already spoken to Senhora Ferrera. She gave us directions to their home in Madalena, so we'll catch a taxi when we get off the ferry. The driver won't have any trouble finding the address. Madalena's population is only about six thousand."

"When do you expect to meet with them?" Cleo asked.

"Tomorrow, I hope, but right now, we all need to get some rest. It's been a long two days."

"Okay, I'll keep you updated and you do the same." I heard her sigh. "This isn't exactly the romantic get-away you and Nick had in mind, is it?"

"Hardly, but we'll try to salvage some time for each other."

Next I put in a quick call to Amah and Jack, who assured me that Harry was on call for any help they might need while I was away. When we'd finished phone calls and unpacking, Nick and I joined Mom and Dad in their cozy living room to discuss plans for the next day. We all agreed a ferry trip to Pico to visit the Ferreras was our priority. My mother would call them first thing Monday morning to confirm a time to meet with them. With that settled, we called it a night.

MONDAY MORNING, MOM called the Ferreras, who agreed to meet with us at their home on Pico at noon. While my parents were busy arranging for our ferry ride to Madalena, I showed Nick around outside. This was his first time in the Azores, so there was a lot for him to take in.

The house was centered on a large lot, with a lawn in front sloping down toward a whitewashed retaining wall at the street. Manicured hedges topped the front wall, and a stairway of a dozen steps climbed up to the front door from a gate at the street. Closer to the house, two squat palm trees trimmed to resemble pineapples stood sentinel on either side of the steps. A gentle incline behind the house rose to meet a lush greenbelt cloaked in trees of different species and shades of green. The white stucco exterior and red-tiled roof completed the

European look of the home. Knowing it had belonged to my father's family for at least three generations gave it a special place in my heart.

"No wonder your parents love it here," Nick said. "Who wouldn't?"

"And this is just the beginning," I said. "Wait until you see the rest of this island and some of the others."

"Next time we come, we should stay for at least a month."

"We'd better start learning the language if we're going to do that." I liked hearing him mention a next time, and hoped someday Nick and I might have our own little cottage on Faial to use as a vacation home.

Nick pulled a small booklet from his pocket. "Already starting." He held up a small Portuguese phrase book, opened it and spoke slowly. "*Está livre hoje á noite?*"

I took the booklet from his hand. He had turned to the section that listed phrases for dating. I found the translation: *Are you free this evening?*

"Is this when I say, 'I'm free, but I'm not cheap'?"

"That's understood." He leaned in for a kiss just as Mom called to us from the front door.

"Hey, kids, we need to get going if we're going to make the ferry."

A quick drive to the ferry dock, and we were on our way.

WE REACHED PICO in less than an hour, docking at the harbor in Madalena. We found an English-speaking taxi driver who assured us he could find the Ferreras' home from the address we provided. I was amused to see Nick's surprise that Mercedes-Benz was the vehicle of choice for most taxi drivers on the islands. I had been, too, until I did some research and discovered the less expensive models were the vehicle of choice for taxis throughout most of Europe for a variety of reasons, including durability and longevity.

We wound along a paved road bordered by massive hydrangea hedges blooming in hues of blue and purple. At intervals, vistas of the open sea treated us to the spectacle of diving whales, their huge, arching flippers tossing glittering sprays of water like diamonds in the sunlight.

At the first sighting, Nick turned to us from the front of the cab where he was riding. "Did you see that? It was a whale, wasn't it?"

Mom and Dad looked at each other with matching smiles. "Yes, it was," Dad said. "We see that pretty often."

The taxi driver glanced in the rearview mirror. "His first time here?" he asked. Mom and Dad nodded. The driver's broad grin revealed his amusement.

"This place is unreal." Nick turned to me. "We're definitely coming back for a longer stay."

Dad reached up and patted Nick's shoulder. "You're welcome anytime, son."

The driver pulled up in front of a house similar in construction to my parents', with an exterior of white stucco and a red-tile roof. The lot it sat on boasted a rock garden, lovingly landscaped with a variety of sizes and colors of lava rock. I spotted many of the island's native shrubs and small trees, including palms and firs, comingled with blossoming groundcover sporting bright-yellow flowers. The Ferreras obviously cherished their home.

Dad always had euros on hand, so he paid the taxi driver, who gave us his number, asking if we would call him first for our ride back to the harbor.

The Ferreras' front door opened before we reached it, and Liliana's parents stepped outside to greet us. The father—a stocky, balding man of medium height—wore dark trousers and a light-blue cotton shirt. The mother, whose face was etched with worry, wore her dark hair fixed in a coil at the base of her neck. She was as tall as her husband and had on a simple dress in a dark print.

Mom made the introductions, and we all went inside where a tempting aroma told me Senhora Ferrera had been baking. She had coffee ready and set a plate of *sonhos* on their dining room table. The Portuguese cookies were a popular Portuguese delicacy, the name translating to *dreams* in English. In spite of her grief and anxiety, this mother's sense of hospitality had prompted her to create the delicious confections often served to guests. They were similar to a light sugar cookie dipped in a special almond-and-cinnamon-flavored syrup, then rolled in powdered sugar.

After coffee was served, we got right to the point. Mom carried on most of the conversation on our side, while Liliana and Paulo's mother spoke for herself and her husband. My mother interpreted for us as they went along.

We were told that they had just heard an hour ago from the TMC interpreter, who told them Paulo was holding his own. Still in a coma, he was stable, and they had reason to believe he would eventually regain consciousness. The wound to his spine had not severed the cord, so there was hope that once it healed, he would have full use of his limbs.

At that, we switched our questions to their daughter, hoping to gain some solid leads as to where she could be. It occurred to me that we still had no idea what Liliana looked like. I mentioned that to Mom, who asked the Ferreras if we could see a photo. The request brought instant tears to the mother's eyes. She got up and left the room, returning with an album. She sat down, passing her hand across the album's cover, as if she might not have the strength to view a catalog of her missing girl's life. Her husband took it from her, opening it toward the back, where I assumed the most recent photos would be found.

He passed the album to us without a word, his jaw clenched, obviously keeping his own emotions in check. The photo revealed an exceptionally beautiful teenager with a body transitioning gracefully into womanhood. Her flowing dark-chestnut hair gleamed with warm, silky highlights. Stunning emerald-green eyes met the camera with confidence and something more, as if she might be fifteen going on thirty. She knew she was exquisite-looking. That was obvious. What she apparently didn't know was how her beauty might put her life in danger. I took out my phone and asked permission to take a photo of the most recent picture of Liliana. They agreed.

Closing the album, Mom handed it back to Senhor Ferrera and asked his wife to tell us about their daughter. As Mom translated, we heard that Liliana was a good girl, if a bit headstrong. She did well in school and hoped to work in the fashion industry, perhaps as a model, but eventually as a designer. She loved to take the ferry to Faial to visit the boutiques that lined the streets of Horta's shopping district, where many businesses catered to wealthy tourists.

We had to stop at intervals when Senhora Ferrera became too emotional to continue. Each time she dried her eyes, she glanced up at a crucifix on the wall and made the sign of the cross. Her husband made soft, re-assuring sounds, as if comforting a child.

Half an hour later, there was a knock at their front door. Senhora Ferrera went to answer it, returning with a slightly chubby teenage girl close to Liliana's age. She was introduced as Liliana's best friend, Catia. The girl wore her hair in the same style as Liliana's, but the color seemed drab in comparison. Catia glanced around the room with wide, troubled brown eyes and immediately burst into tears.

SEVEN

AN ELDERLY WOMAN walking with a cane followed Catia into the room. Her braided gray hair, wound in circles attached above her ears, made her look like an ancient Princess Leia. She put an arm around the girl's shoulders and shushed her, speaking none too gently a few words in Portuguese. Senhor Ferrera stood, offering the older woman his seat at the table. While he left the room to scare up two more chairs, Senhora Ferrera introduced Catia's grandmother as Senhora Nunes. Liliana's father returned with the extra chairs, and soon the eight of us were seated around the table with scant elbow room.

The elderly woman helped herself to one of the last two *sonhos* from the plate on the table. When Catia reached for the other, her grandmother slapped her wrist and shook her head.

"*Não!*"

I didn't need an interpreter for that. I glanced at Nick to see if he and I were on the same page. He raised an eyebrow. We obviously agreed that whatever Catia's part was in Liliana's disappearance, she was still paying for it two weeks after the fact. Mom gently urged the nervous girl to tell us everything she could remember about the last time she had seen Liliana.

Our questions in English were repeated in Portuguese, answered by Catia, and then interpreted back to us in English. Whenever she stopped, either to wipe her eyes or to let a small sob escape, the grandmother nudged her with an elbow, urging her to "*confessar*," while making the sign of the cross.

I sat next to my mother, and at one point in the story, leaned toward her to ask about Catia's parents. Why weren't they here instead of the grandmother? She relayed my question to Senhora Ferrera, who answered her quietly. Mom murmured back to me that Catia's parents were not in the picture. She had been raised from her toddler years by the grandmother. I guessed that her parenting had been tough love served up in large doses.

After a difficult, hour-long interview, Catia and her grandmother both exhibited signs of fatigue. Catia hunched her shoulders and hung her head, while her grandmother slumped ragdoll-like in her chair. Finally, Senhor Ferrera called a taxi for the two women—one little more than a child, the other slipping into old age. As they made their way out to where the taxi waited, the girl turned back to where Liliana's parents stood and called out in heavily accented English, "I am sorry." Her grandmother urged her into the taxi and soon they were on their way back to the ferry dock and then Faial.

The rest of us refilled our coffee cups and compared notes to see if we had gleaned all we could from Catia's story of the night Liliana went missing. Although the girls were from different islands, they had become friends after meeting the previous August during the annual *Semana do Mar*, which translates as Sea Week. The celebration is a popular draw for tourists and locals alike. Sea Week's premier event is the *Festival do Mar*, or Festival of the Sea, when all types of sea craft depart Horta Marina, filling the channel between Faial and Pico with fluttering sails. Other activities include whale boat races and folklore groups, but the concerts, featuring celebrity musicians, were the girls' favorite part.

Liliana and Catia remained close friends, riding the ferry back and forth between Faial and Pico almost weekly to visit. Liliana particularly encouraged the friendship, as it gave her a reason to make frequent visits to the more sophisticated island of Faial. There the girls browsed the boutiques, checking out the latest fashions. Catia repeated what we had already heard from Liliana's parents about their daughter's dreams of becoming a model or a fashion designer. The girls regularly took their lunches to the Horta Marina, where they watched people coming and going from the yachts, hoping to spot American celebrities. Both dreamed of someday leaving the islands to travel to the United States—specifically, California.

On the day of Liliana's disappearance, the girls had been walking along the Horta Marina when a man stopped to talk to them. He said he was working as part of the crew of a superyacht owned by a wealthy American.

Mom glanced down at the notes she had taken and continued, "According to Catia, the man, who said his name was Miguel, was handsome, clean-cut, and friendly. He told them they could come aboard for a tour." Mom glanced up from her notes. "The girls had seen many yachts moored at the marina, but nothing as enormous and grand as this luxury craft. It was so special that they couldn't resist the invitation. They went aboard and were dazzled by the splendid interior. Neither girl had ever seen anything like it."

My mother had asked Catia if she recalled the name of the yacht. The girl replied that it was an American word she wasn't familiar with. She hadn't paid that much attention when Miguel mentioned it, and had no idea how it was spelled. Miguel invited the girls to return that evening for a yacht party. Giddy with excitement, they accepted.

"That's the point when Catia dissolved into tears again," Mom said. "At the last minute, she had tried to sneak out, but her grandmother caught on and dragged the truth out of her about the yacht-party invitation." Mom finished her distressing summary in a somber tone. "That was when the grandmother broke in to say she had refused to allow Catia to go. Catia told the grandmother that she needed to let her friend know she couldn't go to the party. The grandmother told her to call Liliana, or text her. Catia sent a text, but never heard back."

Mom glanced up from her notes. "Then Senhora Ferrera asked, 'How can that be? Liliana doesn't have a cellphone.'

"Catia admitted that another friend of Liliana's, someone Catia didn't know, had helped Liliana arrange for a cellphone that her parents knew nothing about." Mom hesitated a moment, shaking her head. "The next day, the yacht was gone. No one has seen or heard from Liliana since."

When Mom was finished, everyone at the table was silent for a moment. All of us, I suspected, were wondering about the odds of seeing the girl again.

Dad eventually broke the silence to ask the Ferreras if they had learned anything new during this visit from Catia, other than the news about Liliana's cellphone. They exchanged looks, then shook their heads. Dad filled us in on their answer. They had heard all the rest of it before. They mentioned that back when Liliana first went missing, Paulo had been present when Catia was questioned. At that session, Catia had not admitted to knowing about Liliana's phone.

Paulo had pressed her to try to remember the name

of the yacht, but she insisted she didn't know. Then Paulo had gone to great lengths to see if anyone from either island remembered the yacht. His only clue was the crew member who invited the girls to the party—a young man named Miguel who would have disappeared with the yacht.

"Mom, ask if Liliana had a passport," I said.

She asked, and Mrs. Ferrera nodded.

"She says both of their children have passports," Mom said.

"Did anyone look to see if they're missing?" Nick asked.

Mom relayed his question. The Ferreras both nodded as the mother spoke.

"The police here asked about that right away," Mom said. "Liliana's passport is still in a desk drawer in her bedroom. Paulo took his with him when he left to go looking for her."

"How long after she disappeared did he start looking?"

Mom communicated our questions about Paulo. His mother and father responded at length. When they finished, Mom summarized for us.

"At first, Paulo had organized volunteers who helped search for Liliana on Faial and Pico. He questioned everyone he knew. He combed the Horta Marina asking about her, showing her photo to strangers and anyone who had been moored there at the time of her disappearance."

"Sounds like he was duplicating everything the police here in the Azores were doing," my father said. "If she was taken aboard a yacht that left the islands, she could have ended up anywhere."

"How long after she disappeared did Paulo leave for America?" I asked.

When Mom asked my question, Paulo's mother

glanced at a calendar on the kitchen wall. "*Uma semana*." Her eyes clouded with unshed tears.

"One week," Mom said.

"So Paulo left the Azores one week after his sister went missing. Less than two weeks later, he turned up in Timbergate, a gunshot victim," Nick said. "He must have discovered something that led him there."

I agreed. "We have to find out what it was. The connection to Timbergate might lead us to Liliana."

"Catia claimed the yacht was American," Nick said. "That's what this Miguel told them. And she thought the vessel's name was an American word." He shook his head as if to clear it. "Was Paulo aware of his sister's fascination with California?"

Mom asked the Ferreras.

"*Sim, é claro*," the mother replied.

"Yes, of course," Mom said.

Senhora Ferrera glanced at her husband. They both shook their heads, their expressions drained of hope, unable to hold their bodies upright after a long day of questions about their missing daughter and gravely injured son.

The father spoke, while my mother and father listened intently. This time Dad interpreted.

"They know that their son booked a flight to Boston, and then on to San Francisco. He told them he had an idea, but it was a long shot. A friend he had met working on the docks in Madalena had left Pico a year earlier to emigrate to America. Paulo's friend had found work somewhere in Marin County. He'd been in touch with Paulo several months earlier, telling him it was a great place, that he should come to America, learn the language, and see more of the world than just the Azores. He offered to help him get work."

"What's that got to do with finding Liliana?"

"Paulo suspected the superyacht was from the San Francisco Bay Area, but when his parents asked him to explain why, he said it was just a hunch. If he was right, he thought his contact in Marin County might know of a way to identify the American yacht," Dad said. "Unfortunately, they had lost touch with each other. Paulo insisted on making the trip to California to look up his friend and ask for help."

"Do they know where Paulo's friend works?" Nick asked.

"They assume it's either on a fishing boat or some kind of dock work," Mom said.

"Do they know the friend's name?" Nick asked.

Mom told him Paulo's father didn't remember ever hearing the name.

Senhora Ferrera tapped her husband's arm, and with a heavy accent, said, "*A ghosht.*"

"A ghost?" I repeated. She nodded. I looked at Nick. He shook his head. "Probably something she misunderstood."

"Maybe there's something in Paulo's email that would identify his friend?" I looked at Mom. She spoke to the Ferreras, who shook their heads as the mother replied.

"Paulo didn't use an email account," Mom said. "He preferred to text. Of course, he took his phone with him when he left."

"That's too bad." I tried to hide my disappointment from Senhora Ferrera. "That name might have been helpful to the police here. I wonder how much progress they've made. They must know by now that Paulo is in the hospital in Timbergate with a bullet wound in his spine."

Dad relayed my question. Senhor Ferrera nodded and gave a rapid reply.

"He says the Timbergate police are in contact with the police here in Madalena. Both know about Paulo's situation, and they know he had a friend in Marin County, but so far, they haven't been able to identify him. Paulo had no phone on him when he was brought into the hospital."

"If only Catia could recall the name of that yacht," I said. "Mom, did you ask if she or Liliana took a photo of it?"

"Yes, honey, I asked. Catia didn't, because her phone's battery had died, but Liliana took a few shots with her phone."

"Did she share them with Catia?"

"Catia said no. And she seemed certain that Liliana didn't post the photos on Facebook or anywhere else."

"Where is Liliana's phone?"

"Gone. Apparently, with Liliana."

"What about email? Ask if her parents looked at her email account." Mom relayed my question and both nodded their heads.

"They did, and so did the police here. The family has only one computer. An older model laptop. Liliana used it for email, but she didn't have her own account. The parents insisted she use the family account. Unfortunately, the Horta police found nothing on it that would yield a clue to her disappearance."

"If she's like her brother, and most young people these days, she did most of her communicating by text," Nick said.

Mom reached out and touched my arm. "We can't keep pounding these people with questions, Aimee. Why don't you see if you can reach your hospital colleagues for an update on Paulo's condition? Then we'll return to Horta with a promise to contact the Ferreras right away if there are any new developments."

She was right. Liliana's parents were deathly pale, their shoulders drooping. The mother held a shaky hand to her forehead, while her husband stared down at his empty palms.

"Wendi, I don't want to push this now," Nick said, "but they're going to have to decide soon about returning to the States with us." He asked Mom to let them know they still had a couple of days to make up their minds.

I managed to get a call through to Cleo, who reported that Paulo was no worse physically. In fact, he might be gaining ground, but he was still in a coma. Mom relayed that news to his parents. A quiet sob escaped his mother; his father's lips tightened into a thin line. We said our goodbyes, returned to the dock by taxi, and caught the next ferry back to Horta.

When we reached my parents' house back on Faial, Nick and I declined their dinner invitation. We decided to eat out at one of the thirty restaurants in Horta boasting four or five stars—quite a testament to the thriving tourist population on the island. Before choosing where to eat, we walked down to the Horta Marina to have a look around while we still had the late-afternoon light.

As we strolled along, we marveled at the thousands of colorful paintings and designs on the concrete walkways and walls of the jetty.

"So, what's the story behind all this?" Nick asked.

I was eager to explain. "The most popular version tells that the walls were originally gray and bare, until one superstitious sailor decided to paint a small picture to commemorate his stay at the harbor. He believed that leaving a visual memento of his presence would ensure that the rest of his voyage would be safe. Apparently, it worked, and word got around. Since then, the captain of almost every vessel that docks at the Horta Marina has left a small drawing or message of some kind on the walkways or walls of the jetty."

"How long has that been going on?"

"I'm not sure, but as you can see, almost every inch of this massive wharf is covered, and in many cases, original paintings and messages are painted over by newer ones."

"Amazing," Nick said. "And this is where the missing girl and her friend used to meet?"

"It must be. Catia said they used to sit on the built-in benches and watch the yachts, hoping to spot celebrities. They probably chose a location where the largest boats would be moored."

"It's a shame the girl couldn't recall the name of the yacht where they were invited to the party. Even worse, we can't access the photos on Liliana's phone." Nick studied the colorful drawings, lines of verse, and symbols under our feet. "I wonder if the brother found a clue hidden somewhere in all this graffiti."

I didn't like characterizing the amazing array of writings and artwork on the wharf as *graffiti*—it implied that the drawings were trite or had defaced the walls—but I couldn't think of a more suitable word. "I can't imagine how Paulo spotted something useful here. There's just too much. It would take months to examine all of it. He must have found a witness who gave him a clue."

"Maybe." Nick studied the array of markings as he walked. "He obviously came up with it somehow. Otherwise, why fly all the way to Marin County?"

"His parents said he has a friend there who offered to help him."

Nick's brow creased in a frown. "*Ghost*. Look how well that turned out."

"The poor guy ended up more than two hundred miles north of Marin in Sawyer County." I watched as a seagull swooped low to catch a meal. "And why land-locked Timbergate, of all places?"

"It's on the Interstate 5 corridor. Who knows where he was headed when his shooter caught up with him?"

"I hadn't thought of that," I said. "Do you think he was headed to a seaport farther up the coast? Maybe Astoria in Oregon, or Seattle?"

"Anything's possible, but for now, let's keep our focus on where we are. We only have a couple more days here on the islands. We don't want to get ahead of ourselves and overlook anything."

A sudden breeze whipped across the marina. Nick saw me shiver and put an arm around my shoulders. "Are you getting cold?"

"A little," I said, snuggling close to him.

The light was fading and we were hungry, so we put our survey of the marina on hold in favor of a visit to Peter's Café Sport, Horta's iconic bar and restaurant. Nick was captivated immediately by the eclectic crowd and the décor, his head swiveling from wall to wall to take in the colorful banners, posters, and artifacts from all over the world.

He finally focused on me and took my hand across our table. "This place is amazing!"

I had to laugh at his reaction. Pete's Café had that effect on most first-timers. We settled in with our beers and made a meal of *pao d'alho*, a delicious garlic bread concoction that brought to mind an expression I'd heard a few times in the past. The bread was almost *better than sex*, but not quite. Not better than sex with Nick.

EIGHT

TUESDAY MORNING MY parents encouraged Nick and me to play tourist. They pointed out that searching the marina for clues would eat away our entire day with little chance of finding anything helpful. The odds were miniscule.

"Aimee, you and Nick are supposed to be on vacation," Mom said. "Please don't give it all up. Spend this day enjoying yourselves. Let the police here and in California do their job."

I was torn at the thought of setting the missing girl's fate aside, even for a day, but my mother's words made sense. It wasn't up to Nick and me to solve this mystery.

There didn't seem to be anything more to learn from the Ferreras. Cleo had my parents' phone number, so they could keep in touch if there were any new developments with Paulo's condition. Nick and I agreed to follow Mom's advice.

Dad offered to loan us his car, so after a breakfast of scrambled eggs and *linguiça*, we headed to the island's Public Library and Regional Archive. Nick wasn't as excited as I was about the visit, until we arrived and he realized we were talking about far more than a collection of dusty old books. The library's history dated back to 1886, which fascinated me, as I'd heard stories about my great-great-grandmother, who as a teenager often rode a ferry from her home on nearby St. George Island to Faial to visit the library in Horta. I loved thinking that the library gene in my family could be traced back over so many generations. With its move to new premises in 2008, the library was vastly expanded. There were exhibit rooms, a cultural shop, an auditorium, an amphitheater, and a multifunctional room, all framed by a beautiful terrace and garden.

We took the morning tour, viewing paintings by a famous artist from the Azores in one room and an intriguing exhibit of audiovisual toys in another. There were other exhibits, but I didn't spend the kind of time there that I would have if I'd been alone. It wasn't fair to Nick. When it was his turn to choose how to spend our afternoon, he opted for the whale-watching trip. I agreed.

We were lucky with our choice of captains. He was determined to find the amazing mammals and didn't give up until we'd had sightings of sperm whales, pilot whales, and three different species of dolphins.

By the time we returned to the dock, the afternoon shadows were leaning toward evening. We were sunburned, wind-blown, and tired, but happy that we'd carved out time for the experience. The marine adventure had been a pleasant diversion from our concerns about Liliana and Paulo Ferrera, but I couldn't keep the siblings out of my thoughts for long. On our drive back to my parents' home, I put in a call to Cleo, who reported again that there was nothing new. Paulo remained in a coma.

Back at the house, I caught the savory aromas of a special meal before we stepped through the front door. I knew right away that Dad had put his cooking class skills to use to create a feast—with a little help from Mom, no doubt. On the menu were savory chicken breasts baked in white wine, green salad with black olives and red onion, and homemade Portuguese yeast bread. I told Nick we were definitely eating with my parents. He didn't object. A whiff or two convinced him that we wouldn't find a better meal in any restaurant on the island.

As we ate, Mom reported that the Ferreras had decided to return to the States with us. Their passports were in order. They would spend Wednesday arranging for neighbors to look after their place while they were gone. The police on Pico and Faial would have the Ferreras' contact information, so they could stay in touch if any news surfaced in the search for Liliana. Her parents still believed there was a possibility that she would show up unharmed somewhere in the Azores. That seemed unlikely, but we understood how important it was for them to hold on to hope.

On a lighter note, Nick and I gave my mother and father a capsule version of our day. The library and the whales and dolphins. They traded knowing smiles that said, *Typical tourists.*

"So, what do you two have planned for tomorrow?" Dad asked. "Looks like you're going to have to pick and choose, since it's your last day."

"I'd have liked to climb Mt. Pico," Nick said, "but that's going to have to wait. We won't have enough time." He looked to me. "Any ideas?"

"We could split up for part of the day. I wouldn't mind exploring the library in more depth, but there might be something you'd enjoy more."

Dad said, "Nick, why don't you and I go for a sail? I'm not scheduled to teach at the dojo until Thursday."

"Lucas, he just spent all afternoon on a whale-watching boat," Mom said.

"That wasn't sailing." Dad leaned toward Nick. "Different thing altogether, you'll see."

I saw Nick's face light up. Sail with Dad or hang around with me while I prowled the library? No problem guessing which he would choose.

"Sailing sounds great," Nick said, "but I have to admit I haven't had a lot of experience. Just a time or two on the lakes back at home."

"Even better. If you like, I'll give you some pointers. But I should warn you, once you experience the feel of wind in the sails, you'll be hooked. There's nothing better than blue water sailing."

With our Wednesday plans settled, we finished our meal. After the table was cleared, Mom produced a plate of delicate Portuguese meringue cookies called *suspiros*, or sighs, and Dad uncorked a bottle of Madeira, the famous amber dessert wine from the island of the same name—in the Azores, of course. A perfect finish to a traditional dinner.

Dad raised his glass in a toast. "Here's to our favorite tourists: come back soon."

I hoped we would. This visit had been too short. Instead of indulging in relaxation and romance, we'd been preoccupied with finding a missing girl and discovering what had happened to her critically wounded brother.

WEDNESDAY MORNING, NICK and my father left early for the Horta Marina, where Dad's sailboat was moored. Mom and I lingered over coffee. I asked if she would like to come along with me to the library.

"I know once you're there, you'll be engrossed in all the place has to offer." She reached over and patted my arm. "I've done that myself. Why don't I let you go alone? We can meet later for lunch. I'm not scheduled to work today."

Good for Mom. She knew her daughter well. We agreed I would text her when I was ready for lunch.

I walked the mile from my parents' house to the library, basking in cool morning sunshine and breathing fresh island air mingled with a hint of ocean breeze.

At the library, I lost track of time while I pored over the collection of materials in the Regional Archive, hoping to learn more of the history of the Azores. Two hours into my morning, my phone buzzed. A text from Mom, but she was early.

I have news. Call me.

I walked outside to make the call. "Hi, what's going on?"

"Catia just texted me. She can get away to meet us while her grandmother is at the dentist. She says she has something to tell us about Liliana that she was afraid to say in front of her grandmother."

"Where does she want to meet?" *Please, let this be important.*

"At the marina entrance. She'll be there in about ten minutes. Do you want me to pick you up?"

"Yes, I'll wait outside and watch for your car."

Mom arrived a few minutes later. We soon reached the marina entrance where Catia waited. Dressed in jeans and a modest white-cotton blouse, she stood hugging herself while a cool breeze lifted strands of her hair.

As we approached, Catia ran toward my mother. Tears streaming down her cheeks, she said, "*Minha culpa.*"

Mom glanced at me. I nodded. The translation was obvious. *My fault.* Why was this girl blaming herself for

Liliana's disappearance? And why couldn't she explain it the day before, when we had questioned her so thoroughly? *Because the grandmother had been there.* The enlarged pupils of her red-rimmed brown eyes told me Catia was frightened. Frightened of her grandmother... or worse?

I pointed at my watch. Mom asked Catia when she had to be back. The answer was an hour. I had a feeling that whatever we were going to learn from the girl, this was our last chance. The first thing I wanted to know was the exact location on the marina where the girls had seen the yacht in question.

Catia walked us to the section of the marina that accommodated the largest vessels. She glanced around, as if unsure of exactly where it had been moored. She made a wide gesture with her arm and spoke. *"Aqui, em algum lugar."*

Mom raised an eyebrow at me. "'Here, somewhere,' she says."

Mom drove the three of us to a quiet bistro a short distance from the dentist's office. She ordered three hot teas with milk and honey. When Catia's eyes were dry and she seemed composed enough to tell her tale, Mom asked her about the missing parts of her story. That prompted Catia to ask for our promise that her grandmother not be told what she was going to relate. She was already breaking her promise to Liliana. This was to have been their secret.

We agreed, although I had reservations, and I was sure Mom did as well. If what we heard put Liliana's life in danger, we might have to break our promises, too.

Catia spoke in rapid Portuguese, leaving me in the dark, except for a random word here and there. Mom kept a calming and reassuring demeanor throughout their exchange. After about ten minutes, they finished. Mom patted Catia's arm and said softly, *"Obrigado."* Thank you.

Mom turned to me. "Well, this puts a new spin on things. I understand why she's reluctant to have her grandmother hear this part of the story. It helps to know that Catia was born out of wedlock. Her sixteen-year-old mother was disowned by the grandmother, who took the infant child in when her mother left the Azores to live on mainland Portugal. The grandmother has kept a tight rein on Catia, using the family disgrace to illustrate the perils of hanging out with boys or of day-dreaming about romance. She even hopes to convince Catia to become a nun."

"Oh, my God," I said. "The poor girl."

Mom paid for our tea, and the three of us took our drinks outside, where we sat at a table in the bistro's courtyard. Mom and Catia went on with their dialogue while I jotted questions as they came to mind.

After several minutes, Mom apparently told Catia to take a break so I could be brought up to speed. The girl nibbled at her nails while Mom interpreted for me.

"We already knew the girls liked to sit on the marina benches to people-watch—their particular interest being the area where the largest yachts were moored."

"Of course," I said. "They were always on the look-out for celebrities."

"What we hadn't heard before was that the man who invited them to the yacht party also told them that the captain of the American yacht was seeking young women who might be interested in hiring on as members of the crew. He mentioned working as a maid or in the galley, doing chores that wouldn't require any special training." Mom reached over to give Catia's arm a reassuring pat. I knew she felt the same sense of help-lessness that I was experiencing.

For impressionable young girls, that was a delicious, almost irresistible temptation. For me, and other skep-tical adults, it was a huge red flag.

"Is that what happened?" I asked. "She thinks Lili-ana left on that yacht voluntarily?"

"She's not sure, but it's possible. Liliana had a rea-son to take that risk. She desperately wanted to get to America."

"Why?"

"The classic reason. A boy. Liliana met him online through Facebook several months ago. He said he was eighteen and lived in Sausalito, California, with his par-ents. He had been tutoring her in English via emails. He kept urging her to come to America, filling her with dreams of getting engaged."

"So Catia thinks Liliana saw the American yacht as her chance to meet her online boyfriend in person?"

"I'm afraid so."

"But the Ferreras said nothing was found in Liliana's emails that looked suspicious. According to them, she didn't have a Facebook account. How is that possible if she was trading messages with this boy in America?"

"I asked Catia about that. She says Liliana did have a Facebook account, but her parents didn't know about it. She complained to Catia that her parents checked up on her family email account, so to avoid their scrutiny, she created a secret email account with the help of an-other girl. Catia doesn't know who she is. She just re-ferred to her as *garota safada*." Mom's lips twisted. "It means 'naughty girl.'"

"Sounds like Liliana was itching to break free of parental control," I said. "She went to all kinds of trouble to set up a secret email account and a secret phone."

"Exactly," Mom said. "When Liliana spotted the American boy on Facebook, she became intrigued. She used her secret email account exclusively to exchange messages with him. The boy warned Liliana not to tell anyone her secret email address or her password. She wouldn't even tell Catia." Mom sighed. "It turns out it was the online boyfriend who provided Liliana with a cellphone. He put her on his account and sent her the phone at the naughty girl's address."

"Ah, that makes sense. I was wondering how she could have been paying for it without her parents knowing. Does Catia know the phone number of Liliana's cell?"

"No. She swears Liliana wouldn't tell her. Once Liliana linked her email account to that phone, she shut down her Facebook account. Her online social life was all about trading email and texts with this boy."

"Any idea what it was about him that captured Liliana's fancy?"

"Some common interest in music. Not unusual at Liliana's age." Mom glanced at her watch. "We're running out of time, Aimee. We needed to get Catia back to her grandmother's dental office."

Mom assured Catia that we wouldn't reveal what had been discussed during this meeting to her grandmother, but that we would have to divulge it to the police. She elicited Catia's promise to get in touch with Liliana's parents if she thought of any other clues to Liliana's whereabouts, and especially if she should hear directly from her friend. That way, the Ferreras could inform the police, perhaps leaving Catia's grandmother out of the loop. Catia agreed, but before we dropped the girl at the dentist's office, I thought of one last question.

"Mom, ask her if Liliana told her the online boyfriend's name."

She asked. Catia answered.

"She says Liliana called him Francisco."

"We need to know if Catia told any of this to Liliana's brother. Paulo must have learned something that caused him to show up in Northern California."

"Good point." Mom quickly asked my question.

Catia shook her head vigorously. "*Nao.*" She hopped from Mom's car and hurried to the entrance of the dental office building.

I turned to Mom. "So, all we know about this mysterious online boyfriend is that his name—at least the name he gave to Liliana—is Francisco."

"I'd be surprised if he exists at all." Mom winced, obviously considering worst-case scenarios. "Liliana was in way over her head in every part of this calamity. Do you have any other ideas about gathering clues?"

"Not really, but I keep thinking maybe we should walk the marina to the area where that American yacht was moored when the crew member invited the girls to the party."

"The section of marina that Catia showed us covers a lot of space," Mom said. "But that reminds me, if Liliana had been learning English from her online boyfriend, you'd think she might have recognized the name of that yacht."

"True," Mom said. "But if Liliana did know the name, she apparently didn't translate it for Catia."

Frustration crept into my reply. "This mystery would be a lot easier to unravel without the language barrier."

"You're just *now* realizing that?" Mom laughed gently, reminding me that she was the one who carried the burden of interpreting. She pulled her car around and we headed back to the marina. On the way, I had a depressing thought. "That superyacht has been gone for two and a half weeks. It's not very likely we'll find anything useful at the marina."

Mom turned to me and smiled. "Stay positive. It's worth a shot. Mariners are a superstitious bunch. You know the tradition. Most captains leave a memento there. Either by painting a design or by writing some sort of message that identifies their vessel."

"Of course, but why would the yacht we're after do that if they were up to something illegal?"

"You never know. This was your idea, and we have time. Your father and Nick didn't say when they would be back from their sail. It could be another couple of hours."

"Let's go, then. At least we know it was somewhere near one of the benches."

We walked the pier to the area Catia had pointed out. An endless variety of drawings, paintings, and messages decorated every inch of the walkway under our feet and coated the marina walls and built-in concrete benches. There were colorful designs—some basic and child-like, others showing true artistic talent. Messages in countless languages left even my mother unable to translate.

"Let's look for anything with a recent date that might hint at an American yacht," I said.

"I'm looking," Mom said, "but don't get your hopes up. This really is a needle-in-a-haystack exercise."

After an hour of searching in the area where the yacht had been moored, we were both feeling the effects of the afternoon sun and hoping a cooling sea breeze would stir up some relief. We were about to give up when I spotted a tiny patch of bright-red paint that looked fresh. It was in the shape of a pennant, but very small, no more than five inches from the straight edge to the point. I knelt for a closer look. It bore stylized initials in navy blue that read: BWYC. The date was etched in miniscule scratches: *6/3*. I jumped up and waved Mom over.

"Come quick, look at this."

She hurried to where I stood. "What is it?"

I pointed at the small drawing. "That's a replica of the Bay Wind Yacht Club burgee. The same one that Buck Sawyer's yacht flies. See how fresh the paint is? Look at that date. It's the last day Liliana was seen."

Mom had lived in Horta long enough to know that yacht clubs each had a special flag called a burgee that their members flew from their masts to identify themselves as members.

"So it's likely a yacht from Marin County was moored here on that day. Is that what you're thinking?"

"It seems like a good bet. I'm sure it's same flag I've seen on Buck's yacht. Whenever Nick and I are in the San Francisco Bay Area for a weekend, Buck lets us use his yacht as a free hotel."

Mom played skeptic. "But you said it yourself: if the yacht captain who invited the girls to a party was into something illegal, why leave this evidence he was here?"

"And you're the one who said mariners are superstitious." I took a photo of the little drawing with my phone. "It had to be someone who knew about the legend and wanted to ensure a safe voyage. Someone who didn't know the captain was into something criminal."

"That seems like a bit of a stretch."

"I agree." Then another possibility hit me with an almost physical shock. "Mom, maybe the person who drew this had a compelling reason to ensure a safe voyage."

"Oh, my goodness, Aimee. Do you mean what I think you do?"

"I'm afraid so. I think it was Liliana."

"That's taking a lot for granted."

My mother had a point, but I wasn't ready to give up. "Mom, we need to know whether the police here on Faial have talked to the harbormaster. There might be a way to identify the yacht through their records."

"Dad already thought of that. He called Senhora Ferrera this morning. The police told her and her husband that the harbormaster's office had no record of the yacht Catia described. They surmised that it refueled the afternoon it arrived and somehow managed to depart that same night without checking in at the harbormaster's office or at the customs office."

"How would that be possible?" I asked. "There had to be a record of paying for the fuel. A credit card, or some sort of running account, maybe?"

"Not if it was a cash transaction involving a hefty bribe," Mom said. "Sorry to point that out, but the police have to consider the possibility, especially if that yacht was up to no good."

"Then we're back to the painted burgee," I said. "It's not a slam dunk, but it's something."

Mom and I headed back to her car. She insisted that we stop in at Pete's Café to talk over Catia's news about the boyfriend and the secret email account.

"We have to tell Liliana's parents Catia's news, and I'm sure we should also share our information with the police here and back in Timbergate." Mom found a parking spot not far from Pete's. "And we need to decide whether to tell Catia's grandmother. I'd like to hear what you think."

We entered the door to Pete's, where I was struck

again by the plaques, banners, flags, and exotic art objects that decades of visiting mariners had proudly left on display as evidence of their seafaring adventures.

The place was crowded, as usual. I scanned the room looking for a place to sit and was surprised to see Nick at a table toward the back with three other men. Dad wasn't with them. Nick seemed engrossed in some sort of card game. He glanced up, saw us, and quickly looked down at his cards, giving his head a slight shake, as if the cards were a disappointment. I knew better. Mom saw him, too, and nudged me with her elbow.

"Look, there's—"

"Shhh," I took her arm and turned her toward the door, saying in a loud voice, "It's too crowded in here. Let's go home."

"But, we were—"

"We'll come back later." I tugged her arm, nearly dragging her out the door.

Outside, I walked swiftly to Mom's car, while she hurried to keep up. When we reached the car, she stood with her hands on her hips and glared at me. "Aimee, what's the matter with you?"

"Mom, I know Nick, and I know he was sending me a signal to stay away. He's in there fishing for information."

"Then where's your father?" Mom looked around as if Dad might materialize before our eyes.

"Home, would be my guess. He and Nick must have this under control."

Mom and I slipped into her car. She started the engine. "Do you think Nick has a lead about the missing girl?"

"Maybe, or maybe he's just hoping. When we get to the house, we can ask Dad what's going on."

Dad was home, as I'd expected. We asked what was up with Nick, but Dad didn't have much to offer. He said Nick had asked to be dropped off at Pete's Café after their sail. We'd have to wait until he got home to hear what he'd been up to. When we finished filling Dad in on our meeting with Catia, I asked Mom for the password to her Wi-Fi account. With that, I went to the guest room and opened my laptop to do what librarians do. *Research.*

I found several major media stories about crimes on the high seas. One of them pointed out that violent crimes committed in international waters frequently go unreported. I switched my search to yachts and discovered that a ship capable of carrying enough fuel to travel from the Azores to the States would have to be somewhere in the 250-foot range. Curious, I priced yachts that size and came up with a couple of bargains at around 50 million. The most likely route from the Azores would take the yacht to Florida, where it would refuel, then through the Panama Canal, and up the coast to Marin County. That trip could take as long as a month, according to the estimates I found online.

One last fact surprised me. Vessels passing through the Panama Canal cannot just show up, line up, and pass through. They must make arrangements anywhere from three to six months in advance. If this mysterious yacht had done that, it might be arriving back in Marin County at the Bay Wind Yacht Club in just over a week. There was always a chance that Liliana would arrive in Northern California unharmed, meet up with her online boyfriend, and live to tell their grandchildren about her adventure. But I had grave doubts.

Her brother had gone looking for her and ended up a gunshot victim in a coma at Timbergate Medical Center. Where had he been, and who had he spooked to earn a bullet in the back? Had he seen the same painted burgee on the marina that I had spotted? Come to the same conclusion?

If Liliana had remained on that yacht, and it made a straight-on run from the Azores to California, her brother would still have arrived at least two weeks ahead of her—and put a target on his back by questioning the wrong people.

An hour had passed when Nick finally arrived by taxi. Over a dinner of kale soup and cornbread, Mom and I repeated Catia's story for Nick. His reaction only deepened our concerns for Liliana.

"Damn." He filled his lungs and let the breath out slowly. "The online boyfriend scam. The friend thinks Liliana fell for it?"

A shiver of alarm traced across my shoulders. "What are you saying, Nick?"

"I'm saying we don't know what the girl's gotten herself in for. I spent two hours at Pete's listening to horror stories from sailors and yachtsmen. They all seemed like good people, maybe even solid contacts for the future." He gave a rueful smile. "I didn't want to press them too hard, for fear they'd suspect I was a shady character myself."

"Did you get anything that could be a lead about Liliana?" I thought of drug cartels, sex trafficking, and girls sold as ISIS brides. I shuddered at the possibility of Liliana in the hands of terrorists.

He gestured at Mom and me with his spoon. "Nothing as good as what you two turned up. Bay Wind Yacht Club will be on our radar big time when we get back to California."

All of us agreed that we wouldn't need to break our

promise to Catia about keeping her grandmother out of it. At least not yet.

Later, when we were alone in the guest room, I pressed Nick harder for details about his sleuthing.

"I have a feeling there's more on your mind than what you were willing to say in front of my parents. Want to tell me about it?"

He sat on the edge of the bed, slipping off his shoes. "I suppose I should, but you're not going to like it. Those fellows at Pete's left me feeling discouraged about the missing girl's fate. I'd rather not put that in your parents' minds just yet, and I definitely don't want to frighten the Ferreras any more than they already are."

"What did you hear? Anything we can use? Anything that points in the direction of Buck's yacht club in Marin County?"

"I wish it were that specific. They talked in general about how much serious crime goes undetected in international waters. Apparently, thousands of people die under suspicious circumstances every year. The crimes start at heinous and slide up the scale to more evil than you can imagine."

"I just spent part of the afternoon online reading about the same thing." I filled him in on the rest of my laptop searches. "I'm assuming your card-playing companions spoke English. Were they locals or visitors?" I pulled back the covers and dropped onto my side of the bed, leaning back against the plump pillows.

"One from the UK, one from Australia, so language was no problem."

"Did you tell them anything about Liliana or Catia?"

"No. I kept my part of the conversation pretty vague. You know, just a clueless tourist who likes to gab over a few beers." He stripped down to his T-shirt and boxers and slipped under the covers. "Is this how you want to spend our last night in paradise?"

"Not really, but I won't be able to get it off my mind unless we talk it out. So far, all I know is that any number of terrible things could have happened to Liliana if she left the islands on that yacht."

"I'm sorry, but I know you, and you're not going to accept a sugar-coated version."

"Even more reason for us to help, right?"

"Of course, and I have an idea where we can start." Nick took my hand and gave it a squeeze. "According to your research, even if that yacht set a direct course for Marin County when it left Faial, it wouldn't arrive for at least another week."

"That's right. What do you have in mind?"

"I'm thinking we make a trip to the San Francisco Bay Area this weekend."

"But the mystery yacht won't have arrived. If we can't look for it, what's the point?"

"We still might learn something," Nick said. "Thanks to Buck, I'm a member of the Bay Wind Yacht Club. We can start with that. Snoop around a bit. See if we can pick up any information about members cruising to the Azores."

"Good idea. Do you have any thoughts about how to identify the friend Paulo planned to meet?"

"Yes, I'm fairly certain Buck's hull diver is Portuguese. There's at least a chance he'd be acquainted with other young Portuguese men working at the harbors."

"Darn, you had my hopes up for a minute. I thought you were going to suggest that Buck's diver might be Paulo's friend."

"That would be a hell of a coincidence, so I wouldn't count on it."

NINE

MY PARENTS DROVE Nick and me to the airport on Thursday morning. When we arrived, Liliana's mother and father were seated in the waiting area, their faces masks of apprehension. Not surprising, as they were about to place their lives in the hands of a pilot they had met for the first time only three days earlier.

Mom smiled and spoke in reassuring tones, most likely pointing out that Nick was an excellent pilot who had flown us all the way from California in safety and comfort. When she finished, the Ferreras nodded, but still appeared anxious. It touched my heart to know they would face any fear for the chance to see their injured son and to carry on the search for their missing daughter.

I had tucked my Portuguese phrase book and dictionary in my purse, knowing we'd be faced with a language barrier for the duration of the flight. The Ferreras were subdued and quiet most of the way, either from anxiety about flying or sadness about their children. They even dozed for the final few hours. The four-hour time difference put us in Boston at ten in the morning. When we landed, they stayed with me while Nick arranged parking for the plane. We reached our hotel at eleven and found Grandpa and Tanya waiting for us in the dining area.

We had decided to meet there for brunch because Grandpa Machado spoke enough Portuguese to help with translating for the Ferreras. He explained to them that there were large enclaves of Portuguese in Boston, most of them bilingual. Grandpa had already identified three Portuguese-speaking members of the hotel staff who could help the Ferreras out if they needed anything while Nick and I were attending the play that evening.

Tanya pulled two tickets to *Bus Stop* from her purse, saying they were the best seats in the house. When we offered to reimburse her, she said it wasn't necessary. They were complimentary because she and Tony were members of the cast.

The Ferreras seemed content to retire to their room after brunch. They were no doubt fatigued from the flight and the constant worry about Liliana and Paulo. I hoped they would be able to rest.

Nick and I checked into our room and made use of our cellphones. I called my parents first to say we'd arrived safely, and then gave Amah and Jack a capsule version of our past four days. Next I called Cleo, but she was in a meeting and unavailable.

Nick contacted Buck at his hotel across town to arrange the time of our flight back to California the next morning. When he finished his call, I asked if he had filled Buck in about the yacht.

"Did you tell him about the Bay Wind burgee?"

"I did." Nick flopped down next to me on the king-sized bed and kicked off his shoes. "I asked if he knew anyone at his yacht club with a vessel matching the description we have of the superyacht."

"What did he say?"

"He's seen a few come and go, but he doesn't know much about any of them or their owners. He pointed out that it was a stretch to assume the burgee you saw painted on the Horta Marina floor was related to the yacht in question." Nick must have read disappointment in my eyes. He put an arm around my shoulders. "Hey, don't let that bother you. He was making a point, playing devil's advocate, but he's on our side."

We had a few hours to spare before the play, but Nick was tired from flying, and I was feeling more morose than romantic. Sitting together on the bed, we agreed that our best use of the time would be a refreshing nap.

Later, we met Liliana's parents for dinner in the hotel restaurant. Afterward, we escorted them safely back to their room, where we posted the names of the Portuguese-speaking staff members on a list next to the desk phone.

Nick and I took a taxi to the theater, found our seats in the center of the second row, and settled in. While the theater filled, we flipped through our programs. I spotted a name I recognized on the page listing cast and crew, did a double-take, and looked at Nick to see if he had noticed it. He was looking over my head at the person who had entered our row and settled in the empty seat next to mine. I turned to see who it was just as Nick stood, leaned over me, and extended his hand.

"Hello," Nick said. "You're Aimee's friend, James O'Brien, aren't you?"

"That's right." James reached out to shake the offered hand. "And you're Nick…um, Alexander, isn't it?"

I sat between them, watching their clasped hands in front of my face, while the moment seemed to stretch on and on. By the time their handshake finally ended, I had regained enough composure to speak calmly.

"James, I just noticed your name in the program. I had no idea you directed this production."

"That's my fault," he said. "I told your grandfather and Tanya I might not make it to this closing night performance. I thought if I was able to be here, it would be fun to surprise you."

"You definitely pulled it off," Nick said. "Hell of a surprise. Right, Aimee?" Nick's smile wasn't his best effort. His body language remained carefully neutral.

Fun wasn't exactly how I would have described the surprise. It had only been eight months since James flew out to Timbergate from New York during the investigation of his brother's murder. He'd been my girlhood crush about a dozen years ago, and our renewed acquaintance had been a major distraction to the grown-up me. That had been an uncertain time for Nick and me, since we were struggling with where we stood as a couple. Back then, Nick seemed to sense that James could be a serious rival. With Nick and me on solid ground and James a continent away, he had ceased to be an issue.

Even so, sitting between them, my tension level rose immediately. I cast around for some way to relieve it.

"James, I *am* surprised to see you here in Boston. I thought most of your work was based closer to New York."

"There are Equity theaters all over the country that need directors," James said. "I go where the work is."

Nick leaned forward to say, "You said you weren't sure you'd be here. Do you usually attend every performance of the plays you direct?"

"Not at all," James said. "Although that is common in amateur community theater playhouses. In the world of professional theater, the director's job is finished once the play opens."

"But you're here tonight," I said.

"Closing nights are different. I always try to make them. I usually bring token gifts for the cast and crew. Attend the cast party, that sort of thing."

I'd forgotten about the cast party. Grandpa had invited us to attend, but I wondered if Nick would be up for it.

I noticed James hadn't brought a date, but I wasn't going to ask him about that. Not in front of Nick. Once the play began, Nick settled back into his seat on my left, and James did the same on my right. I tried to concentrate on the play and ignore the waves of testosterone that seemed to surround me. James had done well. The production was flawless and the cast was doing a fine job. Grandpa and Tanya were the best, of course.

During intermission, James headed backstage while Nick and I stretched our legs by walking out to the lobby.

"Quite a surprise seeing your old pal James," Nick said. "Do you suppose he had something to do with us being seated next to him?"

"I don't know. They were comp tickets in the VIP section. Maybe it was a coincidence." I didn't want to admit that I'd thought the same thing. *Just how did we end up there?*

I had a chance to ask James when I got back to my seat. Nick was still out in the lobby, tied up on a phone call with Buck, discussing our morning flight to California.

"These are great seats," I said. "Did you have anything to do with that?"

"Guilty. When I heard you might be coming, I made sure you and Nick would have the best seats in the house." The house lights dimmed momentarily and James glanced around at the people returning to their seats. Neither of us spotted Nick.

"Thank you," I said. "That was thoughtful." *Except for sitting next to us*, I added silently.

"The least I could do, considering what both of you did for our family last year."

"We were glad to help." My throat tightened, remembering that difficult time. The lights dimmed again, second warning.

"Aimee," James said in a low, serious tone, "I've thought about you a lot since all of that happened. I want you to look me in the eye while I ask this one last time." My stomach fluttered, but I did as he asked. "Are you sure he's the right choice?"

Was he saying *he* was the other choice? I looked away for a fraction of a second, searching the room for Nick. He was nowhere in sight. I looked back at James. "Nick and I are back together, and it's working. I don't know what else to say."

"I haven't heard anything about a wedding in your future. I thought by now you'd be thinking of starting a family." James seemed determined to look for evidence of any shortcomings in my relationship with Nick.

"We're not in a hurry." I felt my face flush. "I could ask the same about you. You must have found a special woman by now."

"'Fraid not." He leaned in close and said softly, "I had one in mind, but she isn't available."

His implication was too obvious to ignore. "I'm sorry to hear that, James. I'm sure you'll find the right person, and you'll be as happy as Nick and I are. We're committed to each other, and that's enough for now."

"Okay, then. I'll take your word for it, but that doesn't stop me from stepping in as your big brother if I get wind that there's trouble in paradise."

I had to smile at that. I was the oldest sibling in my family. I'd always been Harry's big sister, playing the role of protector. "I'm going to take you up on that," I said. I leaned over and brushed a sisterly kiss on James's cheek—just in time to see Nick walking down the aisle toward us with a clenched jaw and wrinkled brow. Had he seen the kiss? Or was something else troubling him?

The second act was even better than the first, but the

tension between Nick, James, and me put a damper on my enjoyment. Afterward, we went backstage to congratulate Grandpa and Tanya and decline their invitation to the cast party. Considering the tension with James, the party was off the table. And Nick was flying us across the country in the morning; he needed a good night's sleep, alcohol free. We said our goodbyes with hugs and kisses and headed back to our hotel room.

We checked in with the concierge, who told us the staff had called the Ferreras several times to make sure they were comfortable. It was late, past eleven. We didn't want to risk waking them if they'd managed to get to sleep, so we went directly to our room. Nick slipped off his shoes and flopped down on the bed.

"You and O'Brien seemed to enjoy your surprise reunion tonight. I take it you had no warning he'd be there."

"No. I had no idea." I eased onto my side of the bed, plumping the pillows behind my back. "I didn't even know he'd directed the play until I saw the *Playbill*."

"Your grandfather knows how to keep a secret." Nick reached over and took my hand. Flashing a grin, he added, "I realize James O'Brien is an old family friend, but I have to admit, I'd have enjoyed the play a lot more if he'd brought his own date instead of sharing mine."

This was the conversation I'd hoped to avoid, but I figured, in for a dime, in for a dollar. "He *is* a family friend, Nick. That's all he is."

"So that explains the friendly kiss?"

Damn. "Of course. It was the least I could do after he…."

"After he what?" Nick raised his eyebrows. "Sounds like I missed something."

"He has this big brother thing about me. He just wanted to make sure you and I are okay."

"No, Aimee, he wants to make sure *you're* okay. He doesn't give a rat's behind about me." Nick looked down where our hands were still intertwined and rubbed the back of mine with his thumb. "I don't blame him. If I were in his place, I'd be doing the same."

"I told him you and I are together and that we're happy." In the silence that followed, we heard the muffled sounds of the TV in the next room, then soft laughter.

"We are happy, aren't we?" Nick gently pulled me to him. "Let's celebrate that."

TEN

FRIDAY MORNING PASSED in a blur of activity. After joining the Ferreras for breakfast in the hotel dining room, we drove to the airport, where Buck was waiting in the lobby area. Again, I had armed myself with my Portuguese phrase book and dictionary. We were airborne shortly after ten. Nick executed a perfect takeoff. Buck rode shotgun in the cockpit and I sat with our passengers. The Ferreras were still so in awe of the plane's luxurious interior that they would have been speechless even without the language barrier. I texted Quinn, letting him know when we would arrive at Timbergate Medical Center with Paulo's mother and father.

After an uneventful five-hour flight, we touched down at Timbergate Municipal Airport at noon Pacific time. Buck parted company with us at the airport parking lot and headed home. Nick and I drove the Ferreras directly to TMC, where we were met in the lobby by Jared Quinn. He introduced the interpreter, a slender, dark-haired sophomore at the local community college whose name was Ramon Silva. He then introduced TMC's social worker, Mary Barton, a lovely young woman with striking blue eyes and long, honey-blonde hair pulled into a clasp at the nape of her neck.

With Ramon Silva's help, Mary explained to the Ferreras that the hospital provided housing just a block from the hospital, where they could stay as long as necessary during Paulo's hospitalization at TMC.

The Ferreras' faces clouded with concern. Senhora Ferrera murmured something to her husband, who turned to Ramon and said in a low voice, *preco de custo?*

"She's asking about the cost," Ramon said to Quinn.

"It's a minimal charge. We'll work something out."

"That won't be necessary," Nick said. "Buck Sawyer wants to cover their expenses while they're here." He handed Quinn a card. "He'd like to talk with you, see what it takes to make that happen."

Quinn took the card. "This is," he cleared his throat, "very generous of him. I'll call him as soon as I get back to my office." He nodded to Ramon. "Please tell them there will be no charge for their lodging at the family housing facility."

When Ramon translated, the Ferreras were visibly relieved, repeating *obrigado* several times to both Quinn and Nick.

While Ramon continued speaking to Paulo's parents, Quinn filled us in. Ramon was on summer break from college and would be staying at the hospital's housing facility as part of his summer job. He would alternate housekeeping chores with his work as one of TMC's interpreters. As long as their son was hospitalized, the Ferreras could count on him to interpret. Relief passed across the Ferreras' faces as Ramon finished his account.

At that point, Quinn's phone chirped. He read a text and looked up at the rest of us. "Paulo's physician is in ICU. Mary, you and Ramon should take the Ferreras up right away. They'll want to hear what his doctor has to say about their son."

As Mary Barton and Ramon escorted them to the elevator, I asked Quinn for the latest on Paulo's condition.

He tapped his left fist into the palm of his right hand, reminding me he was a lefty. "I wish I could say he's making progress. He's still in a coma, and his status has remained virtually unchanged the entire time you've been gone."

"Who's his primary?" I hoped I'd get the right answer.

"Still Godfrey Carver. Dr. Prine hasn't returned from Florida."

Wrong answer. Dr. *Call-me-God* Carver was on my list of least favorite members of the medical staff, no matter how brilliant he was in the operating room. From what I'd heard, he loved the limelight of surgery, but avoided post-surgical follow-up care the way a precocious child avoids studying. It was all about what he could get away with.

"Any word on when Prine will return?"

Quinn looked down at a spot on the floor, giving his head a little shake. "No word yet, I'm afraid. He's still seeing to his daughter's care."

Nick gave my elbow a gentle squeeze, a subtle reminder that he needed to be going. I told Quinn we had to leave, but we hoped to be informed of Paulo's progress—anything he was at liberty to share.

Quinn thanked Nick for his part in bringing Paulo's parents to Timbergate. He asked him to pass on his thanks to Buck Sawyer for the use of his plane and for his generosity in covering the cost of the Ferreras' lodging.

"I've read up on your employer," Quinn said. He took a folded check from his shirt pocket, handing it to Nick. "This is my personal donation to Mr. Sawyer's foundation. I'm very impressed with his dedication to the fight against drugs. We see the results of illegal drug activity and addiction all too often in this setting."

Nick put the check in his pocket. "I'm sure Mr. Sawyer will appreciate the donation." He reached out to shake Quinn's hand. "I've asked Aimee to let me know if there's anything more we can do for the Ferreras."

With everything settled for the time being, Nick headed out to Buck's house to catch up on whatever the next few weeks had in store for him work-wise. From there, he would pick up Ginger, who was back from doggy detective school. I made my way across the complex to check the state of things in the library. I found the entrance locked, with the *Closed* sign facing out. I checked the time, surprised to find that it was only a little past one o'clock in the afternoon. Jet lag had me feeling as if it should be quitting time.

I unlocked the door and went inside. Since it was Friday, I was still technically on vacation. I wasn't due back at work until the following Monday, but I couldn't resist having a look around. I walked through the stacks and saw that Lola Rampley and Bernie Kluckert, my two senior volunteers, had kept the physical aspects of the place *shipshape*, as Bernie would say. I caught a whiff of his favorite lemon-scented furniture polish and had to smile. Next I booted up my computer to check the inevitable glut of emails. Anything outdated or unimportant could be deleted to lighten my load on Monday.

My desk phone's shrill ring jarred me just as I was opening my email. In one short week of island life, I'd forgotten how that penetrating, high-pitched sound echoed throughout the library during quiet times. I checked the caller ID. *Cleo.* Good, the only person I wanted to talk to on this long, tiring day. I picked up.

"Glad it's you," I said. "How did you know I was here? Or did you? Or do you need something from the library?"

"Whoa, girl. Take a breath. Let me get a word in." I pictured her rolling her eyes. "I don't need anything from the library. I knew you would be there because I heard you were over here in the main tower a little while ago. Wasn't hard to guess that you'd be compelled to check up on things. Did the library survive in your absence?"

"It looks fine. I haven't checked my email yet, so I don't know how much catching up I have to do."

"I can answer part of that," she said. "I guess you've heard that Carver is still following Paulo Ferrera's case."

"Unfortunately, I have." I sat at my desk, pulled out a pen and notepad. "Any chance his CME issue has been resolved?"

"Not a snowball's chance. Our chief of staff polled all the members of the Credentials Committee. They were asked if they'd grant Carver a temporary waiver of his CME requirements if he's still needed on the case after his renewal deadline."

"Seems like a reasonable request. Did it work?"

"They refused. Carver has alienated almost every member of the Credentials Committee with his arrogance and boorishness. They were only too happy to cut him off."

"Isn't there some other way to handle this? For the sake of the patient?"

"You would think so, but it turns out Quinn and the TMC Governing Board stood by the Credentials Committee's action. They think making this exception would set a dangerous precedent."

"I guess they have a point. Now what?"

"Carver has the notion that he can convince you his credits add up to the required minimum. Something about a couple of courses he took by mail. He claims he finished them and submitted the documentation to your office."

"Oh, brother. How did you respond to that?"

"I told him that if you had received that documentation, you'd have forwarded copies to me. I said the medical staff has no choice but to adhere to the bylaws. Meanwhile, Quinn is considering putting Paulo on a medical transport flight to U.C. Davis."

"Why Davis? Why not Sawyer General across town?"

"No can do. Carver doesn't have privileges there. He resigned from their medical staff when several OR nurses filed harassment charges."

"Boy, he doesn't learn, does he?" I searched my mind for other options. "We still have seven days. That's plenty of time for Dr. Prine to get back from Florida."

"That's what Quinn is hoping. His plan is to give it until next Wednesday. If Prine isn't back, and Carver's CME isn't squared away by then, Paulo will be transported."

"Thanks for the heads-up. I'm seeing a barrage of emails from Carver asking me to call him ASAP. I dread dealing with him when I'm so jet-lagged."

"Then give yourself a break. He doesn't know you're back, and there's nothing you can do for him before next week in any case. You might as well wait until Monday. Maybe we'll know more by then."

"That's probably a good idea. Nick and I will be checking things out in the Bay Area all weekend. It might be better to wait, depending on what we learn. In any case, I'll call Carver on Monday."

"Wait. Don't hang up," Cleo said. "I'm dying to hear about your time in the Azores. And what you've learned about Paulo's missing sister. When can we get together?"

"I have to get ready to head out again. I promise we'll have a chance to catch up next week."

I decided to make good my plan to leave the hospital. Problem was, I didn't have a ride. Nick had driven me from the airport, and he'd already left for Buck's place. Both of us had forgotten about that little detail. My cellphone chirped just as I was locking up. A text from Harry.

U need a ride? Nick says.

So Nick remembered, too. I replied with a *yes*.

outside library entrance 5 min?

I sent a K.

Harry's red Jag pulled up exactly five minutes later. "Where to?" he said.

"Home, I guess." I dropped into his soft leather passenger seat. "Sorry to take you away from work. Did Nick fill you in on any of our news from the Azores?"

Harry pulled a right and headed east on the highway to Coyote Creek. "Nope. He just texted asking if I'd give you a lift. He caught me in a lull between snags at the mall site."

Harry's three-story mall project had at least another year to go before completion. As architect and general contractor, he had taken on a massive amount of responsibility for someone so young. I marveled at how well he handled the pressure. Harry was only twenty-seven, at least in his current incarnation, but to me, he was a perfect example of an *old soul*.

We pulled into Amah and Jack's driveway, where we spotted them standing on the front porch. They waved and smiled, gesturing for us to stop and get out of the car. I glanced at Harry. "Did they know we were on our way?"

He turned off the ignition. "Yeah, I called them. You

can imagine how curious they are. I thought you might as well fill us all in at the same time."

The four of us gathered in the family room, where Amah put out a heaping plate of oatmeal cookies.

Jack filled our cups from a fresh pot of coffee. "Let's hear the latest, girl. Catch us up."

I did my best to brief the three of them on everything that had taken place during the past week. The first stop in Boston, our visit to Pico and our time on Faial. Catia's story and the freshly painted yacht-club burgee I'd spotted on the Horta Marina elicited the most interest.

"How do you and Nick plan to follow up on all of that?" Harry asked.

"We just got home. We haven't worked out much in the way of a plan, other than a weekend trip to Marin County."

"Flying or driving?"

"Probably flying. Nick's meeting with Buck as we speak. I suspect we'll be offered the use of one of the Sawyer Foundation planes. Buck's taking this whole situation to heart, as you can imagine."

"What do you mean?" Amah asked. "How does it affect Buck?"

I caught Harry's eye, and he spoke up first. "Buck's foundation is all about fighting drug abuse. He lost his daughter to an overdose when she wasn't a lot older than Liliana is now."

Amah frowned. "I'm confused," she said, turning to me. "Does that mean you suspect drugs play a part in this mystery?"

I didn't want to worry her. "It's just a theory. Buck's mind always turns in that direction." Hoping Harry would back me up, I sent him a silent message. It worked. He backtracked away from the drug connection.

"Aimee's right, Amah, there isn't much to go on at this point, but the police here and in the Azores will follow every lead."

I had a lot more to talk to Harry about, but I didn't want to say too much more in front of Amah and Jack. I steered the conversation back to the stop in Boston on our way back from the Azores. They enjoyed hearing about the play, and about my brief encounter with James O'Brien, whose family still lived in Coyote Creek.

When I wound down, I claimed jet lag, saying I could use a nap, but first I needed Harry to drive me down the lane to the barn. I had crammed my suitcase and carry-on into Harry's car, and I wanted his help getting them up the stairs. I unlocked the door to discover the apartment's interior was not just hot, but musty and stale after being closed up for a week. I went through all the rooms, opening windows and turning on ceiling fans.

"Where do you want these?" Harry still held my bags, one in each hand.

"Master bedroom." I said.

"You could have done this without my help." Harry set the luggage down. "Now what's really on your mind? Something you didn't want to say back at the house?" Harry had an annoying way of reading my mind.

"Just that Nick finally filled me in on the hazardous duties involving his work. I thought you should know I'm up to speed."

"Okay. So how pissed are you?" He couldn't hide the smile twitching at the corners of his mouth.

"A lot, at first. Not so much now, except at you, for thinking it's funny I was the last to know."

"Sorry." Harry returned with me to the dinette table in the kitchen. "Now that we've cleared that up, let's sit down and talk. I know there's more going on with this case than you wanted to say up at the house."

"You'll hear it all from Nick. Probably more than I know. He hung out for a bit at Pete's Café in Horta, where he heard some disturbing stories from a few other patrons in the bar. He claims what they shared was mostly common knowledge, but I'm not convinced he's told me everything. I did some research of my own while we were there. It was disturbing to realize how much crime goes undetected in international waters."

"No wonder you're in a somber mood." Harry put his hand over his chest. "Troubling news aside, I have to say you're breaking my heart even mentioning Pete's. What a great place. Wish I could have been there."

"Sorry I brought it up. You'll have to celebrate with a trip of your own when you finish the mall."

"Count on it." He got up and opened my fridge, pulled out a beer and turned to me. "Okay?"

"Go ahead. I should have offered."

"How about you?"

"Green tea, if there's a cold bottle in there." The apartment had cooled down some, but I was still feeling the change in climate. Coyote Creek's dry heat seemed to start earlier every year.

Harry found an unopened bag of tortilla chips on top of the fridge. He grabbed them and came back to the table. "You said you and Nick are going down to Marin tomorrow, but you haven't worked out a plan, so what's the point?" He popped the bag open.

I took a chip, broke it in two. "There's one thing we know for sure. Liliana was in an online relationship with a boy in Marin County. At least she thought she was. The rest is guesswork." I nibbled the edge of the chip. "We think she went to the yacht party and was talked into leaving on the yacht that same night. That was three weeks ago."

Harry swallowed a sip of beer. "You think there's a chance the online boyfriend is real?"

"I'm not optimistic, but that's one of the things Nick and I hope to determine while we're down there."

"Do you have a name?"

"The girl Mom and I talked to at the Horta Marina said his name is Francisco."

"That's all? Did you get access to the missing girl's phone? What about a computer or a laptop? She must have an email account." Harry was practically bouncing in his chair, his mind spinning with possibilities.

"We asked her parents. They didn't know she had a phone until her friend told us about it. Liliana had arranged for it secretly through the online boyfriend. We're assuming she had it with her the night she disappeared. The parents' home computer was an older model laptop used by the whole family. They all used the same email account. The Azorean police found nothing useful on it." I explained how Liliana had set up her secret Facebook and email, and then shut down her Facebook account at the boyfriend's urging. "As far as we know, at the time she disappeared, Liliana didn't have a laptop of her own or any other device except her cellphone."

"What about her girlfriend? You said they lived on two different islands. They must have communicated."

"They did, but only by email and only using the Ferrera family's account." I told him what Catia had said about Liliana's secret email account. "We were told she used that account only to communicate with the American boyfriend. How is anyone going to figure out how to access that?"

"Good question. It's not going to be simple."

"That seems obvious. How do we start?"

"I have a few ideas." Harry glanced at his phone. "It's four o'clock now. That's ten in the Azores. I'll need the family email account and password the girl was using before she went to the secret one. Find out everything you can about her social media activity. Facebook, Twitter, all of that. If they can't help, get the interpreter to call the other girl—Catia, is it? Do the Ferreras know how to reach her?"

"Yes, but her Facebook is shut down and she wasn't on Twitter or any other social media."

Harry leaned back in his chair. "You know, the police on Faial must have interviewed Liliana's friend early on. They would have asked about email."

"In the beginning, they only knew about her family's account. They didn't know about her secret account or about the boyfriend until we told them."

"Let's hope they're investigating it. What about the police here?" Harry pulled out a pencil and a small pocket tablet and began scribbling notes. "Someone must be leading the investigation into the brother's shooting. Whoever that is would have to be following up on your victim's missing sister."

"I heard it was Kass," I said. "He's the detective who did such a great job leading the investigation involving the hospital a few months ago when Jared Quinn was a murder suspect." I dug around in my purse and came up with a wrinkled card with a smudge that looked like eyebrow pencil. "Here it is: Detective Walter Kass."

Kass was a good man who in the past welcomed any help we offered him.

"You might want to follow up with him when you have something definite," Harry said. "At this point, all you have is speculation and a story from a teenage kid who has already admitted to keeping secrets, if not outright lying for her friend."

Harry finished his beer and took the bottle to the sink. "I'd better get back to work. I left an experienced foreman in charge, but I like to be there at quitting time." He walked to the door. "If you get any info on the missing girl's secret emails or her former Facebook account, give me a shout. And better yet, find out if the parents brought their laptop with them. If they have it here, I'd like to take a look at it."

The door opened as he reached for the knob. He stepped back to let Nick and Ginger enter.

"Hey, Bud, good to see you," Nick said. "I saw your Jag at the main house." They did a fist bump thing that made me smile. How lucky for me that my guy and my brother were best friends.

"You, too," Harry said. "Wish I could stay longer, but duty calls. Aimee can fill you in."

ELEVEN

GINGER PADDED UP to me and sat politely, waiting for an ear scratch. I obliged, happy to see her back from her training session. Nick said, "Lie down," and pointed to her bed in the corner of the kitchen near the door. She obeyed immediately, making a couple of circles before plopping down with a sigh.

"She seems happy to be home," I said.

"So am I." He pulled me into a hug. "Want to debrief me on your conversation with Harry?"

"Sure, he gave me some good ideas. The first is to explore any chance of getting into Liliana's secret email account to see what we can find out about her online boyfriend."

I filled him in on the rest of my conversation with Harry, including the possibility of contacting Detective Kass.

"I agree with Harry," Nick said. "Let's wait until we have something useful for Kass. I suspect the police are already following up on local leads into the shooting. There was at least one witness at that homeless camp by the river. The one who called it in."

"And that caller must have had a cellphone," I said. "Ironic, isn't it? Even the homeless have cellphones."

"It is, until you stop to think how often cellphones are stolen."

"You're painting everyone with the same brush, Nick. Not all homeless people are thieves."

"You're right. That wasn't fair." Nick pulled a bottle of beer from the fridge. "Coincidentally, I picked up a bit of news from Buck this afternoon that we didn't know until now." He popped the lid and sat across the table from me. "The person who called in the incident wasn't exactly homeless. He's a confidential informant for the Timbergate PD."

"Really? Why would Buck know about that?"

"Because the CI is Tango Bueller."

"Tango? He and his sicko buddy could have killed me if it hadn't been for Harry." I took a moment to absorb what Nick had said. "You're saying Tango is a CI?"

Tango had served prison time since attacking me several years ago, and I knew that after his release, he was on the straight-and-narrow, faithful to his twelve-step program. He had even tried, indirectly, to make amends with me. I would not have guessed that he was working undercover with the Timbergate Police Department. His brother Marco, one of TPD's investigators, must have arranged that. I was aware that Marco still had no love lost for either Harry or me. We'd been instrumental in getting Tango sent to prison.

"You know how involved Tango is in Buck's local drug rehab efforts," Nick said. "Turns out, Buck's become a sort of mentor where Tango's concerned."

"That's how you know about Tango's CI status— Buck told you?" This whole new framework for Nick's job and Buck's clandestine operation was taking its toll. "Jeez, do you have any more surprises for me?"

"If I said *no*, would you believe me?" He took a long pull from the beer. "Any thoughts about dinner?"

"Not yet." I looked at our wall clock. "I still need to call the Ferreras' interpreter. Harry wants to look at their laptop, if they brought it with them. Did you happen to notice?"

"No. They had only one piece of luggage. Maybe it was in there."

"Then I'll have the interpreter ask them."

"I'll do chores while you take care of that." Nick headed down to the barnyard.

I called the TMC housing facility where I reached the interpreter, Ramon Silva. He promised to get back to me within an hour. It wasn't long before Nick returned from chores carrying a baking dish and wearing a big smile.

"I scored dinner. Jack caught up with me out by the llamas' watering trough. He said your grandmother made extra lasagna. Says it's ready to bake at four hundred degrees for thirty minutes."

Ginger jumped up from her bed, sniffing at the dish. Nick pulled it up out of reach of her nose, handing it to me. "Here, put it someplace safe."

I put the lasagna in the fridge just as my cellphone rang. It was Ramon Silva.

He confirmed that the Ferreras had brought their laptop, but they had already turned it over to the Timbergate police. They had not been told when they would have it back. Ramon gave me their family email address and password. They used a free provider that ended in the extension *mail.pt. Pt* was the extension for Portugal.

I thanked Ramon and then reported what he'd said to Nick. "What do you think? Is there time to do any other sort of follow-up on Liliana's secret email account before we take off for Marin County tomorrow?"

"Let's see what Harry thinks after you tell him TPD has the laptop."

I phoned Harry with what I'd heard from Ramon. He

responded with a word I wouldn't have used, then went on to say he'd work with what we had for the time being.

Nick cast me an inquiring look and rubbed his stomach, so I turned on the oven and set it for four hundred degrees. I relayed Harry's comments, minus the profanity. "By the way, Harry wondered if we're flying down to the Bay Area or driving."

"Driving eats up almost four hours. We'll fly. Buck's hoping Liliana will be found alive and unharmed. It won't bring his own daughter back, but it'll bring him some consolation if she's found safe."

I took the lasagna out of the fridge and slipped it into the oven. "Here you go." I handed Nick a bottle of Merlot and an opener. "Do the honors?"

He pulled the cork and poured for both of us. "The oven says another twenty minutes. Let's use it to—"

My landline phone rang before he could finish his thought. It was the number TMC had on file for me in the personnel office. If it wasn't Amah or Jack, it was probably someone calling from work. Everyone else called me on my cell. I picked up and heard the last voice I expected.

"Is this Aimee Machado?" He didn't identify himself, but I knew right away that *God* was calling. So much for waiting until Monday.

"Yes, this is Aimee. Can I help you?" I glanced at Nick, shook my head and rolled my eyes. He saw the tension in my face, and before I could object, he reached over and put the phone on speaker mode.

"This is Godfrey Carver. I'm primary on the Portuguese coma patient in the ICU, which you should know by now. And yes, you can damn well help me, Machado. I've been chasing your ass for a freaking week trying to get my CME credits straightened out, and I've just about had it." He paused, wheezing for a moment, then went on, "My office girl sent my CME crap to you, and now you're claiming you don't have it. You're either lying for some reason, or you're an incompetent nitwit." My body stiffened with anger at his rant. I took a deep breath and let it out slowly.

"Dr. Carver, I was under the impression that you knew I've been out of the country on vacation since last weekend. I'll be happy to meet with you on Monday. Would you like to set up an appointment?"

"I won't say what I'd *like* to do, but I'll be damned if I'll wait another two days. I expect to see you at your desk in that pathetic little library of yours tomorrow morning at eight o'clock. We'll find those documents if we have to tear the place apart."

Nick leaned over the phone, steel in his eyes. "Listen, *Doctor*, I don't know what makes you think you can talk to Aimee like that, but I suggest you take it down several notches or you'll have a problem a lot bigger than whatever it is you're calling about now."

"Who is this?" Carver demanded.

"Not important, Doc. Aimee will be out of town this weekend. So either you make an appointment to meet with her on Monday morning when she's due back at work, or you don't. Your choice."

"Freaking jerk. What are you, some kind of bodyguard?"

Nick laughed out loud. "Aimee is her own bodyguard. If you don't know that about her, I feel sorry for you." Nick nodded toward me. I switched the phone off speaker mode.

"Dr. Carver, I can meet with you in the library at nine thirty Monday. Will that work for you?"

"Hell, no. Meet me at nine thirty in Quinn's office.

Your job is on the line, and don't think I can't get you canned." He hung up without waiting for my reply. My legs went rubbery. I slipped into a chair.

"What?" Nick said.

"He's threatening to have me fired." I tried to laugh, but wasn't successful.

"Who in hell does this Dr. Carver think he is? And what did he want?"

"He's… I…it's a medical staff situation. I shouldn't say anything."

Nick leveled a look at me. "The man is *threatening* you. For God's sake, Aimee, I already know his name, that he's primary on the Ferrera case, and is having some sort of problem with CME credits. All you have to do is tell me why he's pissed at you. If you won't, I'll take it up with him, and it won't be pretty."

He had a point. Carver had already blurted out the whole situation. "All right, but you have to keep it to yourself."

"That's understood."

I explained about the problem with Carver's CME credits, and that he had taken over as Paulo Ferrera's primary physician a few days earlier. I was stuck in a no-win situation. Either I took Carver's word about his CME credits and vouched for him with the Credentials Committee, or he'd be suspended and we'd have no one in town who could follow Paulo's case if Dr. Prine didn't return in time.

"Let me get this straight," Nick said. "This patient, Liliana's brother, is being cared for by the jackass who just called you?"

"That's right. As strange as it seems, sometimes the most skilled medical practitioners are sadly lacking in people skills. Dr. Godfrey Carver is the poster boy for bad behavior—a real enfant terrible."

"I have another name for it. He'll be *hamburger* if he tries to intimidate you again." Nick glanced at Ginger, who had raised her head to stare at him. "Sorry, girl. No hamburger."

"She knows the word?" I laughed. A sign that I'd recovered from my reaction to Carver's tirade. The oven bell dinged, and I served the lasagna while Nick topped off our wineglasses.

"One more question about the doctor's problem," Nick said. "Why should you be the one to pull him out of the fire?"

"I'm not. He should be taking responsibility for the mix-up, if he's telling the truth. Cleo and I both think it's more likely he's bluffing."

"As in *lying*," Nick said.

I raised my glass. "Yes, but let's drop this subject and eat before our dinner gets cold."

After a couple of bites, Nick put down his fork. "You haven't slapped my wrist for stepping in on that phone call. I know you didn't need to be rescued, but I couldn't stand there listening to that. Do I need to apologize?"

I smiled. "No, don't apologize. Sometimes it's good to have an ally. It'll be all I can do to deal with him on Monday."

"Are you worried?"

"Not much. I trust Quinn. He knows Carver's temperament. I suspect he'll negotiate some sort of a truce." I took a sip of wine. "My only worry is about our patient. If Carver takes himself off the case as some sort of vindictive ploy, we'll need to transfer Paulo right away, probably to U.C. Davis. That's not altogether a bad thing, but think of his parents. They've been through so much already. I'd hate to see them more upset."

Nick nodded. "At least we have the weekend to try and sort some of this out."

Harry called just before we went to bed. I was brushing my teeth, so Nick answered. After their brief conversation, he filled me in.

"Harry says, keep tabs on the laptop. He wants to know right away if the Ferreras get it back from the TPD. Meanwhile, he's going to start working with what we have tonight. He'll follow up with us right away if he comes up with anything while we're down in Marin, but he's not optimistic it'll be that soon."

"Too bad. I hope we'll bring back something useful for Detective Kass." I set my toothbrush aside. "I'd better call Cleo and Quinn and fill them in on what just happened with Carver. They'll both want to stay on top of this while you and I are out of town."

I finished my calls, with Cleo and Quinn each assuring me they'd stay in touch as needed. I went back to brushing my teeth while Nick was locking up and getting Ginger settled for the night in her doggy bed near the kitchen door.

Before lights out, Nick wiped a trace of toothpaste from the corner of my mouth and leaned in for a kiss. "Um, minty," he said. Then we stopped talking.

TWELVE

NICK AND I boarded Buck's six-passenger Cessna 206 early Saturday morning, bound for SFO. I rode in the co-pilot seat. Ginger was securely stowed in her carrier in one of the passenger seats behind us. The trip from Timbergate took just over an hour, putting us down at San Francisco International's general aviation terminal at nine o'clock. At the first gust of crisp ocean air, I was reminded of the climate we'd left behind in the Azores. Both were far different from the dry heat of Timbergate.

Nick drove us through San Francisco in the little hybrid Buck kept parked at the airport, while I took in the sights and sounds of my favorite city. I appreciated the diverse population of citizens walking the sidewalks in the shaded canyons of downtown, reminding me that this urban environment was a true microcosm of the world.

I rolled down my window to catch the aromas from food stands and the scent of flowers—the wares of vendors who claimed space on street corners. Ginger stirred in her carrier in the backseat, sniffing vigorously. I thought about her drug detection training. Was she was trying to identify the various origins of the olfactory stew? When I rolled up the window, she settled down right away.

Soon we crossed the breathtaking expanse of the Golden Gate Bridge, drove through the recently renamed Robin Williams Tunnel toward Sausalito, and arrived at the harbor where Buck's yacht was moored.

As we walked the dock, I carried our overnight bag while Nick gripped Ginger's leash in one hand and used his other to tote her empty carrier.

Along the way, I looked to see if any power yachts displayed the red burgee of the Bay Wind Yacht Club. Given that it might take a superyacht like the one Catia had described a month to make the return trip from Faial to Marin County, we were a week short. Still, the timing was only an estimate. I couldn't help wondering if the yacht had returned ahead of schedule.

Nick released Ginger from the leash and hoisted her onto the deck, where she immediately began sniffing and exploring. Her first time on the boat had both of us curious about how she would react. The last thing we wanted was for her to decide to dive into the waters of the basin for a swim. While we watched, a seagull flew down and perched for a moment on a large storage box attached to the dock near the bow of the boat. Ginger immediately froze in place, staring at the bird.

Nick reacted with a quick command. "Leave it, Ginger."

The poor dog trembled with indecision for a moment, then turned to look at her master as if to say, "Are you sure?"

I laughed out loud, which startled the seagull into flight and caused Ginger to emit a halfhearted yelp. Nick went to the dog, clipped on her leash, and guided her to the hatch leading down below. He arranged a blanket for her on the floor in a corner of the main saloon.

I unpacked our bag in the forward berth, stowing the clothes in a closet and the toiletries in the head. Back in the galley, I found Nick making coffee. A glance at Ginger told me Nick had remembered to bring along her favorite toy, a replica of Chewbacca. With our chores finished and Ginger settled, Nick and I took our coffee to the settee. It was time to come up with a strategy for the weekend.

"You want to start?" Nick asked.

"Sure." I pulled a few small sheets of paper from my purse. "I've made some notes, but they're sort of a mess. Back in the Azores, I scribbled on anything I could grab."

"Good enough." Nick walked over to the chart table and lifted the hinged lid. He pulled out a lined notepad and brought it back to the table where I sat. "Hit me with what you've got."

"Priority one: find out who owns the yacht in question."

"Tall order without a photo," Nick said. "We're giving a lot of weight to that painted replica of a Bay Wind burgee you spotted at Horta Marina."

"I know. For now, though, it's something, instead of the nothing we had to go on before. Catia said the yacht had an American name."

"That and the burgee *could* help us identify the mystery yacht, but I'm adding a question mark."

I glanced at my notes. "Priority two: access Liliana's secret email account."

"We know Harry's on that." Nick said.

"Yes, but only since late yesterday. We don't know how or when he's going to succeed, if ever."

"Give him credit. If there's a way, he'll find it." Nick got up and went to the galley. "Are you hungry?" He opened the cupboards one at a time, looking in each one. "Man, bare as Mother Hubbard's. We need to eat." He glanced at Buck's wall clock. "Look at that. It's almost two and we haven't eaten since six this morning. No wonder my stomach's making noises."

"We could go shopping at the Harbor Market," I said. "Do you think Ginger will be okay left alone here for a while?"

"She will if I put her in the carrier. She knows that means to shelter in place."

"Maybe you should take her up to the parking area first. She might need a potty break."

"I will. And after that, I'll scout the rest of this harbor, although I'm not sure it would accommodate a yacht like the one Catia described."

"So you're thinking like I am," I said. "There's a chance that yacht is already here."

"We don't have the precise timing, and we're not even sure that yacht was headed here," Nick said, "but we might as well keep our eyes open."

"My thoughts exactly."

Nick clipped the leash on his dog's collar. "You want to make a shopping list while I do this?"

As soon as they left, I snooped around in the galley to see what sort of staples were still on board and not outdated. I dumped a few things in a garbage bag and finished my list.

When Nick returned, we secured Ginger in her carrier, locked up, and made the short drive to the Harbor Market.

On the way, I questioned Nick about his scrutiny of the harbor. "Did you see any possibilities?"

"No. This harbor is designed for smaller vessels. The craft we're looking for would be moored in a harbor somewhere in the Bay Area that caters to the larger yachts. If we don't get any leads this evening, we'll have to spend tomorrow sightseeing."

After we filled a small basket with enough groceries to get us through the weekend, we picked out a nice bottle of Pinot Noir. At the checkout stand, I glanced around at other customers while I waited for Nick to pay. A dark-haired young woman in another checkout lane caught my eye. She and the man she was with were flirting and laughing, obviously enjoying each other's company. I looked away, trying not to stare, but something kept me returning to the couple. She reminded me of someone, but out of context, I couldn't place her.

Then it came to me. Her name was Kiri D'Costa. She was the cousin of TMC's assistant administrator, Sanjay D'Costa. In the States on a work visa from India, she was employed as a temporary member of the office staff in Dr. Godfrey Carver's neurosurgery practice. She'd dropped by the library a time or two to pick up materials for Carver, but beyond that, I had no contact with her.

Kiri and her companion finished their checkout at the same time as Nick and I, and we all headed toward the exit doors at the same time. Considering how Carver and I had left things during our exchange on the telephone, I wasn't eager to meet up with anyone who worked in his office. I hoped she wouldn't recognize me. Then she spoke.

"Aimee Machado, is that you?"

I pasted on a surprised smile. "Oh, hello. You're Kiri D'Costa, right? Sanjay's cousin."

"Yes. What a coincidence seeing you here." She gestured toward the attractive, olive-skinned man who stood by her side. "This is my friend, Gus Barba."

Nick reached out to shake hands with the young man. "Gus, good to see you. How's it going?" I looked at Nick with eyebrows raised. How did he know Kiri's friend?

Nick turned to me. "Gus is a hull diver, Aimee. He's the man who keeps barnacles from forming and fouling the instruments on the bottom of Buck's boat—along with quite a few other yachts, I suspect."

"That's right," Gus said, speaking with the Portuguese accent I'd heard all my life from various relatives on my father's side of the family. "A demanding job, but I enjoy it," he glanced at Kiri, "for many reasons."

Kiri blushed, while at the same time a smile lit up her delicate features, revealing her perfect white teeth.

We followed the couple outside, where I hugged myself against the chill of a crisp ocean breeze. Typically, in summertime, the winds picked up velocity throughout the afternoon.

Gus leaned toward Nick. "Is Mr. Sawyer happy with my work?"

"He's very pleased," Nick said. "I believe he's recommended you to a few of his friends at the yacht club."

Gus broke into a smile. "That's good. I appreciate the work. Tell me of anything extra you might need." Kiri and Gus walked toward a scooter at the opposite end of the lot from where we were parked.

As we drove back to the yacht harbor, I explained that Kiri was one of Godfrey Carver's office staff.

"She works for that jerk?" Nick pulled into a space at the harbor parking lot. He cut the engine and turned to me. "How do you suppose she met Gus?"

"I have no idea. I barely know her. I heard Sanjay was instrumental in bringing her to the States on a work visa. I can't imagine how she and Gus met."

Does her cousin keep a boat down here?"

"On his salary? Not likely," I said.

"What about Carver?"

"That wouldn't surprise me. From what I've heard, he could easily afford it."

"If he does, she might be doing the same thing we're doing."

"You mean using Carver's yacht as a free hotel?"

"Could be. When we get home, why don't you see if you can find out?" Nick took our bags from the car. "I'd like to know if there's a chance we'll ever run into her obnoxious pinhead of a boss down here."

"I'll ask Cleo. She'd know, if anyone does." I glanced at Nick. "We were told that Paulo Ferrera has a friend from the Azores who works down here. Paulo was headed here to ask for his friend's help. Do you think...?"

"We're on the same page," Nick said. "Actually, I'm a page ahead of you. I've already thought about Gus. He's obviously Portuguese. Probably a little older than Paulo."

"Are you planning to ask him if he knows Paulo?"

"I hope to. Not sure how I wanted to approach him. Now that we know he has a connection to your boorish Dr. Carver, I'm even more hesitant. I'm going to hold off on that option for now."

Alarmed, I hoped Kiri wouldn't be the next young woman to vanish. "Is there some reason for you to think Gus is mixed up in Liliana's disappearance?"

"I sure hope not." Nick pulled into the harbor parking lot. "I'll talk to Buck later. See how much he knows about Gus."

We carried our groceries to the basin entrance, where Nick used Buck's passkey to unlock the security gate. We made our way along the dock. I was anxious to know how Ginger had handled being left alone. I was sure Nick was curious, too.

Down below, Ginger emitted a soft *woof* when Nick let her out of her carrier. I picked up her toy, which she'd evidently made good use of while we were gone. She'd put out both of Chewbacca's eyes, but other than that, the toy had held up fairly well. Nick took Ginger up to the parking area for a short walk and a pit stop while I put away our groceries. I had just finished when my cell alerted me to a text from Harry.

Working on it tonight. Will call when I have news.

I texted Thanks.

With luck, we'd get some useful information about Liliana's mystery boyfriend while we still had part of the weekend to follow it up. He claimed to be from the San Francisco Bay Area. That might be true, but I didn't believe for a minute that his name was really Francisco. Coincidence happens, but really?

The wall clock showed the time was close to six thirty. As I stood wondering if I'd hear back from Harry before morning, I felt the boat rock gently. Nick and Ginger had returned. Nick came down the hatch ladder first, then stood at the bottom to guide his dog slowly, preventing her from making her entrance in one giant leap.

When Ginger had settled on her blanket with Chewbacca between her paws, I told Nick about Harry's text. We agreed it was pointless to sit around waiting for more news. We could kill two birds with one visit to the Bay Wind Yacht Club, where we could multitask both dinner and sleuthing.

Nick showed his membership card to the man on duty at the yacht club door. Despite the negatives in Nick's job, there were definite perks to being employed by a billionaire. The Saturday night dinner scene was in full swing, with liquor and yachting stories flowing. Neither of us was acquainted with the other members, so we headed to a small table for two by the wall of windows overlooking a large deck and the expanse of bay beyond. A few boats were still out, using night-time navigation lights to keep them on course and visible to other marine traffic.

I waited at our table while Nick went to the bar for drinks and to place our dinner order. He came back with a beer for himself and a glass of white wine for me.

"They're out of halibut, so I ordered two grilled shrimp dinners. Hope that's okay?"

"Fine with me." I took a sip of my wine and looked around the room. "See anything that gives you an idea?"

"'Fraid not." Nick glanced at his phone and shook his head. "Nothing. Is your phone on?"

"It is. I keep hoping Harry will call one of us."

"I have an idea to check out in the meantime." Nick leaned in toward me, almost nuzzling my ear. "I doubt anyone in here is paying the slightest attention to us, but just in case, we should probably keep our voices down."

"Agreed. What's your idea?"

"When I told Buck about the yacht party and the missing girl, he mentioned that most yacht clubs have something called a cruise director who's responsible for setting up cruises for the club members. Buck says they might cruise across the bay, or out the Golden Gate and up or down the coast. Even to Hawaii. The cruise directors become pretty knowledgeable about the various members and their vessels."

"So, if the owner of the yacht we're looking for does belong to this club, the cruise director could probably narrow things down for us?"

"It's possible. We know a yacht that size wouldn't be moored where Buck's yacht is. We're going to have to explore the other harbors and basins in the area. Of course, there's always a chance that yacht isn't coming here. It could have headed anywhere when it left the Horta Marina."

My heart dropped. "Oh, Nick, I know that's true, but I hate to think Liliana could still be out there somewhere, held hostage for who knows what."

"When you did that online search back in the Azores, didn't you say that yacht would have stopped to refuel somewhere in Florida if it was coming this way?"

"Yes, and it would have refueled again when it reached the Panama Canal." The direction of our conversation was spoiling my appetite. "You think there are at least two places where she could have been handed off?"

"At least. Think of all the stops they could make coming up the West Coast."

"Or even farther north from where we are. Her brother turned up in Timbergate for some unknown reason."

Nick leaned closer to me, his voice even lower. "We'll keep that in mind, but for now, let's concentrate on where we are and what we do know."

"We don't really know much, do we? Most of it is the sketchy story we got from a teenager terrified of her grandmother."

"Think about the patient in Intensive Care. The bullet that injured his spine is about a real as it gets." Nick picked up his fork. "Let's finish our meal and try to stay positive. Maybe this cruise director will give us something."

"If we manage to meet him, are you going to tell him why you're asking about the Azores?"

"No. I don't want to start spilling information that might interfere with what the police are doing. I'll keep my questions simple."

Nick finished his food. I made limited progress with mine. We agreed that there wasn't much to be gained by hanging around the yacht club. On our way out, we stopped to ask the bartender for the name of the cruise director. He reached into a small rack behind his back and handed Nick a printed brochure about the yacht club.

"It's all on there," the barman said.

Nick thanked him and we made our exit.

THIRTEEN

THE EVENING BREEZE had died down by the time we returned to the harbor. A cloudless night gave us a spectacular view of the lights of San Francisco glittering across the bay.

Down below, we let Ginger out of her carrier. The three of us went topside to enjoy the evening on the water. Nick and I sat in the cockpit sipping decaf and munching cherry-topped macaroons from the Harbor Market, while keeping a wary eye on the dog. She padded along the deck, sniffing and exploring. At one point, a couple from another yacht stumbled along the dock in our direction, giggling and clutching at each other. A strong gust of pot smoke wafted toward us.

Ginger suddenly ran to the bow of the yacht, barking at them as they approached, and then turning back to shoot a look at Nick.

The couple stopped in their tracks. "What the hell?" the man said. "He gonna attack?"

Nick put down his cup and went to the dog, taking her by the collar. "It's okay, folks. She's harmless. Just not used to boats. It's all new to her." He reached in his pocket and offered Ginger a doggy treat, saying "Good girl."

The guy fumbled for the woman's hand, and they went back the way they had come.

"What set her off?" I asked.

"The pot. She'll also react to meth, heroin, and co-caine."

"Of course, I forgot for a moment about her drug school." Ginger had settled down on the floor of the cockpit, chewing on Chewbacca. "You didn't mention her training to the couple."

"They didn't need to know." Nick reached over to scratch Ginger behind her ears. "We'll keep that to our-selves, won't we girl?" He looked up at me. "Keep in mind that she's working undercover."

How long would it take me to get used to that idea? Confidentiality at the hospital was one thing, masquer-ading as a wealthy young couple with an overindulged dog was something else.

Nick used a penlight to scan the brochure the bar-tender had given him.

"Anything about a cruise director?" I asked.

"Just spotted it." He pointed to the back panel of the tri-fold handout. "He's listed as an elected official called the cruising captain, along with the commodore, a sail-ing secretary and a racing captain. Interesting stuff. Looks like these folks take their club pretty seriously."

"What's his name?"

"Errol Parkington the Second." Nick laughed. "Sound snooty enough to be a yacht club big shot?"

I laughed, too. "Wasn't he the millionaire shipwrecked on Gilligan's Island?"

"No, that was Thurston Howell the Third."

"Close enough." A bay breeze traced across my shoulders, causing a shiver.

Nick noticed. "Looks like you're getting cold. Are you ready to go below?"

"Either that, or I'll pull on a sweater."

"Let's go down and close up the hatch for the night.

I need to make a couple of calls, and I'm guessing you do, too."

I went below and made sure everything was tidy and secure in the galley, while Nick took Ginger up to the parking lot for her final walk of the evening. By the time he returned, helping Ginger down the hatch ladder, I'd already checked in with Cleo and Amah.

I told Nick that Cleo had nothing new to report. She'd been in touch with Quinn, who told her the weekend hadn't produced any change in Paulo's status. He remained in a coma, and Carver was still the primary on his case. As recently as a couple of hours ago, the police had not been in touch with Quinn.

Amah's report was similar. She had talked to Ramon, the Ferreras' interpreter, who said the Ferreras had been to visit their son in the ICU several times during the day. They had heard nothing new from the police in Timbergate or in the Azores.

Nick put in a call to Buck, asking him if he was acquainted with the BWYC cruising captain. I watched him as he listened, nodded, then broke into a smile. When he ended his call, I knew he must have gleaned something from Buck.

I parked myself on the couch in the main saloon, patting the space next to me. "Sit, and give."

Nick plopped down by my side. "Seems Buck and old Errol Parkington the Second are not the best of buds. Parkington likes to be called by his nickname, *Epic*. Buck says *Ipecac* would be more appropriate. I'm not sure what he was talking about."

"It's a syrup that induces vomiting," I said. "It's rarely recommended these days. Too many cases of ipecac poisoning, but it would have been fairly common back when Buck was young."

Nick laughed. "Even if that's Buck's opinion of this cruising captain, I'd like to get a chance to talk to the guy. If he helped arrange a recent cruise to the Azores for anyone with a Bay Wind membership, we might have something to go on."

"I have to be back at work Monday morning, so we only have tomorrow to make that happen. Do you think it's likely Captain Epic will show up at the club on a Sunday?"

"Buck seemed to think so." Nick pointed to the yacht club brochure he'd left on the table. "The members often spend Sunday mornings sailing on the bay. Most of them congregate at the club for a late lunch or drinks and an early dinner."

"Then let's spend Sunday morning searching the other harbors in the area for any yacht that might match Catia's description."

"Too bad she didn't have any photos," Nick said.

I yawned, feeling the effects of the late hour. "Too bad we can't access the photos Liliana took. If we could get into her secret email account…."

Nick responded with a yawn of his own. "I agree. If Harry's able to crack that, we might find them there."

"Did you happen to ask Buck about Gus Barba?"

"I mentioned I'd like to know more about him. He's going to look into it."

We sat up at the table in the main saloon for another hour, rehashing everything we could think of about Liliana's disappearance. We discussed the best use of our Sunday morning. There were at least half a dozen harbors nearby where the yacht in question could be moored. If we strolled along their perimeters, we might get lucky enough to gain access to the docks. Even from a distance, a yacht like the one Catia described would stand out.

Nick and I had finally snuggled into the forward berth when his cell rang. He took it from the small table next to the bed, looked at the screen and answered with a quick, "Talk to me."

I listened to his end of the conversation, which consisted of a "Yes," and a "Thanks." After the call, he turned to me.

"That was Harry. Still working on Liliana's secret email."

"What did he say? Did he get into the account?"

"Afraid not. He said your girl, Liliana, made it very difficult. He tried several variations on her family's email account ID and password and came up with nothing."

"Then where do we stand? Did Harry say what else he could try?"

I didn't like the expression on Nick's face, nor did I like his answer. "It's not a simple matter. Harry isn't sure how difficult it will be even if he does get his hands on the family's laptop."

"What about the Timbergate police? They have the laptop and they know about the secret account. They must be working on it, too."

"We're not hearing much about what they're doing," Nick said. "The TPD may not have a budget for the kind of cyber-sleuthing this requires. If they have to depend on outside help from another agency, it could take a while. You'll want to talk to your boss when you get back to work on Monday. See if he's hearing anything from Detective Kass."

His mention of Monday morning reminded me that I would be in Quinn's office facing a confrontation with Carver about his CME credits. Not something I looked forward to.

Nick kissed my cheek and pulled the comforter up over both of us. "We have a busy day tomorrow."

I told myself the only thing in my control at the moment was to get some sleep, but it was slow coming. I couldn't stop thinking about Harry's report. Three weeks after her disappearance, we were still no closer to finding Liliana. We seemed to take one step forward and two steps back.

FOURTEEN

EARLY SUNDAY MORNING, we fixed a quick breakfast of cereal and toast in the galley; then, taking Ginger along, we headed out to explore the other half-dozen harbors where the mystery yacht might be spotted. We completed our masquerade as members of the yachting community by donning the deck shoes we usually wore on the boat and dressing in khaki slacks and sporty polo shirts.

The first two harbors we visited were in areas where we could gain an overview of the yachts berthed there without needing to go through security gates. Each harbor ate away an hour of our morning. Nothing we saw matched Catia's description of the superyacht she'd seen in the Azores.

We visited two more harbors with the same result, losing another two hours. It was after one o'clock when we stopped for a quick lunch at the Bay Wind Yacht Club, thinking the cruising captain might show up there. We hoped he would tell us if any Bay Wind members had made a trip to the Azores around the time of Liliana's disappearance. We agreed to approach him with caution. After the way Buck had characterized the man, we weren't about to divulge our real reason for questioning him.

The day was cool and overcast, so we left Ginger in the car at the yacht club parking lot. Inside, we took a table and ordered cocoanut shrimp appetizers. Nick asked the waiter if Captain Parkington was around. We were told he usually came in for lunch on Sundays, but hadn't arrived yet. We tried to time our lunch to avoid finishing too soon. Both of us were on edge, knowing we had two more harbors to visit before flying back to Timbergate. We were about to give up when Parkington made his appearance.

He strode in with a decorative red-haired woman on his arm, easily young enough to be his granddaughter. He looked the part of a yachtsman, with a trim build, a full head of white hair, and a matching white moustache. His female companion wore enough gold and diamonds on her ears, throat, and arms to finance a small nation for a year.

They sailed past our table, waving and nodding to the assembled diners. The man was instantly recognizable from his picture on the club's brochure.

When the couple had seated themselves, I asked Nick how he wanted to proceed.

"We don't have a lot of time for subtlety," he said. "I'll just go over, introduce myself and say I'm inquiring for a friend who wants to cruise to the Azores." He stood and dropped his napkin on the table.

"Good luck," I mouthed.

A few minutes later, he came back and sat down, frowning.

"Well?" I said.

"Struck out." Nick fingered the edge of his napkin. "Said he's never been to the Azores, doesn't know of any members who've made that trip."

"Did you believe him?" I asked.

"I haven't decided."

"Then I'm assuming you didn't mention the burgee I saw painted on the Horta Marina."

"You're correct." Nick dropped some bills on our table. "Let's go. We still have two harbors to visit, and that's going to take some time."

Outside, we talked it over and decided to save time by splitting up. Nick dropped me off at one of the two remaining harbors and drove on to the other, taking Ginger with him. I strolled along the walkway leading to the main dock, hoping to look as if I belonged. When the couple ahead of me went through the security gate, I followed along behind them with a quick "Thanks," as if they'd saved me the trouble of using my own passkey. When they went one way, I went the other.

The harbor was large. It was going to take some time to walk all the docks, so I picked up my pace, passing the sailboats quickly and moving on toward the outer edges where the largest of the power cruisers were moored. Nothing I spotted fit Catia's description, although some of the yachts were twice the size of Buck's. I had stopped to admire one of them when I heard loud voices farther down the dock. Two men were shouting at each other in what sounded like a heated confrontation. They stood on a large power yacht moored at the far end of the dock.

I stepped away from the main walkway onto the narrower finger of dock that separated two adjacent boats. From there, I could listen without being seen. The voices rose. I could tell they were male, but I couldn't make out their words. A gusting wind had come up, causing the riggings of every sailboat in the harbor to jiggle and clank. I was about to step out from my hiding place when I felt the floating dock sway and caught the rhythmic beat of footsteps running in my direction. I edged farther back, away from the main dock.

I heard a loud report like a gunshot and saw a running man suddenly trip on a coil of rope and fall hard on the dock, just across from where I stood. Lying flat on his stomach, he turned his head toward me and our eyes met briefly. He looked young and scared. Blood trickled from his forehead.

I quickly hoisted myself up onto the nearest yacht, praying no one was on board. I dropped down and crouched in the cockpit, listening, straining to hear over the gusting wind and clanking riggings. I waited a few moments, but heard nothing more. I risked rising up slowly to take a look. The man lay still, eyes closed. No one else was around. As soon as I was sure it was safe, I would call 911 for medical help.

I ducked back down and listened intently for another two minutes. With my phone at the ready, I rose again and peeked at the spot where the victim had fallen.

No one was there.

After looking in the surrounding water and seeing no sign of him, I left the harbor, dialing Nick's cell as I walked toward the café we'd designated as our meeting place. I gave him a brief version of what I'd seen. Since his own searching had proved fruitless, he broke it off and hurried to meet me.

It was almost five o'clock, so we decided to grab a quick sandwich before closing up Buck's yacht and flying back to Timbergate. We sat at a sidewalk table, where I kept Ginger company while Nick went inside to place our orders. He came back with Reuben sandwiches, two Caesar salads, and coffees. Ginger immediately responded to the aroma of corned beef. Nick appeased her with doggy treats from a stash in the pocket of his windbreaker.

"Tell me the whole thing." Nick glanced around, confirming that we were the only patrons sitting outside. "Start with what this guy looked like."

"He was young, dark-haired, slim. At first, I thought my eyes were playing tricks on me. He reminded me a little of Buck's hull diver."

"Gus Barba? Are you sure?" Nick's voice rose in surprise.

"No, I'm not. That's the problem. He also looked a lot like the picture that we were shown of Paulo Ferrera, Liliana's brother."

"You mean the coma patient? Well, we know that's impossible." Nick cocked his head at me. "I'm surprised at you, of all people. You can't mean to tell me that all young Portuguese men look alike to you."

"Of course not, but there are bound to be some who do."

Nick unwrapped his sandwich. "What about the blood on his face? Did you say you heard a shot?"

"There was so much noise from the wind and the riggings, I can't be sure."

"But you said you heard running footsteps. How could you hear that and not hear a gunshot?" Nick asked.

"I caught some of the rapid footsteps between gusts, but mostly I felt them. Wooden docks float, and he was running flat out, causing it to rock."

"So, you're not sure if he was shot, or if he simply tripped on the rope and injured his head when he fell?"

"That's right. It could have happened either way." I took a bite of my sandwich. Nick did, too, both of us deep in thought while we tried to ignore Ginger's pleading stare.

We ate quickly, conscious of the time. When we finished, Nick asked if I felt comfortable going back to the dock where the incident had taken place. I was almost certain no one except the fallen man had spotted me there earlier, so I agreed.

Nick easily charmed a lone, thirty-something woman into letting us follow her through the security gate. We walked to the spot where I'd seen the man fall.

"There's still a trace of blood here," I said. "I'm going to try to retrieve a sample."

"You're thinking forensic evidence?" Nick pulled Ginger back from where she stood sniffing at the dark patch on the dock. "It's been there for almost an hour. Isn't it too late? It might be contaminated by now."

"I hope not." I took a small kit from my purse and used a Q-Tip to dab up some traces of the blood. I transferred it to a vial, put it in the kit and put the kit back in my purse.

Nick raised his eyebrows at me. "When did you start carrying that stuff around with you?"

"It's been a while. I pick up a lot of ideas at work. I like to put them into practice whenever I get a chance."

"That forensic library stuff is rubbing off on you, isn't it?"

"Hey, you're one to talk," I said. "You and your secret missions, Mister Spy Pilot."

"Why don't we call a truce and move on? Can you point out the boat where that argument was taking place?"

I shaded my eyes and lifted my chin slightly toward the yacht. I didn't want to make myself too obvious by pointing. "Yes. I saw them standing on the one moored at the far end of this section of dock."

"Then let's keep walking in that direction, but slowly. I want to be able to keep Ginger in check right away if she picks up a scent."

We walked only close enough to the boat to see that

the burgee on its bow staff displayed the ensign of the Bay Wind Yacht Club.

Nick leaned toward me. "You're sure that's the one where the argument happened?"

"Yes." I did an about-face. "Let's start back. I'm not comfortable here."

"Too bad we can't see the name of the vessel from where we're standing." Nick took my hand. "Let's walk to the end of the next dock over, the one that parallels this one. Maybe from there we can get a look at the stern." We strolled back the way we had come.

Before we reached the point where the dock angled to the right, we spotted a woman walking toward us. When she came closer, I recognized Kiri D'Costa. She gave us a friendly smile.

"Aimee. Hi, we meet again." She looked down at Ginger, who was sitting at attention at Nick's side. "What a cute dog. May I pet him?"

Nick nodded. "Sure."

"Nice dog." Kiri stroked Ginger's fur gently. "What is his name?"

"Bruno," Nick said. "I noticed he didn't correct her mistaken assumption about the dog's gender. Assuming he had a reason for that and the fake name, I let it go and changed the subject.

"Are you here on vacation?" I asked.

"No, just playing tourist for the weekend. I must be back at work tomorrow. Dr. Carver has generously allowed me to stay on his yacht. Hotels in this area are so expensive."

"Yes, they are," I said. "Well, have a safe trip home."

"Thank you," she said. "The same to you."

As she continued down the dock, Nick and I lingered, trying to be inconspicuous as we watched to see which yacht she boarded. I caught my breath. It was the same one that the running man had bolted from.

"That does it," Nick said. "We have to get a look at the name of that boat."

We walked to the end of the parallel section of dock until we could get a visual of the stern of Carver's yacht. The name of the vessel was *God's Gift*.

"Did you buy her tourist story?" Nick said.

"More likely she's down here to meet up with Gus Barba." I said. "I have a bad feeling about that."

"Not much we can do about it now," Nick said. "I'll talk to Buck. See what he knows."

"We could offer her a ride home."

Nick glanced toward *God's Gift*, his eyes narrowed. "Look," he said. "Is that one of the two men you saw arguing?"

Kiri stood on the deck of the yacht next to a dark-haired man. He reached out, handing her what looked like an overnight bag.

I shaded my eyes. "It could be, but I only saw him from a distance."

Kiri took the bag and walked back up the dock toward the harbor parking lot. We kept pace on the parallel dock and watched until she unlocked a small blue car, slipped inside, and pulled away.

"There's your answer," Nick said. "She's headed home without our help."

I hoped he was right, but I'd feel better once I knew she was safely back in Timbergate.

AFTER OUR UNEVENTFUL flight home, we drove to Coyote Creek and checked in with Amah and Jack. They had heard nothing from the Ferreras' interpreter. Nick called Harry, who had made no headway in his search for Liliana's secret email account. I called Cleo, who told me Paulo Ferrera's medical status was unchanged. I filled her in on everything that had happened in Marin County.

Nick touched base with Buck, asking if he knew anything about a yacht named *God's Gift*. Buck said no. Nick asked how Buck happened to hire Gus. Buck answered that Gus had been recommended by another Bay Wind Yacht Club member. He didn't recall who it was but offered to look it up.

It was bedtime by then, and we were wrung out from the mystery and all our unanswered questions. We agreed to sleep on it. Maybe if it all sat on the back burner for a while, something useful would bubble to the top.

My sleepy brain refused to give up. As I lay in the dark, one stubborn question lingered.

Liliana, where are you?

FIFTEEN

MONDAY MORNING IN the library I hardly had time to finish checking my email before Jared Quinn came through the door, expression grim and eyes steely. I straightened my shoulders and prepared for the worst.

He glanced at his watch. "Carver will be in my office in twenty minutes, expecting to hear me tell you that you're history if you don't make his CME problem go away."

"I can't do that, unless he can show proof that he's earned his fifty credits."

"If you don't, he's going to raise holy hell."

"What do you want from me? All I do is keep a record of the CME credits that our doctors submit to me. I forward them to Cleo when she processes their medical staff membership renewals."

"He claims he's done the work and sent proof to you," Quinn said. "If that's true, maybe the documentation slipped through the cracks. We have to hear Carver out. We need to do whatever we can to keep him on the Ferrera case until Dr. Prine returns. That young man is stabilized for now. His parents are here from halfway around the world, holding vigil for their only son and worrying about their missing only daughter." Quinn shook his head. "I can't imagine the stress they're under."

"What are you hearing from Prine? How soon can he be back?"

"I wish I knew. There's some complication with his daughter's case. He isn't willing to leave Florida until it's resolved."

"Then what do you want me to do about Carver? Suggest that his documentation was lost? Cleo says he's deficient by fifteen credits. I can't vouch for him without proof. No matter what he sent or where he sent it, he should have copies for his records."

"Even so, it's possible he's telling the truth. You know more than I do about all the options doctors have these days for earning their CME credits."

"I know they can attend conferences, do CME courses online, or order courses by mail—either audio, video, or in print." I decided to share my doubts with Quinn. "All we have is his word."

"Nevertheless, we'll meet with him and see how it goes. He either has the necessary documentation, or he doesn't. I'll see you in my office in ten minutes."

"Okay, then, let's get it over with."

Quinn walked to the exit, where he turned and leveled a look at me. "I know you prefer to take the high moral ground, and that's why I have so much respect for you, but sometimes we have to choose our battles. If we can help him with this, we have to try."

I watched Quinn's back as he left the library. Then the irony occurred to me. Watch your leader's back. That's what a good soldier does.

Lola Rampley, my elderly and over-qualified volunteer, arrived at nine on the dot, exuding good cheer, as always. After conferring with her about the morning's duties, I left her in charge. On my walk across the complex, I began perspiring, even though I was wearing only a white, sleeveless cotton dress and sandals. I sucked in Timbergate's tepid morning air and found myself wishing we could have bottled the temperate Azorean climate and brought it home with us.

When I reached Quinn's office, TMC's assistant administrator, Sanjay D'Costa, was standing next to Varsha Singh's desk in the air-conditioned chill of her reception area, pointing over her shoulder at a document. He looked up and greeted me with a bright smile.

"Aimee, so nice to see you," he said. "My cousin Kiri tells me she saw you down in Marin County last weekend." He picked up the document on Varsha's desk, thanked her, and returned to his office. At least I had the consolation of knowing Kiri had returned safely to Timbergate.

"Good morning, Aimee." Varsha stood and walked to Quinn's office door. The apprehensive look clouding her expressive dark eyes told me the three-way meeting with Quinn, Carver, and myself would be contentious at best. The raised voices coming from Quinn's office confirmed it. Varsha opened the door for me. "You can go on in."

Quinn sat behind his desk. Carver sat in front of it in one of the visitors' chairs. Quinn gestured for me to sit in the other one. I pulled the chair several inches away from Carver and sat, still feeling we were too close.

"Aimee, you know Dr. Carver, of course."

"Yes, we've—"

"Skip the BS, Quinn," Carver said. "She knows me, and I know her. What I want to know is how well she knows her job."

Heat rushed to my cheeks in a flash of anger I struggled to control. I held my tongue and waited for Quinn to react. I wasn't disappointed.

"Godfrey," he said, "you're on my turf right now. I'd suggest you temper your language and your attitude if you expect to receive the help you need from Aimee or from me. Either take it down several notches or this meeting is over."

Carver shot up from his chair. "Who do you think you're talking to? Some upstart fresh out of med school?"

Quinn stayed seated. Picking up his phone, he held his gaze on Carver. Quinn's expression brooked no argument. "Last chance, Godfrey. Play nice or Security will escort you from the building."

Then who will take care of Paulo Ferrera?

Carver's face flushed nearly purple. In his late fifties, he was plenty old enough to have a massive stroke if his blood pressure rose any higher. I saw him reach the fingers of his right hand to touch his left wrist. I counted to ten in my head while he checked his pulse. *Good idea.*

He sat down, propping his elbows on the arms of his chair. "Let's get on with this, Jared. I have patients to see." His rosy color faded somewhat, but he still looked a little too pink.

Quinn placed the phone back in its cradle. "Thank you, Dr. Carver. I'm ready to hear you out. How about you, Aimee?"

"Yes, of course," I said, holding my pen poised over the notepad I'd brought along.

Carver proceeded to tell us he'd done part of his continuing education via online classes, and the rest through courses he'd ordered by mail, including a course in managing spinal and peripheral nerve problems.

He insisted he'd fulfilled his fifty credits, the required number for the two-year time frame between medical staff membership renewals.

"If that's the case, can you explain why Aimee wouldn't have that information on file for you?" Quinn asked.

"That's the hell of it. One of the girls in my office takes care of all that. Either she screwed up, or someone else did." He sent a glare in my direction. I kept my focus on my notepad.

"Aimee," Quinn said. "Do you have any questions?"

I cleared my throat. "Um, yes." I turned to Carver. "My records show you're deficient by fifteen CME credits. I'd like the name of the person in your office who oversees documenting your credits and forwarding them to me. I'm thinking she and I can work together to get this straightened out."

Carver frowned at me, turned to Quinn. "Why the hell…." He stopped himself mid-sentence and started over. "Jared, why am I dealing with this *secretary*? Dr. Poole is the chairman of our CME Committee. Why isn't she here?"

"Let's get this straight, Godfrey." Quinn stood, leaning his arms on his desk, looking Carver in the eye. "Aimee is no one's secretary. She's a member of the professional administrative staff of this hospital. She's here because your problem falls under her job description. Phyllis Poole chairs the CME Committee, but it's not her responsibility to pull you out of the shit storm you're in."

Carver rose from his chair, placing his palms on Quinn's desk, facing him eyeball to eyeball. "You're making a mistake, Jared. That young man from the Azores has made good progress. If I'm taken off his case before Prine returns, we're going to lose a lot of ground. He may never recover."

"Are you keeping Prine apprised?" Quinn asked.

"I've told him the patient is showing signs of emerging from the coma. I've assured Prine that I'll be on hand if he isn't able to return before that happens." Carver stalked to Quinn's office door, where he stopped and turned to me. "I'll have my office manager contact you. She'll know which one of my girls you need to talk to."

I was relieved when he finally left, closing the door with more force than necessary. If I'd heard him call his employees his *girls* one more time, I'd have been the next one uttering profanities.

Quinn leaned back in his chair and smiled. "That went well, don't you think?"

"I know you're joking, but at least we have someplace to start. I'd better get back to the library. We only have four days to get this done. I don't want to miss that call from his office."

"I hear you," Quinn said. "Thursday is his last day, right?"

"Right. He'll have no medical staff membership or privileges after Thursday, unless he comes up with his missing credits."

"Then I'd better pave the way for getting Paulo Ferrera transferred to U.C. Davis. I want everything in place by Wednesday, just in case Prine isn't back by then."

"What are you hearing from Dr. Prine?" I hoped we could avoid a transfer. "He's been gone for ten days. It seems like his daughter would be stable by now."

"Apparently, his daughter is out of danger, but still hospitalized." Quinn drummed his fingers on his desk. "Prine is aware of the situation with Carver's pending membership renewal, and he also knows Paulo is still in a coma." Quinn hesitated for a moment. "Although

what Carver just said is news to me. I hadn't heard that
Paulo Ferrera was showing signs of waking up."

"Neither had I, but that's good news. Maybe that's
what Carver meant about the danger of a transfer to
Davis. I suppose it could cause a setback in his recovery."

"Prine keeps saying he'll be back at TMC before
Thursday," Quinn said. "I wish I could depend on that,
but we have to keep transfer in mind as a backup."

"There's always a chance Carver's telling the truth
about his CME credits."

Quinn shook his head. "There's a chance pigs can
fly, too, but go ahead and talk to his office manager.
We might as well see where that goes."

Back in the library, I was relieved when Lola reported that Carver's office had already called. The name
she had jotted on a message slip was Kiri D'Costa.

I called Kiri back immediately. She agreed to set
aside a time for the two of us to meet in Carver's office
toward the end of the workday.

Next, I called Cleo. She knew more about the nearly
three hundred doctors on the TMC medical staff than
anyone else. I needed her take on just how dangerous it
would be to cross Carver. How miserable could he make
my life? As Quinn said, we had to choose our battles.

CLEO AND I met for a late lunch at Margie's Bean Pot, a
popular diner across the street and down the block from
the hospital. She unfolded her paper napkin, using it to
polish her soup spoon. "How unpleasant was the war
of words in Quinn's office this morning?"

I gave it to her in a nutshell, stressing that I would
be working with Kiri D'Costa to see if we could find
proof of Carver's claim about unreported CME credits.

"I'm meeting with Kiri later today, after Carver's office hours. I'll look at the paperwork they have on file there."

"What else is new?" Cleo asked. "Any word on when Dr. Prine will be back from Florida?"

"That's still an unknown, although he told Quinn he'd be back by Wednesday. Apparently, his daughter's case is more complicated than expected."

"I'm pleased and a little surprised he's taking such a paternal interest in her," Cleo said. "From what I've heard, he and her mother split up when she was a toddler. Her mother remarried and moved out of state fifteen years ago. I didn't realize Prine had remained close to the girl all these years."

"Does he have other children?"

"Not that I know of." Cleo glanced at the tables nearest ours, then added softly, "Prine keeps his personal life under wraps, which isn't easy to do in a medical community. Most people assume there are women, just not here in Timbergate." Cleo tapped a finger to her chin. "He does like to travel. Could be there's someone in another city."

"Maybe there's a woman in Florida," I said. "If that were the case, he'd be tempted to milk his daughter's accident for a little extra time off."

Cleo smiled. "Listen to how cynical you've become. Is this job is robbing you of your innocence?"

"Maybe a little. You can't blame the man for wanting a break from the constant demands of a medical practice. Especially if it involves romance."

"Still," Cleo said, "if the Portuguese patient *is* emerging from his coma, that's a big step toward recovery. I'd expect Prine to hightail it back here."

"Yes, but from what I've seen in medical literature,

emerging from a coma isn't as simple as waking up from a nap. It can be a long process."

I agreed to fill her in on whatever I discovered about Carver's CME credits. With that out of the way, Cleo switched topics. As always, she prodded me about Nick. Were we any closer to making wedding plans, or at least a formal engagement? I evaded that question, but satisfied her need for "girl talk" by telling her how Nick and I had run into James O'Brien at the theater in Boston.

"Oh, boy," Cleo's eyebrows shot up. "Nick saw you plant a kiss on James?"

"On his *cheek*. A *friendly* kiss," I said.

"Sure, *friendly*," Cleo gestured air quotes. "Talk about hotties! James O'Brien is tough competition. Nick had better pick up his pace."

I didn't bother to respond. Trying to reason with a romantic like Cleo was useless.

SIXTEEN

MONDAY AFTERNOON I closed the library an hour early. I drove a few short blocks and pulled into the parking lot of Carver's new office building overlooking the Sacramento River. It was centrally located in Timbergate, within easy reach of both of the city's acute care hospitals. I made my way to the door displaying Dr. Godfrey Carver's name and office hours. I stepped into an empty waiting room and walked to the reception area. A middle-aged woman with strands of lank gray hair drooping against her neck looked up, startled. She glanced at her computer screen, then back at me.

"Do you have an appointment?" she said.

"Yes. I'm here to see Kiri D'Costa." I tried to maintain a pleasant affect, despite what appeared to be a permanent frown creasing her forehead.

"Are you sure it's today?" She squinted at the monitor. "I don't have you on the schedule."

"Is Kiri here?" I asked.

The woman boosted herself off her chair. "I'll go check."

I waited at the front counter as she headed into the hallway behind the reception area. She came back a couple of minutes later.

"She's already gone. Something I can do for you?"

"Oh, I'm surprised. I was sure we'd agreed to meet at four thirty. Will she be back? It's very important that I speak with her."

"Not today. She must have forgotten. She left a few minutes ago. Doctor sent her to drop our mail off at the post office." The woman's direct look held more than a hint of meaning. "We're just about to close up. Doctor's already seen his last patient."

"Is he here?"

"Sorry, no."

I pulled a card from my purse. "Then please give this to Kiri. Tell her I stopped by, and ask her to call me tomorrow to reschedule our meeting."

The woman looked at the card with suspicion, holding it by its edges as if it might be laced with some deadly poison. "You sure I can't help you?"

"I'm afraid not, but thanks," I said.

Outside in my car, I called Quinn, reporting that Kiri had missed our meeting.

"You think it was deliberate?" Quinn asked.

"Hard to tell. The receptionist said Carver sent Kiri to the post office."

"She didn't call or text you to reschedule?"

"She hadn't called before I left work, and there's no message on my cell."

I heard Quinn take in a breath and exhale a profanity. "Could be a simple mix-up. Go on home. You can sort it out with Kiri tomorrow, but please follow up as soon as you can and let me know how it's going."

THAT EVENING AT HOME, Nick and I dined on fresh-caught trout. Jack had offered the fish when he found Nick out in the pasture cleaning watering troughs. We lingered over wine, Waldorf salad, and breadsticks, taking turns telling our day's news. Mine included the tense meeting with Quinn and Carver, as well as the odd incident when I arrived to meet with Kiri and found her already gone.

"Sounds like you're reinforcing my opinion of the jackass. Carver probably sent that woman out of his office early just to spite you."

"Seems that way, doesn't it?" I took a small sip of wine. "I'll see what happens tomorrow."

"You had some good news, though. Dr. Pain-In-The-Ass did say the Ferreras' son is showing improvement. Maybe even to the point of coming out of the coma."

"I hope he's right," I said. "Just think how much we'd learn about Liliana if Paulo could talk to us."

"And you said there's a chance the other doctor will return from Florida as early as this week?"

"That, too. Then we'd have the best of both worlds. The Ferrera boy emerging from his coma and his primary doctor back on the case."

Nick raised up his wineglass. "I'll toast to that. If it happens, you can let this Carver creep take care of his own CME mess, right?"

"Up to a point," I said. "Now it's your turn. Have you heard anything from Harry today? I haven't had a chance to get in touch with him about that secret email account of Liliana's."

"Nothing so far. The problem is figuring out what email address she used when she set up the account. Harry's tried the obvious, using her first and last name and birth year, which he got from her parents through their interpreter. Amazing how many people use that combination. That didn't work, of course."

"What else has he tried?"

"Her last name, the name of her hometown, lots of variations on the word California."

"What about her interest in modeling and fashion? That was her dream—coming to America to be a designer or a model." I picked up my Portuguese/English dictionary. "*Supermodelo* or *desenhista*. He should try those. Then maybe add some combination of her birth date."

"Good thinking. I'll call him." Nick picked up his phone and walked out onto the deck.

I'd cleared the table and turned on the TV to watch the news when my cell rang. *Cleo.*

"Aimee, have you heard?" she asked.

"I guess not. What are you talking about?"

"Dr. Prine is flying home from Florida tomorrow. He'll be back at work Wednesday."

"Thank heavens." A rush of relief spread through my body. "When did you hear?"

"He just called Jared Quinn. Apparently, Carver contacted Prine in Florida to tell him Paulo is showing definite signs of emerging from the coma. Prine wants to be here when that happens."

"This is great news. Quinn told me this morning that Prine wasn't sure when he'd be back. There was some complication in his daughter's case."

"Apparently, that's been addressed," Cleo said. "What's it been? A week and a half since she was injured? If Prine isn't satisfied with her care, I doubt he'd be coming home."

"Finally, something is going our way," I said. "Prine will be here to take over before Carver's medical staff membership expires."

"Takes some of the pressure off, but Carver's still going to be ticked at all of us if his membership and privileges aren't renewed. You'll be on top of his you-know-what list."

I sighed. "Hey, I tried to meet with Kiri D'Costa this afternoon. She missed our appointment. I'm not sure what's going on with her and Dr. Carver."

"Better make it happen. Regardless of Paulo Ferrera, Carver's going to keep raising a stink until his CME issue is resolved."

"I was trying to focus on the good news. I'm going to make every effort to get this situation taken care of."

"Then how about this?" Cleo said. "When Paulo regains consciousness, the police will finally be able to question him thoroughly. His answers could lead them to his sister."

I didn't like bursting Cleo's bubble, but I needed to caution her. "You know, emerging from a coma isn't like what you see on television. He isn't going to wake up, smile, get dressed, and check out of the hospital."

"Of course not. But won't he be able to tell his story to the police?" Cleo asked.

"I spent part of the afternoon researching the process. It usually happens in stages."

"So how long, then, before he can fully communicate?"

"According to what I found, speech isn't the first step in the process. In fact, purposeful speech could take several days, if not longer. It usually happens only after the patient shows movement in response to stimulation."

"Then it's even more important that Dr. Prine will be back on the case," Cleo said. "I have a bad feeling about Carver after what you saw on his yacht. Kiri's odd skipping out on your appointment makes it even worse."

"Have you thought of talking to Sanjay about Kiri? Seems like he'd want to know if his cousin's getting in over her head. He must have arranged for her work visa."

"Yes, but her employer of record is Dr. Godfrey Carver. If she leaves his employ, I don't know if she can stay in the States." I heard Cleo's muffled voice saying, "We're almost finished." Probably her husband, Sig, wondering how much longer she'd be on the phone.

"Let's see if I can get together with Kiri about Carver's CME credits before it's too late. This is Monday. As it stands, Carver's in good standing through Thursday."

"What a pickle," Cleo said. "If Carver's suspended, he'll be ticked off at everyone at TMC, including Sanjay. You can bet Kiri will need to find another employer."

Nick came in from the deck just as I signed off with Cleo. I filled him in, including Paulo's signs of emerging from his coma and Dr. Prine's decision to return from Florida. Like Cleo, Nick expected Paulo to be able to talk to the police right away. I explained why that was unlikely.

"Darn shame," he said. "This whole mystery might be solved in minutes if that young man could talk."

"What did you hear from Harry?" I asked. "Has he come up with any ideas about retrieving Liliana's secret email account?"

"He's had no luck so far. I gave him the two Portuguese words you mentioned—the ones that translate as *supermodel* and *designer*. He tried those, along with her birth date, while I was on the phone with him. Didn't work, but he's going to keep trying other variations this evening." Nick read the disappointment on my face. He leaned in to kiss my forehead.

I remembered something Nick and I had talked about when we were in Marin County.

"Nick, has Buck dug up the recommendation he was given on Gus Barba?"

"Yes. Buck said Gus was recommended by the Bay Wind cruising captain."

"Errol Parkington? I thought Buck didn't care for the man."

Nick smiled. "He doesn't, but that's because he's not fond of overinflated egos. When you're traveling in yacht club circles, that personality type is hard to avoid."

"Did Buck have any reservations about Gus?"

"None. He said Gus came with other topnotch recommendations in addition to Parkington's. Buck's had no problems with Gus and no complaints. You'll love this. He said some of the references mentioned Gus's impressive 'Portuguese work ethic.'"

"Really? The Portuguese have their own work ethic?"

"Hey, don't blame Buck. He's just the messenger."

Buck's comment reminded me again of how many young Portuguese men were involved in the mystery surrounding Liliana's disappearance. Her brother, Paulo, of course. Miguel, the young man at the Horta Marina who invited the girls to the yacht party. And of course, the online boyfriend, Francisco, who probably wasn't real.

Then there was Paulo's unidentified diver friend in Marin County. Paulo had counted on that connection to help him find Liliana. Unfortunately, that diver's name was unknown, unless Senhora Ferrera had been right when she said his name was *Ghost*. Even Ramon Silva, the Ferreras' interpreter, was a young Portuguese man. He was the most accessible, but also the least likely to be part of the mystery. The only other person on the list who *was* accessible to us was Gus Barba, who appeared to be in a romantic relationship with Kiri D'Costa.

"Nick, what do you think about talking to Gus Barba? There can't be that many young Portuguese men working the docks or as hull divers in Marin County. Maybe Gus knows of someone from the Azores."

"If I were sure Gus was the right guy to approach, I'd do it. We don't even know where *he's* from. Could be Portugal, could be the Azores. I did ask Buck if we could get a more thorough background check on Gus, but until we know more about him, I don't want to tip our hand."

"You suspect he's involved somehow in what happened to Liliana and Paulo?" I rinsed our dinner dishes while we talked.

"We can't overlook anyone," Nick said. "Let's think about Gus. Maybe he's hiding in plain sight. He's involved with the D'Costa woman, who works for your hospital's problem child, Dr. Carver, whose yacht was the scene of the altercation you witnessed. Didn't you say the wounded man who fell on the dock was running from Carver's boat?"

"Yes. I'm positive."

"And we have no idea what that argument was about." Nick opened the dishwasher and started loading what I'd rinsed. "Plus, Paulo Ferrera's recovery is still in Carver's hands, and Carver is pissed at you over his problems with his CME credits."

"You're right. What a tangle. I keep wishing I knew more about Kiri D'Costa."

Nick gave me a puzzled look. "What do you mean?"

"I'm not sure. It's troubling me that she was staying for the weekend on the yacht where I saw that confrontation. Doesn't that seem odd? Two men argue, one runs, falls with a bloody head wound, possibly shot, and then disappears. The next day, we see Kiri, relaxed and in good spirits, although she's been staying on the same yacht."

"I'd agree with you, except for one thing. She was obviously down in the Bay Area to spend time with Gus

Barba. I suspect she didn't spend her nights on Carver's yacht. She probably spent them with Gus."

"You're thinking it's likely she wasn't aware of the confrontation I witnessed?"

"We have to consider that." Nick put the last of our silverware in the dishwasher.

"I'd agree, except that we both saw that man hand her an overnight bag when she left the yacht. That doesn't fit with your theory. Her bag wouldn't have been there if she'd been staying somewhere else with Gus."

"True," Nick said. On the other hand, we don't know what was in that bag. Maybe it wasn't pajamas and her toothbrush."

"What are you suggesting? She's a secret courier toting a bag full of diamonds?"

"Maybe diamonds, maybe something else. Lots of illicit things could fit in a bag that size. Even a lot of cash."

"You're saying Sanjay's cousin is a smuggler?" My mind started spinning in a staggering new direction. "Thanks for planting that idea. Now I'll be awake all night."

"Sorry. Just trying to think outside the box. If I hadn't thought of it, you know Harry would have." Nick took my hand and led me to the couch in the living room. "KP's done. Let's relax for a while."

"Good luck with that." I paced the room while Nick sat watching me. "I'm still hoping to pin down a meeting with Kiri D'Costa to sort out Carver's CME credits by Thursday. Imagine how distracting it'll be, sitting down to that task with someone who might know who shot Paulo Ferrera and abducted his sister."

Nick sighed, got up and stood blocking my path. "Hold it, sweetheart. Let's back up a couple of steps."

He took me by my shoulders, gently steering me backward until I sat down. He sat next to me, kneading my trapezius muscles. "I'm sorry I brought up the idea of the D'Costa woman being involved in this mystery. It was just an example of casting a wide net. We have to consider every possibility, but I didn't mean for it to keep you awake all night."

My body slowly released tension. "I know, but I can't stop thinking that even if Paulo is on the road to recovery, time is running out for his sister."

"Speaking of time," Nick said, "we can still visit the dojo. That might be a perfect way to wind down."

I didn't want the massage to end, but he was right. We hadn't been there for two weeks. We were overdue for a workout.

SEVENTEEN

CLEO STARTED MY workday on Tuesday morning with a phone call to confirm that Dr. Prine was back on Paulo Ferrera's case.

"What a relief." I felt pounds lighter. "That takes some pressure off our situation with Carver's medical staff membership. We can stop worrying about transferring Paulo to U.C. Davis."

"True," Cleo agreed, "but you're still going to have plenty of pressure from Carver. Have you tried to set up another meeting with Kiri?"

"Not yet. Carver's office doesn't open until nine. I'll put in a call this morning and make sure it's confirmed." I again pictured Kiri at the yacht harbor, being handed a bag by someone on Carver's yacht. There was no point troubling Cleo with Nick's suspicions.

"Better get together with Kiri on the double," Cleo said. "This is Tuesday. You only have until the end of the day Thursday to get it done."

"I know, and I understand how important it is to get this cleared up. If only Carver weren't so arrogant and difficult to work with. It's hard to believe he cares about the hospital and our patients as much as we do."

"I hear you," Cleo said, "but Carver and Prine are the only board-certified neurosurgeons in town. Leaving personalities aside, they both provide good care to our patients."

"I'm sure you're right, and I'll make every effort to meet with Kiri today."

An hour later I had plowed through morning emails and printed out requests for library materials. At nine o'clock sharp, my Tuesday volunteer, Bernie Kluckert, ambled in with his usual greeting.

"Top o' the morning, Miss Machado." Bernie tilted his gnarled hand in a quick salute. "Lola tells me the plants are looking forward to some TLC."

Bernie and my other volunteer, Lola Rampley, had become permanently engaged a few months earlier. The status of their relationship seemed to suit both of them. With Lola in her eighties and Bernie approaching ninety, they had decided to forgo marriage and all the legal and financial complications it would place on their heirs.

Back when Lola explained their situation, I had responded with a medical librarian's curiosity by doing some research on the topic. I discovered that more than a million couples in America in the sixty-plus age group were living together for financial reasons related to aging and health, even though they would prefer to be married. Turned out she and Bernie had done their homework and made the decision that was right for them.

Bernie busied himself with feeding and watering our plants and polishing their leaves, while I got on with my day and the chore I looked forward to least.

I dialed Carver's office, introduced myself, and asked to speak to Kiri D'Costa.

"She's out," the voice on the other end of the phone said. "Something someone else can do for you?"

"I'm not sure," I said. "I was told she's responsible

for keeping track of Dr. Carver's continuing education credits. Can someone else help me with that?"

"I have no idea. Hold on." I was forced to listen to piped-in elevator music for much too long. As I was about to hang up, the woman's voice came back on the line. "Sorry, nobody here knows how to look up what you want."

I asked the woman if I could speak to the office manager.

"I'm it," she said.

I'd been exposed to my share of poor telephone etiquette, but this was a new low.

"May I ask your name?" I said.

"Won't matter," she said. "I'm a temp. Leaving at the end of the week. The real office manager quit without notice a short time ago."

My best bet was then to track down Carver and tell him I was getting nowhere with his office staff. If he wanted his CME straightened out, he was going to have to intervene. I put in a call to Dr. Phyllis Poole's office. When she came on the line, I explained the problem and asked if she might be willing to touch base with Carver.

"You want me to light a fire under him?" Poole asked.

"If necessary," I said. "He's already implied that you should be involved."

"Because I'm chair of the Continuing Education Committee?"

"Exactly. Mr. Quinn tried to explain that clearing up the issue of CME credits was my responsibility, not yours, but Carver didn't want to hear that."

"Where do things stand now?" Poole asked.

"I don't know if Carver's aware that I'm being stonewalled. It's easy to assume that there's a problem about the credits he claims he's earned because of how he's responding to our request for verification. He insists that we take him at his word, but his righteous anger is so out of proportion that it makes us even more suspicious."

Poole laughed. "You can dispense with the diplomatic speak, Aimee. It certainly sounds like the man's lying, doesn't it?"

"I don't know what else to think. If he has earned the credits, he should be doing everything he can to help me get together with Kiri and sort the problem out. He's running out of time."

"All right, then. I'll see what I can do."

Poole's offer of help started me wondering what else *I* could do. With Dr. Prine back in town, we had Paulo's situation under control, but only up to a point. Unless he emerged from the coma to a level where he could tell his story, we still had little hope of finding his sister.

Were the police having any better luck? I put in a call to Quinn asking what he had heard about Paulo's case, and by extension, about Liliana.

"They're not giving me a blow by blow, of course," Quinn said. "All I'm being told is that they're checking leads."

"Any idea what kind of leads?"

"They're questioning people who were at the homeless camp when Paulo was shot. So far, no one admits seeing the shooter. They heard shots, saw the victim running, then falling. The TPD's confidential informant happened to be there, part of a sting operation involving drugs. He's the guy who called the shooting in to the police."

I knew who Quinn was talking about. Tango Bueller, the rehabilitated ex-con who had gone to prison several years earlier for attacking me. I didn't let on to Quinn that I knew the CI's name. Not my place to reveal that.

"Have they mentioned any other leads? Are they trying to identify the yacht where Liliana went to the party?"

"I'm sure they are," Quinn said, "but they're not saying much about that. All I've been told is no one can confirm that she left on that yacht. Without the name and the hull ID number, they can't even get the Coast Guard on the lookout. All I'm told is they can find no trace of the girl since the night she went to the party in the Azores."

"The police have to know about the online boyfriend, Francisco. He started this whole mess. It seems like they'd have some way of tracking him down."

"If that so-called *boyfriend* exists at all, he's clever enough to cover his tracks. At least, that's what Detective Kass is saying." I heard Quinn's muffled voice thank Varsha for something. "Aimee, I have to go. Trust the police. They're doing everything they can. All we can do is take care of Paulo Ferrera and make his parents as comfortable as possible while they wait for their son to recover."

I hung up, mulling over his last comments. All we could do? It didn't seem like enough. Could Harry dig deeper than the people the police were using? Harry had been trying for almost five days to search out Liliana's secret email account. Why was it taking so long?

And how long would it take Buck to do a background check on Gus Barba? I glanced at the time. Almost noon. Nick wasn't flying this week. He'd said he would be spending most of it in training sessions with Ginger. I texted, asking if he had any free time to talk.

He replied, Lunch?

We agreed on Margie's Bean Pot at noon. I arrived first, surprised to spot Godfrey Carver and Kiri D'Costa sitting across from each other in a booth. They were deep in conversation. Neither of them noticed me as I made my way to a table at the back of the room. I sat there debating whether to confront them about Kiri skipping out on me the day before. While I was trying to make up my mind, Nick walked in, spotted me, and came over.

As he sat, I said in a low voice, "Don't look now, but we have a situation here."

Nick's eyes widened, but he managed to keep his focus on me and reply in low tones, "Is danger involved?"

"Not that kind of situation." I reminded him of my efforts to meet with Kiri. "She's sitting right across the room with Carver. Doesn't that seem kind of odd?"

Nick smiled. "I'm not sure. Help me out here."

I explained about trying to make another appointment with Kiri earlier in the morning. "I was told she was out, yet here she is, having lunch with her boss."

"You think it's romantic?"

"*Ick*. Look at her. Young and pretty. Then look at him. Old and bald with bushy eyebrows. Besides, from what we saw last weekend, she already has a boyfriend."

"Gus Barba."

"Yes, and while we're on that subject, has Buck turned up anything on Gus Barba's background?"

"Nothing sinister. He's Portuguese, of course. Late twenties, from Lisbon. Came to America a year ago on a work visa and has applied for a green card. Apparently, he's clean as a whistle."

"If that's the case, maybe you should ask him to help us identify Paulo's Bay Area connection."

"I'll wait a little longer before deciding what to do about Gus," Nick said. "I'd like to be sure he's what he appears to be and nothing more."

"If he is, he'd be a great catch for Kiri. Handsome and the right age. Why would she throw him over for Carver?"

Nick shrugged. "Money?"

"I doubt that would do it." I shivered at the thought of being touched by Godfrey Carver.

"Then it's a business lunch," Nick said. "Maybe they're discussing you. How to fool you into thinking Carver's been doing his CME homework."

"That, I can believe."

"Are you going to go over and ask them why they keep putting you off?"

"I'm debating." I leaned closer to Nick. "You had doubts about Kiri last weekend when we saw that bag she took from the man on Carver's yacht."

"Maybe I shouldn't have said what I did. I'd be surprised if she's a smuggler or any other kind of villain. I was just reminding you to—"

"I know, think outside the box, but now my mind is wandering around out there, and I can't get it back inside. Anybody could be mixed up in this mystery."

"Go over to that table, Aimee. Talk to them. Keep reminding yourself you're just doing your job, not solving a crime."

"You think I should?"

"What have you got to lose? Now that the other doctor is back and taking care of the Ferreras' son, Carver's status with the hospital isn't the dilemma it was before."

"True. If he's suspended, he'll have to do whatever it takes to get reinstated."

"And he can do that in his own sweet time. He's the

one with the problem. Why not let him come to you if he needs your help?" Nick grinned. "It'd do the creep good to eat a little crow."

"I'd agree, but Cleo reminded me that since we have only two board-certified neurosurgeons in town, it's dangerous to go without a backup. What if Dr. Prine decides to take off again?"

"Ah," Nick nodded. "I see your point. Maybe you should do a little tablehopping before they have a chance to leave." He stood and brushed my forehead with a quick kiss. "You're busy here, and I'm going to head out. I'll leave you to it. Good luck."

EIGHTEEN

KIRI AND CARVER seemed in no hurry to finish their lunch. I stayed at our table for a few moments after Nick left, thinking how best to approach them. Nothing confrontational, I decided. I hoped Dr. Poole had managed to explain to Carver the wisdom of cooperating with me. Either way, they were there, Kiri and her boss together, and this was my chance. I walked over to their table and said hello.

"Aimee," Kiri said. "It was good to see you at the marina last weekend. Did you enjoy yourself in the Bay Area?" I wished she hadn't blurted that out right in front of Carver.

"Yes, of course," I said.

"You own a boat?" Carver raised his shaggy eyebrows in surprise. Probably thought I couldn't afford the yachting life. He was right, but still, it was rude to make assumptions.

"No, Dr. Carver. My boyfriend and I stay on a friend's yacht occasionally. We enjoy the cooler weather down there. It's a nice change from our heat here in Timbergate."

"Who's your friend?" Carver asked. "Maybe I know him."

"I doubt it. She's a very private person." *Keep Buck out of this.*

"A woman, huh? I know a couple of gals with boats.

They both named 'em *Community Property*." Carver chuckled at his own little joke. Neither Kiri nor I joined in.

Carver shot a dour look my way. "Well, you might as well get to the point. You didn't come over to our table for girl talk." *Girl*. The man couldn't seem to speak without using his favorite word, but he had given me an opening, and I took it.

"Dr. Carver, you must know I've been trying to set up a time to meet with Kiri to sort out your CME problem. Would it be convenient if I came over to your office sometime this afternoon?"

"Convenient?" His eyebrows lowered in a frown. I tried not to look at them. They almost seemed alive, like some sort of hairy, wiggly caterpillars. "No, it wouldn't be *convenient*," he said, "but since you and Quinn obviously sicced Dr. Poole on me, I suppose you might as well get it over with." He stood, pulled out his wallet and handed some bills to Kiri. "I've got to go. Settle this up, will you? And have the girl box up the rest of my food so you can bring it back to the office."

After Kiri did as he'd asked, the two of us walked the short block to the TMC parking lot and took my car to Carver's office building. I mentioned that I'd been told Kiri had the day off.

"No. I was just out of the office this morning running errands for Dr. Carver," she said. I didn't ask if they were job-related. Knowing him, she was probably picking up his dry-cleaning.

The woman seemed oblivious to the implications of Carver's problem. It was time to enlighten her. I parked at Carver's office, but instead of getting out of my car, I stopped Kiri when she reached for her door handle.

"Kiri, wait a moment before we go inside, would you?"

She sat back. "What is it?"

"I have to ask whether Dr. Carver told you that he'll lose his admitting privileges at TMC if this doesn't get this resolved before Thursday. That's only two days from now. Do you understand how important this is?" I tried to soften my tone, while impressing upon her the seriousness of this problem. Kiri shook her head. "I'm afraid I'm new at this. I've never worked in a medical office before. Dr. Carver insists he has proof of those fifteen missing credits. What will happen if we don't find it?"

I explained that he would no longer have privileges at either hospital in town, and that being the case, not only would his income and his patients be affected, but TMC would be left with just one doctor to perform neurosurgeries or to follow the care of patients like Paulo Ferrera.

"I see," she said. "No wonder he's been so temperamental."

I somehow refrained from telling her that his temperament was foul even on the best of days.

Inside, Kiri led the way to her work station. Gray partitions separated her and each of the four other women in the workroom into separate cubicles.

"This desk was used by the office manager until I began working here," Kiri said. "It seems as if Dorothy—that was her name—had simply stuffed any unfinished work into bottom drawers. It piled up over several months until she forgot about it." Kiri opened the drawers to show me the jumbled mess. "You see how much there is to sort out. Because I'm the newest employee, Dr. Carver assigned that chore to me. My other duties have left me with very little time to go through everything."

"Did you ever try to contact Dorothy? Ask her about the missing paperwork?"

"No. We never even met. She was gone before I was hired, but I was told that one of Dr. Carver's staff had contacted her."

"Any luck with that?"

"No. Dorothy claimed she didn't know anything about the missing CME documents."

What the former employee had done seemed unconscionable. I didn't envy Kiri such a dismal task. I wondered if it were possible that Carver was telling the truth. Was his missing CME documentation buried somewhere in this cluttered heap of papers and folders? But how could something so crucial to his practice have been treated so negligently?

"Have you seen anything about continuing education in what you've gone through so far?" I asked. "This is so important, and there's so little time."

"I have been doing my best," Kiri said, "but I don't know exactly what I'm looking for. Dr. Carver did insist that he filled out the proper paperwork to be submitted to you for the missing fifteen credits." Her pretty face looked grim, but at the same time, my mind kept replaying the image of her down in Marin County at the yacht harbor. I was still wondering what was in the bag that was handed off to her from Carver's yacht.

I offered to come by after hours again to help her search. It seemed a waste of time, but I had to make one last effort, for myself and for the hospital.

"Kiri, what has Dr. Carver told you about why his CME documentation is so important?"

"Actually, that's what we talked about at lunch." She gestured to me to follow her to a small break room where we sat out of earshot from her coworkers. "He says it's a ridiculous waste of time. That the state board has accepted his word that he's done the required continuing education, and that should be good enough for TMC." She blushed. "Even after what you've said, I'm afraid I don't see the problem."

"Did he mention the potential of an audit?"

Kiri frowned. "No. What do you mean?"

"The state board requires doctors to keep proof of their past four years of CME credits in case they're chosen for an audit. A situation came up at TMC a few years ago where one of the medical staff lied about his CME credits, had his license renewed, and subsequently failed an audit by the state board. His TMC membership and privileges had been renewed. He'd been admitting and treating TMC patients until someone leaked the information that he'd been caught cheating. It made the news and resulted in more than one malpractice lawsuit. You can see why this documentation is so important for TMC and Dr. Carver."

"I do see." Kiri nodded her understanding. "That's when TMC began enforcing the strict requirement for CME documentation?"

"That's right. Dr. Carver's state license will renew for two years as of this Thursday simply because he has certified that he's done the required credits. He can see office patients, prescribe, do everything his practice allows. Even so, he won't be admitting or treating patients at TMC after midnight Thursday night unless he proves he's done his homework. We're trying to make this work for him as well as the hospital."

"I'll have to call Dr. Carver and find out how he wants to proceed." Kiri rose and walked me out the front door. "Thanks for giving me the rest of the story," she said.

Her response seemed strangely noncommittal, given the situation her boss was facing. What was up with her and Carver?

Driving back to the hospital, I pondered my next steps. There was my concern for the hospital, but I also had nagging doubts about Kiri. Should I speak frankly to Sanjay D'Costa about his cousin?

Maybe he could shed some light on the woman. How well did he really know Kiri? If she was leading some sort of criminal double life, had she pulled the wool over his eyes? I decided to talk to Cleo first. If she agreed with me, I could count on her to help me persuade Quinn that we needed to have a talk with Sanjay.

I stopped by Cleo's office before returning to the library. She heard me out but admitted she had reservations about going to Quinn.

"This is bad timing, Aimee. Quinn's not going to want to intervene unless you have something more tangible to offer him about Kiri. He's developed a good working relationship with Sanjay. You must recall that the poor guy got off to a rough start here."

"I do. And I agree. Sanjay's come along well these past months. It's just that his own life will be impacted if it turns out Kiri is mixed up in criminal activities involving the Ferrera family."

"Take the rest of the afternoon to think it over," Cleo said. "I'll give you the same advice I give TMC employees when they come to me with a gripe about one of our doctors. Document everything you can think of that could be considered hard evidence of wrongdoing. Then look at the list. Decide what your list proves, if anything."

"Sometimes we follow our intuition," I said.

"I understand, but in this situation, I think you have

to follow your intuition until it leads you to something concrete." Cleo leaned over her desk to pat my hand. "I'm on your side, and I trust your judgment, but we need a damned good reason if we're going to ask Quinn to confront Sanjay about Kiri."

I did as Cleo suggested with the remains of the afternoon. I made a list of my suspicions about Kiri and tried to view it through Quinn's eyes. It didn't pass the test.

The bare facts were that Kiri had spent the weekend in Marin County. She had been seen with the hull diver who cleaned the bottoms of both Godfrey Carver's and Buck Sawyer's yachts. She had been seen leaving Carver's yacht on Sunday afternoon, after being handed what appeared to be an overnight bag. That was it. Everything else was conjecture. Obviously, Cleo was right. There was no point in bothering Quinn. Not yet.

At quitting time, I had reached the library's exit door when my desk phone rang. I hesitated, wondering how much my conscience would bother me if I left without answering it. *Enough.*

I went back to my desk and picked up. It was Cleo, with unwelcome news.

"So sorry to be the bearer of bad tidings, but I thought you'd want to know."

My breath caught in my chest. "What is it?"

"It's Paulo Ferrera. He's taken a turn for the worse."

"He's worse? How did that happen? I thought he was showing signs of emerging from the coma."

"His coma has deepened again, but I don't know anything more specific. Quinn's been in close touch with Dr. Prine, who suspects there was something in Carver's treatment regimen that backfired and complicated Paulo's recovery. Quinn's trying to reassure the parents that Prine can get things back on track."

"I hope he's right. Those poor people have been through so much."

"This doesn't look good for Godfrey Carver," she said. "On top of his CME problems, he'll have to answer some difficult questions about this case."

"Unless he comes up with proof of the missing CME credits, he's only going to be on the medical staff for two more days. After that, it'll be moot, won't it?"

Cleo hedged, keeping her confidentiality obligation in mind. "I can't say any more, but trust me, he'll be held accountable if we lose Paulo Ferrera."

As soon as I reached home Tuesday night, I told Nick what had happened with Paulo at the hospital. I added that I had not heard a word from Kiri about Dr. Carver's CME documents.

"I'm sorry. That's bad news on both counts." He gave me a quick kiss. "Chores are done and dinner is courtesy of the Coyote Creek Deli. Want to talk it over? Try to unwind with a drink before we eat?"

"Yes, please. White wine would be nice. I'll change and meet you on the deck."

I slipped into cutoff jeans and a T-shirt and caught up with Nick outside, where he was talking on his cell. I waited while he finished the call, knowing from his end of the conversation that it was Harry.

"What was that about?" I asked.

"I told him the Portuguese patient is worse. We need the sister's email account more than ever. Harry's going to come out to Coyote Creek and huddle with us."

"Is Rella coming, too?"

"No, she's working." Nick shook his head and smiled. "If you call hanging out in Miami Beach work. She flew Buck to Florida this week. He's looking to invest in some real estate down there."

"Has Harry told her what's going on with the Ferrera family?"

"I haven't asked him about that. We'll find out when he gets here. I'm more interested in whether he's any closer to identifying the Ferrera girl's online boyfriend."

"So am I. I'm afraid the police here and in the Azores are going to consider this a cold case if there aren't any new leads fairly soon."

"That could happen eventually," Nick said, "but it's been less than two weeks since the brother was shot."

"But it's been three and a half weeks since his sister went missing. A lot of other local crimes have been in the news since then." I worked my shoulders to relieve the tension from a stressful day. "When do the police decide it's time to shift their resources to the next case?"

"I don't know the answer to that, but speaking of police, I wonder if the TPD has contacted their counterparts down in the Bay Area." Nick tapped his phone.

"What are you looking for?"

"Just a sec." He scrolled until he found what he wanted. "Here it is. I'm looking at the law enforcement agencies in Marin County. Looks like there's a county sheriff's office, and each city has its own police department."

"What does that imply?" I asked.

"Not sure." Nick's brow furrowed. "I was wondering what Marin County agency our police department would be contacting, if any."

"How about someone in charge of Bay Area harbors and marinas? Someone who could keep an eye out for the yacht she's on."

"I'd agree, if there was any way to confirm that she's on that yacht."

"Oh, Nick, you're right. We can't prove it, but I feel it, deep in my bones. She left the Azores on that yacht."

"Detective Kass is leading the case. He must be doing something to cover every possible contingency," Nick said.

"Maybe there's some way to alert all the harbormasters in Marin County to be on the lookout for a yacht matching Catia's description and flying the Bay Wind burgee."

"Not a bad idea, although we're only guessing it flies that ensign." Nick tapped his phone again, found what he wanted, and shook his head. "Not sure how helpful that would be. Marin County has one harbormaster covering at least fourteen yacht harbors and marinas."

"Really? Does it say what the harbormaster actually does?"

Nick read from his phone. "Yep. Found a description of duties. In a nutshell, he assigns berth spaces, checks documentation and registration, and collects fees." He put his phone down and picked up his wineglass.

"That's disappointing." I set my glass aside. "Unless the harbormaster has something concrete from the police or sheriff, I doubt he'll be able to help."

Nick nodded. "And so far, there's no evidence any crime was committed in Marin County. The brother was shot in Timbergate. It's up to our local police department to take the lead, and in the eyes of the police, here and in the Azores, the sister's disappearance may not even be a crime. No one can prove she left on that yacht against her will. They can't prove she left on it at all. Even if she did, the police would have to consider that she's a runaway who will eventually go home."

"But there *was* a crime," I said. "Her brother came to California to find her and ended up shot. That definitely increases the odds that the girl is in trouble."

"Still, the authorities in the Bay Area would need probable cause for a warrant before they could board a yacht and start nosing around."

"Meanwhile, the best way we can help find that girl is to find her secret email account and hope it leads us to the bogus online boyfriend. If the police had him, this case would heat up like a wildfire."

"I agree with you." Nick shaded his eyes toward the horizon, where the lowering sun tinted the sky over the western mountains. "We have to trust that Detective Kass sees it that way."

"Then that's where we need to focus." I took a sip of wine, hoping to ease my anxiety. "We're still taking one step forward, and two steps back. We must do something soon. Without Paulo, the odds of finding Liliana are desperately low. The Ferreras are going to lose both their children."

Nick stood up and pulled me into a comforting hug. "Let's wait until we hear what Harry's been doing. Maybe he's making some progress."

It wasn't long before we saw Harry's red Jag approaching down the lane toward the barn. I began questioning him even before he reached the deck at the top of our outdoor staircase.

"Have you had any luck with the email account?"

"Whoa, Sis, at least let me say hello." Harry nodded to Nick, who stood holding open the door to our kitchen.

"Come on in." Nick crooked a thumb toward our dinette table. "We're about to eat. There's plenty if you're hungry. I ordered a monster sub sandwich and a tub of potato salad."

"If it's from the Coyote Creek Deli, I'm in," Harry said.

Harry grabbed a beer from the fridge. We split the sub into three parts, heaped potato salad on our plates and sat at our small table. I told Harry what little I could about Paulo Ferrera's worsening condition. It wasn't much and didn't rise to the level of breaching confidentiality. Paulo had shown signs of emerging from the coma for a few days, then his progress reversed. His coma deepened, and just in time, Carver was relieved of the case by Dr. Prine.

"Everyone at the hospital was grateful that Prine was back," I said.

"Any up-to-the-minute word on the patient?" Harry asked.

"No. I won't know anything until I get to work tomorrow." Anxious, I asked Harry for a progress report on the email search.

Between bites, he replied, "We're not there yet, but I think we're closing in on it."

Nick held up a finger. "Wait a minute. Who's *we*?"

I knew why he asked. We didn't need any outsiders in the mix.

"No worries," Harry said. "My cyber-security skills are a little rusty, so I contacted a couple of guys—actually a guy and a gal—who used to be part of a harmless little group I belonged to back in the day."

"You were in a hacker group?" I said. "When? Did Mom and Dad know?"

Harry gave me a look. Not quite condescending, but close. "Back in high school, Aimless. While you were using your spare time taking dancing lessons, I had my own hobby."

Nick broke up the sibling banter. "Okay, Harry, let's hear the rest. Are your consultants in prison now?"

"Not hardly. They're up-to-date pros, working for legit corporations. They've brought me up to speed with the kind of tools I need to get this done."

"How soon?"

"No guarantees, but if I can't do it, Dick and Jane," Harry paused and grinned, "not their real names of course, have offered to help me crack the secret email, just for the fun of it."

"Harry, tell us how long it's going to take," I pressed. "If Liliana is on that yacht, and the yacht really is headed for Marin County, it's going to arrive any day. We're almost out of time."

He swallowed a bite of sandwich. "After I talked to my friends, I quit trying to use simple guesswork to figure out what email address Liliana used to set up the account. They helped me set up an algorithm using everything we know about her. It's running as we speak." He glanced up at our kitchen clock." I'll call you any time, day or night, if I get a hit."

"If you do, what happens next?" Nick asked.

"Then it gets easier." Harry leaned back, took a sip of his beer. "Once we have her account ID, we use a nifty feature called a password cracker to open it. Then we look for any mail from this Francisco character. With luck, she'll have saved some of her messages from him. We'll also read everything she sent to him."

"That's it?" I said. "I thought you could do more."

"I can." Harry gave me a frustrated sigh. "I wasn't quite finished. If we get into her account and see messages from the boyfriend, I'll have an email address for him. Then I can sniff out his IP address, which in turn could lead us right to his front door."

"Wait a minute," Nick said. "I know about IP sniffers, but what if he's spoofed his IP?"

I held up my hand. "I've heard of IP sniffers. Not sure about the spoofer. Please explain."

Nick complied. "When a sender doesn't want to be identified, he—or she—can trip up the sniffer by spoofing, which means bouncing the email around the globe from one IP address to another before it reaches its target." Nick looked to Harry. "Did I get that right?"

"Close enough," Harry said. "Let's just hope that didn't happen. If our boy, Francisco, is part of some major crime organization that's abducting women for sex trafficking, you can count on the IP address being spoofed. If he's just some jerk-off preying on naïve teenagers, he's probably not that sophisticated."

Harry left, promising again to alert us if he succeeded with Liliana's email account.

NINETEEN

NICK AND I were both too restless to settle down for the evening. We had a couple of hours before bedtime, so we decided to walk up to the main house and see what Amah and Jack were doing. We found them sitting on the veranda overlooking their backyard vegetable garden. They were sorting what they'd picked into separate baskets.

"Hi, kids, what's going on?" Jack waved to us with a zucchini in one hand and a cigar in the other. "We saw Harry's car leave. Thought he'd stop in and say hello, but he kept on going."

"And we were going to offer him some veggies. His loss," Amah said. "You should take some of this back to your place. I'll get a bag." She hopped up and hurried inside, probably hoping to foist some zucchini on us before we could get away.

Amah returned and started filling a bag with an assortment of garden produce, while Jack nodded, satisfied with her choices.

"Grab a couple of chairs and tell us the latest," he said. "How's the Portuguese patient doing? Any luck with finding the sister?"

"I wish I had better news," I said. "The brother was improving, but now he's losing ground. And there's still no trace of the sister."

Amah exhaled a breath. "Oh, I'm so sorry. Your parents had such high hopes for that family."

"We all did. Still do," Nick said. "That's probably why Harry didn't stop to chat. He's doing some cyber-investigating, hoping to turn up clues as to the girl's whereabouts."

"I thought she was supposed to be on a yacht some-where," Jack said.

"That's our best guess," Nick said. "Trouble is, no one can verify that."

"Unless we can access her secret email," I said. "That might give us more to go on. Harry thinks he's found a way to do that."

"He's something else with the cyber stuff," Jack said. "Has been since he was little." He turned to Amah. "What was he, about ten years old when he taught me how to use email?"

Amah grinned. "That sounds right. Now he's teach-ing you how to use PowerPoint for your seminars on turkey hunting."

"Damn technology." Jack flicked the ash from his cigar. "Wasn't anything wrong with doing slide shows with a projector and screen back in the day. No one can get away with that these days. PowerPoint's the only way to go."

"Back to the Ferreras," Amah said. "We've been in touch with your mom and dad, Aimee, so we're fairly well caught up with everything that happened while you were in the Azores. Didn't the missing girl have a friend who told you about the secret email account?"

"She did." I said. "As far as we know, the friend, Catia, was the only person who knew about it."

"But she didn't know details?" Amah said.

"No. If she had, I'm sure the police in the Azores would have followed up on that lead right away."

"Yes, of course." Amah stared thoughtfully out toward the garden. "Did you ask the friend for her email address or phone number? Or leave yours with her?"

"No, it didn't occur to me, because Catia swore she'd told us everything she knew. The police in the Azores would have her contact information. And Catia called Mom to tell us about Francisco, so Mom probably has her cellphone number."

Jack tamped out his cigar and cocked his head toward Amah. "You're thinking, aren't you Rosa?" He smiled at Nick and me. "Yep. She's thinking. Look out."

"Oh, stop it, Jack." She swatted at his arm. "I was just wondering. If the girl, Liliana, knows she's in trouble, she's going to reach out to anyone she can. Who knows how she'll communicate? Or with whom?"

"She had a cellphone, but we already know it hasn't been used since she disappeared," Nick said. "She hasn't emailed her family, either. There's been no way to tell her that her brother's injured and her parents are in the States—right here in Timbergate."

"So if she could, she might try calling or emailing her parents, her brother, or her friend in the Azores," Amah said.

I cut in. "Exactly, but as far as anyone knows, she hasn't. Her brother had no phone when he was brought in to the hospital. The parents said he never used email. The TPD police have the Ferreras' laptop, so they'll keep checking that."

Amah pointed skyward. "First evening star. Make a wish." She smiled. "Never mind, I already know what we're all wishing for."

I reached over and touched Amah's arm. "I know where you were going with your questions about Catia's email and phone. You're thinking that if Liliana is still okay, still feeling safe, and has no idea Paulo's hurt and that her parents are here, then she's assuming everything is status quo back in the Azores. She can stay on whatever course she's chosen to take."

"Yes, that sums up the best-case scenario," Amah said. "But even if it's the correct one, wouldn't she be feeling at least a little guilty about running away?"

"I would," I said, "but I'm not an impetuous fifteen-year-old."

"No, but try thinking like one," Nick said. "Follow Rosa's logic, Aimee. What would Liliana do if she's feeling guilty or having doubts?"

"She's probably try to communicate secretly with Catia, if only to find out how much trouble she'd be in if she returned home."

"I agree," Amah said. "From what I gather, girls that age now communicate every moment of their lives to their best friends. Liliana's conscience must surely be troubling her. Don't you think she'd unload on the girl who promised to keep her secrets?"

"Of course, but only if Catia can be contacted." I glanced at Nick. "Her grandmother shut her down completely. No phone, no email."

"I have another thought," Nick said. "The police in the Azores must have access to Catia's email and phone, even if she's not allowed to use them. They'd want to intercept any messages or texts Liliana tried to send Catia."

"There you go, Amah. If Liliana tries to contact Catia, the Horta police will intercept the message." I was developing a headache from all the ping-ponging back and forth.

"Of course, we can't overlook another possibility," Nick said. "What if Catia has a second email account?"

The question caught me off-guard. "Oh, my God,

Nick. You're right. Liliana set up a secret email account at a cyber café. Catia might have done the same thing, and if she did, her grandmother and the police wouldn't have a clue." Then a depressing thought hit me. "Great. If she did that, we now have two secret accounts to uncover."

"But why wouldn't the friend alert the police if she heard from Liliana?" Amah asked. "Surely she'd want to help."

"Depends on what Liliana's situation is," Nick said. "Assuming she's safe and whole, still looking forward to meeting her boyfriend, Francisco, she'd probably ask Catia to keep quiet."

"Wait," I said. My head was pounding. "Let's stop for a minute. I'm getting dizzy. The *ifs* are flying around this veranda like a swarm of gnats. *If* Catia has a secret account, and *if*, somehow, Liliana knows about it, and *if* they've been in touch, then Catia would have told Liliana that Paulo is in critical condition in a hospital in California and that their parents are also here, holding vigil and praying for his recovery." I stopped for breath. "So *if* all that is true, and *if* Liliana is safe, why hasn't she contacted her parents?"

"Because she no longer has her phone," Jack jumped in. "That's the most obvious answer. Her captors got it away from her somehow. Probably tricked her into thinking she lost it."

"He's right," Nick said. "That is the most obvious answer, and it puts us a back at square one. Liliana vanished from the Azores; her brother set out to find her. Raise your hand if you think his being shot in Timbergate was a random coincidence."

Jack raised his hand. "Nope, I don't think it's a coincidence. I just wanted to speak again."

"Please do," Nick said. "Aimee and I have gone over this so many times, we could really use another point of view."

"Okay," Jack leaned in. "Being a hunter, of course I'm familiar with firearms, so I keep coming back to the gunshot part of this story. What I'm wondering is, who was hunting down the brother? Sounds like we already know the *why* of it. He was on to some pretty strong clues as to what happened to his sister." Jack looked at me. "Sorry, honey, but that little gal is not safe. Take my word for it. She may not know it yet, but sure as heck, she's in deep, deep trouble."

"You're saying we should start with why the patient was shot," Nick said. "But he's in a coma."

"'Course." Jack nodded. "We know that. But all those homeless people in that camp who saw the incident aren't in comas."

"I'm sure they've already been questioned," I said. "Our TPD would have done that immediately."

"All of 'em?" Jack said. "Don't bet your bottom dollar they got to *all* of 'em."

"I don't know, Jack." I massaged my throbbing temples. "The police had a CI working the camp that night. He's the one who called it in. With his account of the incident, they should have gleaned everything they could from all the witnesses."

"Then how about this? Either of you know this guy? This CI?" Jack asked.

I didn't want to answer that. I looked to Nick. Should we tell Jack the CI was Tango Bueller, the ex-con who had attacked me with intent to rape five years ago?

"We know *of* him," Nick said. "Why do you ask?"

"Just a thought. It might be interesting to look at the crime scene. Especially if the CI could accompany you and point out the particulars of what happened. Maybe he missed something. Had to be a reason that injured boy was shot where he was."

Nick's eyes narrowed in a way that guaranteed he was going to do exactly what Jack suggested. And that he would try to discourage me from going along. He wouldn't want me anywhere near Tango Bueller. *Too bad.* I'd already made up my mind. I'd perused more than one of the books on crime scene investigation in the TMC library's forensic collection. That didn't make me any kind of expert, but it did make me inquisitive.

Nick and I thanked my grandparents for letting us use them as a sounding board, and for the load of garden produce they insisted we take back to our apartment over the barn. On the short walk down the lane, I waited to hear how Nick would voice his objection to my going along to the homeless camp. I didn't have to wait long.

"I know what you're thinking, and my answer is *hell, no*," he said.

"Not your decision." I said.

"No, but Tango is still on parole. What do you bet he's not supposed to be anywhere near you?"

"It would be easy to find out." We reached the stairs to the deck. I went up first. "I'll check with Detective Kass. See if he can clear it with Tango's parole officer."

Nick came up behind me. "Okay. If you're determined to do that, why don't we invite Kass along? He seems like a reasonable guy."

I CALLED KASS from the library on Wednesday morning to explain what Nick and I wanted to do. He hesitated at first, but when I reminded him that TPD's crime victim was still in a coma in the Timbergate Medical Center ICU, he softened up.

"I'm not saying we can't do this," Kass said, "but I wonder what you and your boyfriend think you can do that my men haven't already done?"

"Probably nothing." I pushed on. "It's just that we have such a close connection with the victim's parents. We promised them we'd go to the location where their son was wounded. Even if it's a futile gesture, it will make them feel like someone cares."

I kept my fingers crossed during that little speech. It was such a good white lie, I decided to make it true. Kass agreed to call me back if he could arrange something with Tango's parole officer. I texted Nick to say we were halfway there.

Lola Rampley arrived a few minutes later for her volunteer shift, looking as if she'd youthened five or ten years. She wore her short hair in soft curls, framing her face like a gentle white cloud. Her subtle makeup tinted her cheeks slightly pink and her lips a shade darker. Her dowager's hump was pronounced, but it didn't seem to affect her attitude or her mobility. I marveled at her energy and hoped I'd fare as well when I reached my eighties.

"What's on our schedule today, Miss Machado?" Lola enjoyed every aspect of library work, but I knew her favorite was filling requests for articles from our journals and databases. She would either email them as attachments or print them and have them delivered by courier.

"I've set aside the journal requests," I said. "They're on your desk." Her beaming smile gave my day a lift.

I left Lola to her chore and turned my attention to the matter that needed it most: Dr. Godfrey Carver's shortage of CME credits. What was left for me to do? The visit to his office the day before had been fruitless. The mess his former office manager left behind was almost enough to convince me that he *had* done the work. If so, he'd used incredibly poor judgment in trusting that woman to send his documents to me instead of submitting them himself. It made matters worse that Dorothy, the ex-employee, either couldn't or wouldn't help.

I thought again about Kiri trying to create order from the chaos she'd inherited. I almost felt sorry for her until I once again recalled seeing her on the dock down in the Bay Area. The image of her being handed that overnight bag kept popping into my mind, along with Nick saying, *We don't know what's in that bag.*

Although I'd decided not to question Sanjay about his cousin, I did find it odd that in all the months he had been TMC's assistant administrator, I'd never heard him mention her. I had no idea she existed until she suddenly appeared in Timbergate as a new hire in Carver's office. No, I wouldn't involve Sanjay. He'd only wonder why I was asking, and I had no good answer.

Instead, I placed a call to Kiri to ask if she had made progress in her search.

"She's not in." *Not this again.* The same shabby telephone etiquette from the same hopeless temp I'd spoken to at Carver's office the day before.

"Could you please take a message? I'd like to hear from her when she gets in. As soon as possible." I tried to keep the irritation out of my voice.

"No guarantees, but go ahead and give me your number."

I gave her my number and my cell number, and then asked when I might expect to hear from Kiri. The temp had no idea, an answer that I found particularly difficult. I gave up on making any further headway with the woman, deciding it would be more productive to go directly to Carver and warn him that his office staff was making it impossible for me to help him.

Before I did that, I would get Cleo's go-ahead. She was just as involved in the fuss over Carver's medical staff status as I was. I called to tell her I was on my way. Leaving the library in Lola's capable hands, I trekked across the complex to Cleo's office in the main tower. Before I brought up Carver's situation, I asked if Cleo had heard any news about Paulo Ferrera.

"Unfortunately, I have." She nodded toward her phone. "I just heard from Quinn, who's keeping close tabs on the case. He says the young man is still losing ground, and Dr. Prine hasn't been able to pinpoint the problem. He suspects it has something to do with the treatment regimen Carver was using. Quinn quoted Prine as saying he wished he'd come home from Florida sooner."

"Sounds like Prine is suggesting that Carver did the patient more harm than good."

Cleo's eyes widened. She glanced at her office door, then said softly, "*Shhh*, that's not the kind of talk we'd want overheard."

"Sorry," I said. "It's just so frustrating. How long will it take Prine to regain the ground Carver lost?"

Cleo dropped her half-moons on her desk. I saw sympathy in her eyes. "Aimee, I know the Ferreras are almost like family. This case is personal for you, but you can't let it cloud your judgment about the members of our medical staff. Godfrey Carver is a good doctor. He's eminently qualified to take the lead on a case like Paulo's. I'm not sure what Dr. Prine's comment meant, so let's not read more into it than necessary." She put her glasses on and leaned back in her chair. "When you called, you said you had a question about Carver's CME status. What was that about?"

I filled Cleo in with the latest in my efforts to help uncover the missing continuing education credits Carver kept insisting he'd earned.

"That's odd," Cleo said. "You're still having trouble pinning Kiri down? I thought she'd welcome your offer of help. If something isn't done by tomorrow, Carver's staff membership will be suspended."

"I know. And I'm new enough that I've never had to deal with a case like his, so here's my question. Should I tell Carver that I can't help him because I'm not getting the cooperation I need from Kiri?"

"Tattle on her to her boss?" Cleo wiggled her pen in her hand. "That's a tough one, but the circumstances might require it. In forty-eight hours, we're going to lose an indispensable member of our medical staff. If proof of his fifteen CME credits exists, finding it is critical. Think of worst-case scenarios. Paulo Ferrera is failing and may need another surgery any day now. We have Prine back from Florida, but if anything happened to put him out of commission in the next few days, Paulo would have no one, and neither would any other neurosurgery patient in Timbergate."

"Then what do you suggest? Do I speak to Carver? Or to Quinn and Sanjay?"

"Let me give it some thought. I'll call you at the library in ten minutes."

TWENTY

LOLA HAD FINISHED processing the requested articles when I returned to the library. I spotted her in the stacks, helping a patron find the section where we shelved nursing journals.

A phone message on my desk, written in Lola's precise hand, said *Call Nick*. He answered right away, asking for the status of our trip to the homeless camp. I told him I was waiting to hear back from Detective Kass, but the odds were good.

"Okay, then, here's what I'm hoping you can do in the meantime." Nick hesitated. "I'd do it myself, but I don't think that would work."

He explained that our walk through that camp would be more productive if he brought his dog along, but we would need an item that carried Paulo's scent. He suggested I visit the Ferreras at TMC's family housing facility. They might have something we could use.

I had my doubts. "Nick, the police would have all of that, wouldn't they? They've probably already scoured the crime scene with their own dogs."

"I imagine they have," Nick said, "but it would be a great chance for me to put Ginger through her paces. Maybe if I put it that way, Kass won't take it as a criticism of his investigation."

"I hope so. Do you really think she might pick up a scent another dog would miss?"

"I honestly don't know, but here's the thing. We don't

have access to the details of the police investigation. Even if Ginger reacts the same as the TPD dogs, we'll have more firsthand information than we do now."

"Nick, hold on." My second phone line was blinking. I put him on hold and picked up the other call. It was Kass. I asked him to hold, picked up Nick's line and said, "Kass is on my other line. I'll call you back."

Kass had good news. He'd cleared it with Tango's parole officer. He asked if Nick and I could meet him at the homeless camp at one o'clock. I told him we would be there. I didn't elaborate about bringing the dog. Let Nick handle that.

I got back to Nick, who urged me again to bring something that held Paulo's scent. I searched my mind for ideas. Surely the police would have taken his clothes and shoes for forensic examination. I wasn't about to ask Kass to bring any of that along. I was already uncomfortable that we were bringing Ginger with us. I wasn't about to tip him off ahead of time.

What else could we use that might have Paulo's scent? Nothing came to mind. I would have to ask his parents if they could think of something.

I'd just managed to get my mind back on library business when Cleo called as promised with a message that piqued my curiosity.

"Aimee, you asked if we should confront Carver about Kiri and the missing CME credits. Or maybe talk to Quinn or Sanjay. Let's hold off on that. I have something else going on that might be relevant."

"What is it?"

"I don't have time right now. Stop by later this afternoon and I'll explain."

I puzzled over that until noon finally came, and with it the end of Lola's shift. As soon as she left, I grabbed my purse, closed the library and walked the quick block to the TMC's family housing building.

The Ferreras were coming out the front door just as I arrived. The interpreter was not with them. With the help of the Portuguese dictionary in my purse and some pointing, I confirmed that they were on their way to the hospital. Their somber expressions conveyed their worry. Their son was getting worse, not better.

I tagged along with them, dictionary in my hand, looking for some way to communicate what I needed. We had reached the main lobby when I spotted Ramon Silva, their interpreter, coming off an elevator. I waved him over and explained what I needed without going into detail.

Ramon spoke in rapid Portuguese, holding his hand up to his nose and sniffing. I saw light dawn in Senhora Ferrera's eyes. She opened her purse, pulled out a hairbrush, and handed it to me. When I took it from her, she clasped my hand in both of hers.

"*Por favor*," she said, followed by two words I didn't understand.

Ramon filled in the blanks. "She says, 'Please save our children.'" A lump lodged in my throat, making it impossible to speak. I could only nod and hope she understood how much I wanted to do just that.

Senhora Ferrera spoke again, and Ramon explained that she gave me the hairbrush because every time she and her husband sat at their son's bedside in the ICU, she used it brush his hair. No doubt it would carry his scent.

WITH THAT DONE, I headed to the location where Paulo had been shot. Nick arrived just as I did, followed by Detective Kass and Tango. As they emerged from Kass's unmarked car, Tango spotted me and immediately cast his eyes down at the ground. I felt a bolt of adrenaline surge through my chest and almost lost my balance as the memory of his attack five years ago flashed through my mind. Nick sensed my reaction and called me over to him, asking if I would stay with Ginger while he talked with Kass and Tango.

I agreed and thanked him for giving me a moment to regain my composure. While he spoke to the two men, I took Paulo's hairbrush out of my purse. After the three of them broke their huddle, Tango and Kass took the lead, heading toward the homeless camp. Tango relied heavily on his cane, his limp as severe as ever. It brought back a vivid memory of the dark night when he and his criminal accomplice had stunned me with a tire iron and dragged me from my disabled car. Harry had arrived just in time to cripple both of my attackers and probably save my life.

Pulling myself back to the present, I handed Paulo's hairbrush to Nick, who offered it to Ginger to sniff. I heard him give her a "find it" command. Nick put the brush in his back pocket, and we walked quickly to catch up with the other two. The sun was still high enough to keep the day's temperature above ninety degrees. A slight breeze off the flowing river gave scant relief.

The camp was empty, but the litter and trash left behind created a nasty picture. Cardboard boxes, crumpled newspaper, a few broken-down shopping carts, and drug paraphernalia. Even soiled toilet paper was scattered among the river rocks.

We stepped carefully to avoid needles and broken glass, but I worried about the dog's paws until I realized Nick had come prepared. He called for me to wait up while he pulled a set of protective dog boots from the small backpack he was wearing. He fastened them on all four of Ginger's paws. With that done, we set off again, following Ginger, who followed her nose. The smells from the debris and detritus of the camp were so repulsive, I couldn't imagine how the dog could identify one specific scent from the malodorous hodgepodge.

Up ahead, Tango was talking to Kass, pointing to one spot and then another. When we reached them, the four of us were standing directly under the bridge of a busy four-lane street. The traffic noise made it impossible to hear what Tango was saying.

Nick and I followed Kass and Tango as they retraced their steps several times. Ginger kept her nose to the ground and seemed only slightly more interested when she came to the spot where Paulo had fallen.

"Do you think too much time has passed?" I asked Nick. "Maybe the scent has gone cold."

"I don't know; this is her first real-life field test." He took Paulo's hairbrush from his pocket and held it to Ginger's nose again, giving her the same command: "Find it."

Just then a jackrabbit scampered by, heading away from the camp toward a slope thick with brush that led upward to the professional buildings lining the riverbank. Ginger strained at the leash, but Nick redirected her attention, trying to keep her focus on the areas Kass and Tango were pointing out. I glanced at Nick's grim expression. Ginger's first field test. Was he disappointed with her performance?

After half an hour, we had accomplished nothing. There were no people at the camp to question. We'd seen nothing resembling a clue. Kass had to leave to follow up on another case. Tango had ridden with him, so they left together. Nick watched them drive away. He looked down at his dog, and then at me.

"I'm going to stay a little longer," he said, "but I don't want to keep you here if you're getting tired of this."

"I'd like to stay. Do you have any ideas we haven't already tried?"

Nick patted Ginger's head. "Only one. I'd like to take her to that area where she wanted to follow the rabbit. She's not supposed to get distracted that easily." He held the brush for her to sniff again.

We walked toward the spot near the steep grade where the dog had headed before Nick pulled her back. Her nose went to work and she picked up speed, heading up the slope that led to the professional buildings. It was thick with tangled brush, making it difficult to navigate. Nick and I both snagged our clothes trying to keep up. We were halfway to the top when Ginger stopped abruptly, sniffing at a bush where a torn bit of cloth flapped in the breeze. After a moment, she sat there alert, as if her work was done. I looked at Nick.

"She's definitely reacting to that scrap." Nick smiled like a proud father. "It wasn't the rabbit after all." He used his phone to take photos of the spot from several angles.

"Let's bag that," I said.

Nick looked at me and laughed. "Did I just hear you say that? You sound like one of those woman detectives on TV who wear five-inch heels to crime scenes."

"And you sound like a pain in the rear." I took a small paper bag from my purse. "Here, hold this open." I used tweezers to pull the cloth from the bush and drop it in the bag.

Nick folded the bag and handed it to me. "Ginger found it—that's a good sign it's from whatever shirt

Paulo was wearing when he was shot. Let's get out of this thicket and go home."

"Out of the thicket, yes, but home, no. We need to identify those buildings."

"Okay, but don't assume too much from that. If Paulo was on the run, being chased, he'd have covered a lot of ground before he got this far."

"Still, I want to check something. I can't be sure from here, but one of those buildings looks familiar."

We scrambled back down to our cars. Nick unfastened Ginger's boots and loaded her in her kennel in the bed of his pickup. We left my car where it was parked and used his truck to wind our way up and around to the buildings we'd seen from below. Nick parked across the street.

"Well?" he said.

"I was right." A chill ran through me. "The building nearest where we found that bit of cloth is Dr. Godfrey Carver's new office."

TWENTY-ONE

NICK DROVE ME back to where I had parked my car near the homeless camp. On the way, we agreed that we should ask the Ferreras if they could identify the scrap of material we had found.

"I'll do that right away." I opened my purse, assuring myself that the torn material was still in the little paper bag.

Nick pulled up and stopped next to my car. "If the Ferreras recognize that fabric, we'll call Kass as soon as you get home." He leaned over to kiss my cheek. "Don't get your hopes up, though. It most likely can't be considered evidence in a legal sense, because it wasn't found by the police."

"But you did take photos, and Kass can compare the scrap with the shirt Paulo was wearing when he was shot. That will tell him the same thing it's telling us. Paulo probably ran down that slope just before he was shot at the homeless camp."

"Agreed, but keep in mind that Kass has no reason to suspect your Dr. Carver of being involved in this mystery."

"Not yet," I said, "but the scrap could help him make that connection."

"Maybe, but we can't be making accusations based on vague suspicions and speculation. For now, let's just see what you find out from the Ferreras."

"I'm not sure how long it'll take." I got out of Nick's

pickup and walked around to his driver's side window. "You'll probably have to do the chores without me."

"Take as much time as you need. Jack wants me to help him trim llama hooves this evening. I expect I'll be busy until you get home."

Nick took off, and I headed to the TMC family housing facility, hoping to find the Ferreras. I was disappointed. They were probably at their son's bedside in ICU. I hoped that meant Paulo had taken a turn for the better. I hurried over to the hospital, reminding myself to return the hairbrush to his mother. I was met with another disappointment when I stopped by Cleo's office on my way to the ICU.

"He's no better," she said, when I asked about Paulo. "In fact, Dr. Prine is stymied. He's all but given up."

I slumped into a chair across from Cleo's desk. "We had such high hopes when Prine took over. Have you heard anything to explain why that poor patient regressed?"

"No." Cleo shrugged. "I'm not privy to all the details of his care at this point."

"That reminds me, this morning you said we should hold off confronting Carver about Kiri and the missing CME credits. Or talking to Quinn or Sanjay. You told me something had come up. What was that about?"

"Dr. Prine called this morning to arrange an appointment with me. He's coming by to talk about Godfrey Carver." She glanced at her watch. "He'll be showing up here any minute."

"Then I should leave."

Cleo sighed. "Yes, you should. I suspect Prine is gunning for Carver. He'll want privacy." She gave me a weary look. "I'll call you later if there's anything I can tell you in good conscience."

The hallway outside Cleo's office was empty as I hurried, head down and heart heavy, toward the ICU. Turning a corner, I collided with Dr. Oliver Prine. His stethoscope flew from around his neck and landed on the floor. Bending down to pick it up, we nearly head-butted each other. We both apologized in an awkward duet that had us saying *Sorry* and *Excuse me* at the same time.

When we straightened up, Prine towered over me. I sidestepped out of his way, eager to avoid any further embarrassment.

"Wait." He reached out, touching my arm. "You're the new librarian, aren't you?" His deep tan and full head of light-brown, sun-streaked hair reminded me that he had spent the last week and a half in Florida. We had never been formally introduced, but I was surprised that he referred to me as *new* when I had worked at TMC for almost a year.

"Yes, I'm Aimee Machado. I'm TMC's librarian and continuing education coordinator."

His expression reflected more than casual interest. "You're in charge of CME?"

"Yes." I immediately wished I hadn't mentioned that. According to Cleo, Dr. Prine was already gunning for Carver. I tried to change the subject.

"How is your daughter, Dr. Prine?"

"I'm sorry?" Prine's brow wrinkled slightly.

"Your daughter in Florida," I said. "I hope she's recovering from her accident."

"Oh, yes," he said. "You caught me off guard there. I didn't realize her accident was common knowledge among our employees here."

I felt my face flush. I couldn't seem to speak to this

man without embarrassing myself. I began to back away, but he stopped me again.

"Miss…sorry, I'm afraid I don't know your last name."

"*Ma-SHAW-doe.*" I pronounced it for him.

"Well, Miss Machado. It was nice to meet you. And thanks for asking about my daughter. I'm sure she's going to be fine."

Dr. Prine finally moved on, leaving me to finish my trek to the Intensive Care Unit. I used the in-house phone to ask Paulo's ICU nurse if his parents were with him. She confirmed that they were. When I told her I had something for Mrs. Ferrera, she said she'd get the interpreter on the line. He would ask Mrs. Ferrera to come out to talk to me.

While I waited, I opened my little dictionary and phrase book, searching for the words I needed. I managed to come up with a sentence that said: Does your son have a shirt made of this fabric? *Seu filho tem uma camisa feita deste tecido.*

The doors to the ICU finally opened, and both Senhor and Senhora Ferrera came slowly toward me, looking more devastated than I'd ever seen them. I loathed the idea that my question might cause them more pain, but I went ahead, showing them the fabric and trying to pronounce my question clearly. They looked at each other, nodded, then Senhora Ferrera said in a voice choked with emotion, "*Sim, é sua camisa favorita.*" I knew right away that she was telling me the fabric was from her son's favorite shirt.

I thanked them both, handed the hairbrush back to Paulo's mother, and used the house phone to tell the ICU nurse to let them back into the unit.

On my way out of the building, I tried to fathom the

grief Senhora Ferrera and her husband must be feeling. I knew I couldn't come close. What they were going through was heartbreaking. My throat burned with the effort it took to keep from sobbing as I raced to my car. I was desperate to get home to Nick and my grandparents. I wanted to hold them close and assure myself that my loved ones were all safe and well.

AT THE RANCH, I drove down the lane toward the barn, where I spotted Nick and Jack in the corral with two of the llamas tethered to posts. Jack was holding one of them steady while Nick worked the clippers on the toenails of the animal's split hooves.

I hurried up to our apartment and quickly changed into cut-offs and a T-shirt. My cell rang as I was opening the fridge to grab a bottle of green tea. Harry was calling. I put the drink down and answered with my fingers crossed.

"Any news?"

"Not yet," he said. "Just calling to ask about the brother. Any good news there?"

"No, but Nick and I did make a discovery that might help the police." I told him about our trip to the crime scene and the scrap of fabric that Ginger found down the slope behind Carver's building.

"Sounds like it came from the victim's shirt."

"I'm almost certain it did. Paulo's parents said they recognized it."

"Excellent!" Harry said. "Doggy detective school is paying off. Did you take that scrap to Detective Kass?"

"Not yet. I just got home. I haven't even had a chance to tell Nick yet."

"Do it soon. If it's a match, Kass might convince a judge that he has probable cause for a search warrant."

"You mean he'd go in and search Carver's office?"

"No. I was thinking he'd start with the security cameras on that building," Harry said. "He could do that without alerting the doctor that he's a suspect."

"You mean, act as if it's just a coincidence that a crime took place near Carver's office?"

"Why not?" Harry said. "Happens all the time. Kass could just ask the doc to be helpful—do his civic duty."

"Good idea. Then if Carver balks out of fear of what's on the cameras, Kass will pick up on it."

"There are a couple of downsides," Harry said. "If there was something on there that would incriminate Carver, he would have ditched it by now. Unless he's dumb, and I doubt that."

"What's the other downside?"

I heard Harry clear his throat. "That would be your worst case. Is there any chance the camera behind that building recorded you and Nick and his dog when you found that scrap of material? If it did, you've already attracted Carver's attention."

My stomach lurched at the thought. "Good question, but I'm sure we're in the clear. We found it before we got close to the building, and the angle of that slope couldn't have provided a sight line to where we were."

"Glad to hear that," he said. "Good luck, then."

"Thanks." I looked out my kitchen window. "Nick's helping Jack trim llama hooves, but I'll tell him you called. And please keep trying to find that email account for Liliana."

"Working on it. Don't give up hope."

Another thought struck me. "Wait... I have a question. How hard would it be to look up the registration information for a yacht?"

"Not too hard. All you'd need is the hull number."

"I don't have that. Is there any other way?"

"The name of the vessel would be a start. But you have to consider that any number of yachts could have the same name. It's the hull number that's tied to the registration."

"I know that," I said. "What if all you have is a description?"

"If the yacht that girl from the Azores is presumed to be on moors at any of the harbors or marinas in the Bay Area, it should be easy to spot. Something that size doesn't show up every day."

"But I'm thinking of another, smaller one," I said. "One of the doctors on our medical staff owns it."

"If you know who owns it, why do you need to look up the registration?"

"It's probably nothing." I didn't blame Harry for sounding puzzled. "Sometimes there's more than one owner. I'd like to know if this doctor has a partner in ownership. That might explain the argument I witnessed on Carver's boat. If the boat had a second owner, that incident might have had nothing to do with Carver or our missing girl."

"Got it," Harry said. "What's the yacht's name?"

"*God's Gift.*"

"Hold on a sec." I heard keys clicking. "I'm back," Harry said. "That name is more common than I would have thought. Do you have any other info that would narrow it down?"

"Its owner is a member of the Bay Wind Yacht Club," I said. "Does that help?"

"Probably. Their membership info might be protected. I'll see what I can do and get back to you."

Just as I finished talking to Harry, Nick came through the kitchen door looking dusty and overheated.

I filled him in on our conversation, then told him the Ferreras' reaction to seeing the scrap of fabric.

"What do you think? Should we try to contact Kass tonight?"

"We might as well." Nick pulled his sweaty shirt away from his body. "While you do that, I need to clean up. Those llamas are dusty critters."

While the shower was running, I left a message for Kass, asking him to return my call. With that done, I explored our fridge for inspiration. I found cheese, pickles, and chocolate syrup. There was half a carton of vanilla ice cream in the freezer compartment, and half a loaf of sourdough in the bread box, so no problem. Grilled cheese sandwiches and sundaes. Perfect for a hot summer evening's meal.

Nick came into the kitchen smelling all soapy clean and looking scrumptious. "Any word from Kass?"

"Not yet. I left a message. I didn't go into detail, just said it was about the Ferrera case."

"That's all we can do for now." Nick saw me put a skillet on the stove. "You're cooking?"

"Sort of. Grilled cheese."

"Make two for me," he said. "I worked up an appetite trying to keep up with Jack."

I loved that Nick pitched in with some of the more difficult llama tasks. Jack was still strong and capable, but trimming the hooves on the newer, more high-strung llamas was a lot safer as a two-person job. One well-aimed kick at lightning speed could result in a swift trip to the Emergency Room.

"How many sets of hooves did you do?"

"We took care of the two that needed trimming."

"Thank you for helping," I said. "Jack's a man of few words, but you must know how much he appreciates it."

"I know. He did mumble something that sounded like a thank you. The gist was that he thinks I've got the hang of it now." Nick stood behind me and nuzzled my neck. "Maybe you can add your thanks later."

A shiver went up my neck and into my scalp. "Back off, buddy. I'm holding a hot skillet here."

Nick set the dinette table with placemats and napkins. Ginger wandered in from the living room, tail wagging. *Doggy dinnertime.*

While I plated our sandwiches and poured iced tea, Nick fed the dog. Finally we sat down to eat and decide what to do next.

"If we don't hear from Kass tonight, we should try again first thing tomorrow," I said.

"Absolutely. You have to be at work. If I can't get him on the phone, I'll run by the police department."

"If you do talk to Kass, will you ask him about checking the security cameras on Carver's building?"

"Only if he doesn't come up with that himself." Nick swallowed a bite of pickle. "He's a good guy, but he wouldn't appreciate me telling him how to do his job."

"Nick, I just thought of something else you can take to Kass tomorrow." I jumped up and ran into the bedroom for my purse. I came back to the table with my forensic kit. "Remember the man who fell bleeding on the dock last weekend?" I held the blood sample out to him.

"What do you want Kass to do with this?"

"Whatever he can, as fast as he can, to identify the man I saw." My heart raced with the anxious thought that I'd almost forgotten about that blood sample. "Ask him to call me if he needs my description of what I witnessed on that dock."

Nick wiped his mouth with a paper napkin. "You realize he'll need to be brought up to speed concerning your theory about Carver's yacht."

"If he'll take the time to hear you out, you can explain it, can't you?"

"I can try, but you were the witness." Nick shook his head. "I suspect he'll want to hear it firsthand, if he thinks it's important."

"If he does, ask him to please call me. I'll explain everything in as much detail as he wants."

After we cleaned up the kitchen, Nick poured each of us a glass of wine. We went out to the deck to watch the sunset. As the last flush of flame-colored light faded from the sky, Jack's turkeys flew to the upper reaches of the pasture's blue oak trees to roost for the night.

We had settled into a companionable silence when I heard my phone ringing inside. I considered ignoring it, but curiosity kicked in. There were too many things going on in our lives. Too many people who might have important news about Paulo or Liliana Ferrera. I ran inside to answer the call.

"Aimee," Cleo said, "hope I'm not interrupting anything."

"No, what's up." A terrible thought struck. "Is it Paulo? Is he—?"

"No. No change there. But the reason I called is related to his case. I thought you might want to hear about my meeting with Dr. Prine."

"Absolutely." I'd had so much on my mind that I'd almost forgotten. I told Cleo about literally running into Dr. Prine just outside her office. "It was almost as if he had no idea who I was until I reminded him that I'm in charge of the medical staff's CME business," I said. "What did he want with you? Was it what you thought? Something about Carver and Paulo Ferrera?"

"That was it. He's not at all happy with what he came home to. Says he's letting everyone at TMC know that Carver is not to go anywhere near Paulo or even have access to his medical record."

"I guess we can't blame him," I said. "Anything else?"

"Back when Prine left for Florida, I had already told him about Carver's CME trouble. I reminded him that tomorrow is Carver's last day before his TMC membership and privileges are suspended."

"Which means Carver won't be allowed access to any TMC patient or any medical charts until he's reinstated." I asked the obvious, "Did that satisfy Dr. Prine?"

"You would think so, wouldn't you?" Cleo asked. "But no, he's really on a tear about this. He made it clear that even if Carver digs up his alleged CME hours tomorrow, he's not to have anything to do with Paulo's case."

"Wow, sounds like he's after Carver's hide, doesn't it?"

I heard Cleo push out a heavy sigh. "Can you blame him?"

I surprised myself with my reply. "I don't know, Cleo, I feel uneasy about how this is playing out. I want to make another effort to help Kiri D'Costa wade through all the piles of documents in Carver's office. He keeps insisting he's earned fifteen credits that didn't get reported because the paperwork his office worker sent to me got lost. He's implying that it's my fault. I know that's not true. I never received it, but if there is proof buried somewhere in that mess in his office, we need to know it. Not just for Carver, but for TMC and our patients."

"I hear you, Aimee, but Carver's right down to the wire. With tomorrow being his last day, it seems like an exercise in futility."

"Even so, I won't feel right if I don't at least make the offer."

"Of course," Cleo said. "CME is your responsibility, and you take it seriously." I heard her sigh. "Carver's a gigantic pain in the rear, but he does good work."

"I know. That's why I want to be sure his loathsome personality isn't coloring my judgment. I'd almost be happy to see him kicked off the staff, which makes me determined to give him one last chance to prove his claim."

"Then by all means, if you can get Kiri or anyone else in his office to cooperate, go for it."

I went back out to the deck and told Nick what little I could about Cleo's call without breaching confidentiality. Mostly that Paulo's condition had not improved since Prine had replaced Carver on the case.

"Damn," he said, "too bad he didn't get back from Florida sooner."

"In all fairness, Nick, Carver's never been known for poor patient outcomes."

"It's a shame the patient isn't improving. Maybe the spine damage is more complicated than either of those doctors can handle." Nick reached for my hand. "Do you think the doctor who's back on the case has the know-how to turn things around?"

"Dr. Prine seems determined to do that, but it might be too late."

Nick leaned in and kissed my forehead. "Let's get some sleep. We're both going to have a busy day tomorrow."

"Okay, but first, I should thank you for helping Jack with the llamas."

"Yes indeed." He took me in his arms, nuzzled my neck and murmured, "You surely should."

My restless sleep was filled with dreams of luxury yachts, homeless camps, and Paulo Ferrera lying wounded under a bridge, his blood spilling on bleached river rocks, turning them black with the color of death.

I jerked awake, gasping for breath, at four o'clock, and murmured a prayer that Paulo Ferrera would wake up and tell us how to find his sister.

TWENTY-TWO

IN THE PRE-DAWN hours of Thursday morning, my mind refused to shut down and allow me to go back to sleep. Pieces of the mystery of Liliana and Paulo swirled around in a jumble, refusing to coalesce into a pattern that might lead to answers.

I slipped out of bed, taking care not to wake Nick. At our dinette table, I jotted what we knew, looked at the list and realized it was mostly guesses and suppositions.

The hard fact was that Paulo remained in Intensive Care in a coma, shot by an unknown assailant. We knew he left the Azores to find his sister. That was also a fact. He mentioned a friend in Marin County who might be able to help him. *Fact.* I searched my memory of the past two weeks for any further concrete information and came up with nothing but more questions.

That list was far longer than the first. Did Liliana leave the Azores on a yacht? So far, we had no proof. But if she did, would that yacht arrive in Marin County any day? Or would it head off in some other direction? Was the Bay Wind Yacht Club burgee painted on the floor of the Horta Marina a real clue, or a false lead? Was Liliana's online boyfriend, Francisco, real, or was he a predator with sinister motives?

Who was Paulo's friend in Marin County? Who was the man I saw arguing on Carver's yacht and then running and falling on the dock with a bloody head wound?

Would Detective Kass get a DNA match with the blood sample I collected? How long would that take?

When I reached that question, I opened my laptop to search the timing of DNA results. I recalled seeing a recent article in one of the TMC library's online forensic journals about a new test that might offer almost instant results. After trying a few search terms, I found what I was looking for. A new device that could produce DNA profiles from buccal swabs inside the mouth, and other human samples, including blood, in approximately ninety minutes. It wasn't yet approved for the courtroom because the accuracy rate was only eighty percent, but it would be a good start. If Kass and the TPD had access to that system, we might at least know the identity of the man whose blood I'd collected—if he happened to be in a DNA database.

I printed the article so Nick could take it along when he met with Detective Kass. As I was closing my laptop, Nick wandered into the kitchen at five thirty, yawning and stretching.

"Aimee? What's going on? Why are you up so early?"

I told him about the new DNA identification system and gave him the printed material. He opened his eyes wide, blinking away the last remnants of sleep. "Give me a sec, and some coffee, please." He sat and started reading.

I filled the coffeemaker with water and ground the beans while he perused the article. When he finished, he looked up at me. "Looks good. You think the TPD has this device?"

"I'm hoping." I pushed the brew button. "If not, they might have access to one. It's worth asking Kass about it, don't you think?"

"Sure, but we're back to what we talked about last

night. If he does have access to this method, I'm pretty sure he'll want to hear your story of where the blood came from and how you can help him justify running the analysis."

"He has my cell number. Or he can call me at the hospital library." I poured two cups of coffee and handed one to Nick. "Oh, scratch that. I might not be in the library this afternoon. Better tell him to use my cell if he wants to reach me."

"What's going on with your afternoon?"

"I hope to be helping Kiri D'Costa search for documentation of the CME credits Dr. Carver insists he's earned."

Nick's brows raised at the mention of Kiri. He took a sip from his cup. "Okay, then. I'll tell Kass to call you on your cell."

When I reached the library, I called Cleo to ask about Paulo Ferrera, just as I had every morning for the past two weeks.

"No change," she said. "I spoke to Mary Barton this morning. The parents are getting all the support she can offer from TMC's Social Services Department, but they're having a hard time coping with the limbo they're living in."

"Those poor people. In a strange country, worrying about both their children and dealing with a language barrier. I can't imagine the stress they're under. I wish there were some way to offer them hope."

"Dr. Prine's back on their son's case," Cleo said. "That's something."

"That reminds me. I'm definitely offering to help Kiri, even though Carver's suspension takes effect at the end of the day today. I'll take the high road and at least pretend to believe he earned the missing credits."

"You were contemplating digging around at Carver's office looking for his missing homework. You've decided to go ahead with that?"

"I might as well, if I can get cooperation from his office."

"No reason for Carver to object, is there? If he's telling the truth, he'll want it found. If he's lying, he'll at least be pretending to cooperate."

"That's what I'm thinking."

"You're a better woman than I am," Cleo said. "When are you going to his office?"

"I'll call Kiri right away. If she or anyone else there wants my help, I'll head over to Carver's office after I take care of my morning library routine."

"You're going to close the library?"

"I'll have to, but just for the afternoon. It shouldn't be a problem. Most of my patrons aren't walk-ins. They usually contact me online. I'll have my phone with me in case anything important comes up."

I called Kiri and finally met with success. I arranged to meet her after lunch in Carver's office. Meanwhile, Bernie Kluckert, my Tuesday and Thursday volunteer, arrived. As he started his plant care duties, an unexpected visitor walked into the library. Although Oliver Prine had been on my mind, he was the last person I expected to see striding toward my desk.

"Hello, Dr. Prine." I stood. "Welcome to the library. How can I help you?"

He responded with a good-natured smile. "For starters, let's avoid another collision." I blushed, remembering his stethoscope hitting the floor when I plowed into him outside Cleo's office. Prine glanced across the room, where Bernie stood mixing his weekly concoction of plant food. "I'd prefer to speak to you in private, Miss Machado."

His comment, delivered in a somber tone, aroused my curiosity and at the same time set my nerves tingling. "Of course. We can talk in the break room." I signaled to Bernie, who nodded his understanding.

I led the way for Dr. Prine, who declined my offer of coffee. We sat at the small table in the little room. I clasped my hands in my lap to keep from fidgeting while I waited to hear what he wanted from me. He got right to it.

"I understand you're up to speed on the Ferrera case?" Prine met my eyes with directness and a soothing demeanor. If it represented his normal bedside manner, I could understand why his patients loved him.

"Only up to a point," I said. "I'm not privy to the details of his medical treatment."

"I understand, of course, HIPAA," Prine said. "But you *are* a key figure in the situation regarding Dr. Carver's CME credits?"

"Yes." From Cleo, I knew Prine was "on a tear" about Carver and the Ferrera case. He was using a distinctly different approach with me, but I kept my guard up.

"Miss Machado, I'm here to ask your cooperation." Prine tilted his head slightly, a gesture that, combined with an easy-going smile, implied that we were confidants. "Without going into inappropriate detail, I must warn you that Dr. Carver's medical skills are diminishing. It's possible that his lack of attention to continuing medical education may be the reason."

"Is that what you think caused Paulo Ferrera's setback?" I asked. "Something went wrong with his treatment while you were away?"

"That's the most obvious explanation," Prine said. "If

Godfrey Carver's being honest about keeping up with his CME, then the only other explanation is early-onset dementia or some other type of impairment." He didn't mention drugs or alcohol, but the implication was clear.

"What is it you want from me?" I asked.

"I understand from Ms. Cominoli that you're making a special last-ditch effort to pull Carver out of the fire. She admires your going the extra mile for him." Prine allowed a trace of a frown to cross his forehead. "So do I, as a rule. I'd want the same consideration if I were in his shoes, but this might be a time to let the chips fall where they may."

"Are you saying I shouldn't make the extra effort?" I needed clarification. This conversation was veering into uncharted territory.

"This is a delicate situation," Prine said. "I wouldn't presume to tell you how to do your job. All I'm implying is that the best outcome, particularly at this late hour, would be to ensure that Dr. Carver, or any doctor on TMC's medical staff, is fully fit, *educated*, and qualified to fulfill the needs of our patients."

"But confirming that he's met his education requirements would do that, wouldn't it?"

Prine stood. "One would hope, Miss Machado, but sometimes the proof is in the pudding. You have only to ask Paulo Ferrera's parents if Dr. Carver was meeting their son's needs in my absence."

As soon as he left the library, I chewed an antacid to squelch the bile that burned in my throat. Then I called Cleo.

"What exactly did you tell Dr. Prine about me?" I asked her.

"Nothing too specific. Just that you were bending

over backward to help Carver prove he'd done his home-work. Why?"

"Because he dropped in to have a talk with me." I gave her an almost verbatim account.

"I'm sorry he put you in that position, but with jobs like ours that's part of the territory." I heard Cleo tapping her nails against her desk. "What are you going to do? Cancel your afternoon with Kiri?"

"No. It's probably a fool's errand, but I made a commitment, and Kiri finally seems to be looking forward to my help. I'm going to go over to Carver's office this afternoon and at least go through the motions."

"Better hurry," Cleo said. "You're doing the right thing, but I don't envy you."

Cleo's comment left me with serious doubts about my decision. Why was I going the extra mile for a man who didn't deserve my help? I wasn't doing it for Carver. I thought of Kiri and her connection to TMC through her cousin Sanjay D'Costa, our assistant administrator. I was doing it for Kiri. A simple favor for a young woman hoping to find her way and to build herself a life in a new country.

More importantly, I was doing it because it was my job to help ensure that our patients were receiving treatment only from physicians undeniably qualified for membership on TMC's medical staff. In that, I agreed completely with Dr. Prine.

As I PULLED into an empty parking space at Carver's office, my cell rang. Harry was calling. I hoped he had something to tell me about Liliana's email or Carver's yacht.

"What's up? Did you come up with Liliana's secret email account?"

"Sorry, no. I called about something else, but since you asked, I'd really like to get my hands on the Ferrera family's laptop."

"The TPD is still working on that. Do you think you can find something they can't?"

"Maybe not," Harry said. "Or maybe my IT guys are better than their IT guys. We'd like to try. If it doesn't help, no harm, no foul."

"All right, I'll ask Kass to let me know as soon as they're finished with it. But you said you called about something else?"

"Yeah, I did," Harry said. "Buck and Rella got home from Florida this afternoon."

"Good for you. Your girlfriend is back in town, but what's that got to do with me?" At the moment, I didn't need an account of Rella's whereabouts, or Buck's, for that matter.

"They might have stumbled onto a piece of your puzzle while they were there."

That got my attention. "What are you talking about?" Harry could be annoyingly cryptic at the worst possible times.

"Too complicated to explain on the phone. We need a huddle. You, Nick, Rella, and me."

"Where and when?" I asked.

"Dojo at nine o'clock?"

"Can't we meet sooner? We're almost out of time."

"Can't." He sounded genuinely apologetic. "I'm slammed at work. Inspections are scheduled throughout the afternoon, and then I'm going straight to the dojo to teach my seven o'clock class."

"I'll tell Nick. We'll be there at nine."

"Bring your gi. Nick, too. You could both use a workout."

Normally, I would have contradicted my brother just out of sibling stubbornness, but he was right. I texted Nick, who was spending the afternoon in training sessions with Ginger. He responded that he expected to be home in time for dinner.

I locked my car and walked to Carver's building, battling excitement at Harry's tidbit of news and frustration with the long wait to hear the details. Nine hours stretched out before me. What could Rella and Buck possibly have stumbled on in Florida that might connect to the disappearance of an exquisitely beautiful but headstrong Portuguese teenager?

TWENTY-THREE

THE DOOR TO Carver's office was unlocked, but his waiting room was empty. Probably because he and his staff, except for Kiri, were still on their lunch break. Soothing background music drifted from speakers in the ceiling. I walked to the unoccupied reception counter, hoping to find a way to attract Kiri's attention. I was surprised she wasn't stationed at the front door, watching and waiting for me. I was struck by her lack of concern for her boss's future, considering he was the employer of record for her work visa.

A glance at a large clock on the wall told me it was twelve thirty, the exact time Kiri and I had agreed upon. I considered dropping my keys on the counter and jiggling them, hoping someone in a back room would hear. Kiri saved me the trouble by appearing in the reception area.

"Aimee, you're right on time. Thanks so much for coming." Kiri's smile seemed forced, and she carried her shoulders high and tense.

"No problem," I said. "I'm available all afternoon."

She opened the door leading to the workroom I'd seen on my last visit. We walked to the same unoccupied desk where she had shown me the mess left behind by the disgruntled former office manager.

"Here we are," she said. "I've taken a bit of time each day since you were here last to sort some of this mountain of paper into piles. It's mostly junk mail and letters from patients, both compliments and complaints." Kiri gave a tense little shrug. "Most of this stuff isn't important. I can almost understand why Dorothy put it aside and ignored it." Good, she had shown at least some initiative.

"I hope you've been given the rest of the day to work on this," I said. "Finding that missing CME documentation before the end of the day is Dr. Carver's only hope of avoiding suspension."

Kiri nodded. "Dr. Carver had all of the afternoon patients rescheduled. He gave the other employees the rest of the day off."

"Do they know what's going on?" I asked.

"Apparently not." She sighed. "I have to warn you, since you were here last, I found another stash larger than the first one. It was crammed into the bottom drawer of a horizontal file cabinet. I'm afraid we're facing a hopeless task."

Great. Mission impossible. "Then let's get started."

Kiri sat at her desk, and I claimed the one left behind by Dorothy.

Carver had told Kiri he would be making rounds on his hospital patients, and from there, catching up on errands and business appointments. He had assured her that he would come to the office immediately if we found what we were looking for.

We agreed on a system that minimized the amount of time it took to inspect each item. We stacked anything that might need attention into designated piles. Each of us kept a wastebasket handy for items we judged to be trash.

During the first hour, we worked in silence. I tried to avoid being distracted by my memories of Kiri down in Marin County the previous weekend. I kept recalling those moments. She and Gus Barba, the hull diver who cleaned Buck's boat, seemed to be in a relationship. Then, when Nick and I encountered her alone on the dock, she said she sometimes used Carver's yacht as a free place to spend weekends in the Bay Area. But the image that troubled me most was the unknown man on Carver's yacht handing Kiri an overnight bag. I would have assumed she came back for it at the last minute. Not Nick. He had asked the question that wouldn't go away. What was in that bag?

One hour at Carver's office stretched into two, then three. I had made good progress on my share of the work. I glanced over at Kiri intermittently to see her frowning in concentration. We had agreed that since I was more familiar with CME documents, she would ask me if she found something she couldn't identify. Not once in all that time did she come to me with a question.

Distracted by Harry's earlier call, I couldn't stop myself from checking the time as each hour moved us closer to the end of the workday. I became more discouraged as the day wore on. I was also apprehensive about Kiri's possible role in Carver's practice and in the rest of his life. It just didn't feel right.

"Aimee?" Kiri walked toward me just as I'd glanced again at the time. Four thirty. "Would you take a look at this?" She handed me a printed document.

"Oh, my...." I scanned the pages, did a double-take, stood up, read them more carefully. My heart started pounding and I caught my breath. "Kiri, I think you found it."

She broke into a bright smile. "Really? I hoped I was right, but in a way, I'm almost disappointed."

"I know exactly how you feel," I said. "This vindicates Dr. Carver, which was our goal, but it could have happened to a nicer man."

We both let out a laugh that provided some relief. Kiri hurried to put in a call to Carver.

While he drove to the office, I read through what Kiri had found. The document proved he had done the necessary work to earn his missing fifteen CME credits. Just as he had told Quinn and me, he'd taken an extensive course in the latest techniques for managing the full range of spinal and peripheral nerve problems. The course addressed different surgical procedures, patient selection, preoperative preparation, anesthetic techniques, patient monitoring, and surgical techniques and outcomes. The date next to Carver's signature was recent. Had the office manager buried it as payback for being fired? One of the many unanswered questions about Carver and his CME credits. As we waited for Carver to show up, I texted Cleo, letting her know what Kiri and I had accomplished.

When Carver arrived ten minutes later, his scalp shining with perspiration and his brow furrowed, he herded Kiri and me into his private office.

"Sit, both of you." Not a polite invitation, rather a command, like a surgeon issuing orders to his operating team.

As soon as we were seated across from him, he asked to see what we'd found. I offered the document, which he grabbed from my hand.

"We found it buried in a deep stack of paperwork," Kiri said. "We believe it's the proof you mentioned, but we wanted to be sure."

"Hold on. Let me have a look." Carver gave her a glance that clearly said, *You'll speak when spoken to.* Kiri and I sat silently until he'd perused the few pages she had found. I hoped he'd finish soon.

"I damned well told all of you I'd done my homework, didn't I?" Those words were shot at me with such velocity, I almost ducked, but it didn't stop me from sending a volley back in his direction.

"Yes, you did, but in the future, I suggest you make a point of submitting your CME documentation first-hand, rather than trusting it to a staff member who may not realize its importance." His response was not what I expected.

"Duly noted," Carver muttered. And then he stood up, walked around his desk and held out his hand, first to Kiri, and then to me. "Thank you both for your efforts."

His face flushed pink. Those six words had cost him. He made no apology for his earlier obnoxious behavior, but the *thank you* was more than I'd expected.

While Kiri made a copy of the CME documents, I put in a call to Jared Quinn with the good news. He agreed that Carver's membership and privileges on the TMC medical staff would remain intact.

Outside, standing by my car, I texted Cleo to let her know that Jared Quinn had been notified. I asked her to bring me up to date on Paulo Ferrera's medical status when she had a chance.

I put my phone away and drove home with my stomach in knots, surprised and disoriented from the experience in Carver's office. I was impressed that Kiri had come through. Did it convince me of her good character? Up to a point, but I still sensed an underlying tension between us, as if she were holding back in some way. I reminded myself that my instincts weren't always reliable. I had been wrong about Carver's continuing education, so sure had I been that we would find nothing. I was dead wrong. He had taken the classes he claimed. His CME credits were in order, both for his state license and his membership on TMC's medical staff.

What if everything I had assumed about Carver was wrong? His treatment of the staff at the hospital, including me, had earned him universal enmity. Yet, he had taken excellent care of Paulo while Dr. Prine was away. So why had Paulo's condition taken a nosedive? And why was Prine so certain that the relapse was Carver's fault?

NICK AND GINGER arrived home minutes after I did. He prepared the dog's dinner, which she gobbled down while I filled Nick in. I started with Harry's teaser about Rella and Buck.

"Apparently, they came across something in Florida that might relate to the Ferrera family's mystery. Have you talked to either of them?"

"No, I've been tied up all day. It took some doing to make contact with Detective Kass. He was on his way to Sacramento to appear as a witness in a change of venue case down there. I caught up with him at the airport a few minutes before he boarded his flight."

"How did it go? Did you have time to fill him in?"

"Just. He said he'd have to keep his phone off in court, but we should leave messages in case of updates."

Kass's absence wasn't good news, but at least he was willing to consider the evidence Nick had offered. "Any idea when he'll be back?" I asked. "Or how soon we'll hear about the laptop or the torn shirt fabric?"

"He'll be back Saturday. Not likely we'll hear anything before then."

"Two days. It seems like a long time." Ginger looked up at me, walked over and rested her head in my lap, almost as if she sensed my somber mood.

Nick tossed an affectionate glance at the dog. "Your turn. Did Harry give you any sort of detail about what Buck and Rella unearthed in Florida?"

"No. Just what I've already told you. That was enough to keep me desperately curious all afternoon."

"And you got through the rest of the day without going nuts?" Nick said. "How did you manage that?"

"I was too busy to dwell on it." I wanted to tell him about Carver's narrow escape from being suspended, but that would take me into confidential territory. I'd shared with Nick during a past-crisis situation involving the hospital, but it was always a challenge to decide how much I could say. Sometimes it was helpful to have his perspective, and in that event, I always stressed that what I shared was extremely confidential. This time, since Carver's medical staff status remained the same, Nick didn't need to know the details. At least, not yet.

Nick picked up Ginger's empty bowl and gave her a pat on the head. She settled on her doggy bed with her chew toy, and he came back to sit across from me at our dinette table.

"Any change in the Portuguese brother's status?"

"I don't know." I took out my phone but found no reply from Cleo.

I decided to call Ramon Silva to ask about the Ferreras. He was concerned. Both had lost weight and appeared more depressed each day. Mary Barton had taken them to a nearby Catholic church and introduced them to the priest, but because the priest spoke no Portuguese, there wasn't a lot he could do to offer them comfort or solace.

NICK AND I arrived at the dojo just before nine, as Harry's students were pulling out of the parking lot. Rella drove in and followed us inside, where Harry stood cooling himself in front of a pedestal fan. He stepped away from the fan and greeted Rella with quick peck on the mouth. They both seemed almost shy in front of Nick and me. I thought that was sort of endearing, considering that between the two of them—Harry a high-ranking black belt and Rella, a former fighter pilot—they could probably wipe out a small army. They made a stunning couple: his dark Eurasian looks contrasted with her fair complexion and blond Nordic beauty.

Harry invited us into the sensei's office, where we could sit comfortably around a small table. He opened a bag of organic popcorn and dumped it into a bowl.

"No dinner," he explained. "Help yourselves." He passed around bottled waters and then got down to business, taking on the role of captain of our crew of assorted crime busters. He directed his first question to me.

"Aimee, did you get ahold of the Ferreras' laptop?"

"Not yet, but you have access to the family account and password. Isn't that enough?"

"We could dig deeper if we had that laptop."

"I'll keep trying," I said, "but there's only so much I can do, and we just found out Kass is out of town."

"Then let's get to the main event. Rella, are you ready to tell them about Florida?"

Rella straightened up in her chair. "This might be nothing, Aimee, but Buck thought it was worth mentioning. When I told Harry, he agreed." She glanced at him. "I hope he's right."

"Me, too," I said. "I've been on the edge of my seat all day, trying to imagine what it might be."

Rella began, "You know, of course, that Buck owns a yacht and hangs around yachting types whenever he has a chance." She took a small card from her shirt pocket. "One of the real estate people he met with in Miami also owns a yacht, and as you might guess, belongs to a yacht club there." She looked down at the card.

Nick shifted forward in his chair. "With you so far." I knew he was as eager as I was to hear the rest.

"So this man invited Buck onto his yacht for dinner and drinks," Rella smiled, "hoping, we suspected, to influence Buck into buying whatever he was selling."

"When did this take place?" I asked.

Rella thought for a moment. "This is Thursday, so... night before last."

"Tuesday evening." Harry looked at Nick and me. "Let's keep that in mind." He nodded to Rella. "Go on."

Rella picked up the thread of her story. "The man seemed a little shady to Buck, who began to think there was more than real estate in this guy's portfolio."

"Like some sort of import/export arrangement?" Harry asked.

"As in trafficking?" Nick added.

Rella nodded to both of them. "You know how keen Buck's instinct is for that sort of thing." She continued, "He asked me to go along as his clueless and much younger trophy girlfriend, which allowed me to sit there looking dense while I listened and observed." She glanced at Harry and blushed. "The most difficult part was shopping for a slutty outfit and then actually wearing it all evening."

Nick scooted forward in his chair. "Did the yacht fit the description we have of the one the girls saw in the Azores?"

Rella shook her head. "No, sorry. It was smaller, closer to the size of Buck's. Plush, but too small to make the Atlantic crossing from the Azores."

"Then what would it have to do with the missing girl?" She had my attention, but I was eager for the punch line. "Did you or Buck pick up on something suspicious?"

Rella looked again at the card in her hand. "That's what we need to ask you, Aimee. We met a doctor on that yacht who was a business acquaintance of the real estate tycoon. Buck thought the doctor looked familiar—from the Bay Wind Yacht Club in Marin County. He was sure when he spotted a small pin on the man's jacket displaying a replica of the Bay Wind burgee. It was obvious that the doctor didn't recognize Buck, so knowing what Nick had told him about the missing girl and the yacht from the Azores, Buck kept quiet."

I had to ask. "Are you saying that the doctor Buck met was Dr. Carver? Because that's impossible. Dr. Carver hasn't left Timbergate the whole time you and Buck were gone."

"I know," Rella said. "It wasn't Dr. Carver. It was a doctor named Oliver Prine."

That caught me by surprise, but after a moment, I realized it was easy to explain. "Oh, well, that's simply a coincidence, nothing sinister," I said. "Dr. Prine was still in Florida while you were there. His daughter had been in a highway accident. He flew there almost two weeks ago to be with her. In fact, he just returned home yesterday." Disappointment seeped through me. Rella's news was insignificant after all.

"Wait, there's more." Harry lifted his chin toward Rella. "Go on."

"This Dr. Prine, the one you say has a daughter, didn't mention anything about that. He told Buck he had been in Miami visiting business partners who each own shares in a superyacht. That yacht was due to return to the San Francisco Bay Area from the Azores this weekend."

I sucked in a breath, and a bit of popcorn lodged in my throat. I coughed it out along with a question. "Did he happen to mention the name of the yacht?"

"Yes, in fact, he and the other man made a joke of it. They said they called it *Seashell*."

"*Seashell?*" I said. "What's the joke?"

Harry replied, "The joke is that multiple silent partners own that yacht. It's registered to an offshore corporation, and offshore corporations are commonly called *shell* companies."

"Not uncommon for wealthy people avoiding taxes," Nick said.

Harry held up a hand. "However, it's even more common for criminals who have more than taxes to hide. I wouldn't be surprised if some of those owners used fictitious identities."

"In either case, it sounds like they were pretty loose with that information," Nick said.

"They'd been knocking back vodka for quite a while, plus they thought they were in the company of like-minded fellow yachtsmen." Rella looked at Nick. "You know our boss—he's quick. He smelled something rotten right away, so he dropped a few hints about shady deals of his own. He said maybe they could do business someday. He didn't mention trafficking, but the implication was there."

I couldn't wait any longer to ask the obvious question. "Are you sure the man you're talking about is TMC's Dr. Prine? It could have been another doctor with a similar name."

Rella handed me the card she had been holding. A jolt of vertigo rocked me as I read the name: *Oliver Prine, M.D. FAANS*.

Those initials behind his name that came after M.D. stood for *Fellow of the American Association of Neurologic Surgeons*. The odds were overwhelmingly against there being two Dr. Oliver Prines in the same specialty hanging out in Florida at the same time.

TWENTY-FOUR

RELLA'S DISCLOSURE SPARKED another round of questions. Did this give us anything concrete to take to Detective Kass? We all agreed it did not, but on the other hand, it wouldn't hurt to inform him, in the event it developed into something more.

Did Oliver Prine really have an injured daughter in Florida? If not, why had he headed there when he did, leaving Paulo Ferrera in Carver's care? That was almost two weeks ago, about the same time the yacht carrying Liliana would have stopped in Florida to refuel. As I realized what that implied, I jumped up from my chair.

"Guys, I have an idea. Tell me if I'm grasping at straws."

"I'll bet I know where you're going with this," Nick said, "but you first."

"We have to add new elements to our equation—"

Harry burst out laughing before I could finish. "Look who's using math terms. The only person I know who had to take Beginning Algebra twice."

"Hey, that's my private business." I tossed a piece of popcorn at him, which the showoff caught in his mouth. Nick and Rella stayed out of it. They were used to our sibling sparring.

"Your new elements," Nick said. "Go on, Aimee, finish your thought."

I rubbed at the chill that pimpled my upper arms. "I hope I'm wrong about this, because it's so frightening, but the timing can't be ignored. After Dr. Prine's surgery, Paulo Ferrera remained in a coma until Dr. Prine left. It was only when Carver took over his case that he began to show signs of emerging from the coma."

"Is that unusual?" Rella asked.

"Nothing about a case like Paulo's can be easily predicted," I said.

"How do you know?" she asked. "You've never had medical training."

"I'm not a doctor or a nurse, but I've worked in the medical field for a long time, all the way back to my first job as a medical transcriptionist."

"So, what are you getting at?" Harry asked. "You mentioned timing."

"Two things." I took Harry's wall calendar down from over the sensei's desk and spread it on the table. "Look at this." I pointed to the day Liliana had gone to the yacht party. I picked up a pencil from Harry's desk and marked the date. The first Friday in June.

"Hey," Harry said, "you're messing up my calendar."

I shot him a look. "Really? You're going to whine? I'm using a pencil, Bro. It'll erase."

Harry held up his hands. "Okay, just saying, my students need to use that to keep track of their classes and assignments."

We moved on, and discovered that Dr. Prine had left Timbergate during the time window when the mystery yacht would have reached Florida.

"For what reason?" Nick asked. "If the yacht was bound for the Bay Area, why would he need to rendezvous with it in Miami?"

"That's what we need to find out. If it turns out we're on the right track—"

"It could mean he's a ringleader in the trafficking operation," Harry said.

I nodded. "What if the *Seashell*'s crew needed his instructions? His orders? Something that couldn't wait until she docked in California?"

Rella broke in, "Something unusual, like what to do about Liliana and her brother?"

"Yes."

I went on to point out that we all assumed Paulo had begun emerging from his coma because of Prine's care, and then relapsed a few days after Carver took over. Because of our preconceived notions about both doctors, it didn't occur to us that Paulo's relapse might have begun just *after* Prine returned, not before.

"Come on," Harry said. "Now you're freaking me out. You think the good doctor is Mr. Hyde? That he took off to Florida to check in with his crew on the superyacht and then beat it back to Timbergate to shut the spine patient down before he could be questioned?"

"You're the boy genius who's always harrying the rest of us to think outside the box," I said.

Rella laughed. "Harrying? Is that a word or did you make it up?"

"It's a real word," I said. "It means 'to persistently harass.'"

Harry gave me the stink eye. "Okay, Sis. We're even."

Nick raised a hand. "Let's get out of the third grade and back to the implications of what Aimee's suggesting." He turned to me. "Is there a way your hospital folks can check up on Prine's treatment of the Ferrera boy?"

"I'll ask Cleo," I said. "She'll know how to run it up the chain of command. We'll need to convince Jared Quinn that someone should intervene."

"Will that be difficult?" Rella asked.

"It won't be easy," I admitted. "We'll need more to justify it than we have now."

"Can't your administrator just take Prine off the case?" Nick asked.

"And leave Carver in charge again?" I didn't like that option. "Not until we're sure where Carver fits into the picture. What if he and Prine are mixed up in this together?"

Rella frowned. "But you just said the patient was improving while Carver was on the case. If both doctors are involved in something that happened to the sister, neither of them would want her brother to regain consciousness."

"Yes, but we don't know if both are involved, or if one is willing to go further than the other to keep Paulo Ferrera from telling his story." I took a moment to consider that. "What I do know is that Quinn can't take action against either doctor without a darn good reason. We need more proof of criminal intent, or at least blatant malpractice."

"We also need the sister's secret email account," Harry said. "We still don't know the online boyfriend's role in this, if any. He might just be a creep who's catfishing for an unsuspecting kid."

"Seems more likely he's in cahoots with the owners of the superyacht, scouting girls as pricy pieces of contraband to sell to the highest bidder," Nick added.

"We have to get those answers." I erased my penciled notes and hung Harry's calendar back on the wall. "I'm afraid Paulo Ferrera is not going to wake up while Oliver Prine is in charge of his care."

"And if he doesn't, we won't find his sister." Nick

turned to me. "That superyacht could be arriving in the Bay Area any minute."

"Then let's tell Kass to put out the word to law enforcement down there to watch for it. We know the name is *Seashell*."

Harry stood, making a timeout sign. "That won't work, Aimee. We don't have anything Kass can use as probable cause, and we have to keep in mind more than one vessel could have that name."

"Harry's right," Nick said. "The law requires probable cause *and* the hull number in order to get a search warrant, and we don't have either. At least, not yet. We're going to need to take another trip to Marin County." He turned to me. "You'd better arrange to take tomorrow off. I'll arrange for a plane."

"I'll cover for you with Buck," Rella said.

Harry picked up the empty popcorn bowl. "And I'll exhaust every resource I have to ferret out the online boyfriend."

"That's the one who calls himself Francisco?" Rella asked.

"Yeah," Harry said. "Francisco from San Francisco. Real original. Like a needle in a pile of needles."

TWENTY-FIVE

NICK AND I reached our apartment in Coyote Creek after midnight, both of our minds zinging from considering every angle of the mystery surrounding Paulo and Liliana Ferrera. We agreed that our priority was a reasonable amount of sleep—especially for Nick—who would be flying the plane. We sat up in bed making notes, rehashing our earlier intel-sharing session with Harry and Rella.

"You go first," Nick said. "Your list is longer than mine."

"I'll start with the obvious," I said. "In the morning, I'll go into work to arrange the day off. While I'm there, I'll fill Cleo in on what Rella told us about Dr. Prine. She has the ear of Jared Quinn and the chief of staff of the hospital. She'll know how to motivate them into mandating a third opinion about Paulo Ferrera's case."

"You think she'll get that done right away?" Nick asked.

"Probably not. What we have is speculation. No substance. She'll need something more specific that could be identifiable as outside the normal limits of practice for a coma patient. Besides, anything that would alert Prine or Carver that they're suspected of prolonging Paulo's coma could put that young man in greater danger." Imagining a member of the TMC medical staff capable of foul play made me queasy.

Nick's brows rose. "You think they'd decide to... what? Pull the plug?"

"Not something that obvious. They'd find another way. Something easier to cover up."

"Man, you're making me hope I never end up in a hospital." Nick glanced around the room, as if a homicidal doctor might be hiding in the closet or lurking under our bed. "This is starting to sound like something out of a horror flick."

I laughed. "Nick, hospitals save lives every day. Most of the time, they do patients more good than harm."

He cut a skeptical look at me. "*Most* of the time?"

"Hey, nothing's guaranteed. You're a pilot. You should know that."

"Touché." Nick nodded toward the paper in my hand. "Anything else on your list?"

"No. Your turn."

He read his notes. "Arrange for a plane. Talk to Kass about the security cameras on Carver's building. Get some sleep."

"That's it? Seems like there's something else." Then it came to me. "What about the blood sample I collected on our last trip to Marin? Did you ask him about that ninety-minute DNA machine?"

"Kass took the sample you collected from the dock, but he doesn't have immediate access to one of those machines. His department shares one with another county, so they take turns."

"When is it Kass's turn?"

Nick glanced at the calendar on his phone. "He thinks he can run it on Saturday. I'll ask him about it before we fly out." He put the phone and his notes on his nightstand. "It's almost eleven thirty. Lights out, okay?"

Just then, Ginger wandered into our bedroom, padded over to Nick, and gave him a doggy goodnight kiss on the cheek. "That reminds me," I said. "Are we taking Ginger along this time?"

"No." Nick rubbed at his face with a tissue. "She's staying with Jack and Rosa." He pointed at Ginger's bed across the room. She went over and flopped down. "I thought it should be just the two of us. We might have more ground to cover, and I don't want either of us to be encumbered." With his face clean of doggy saliva, he leaned in for a good night kiss that would have cost us even more lost sleep if we hadn't thought better of it.

I MANAGED TO sneak out of our apartment Friday morning without waking Nick. We had agreed to meet at the airport at noon. I volunteered to bring a quick lunch to eat before takeoff.

My business at the hospital library was completed in short order. After arranging to close early and take the rest of the day off, I dropped in on Cleo. We talked over the news from Rella about Dr. Prine's suspicious visit to Florida. I made breakfast of a few Tootsie Rolls and Junior Mints from the candy bowl on her desk while she searched around online. Then she made a couple of phone calls.

It didn't take long for her to determine that Prine's daughter was *not* living in Florida. She and her mother, Prine's ex-wife, had been living in New York City for fifteen years. After her second phone call, Cleo motioned me over to her desk. I swallowed my last Junior Mint.

"Look at this." She had pulled up a site for a performing arts school in Manhattan. She glanced up to check that her office door was closed. It was, but even so, she spoke softly. "No way Prine's daughter was in a highway accident in Florida on the date he claimed."

The site displayed photos of the cast of a student performance of *A Midsummer Night's Dream* with Prine's daughter, Elsbeth, playing Hippolyta. The play opened the day after Prine left for Florida, and it was still running in Manhattan, with stellar reviews for his daughter.

"Holy cow," I said. "The whole time he was gone, he was faking, pretending to be at his daughter's bedside in Florida."

Cleo checked her desk calendar. "He left here on a Friday, two weeks ago. Got back to work just this past Wednesday."

"So he was gone for a week and a half." I paced her office. "What the heck was he doing?"

Cleo sat back, arms folded. "And why was he lying?"

"Are you going to take this to Jared Quinn? I'll go with you, if you want." I glanced at the time on her designer wall clock. *Almost nine.* Still plenty of time to meet Nick at the airport at noon.

Cleo put on her professional face. "There is nothing about this that shouts malpractice, or even substandard patient care."

"Cleo, he *lied*."

"Lots of men lie when they're hooking up with a woman and want to keep it on the down-low. And that's not the only reason he might have come up with a cover story. Maybe he just wanted some time off."

"But Rella witnessed him talking about shady business deals with that yacht owner in Florida."

"Again, we're not seeing anything that suggests Paulo Ferrera or any of Prine's or Carver's other patients are in danger."

I'd never been angry with Cleo, but this time I was

close. Surely she saw the implications I was seeing. "Isn't there anything we can do?"

"There's something you're not considering, Aimee." Cleo leaned her elbows on her desk. "Dr. Prine operated on Paulo Ferrera. We could even say he saved the young man's life. Why would he do that if he was responsible in some way for the patient being shot in the first place?"

A fair question. I searched for an answer that might make sense. "What were Prine's options? He was on call for neurosurgery cases. He had an OR team watching his every move, including an assistant surgeon with enough savvy to notice if Prine's surgical technique looked inappropriate or suspicious."

Cleo nodded. "I'll give you that."

"Is it enough to take to Quinn?"

"Not yet, but let's follow your reasoning to Prine's post-surgery care. He can't deviate from accepted practice without raising questions. The nursing staff in ICU would surely notice. They take Prine's orders every day and follow them scrupulously. Don't you agree, that at least for now, it stands to reason that Paulo Ferrera is safe?"

I resigned myself to Cleo's logic. "I hope so, but please…." I stopped myself. "Sorry. I know you'll do what's right for the patient. It's just that something tells me we're missing parts of this puzzle that might never be found."

Cleo walked over and stood in front of me with her hands on my shoulders. "I'll keep a close eye on Paulo Ferrera, and I'll talk to Jared. We both know you have good instincts." She studied me for a moment. I'd never seen her look so serious. "Apart from your instinct for self-preservation. Someone out there is doing something that got Paulo Ferrera shot. You must realize that you and Nick could be taking on a dangerous adversary—one quite willing to kill, if necessary."

"I know, and so does Nick." I lifted her hands from my shoulders and gave them a squeeze. "We'll be careful. Just make sure that you keep Paulo safe. How much are you going to tell Quinn about Dr. Prine?"

"I'll tell him everything you've told me, but keep in mind that there's still a lot of *them* against *us* mentality in play when it comes to the roles of hospital administration versus the medical staff organization. Quinn can't take action against a member of the medical staff without a damned compelling reason." Cleo walked back to her desk, dropped her glasses, and massaged her temples. "Even then, Quinn would have to convince the chief of staff to take his side, or the rest of the medical staff would howl in protest."

"Then please start looking for a compelling reason. Nick and I will do the same."

I made certain that Cleo had my cell number and Nick's. She promised to text me with frequent updates on Paulo and his parents.

NICK HAD THE Cessna 206 pulled out of the hangar when I arrived with takeout burgers. We sat in his pickup to eat our lunch, and then parked both our vehicles in the hangar and locked the doors.

Nick wadded our wrappers into a ball and tossed them in a nearby trash bin. "Any morning news items to report before we take off?"

"Just a quick visit with Cleo. I wanted to warn her to keep an eye on Dr. Prine. I don't trust him—or Carver, for that matter—to take care of Paulo Ferrera."

"Can't blame you." Nick walked around the plane

with a clipboard and pencil, performing his pre-flight inspection of the exterior. "Did she take you seriously?"

"Up to a point." I filled him in while he finished his walk around. Satisfied with the condition of the tires, rudder, fuel gauge, wings, propeller, and various other parts, he opened the passenger door and helped me up. Inside the cockpit, he continued his inspection. The last step was to call the tower to make certain that his radio was broadcasting and receiving.

"Looks like we're ready to go." He turned to me. "All set?"

"Not yet. I haven't heard how your morning went. Did you talk to Detective Kass about Carver's security cameras or about the DNA from that blood sample I collected?"

"Didn't have a chance. He's still tied up testifying in Sacramento. The change of venue thing. He won't be back until Saturday."

"Maybe we can reach him in Sac."

"Let's try to contact him when we get to SFO." Nick leaned over to kiss my cheek. "Put on your headphones, woman." He started the engine and we were on our way.

When we reached SFO, Nick tried, without success, to reach Detective Kass, whose voicemail was full.

In the small compact that Buck kept parked at the airport, we crossed the Golden Gate in midafternoon and drove through Sausalito, enjoying the sight of dozens of sailboats taking advantage of the clear weather and a gentle five-knot breeze. We stopped at the Harbor Market for groceries before heading to Buck's yacht.

As we reached the checkout lane, I recalled that just a week earlier we had seen Kiri D'Costa and Gus Barba at the same market. Discreet glances at the other shoppers turned up no one I recognized. Nick seemed to be in the same mode, checking out his surroundings at least as often as I did. Alert, but inconspicuous, he reminded me of actors I'd seen playing Secret Service agents guarding the president.

We stowed our purchases on Buck's yacht, except for brie, crackers, and grapes, which we left out for snacks. Nick stepped up the hatch ladder to gain a view of the harbor outside. He looked down at me. "Want to review our game plan for the rest of the day?"

"Definitely. But let me unpack first." I headed to the forward berth with my tote bag. Nick called after me, "Why not do that later?"

"I just want to get out my sunscreen. The rest can wait." I unzipped the bag and took a step backward. "What the—?" There, nestled among my bras and panties, secure in its inside-the-waistband holster, was my revolver. I thought I'd left the snub-nosed .38 at home in the drawer of my nightstand.

Nick came up behind me. "I was hoping you wouldn't see that until I'd had a chance to explain."

I spun around and faced him, nose to nose. "Explain? Is there something you know about this weekend that you haven't told me?"

"Yes, but before we get into that, I need to ask. Do you have your concealed carry permit with you?"

"It's in my purse. I always keep it with me. Now tell me what this is about."

Nick inhaled a deep breath and held it for so long that I finally poked him in the stomach. He exhaled, took my hand and led me out to the main saloon. "Let's sit for a minute."

With all the patience I could muster, I sat waiting while Nick took out his phone. He scrolled until he found what he wanted, and then looked up at me.

"Here it is," Nick said. "A text came in from Buck just after I dropped Ginger off with Jack and Amah. It added a new wrinkle to our weekend, but I didn't want to get into it with you until after the flight."

"Why not?"

Nick glanced at his phone again. "I wanted to wait until we could focus our complete attention on Buck's new twist. If I'd told you before we took off, it would have distracted both of us, and I don't like to fly distracted."

"Fair enough. I don't like to ride shotgun distracted, but now you're trying my patience. Why did you pack my gun?"

Nick handed me his phone. I read the text from Buck. It said he'd been invited to a private auction of newly minted, unblemished merchandise. It was to take place in the San Francisco Bay Area at ten o'clock Sunday night. Because of the private nature of the auction, its exact location would be revealed only if RSVPs were vetted and approved.

In the attached photo was a young, scantily clad model, holding up a foot-high eagle sculptured in gold and encrusted with diamonds. The starting bid was half a million dollars. "Oh, my God, Nick! That model is Liliana."

"See what I mean?" He took his phone from my hand.

I was so stunned, it took a moment to catch my breath. "What is Buck going to do? Did you tell Kass about this? What are *we* supposed to do?"

"That's what we have to decide. This situation is going to require a lot of thought and careful planning."

He was right, but I couldn't stop thinking the good news was that Liliana was alive—probably somewhere in the Bay Area. Was she aboard a superyacht named *Seashell*?

"Has anyone told the Timbergate police?"

"Not that I know of," Nick said. "So far, no one knows about it except Buck and me…and now, you."

"We have to contact Kass as soon as possible."

"And we will," Nick took the phone from my hand, "but despite what we're seeing here, there's no proof a crime is being committed."

"Liliana was kidnapped, but obviously she doesn't know it," I said. "Somehow, her brother knew it, and he was shot. Of course there's a crime. Two crimes."

"Unfortunately, the invitation to this private auction was sent to Buck from an import/export company that gave no business address. Its origin would be hard to trace by anything less than a top-notch cyber-forensics team."

"Then the sooner we get it to Kass and Harry, the better," I said. "Now that we're down here, what do we do about rescuing Liliana from whoever is behind the auction?" It sickened me to think Prine or Carver might be involved.

"For starters, Buck's going to do his damnedest to arrange for me to attend as his surrogate."

"Am I going, too?"

"No. We're not asking for you to be admitted." Nick reached out and touched my cheek. "Frankly, I'd rather keep you away from that scene, but I'd like for you to be nearby. Liliana might need a woman on hand if things get dicey and she doesn't know who to trust."

The thought sent a chill racing from my scalp to my toes. I picked up Nick's phone and looked again at the photo. The sinking feeling in the pit of my stomach made it hard to ask my next question. "That flyer is advertising more than a priceless sculpture, isn't it?"

"I'm afraid so." His jaw muscles worked. "Those bastards have Liliana fooled into thinking she's just a model, when the truth is, that sculpture isn't the only thing being auctioned on Sunday night."

"She'll go to the highest bidder." My words came out a dry-mouthed whisper.

"*Unblemished merchandise*," Nick said. "Code that says she's still a virgin. Worth half a mil to the right buyer."

"This is why you packed my gun?"

"Do you blame me?" Nick asked.

"No, of course not," I said.

I touched the photo of Liliana, a lovely young teenager, too headstrong and far too naïve for her own good. "How are we going to save her?"

"We have until Sunday night to figure that out." He reached around me and picked up my gun. "You might want to keep this with you. It's going to be one hell of a weekend."

TWENTY-SIX

NICK AND I texted Detective Kass and everyone else involved in putting the pieces of this mystery together. We urged Harry to redouble his efforts to identify Liliana's secret email account and the source of the auction flyer. We told Buck to keep up the pressure to give his *agent*, Nick, priority in the special auction bidding. And to let us know immediately about the location of the auction. We left urgent messages for Detective Kass to get in touch with us as soon as possible.

Finally we sat down to cobble together our game plan. We agreed that another trip to the Bay Wind Yacht Club was imperative. The week before, Cruising Captain Errol Parkington had claimed to have no knowledge of a Bay Wind member cruising to the Azores during the timeframe in question. Yet we now knew the superyacht, *Seashell* had been to the Azores, and that at least one of its owners, Dr. Oliver Prine, was a member of the Bay Wind Yacht Club.

I was still intensely curious about Kiri D'Costa's role in all this. We decided that Nick should contact Buck's hull diver, Gus Barba, under the guise of having a couple of beers and discussing Gus's working arrangement with Buck. While he was at it, Nick could pry into Gus's relationship with Kiri.

Hoping to find more forensic evidence, I suggested going back to the dock where the man had fallen and suffered the bloody head wound. We could at least check around to see if a bullet had lodged nearby, maybe in one of the boats or in a piling. The weekend before, I'd been too focused on the blood to consider that possibility. Nick thought it was a long shot, but I wanted to give it a try.

Feeling organized enough to get started, we each donned BWYC jackets Nick had borrowed from Buck and Delta Sawyer. Dinner at the yacht club was as good a place as any to keep an ear to the ground for references to the mysterious *Seashell*, or better yet, a slip of the tongue about the special private auction set for Sunday night.

We arrived at the yacht club early, our Members Only jackets easily concealing our weapons. The dining room was sparsely occupied. We made our way to a table near the wall of windows overlooking the bay. Awkward and uncomfortable with my gun and holster clipped to the inside of my waistband, I tried to imitate the assertive walk of women cops on TV shows. Would I really pull my weapon and fire it before the weekend was over? I would, if it meant saving Liliana.

I stayed at our table while Nick walked to the bar to order drinks. I watched him speak to the bartender, at the same time sliding several bills across the bar. The man maintained a poker face and scooped up the cash as he replied. With a nod, Nick picked up our drinks and made his way back to our table.

"Did I just see a transaction?" I asked. "You bought more than drinks?"

"Hope so." Nick sipped at the foam on his beer. "We'll see soon enough. Depends which side of the fence that bartender sits on."

"What did you ask him?"

"I said I'd like to buy a drink for the cruising captain if he happened to drop in."

"Parkington? Why?"

"Because he's either lying about no Bay Wind members cruising to the Azores, or he's a figurehead who holds his title in name only and hasn't a clue what's going on around him." Nick picked up a menu from the table. "What are you having?"

"Heartburn."

Nick smiled. "Might as well try to enjoy dinner. This evening may be a complete bust otherwise."

"Then I'll have the halibut." I set the menu aside and took out my phone to check for messages. Nick did the same. I spotted one from Cleo, sent half an hour ago: *Ferrera condition grave.*

Fighting tears, I held the phone out for Nick to see. "We're going to lose both of them, aren't we?"

When our dinners came, I made myself eat, hoping gourmet fare would lift my spirits. We had finished all but our desserts and coffee when Nick glanced toward the bar. I saw the bartender nod at him, then jerk his head toward the other side of the dining room where Parkington sat, the same arm candy from the week before draped over him.

"Looks like that fifty paid off," Nick said. He nodded toward Parkington, who held up his glass in a *thank you* gesture.

"Are you sure that was a good idea?" I murmured.

"Nope, but we're about to find out."

The unnatural contour of the holster clipped to the inside of my waistband was a constant, uneasy reminder that I was carrying. I gave up on finishing my flan and instead sipped at my coffee, while Nick wolfed down his triple chocolate ice cream cake.

Out of the corner of my eye, I observed Parkington and his flashy, red-haired companion. Girlfriend? Wife? Daughter? My money was on the first. No wife or daughter would rate the amount of bling that woman was wearing. Each time I stole a look, she was fingering a necklace, twisting a bracelet, or tossing down another slug of wine. There was no chatting going on between the couple. Parkington was deep in conversation with a man seated at a nearby table. His date looked bored out of her mind.

Nick pulled my attention back to our own table. "Are you going to finish your flan?"

"No." I edged the dessert toward him. "Go ahead."

"Thanks, but that's not why I asked. It's time to fish or cut bait."

"You have a plan?"

"We'll pass his table on our way out. Couldn't hurt to say hello. See what happens."

"You're not going to question him about the super-yacht or the auction, are you?" That seemed like a bad idea.

"Not directly. I'll drop a throwaway word or two. See how he reacts."

"What's my role?"

"You're exotic, sexy, and beautiful—that's a start." He smiled. "I know it's a stretch, but you might try to look almost as dumb as his date."

"I'll try, but I don't have the showy bling. I'm pretty sure a woman's IQ decreases proportionately as the load of jewelry she wears increases."

"Then I won't be buying you any pricey trinkets. I like you smart." Nick put a couple of bills on the table. "Let's get this done."

It isn't so easy to act clueless when you're carrying

a concealed weapon, but I gave it my best shot. Well, my best effort, anyway. I tagged along behind Nick, whose usually supple, masculine walk had morphed into a chauvinistic swagger. As we neared their table, Parkington's date spotted Nick and sat up straighter. She pushed out her chest, nearly causing her nipples to escape from her clingy, strapless top. Nick had that effect on women. Some women. *Most women.*

Parkington picked up on his date's shift in attention. He glanced at her, saw her watching our approach, and plastered on a smile, barely visible under his flamboyant white moustache.

"Evening, folks. Thanks for the drinks." He was obviously trying to work out why he should recognize us, and why Nick would buy him a round.

"Least I can do," Nick said. "I'm hoping to pick your brain about cruising. I suspect you're the man to talk to."

"Anytime, for a fellow mariner."

As Parkington spoke to Nick, he looked me up and down in a speculative, salacious way. Imagining his lewd thoughts brought to mind a slug creeping along, leaving a trail of slime.

"Good to know," Nick said. "I have business to take care of this weekend, but I'd like to set something up for Sunday night, if that works for you."

Parkington seemed to hesitate. "Sorry, that's out, but any other time." He handed Nick his card. "My info's on there."

Nick took the card. "Great. I'll check my schedule. Appreciate it."

"Glad to help." Parkington raised his glass. "Thanks again for the drinks."

Nick parked his hand on my butt and said loudly, for

Parkington's benefit, "Let's go, babe. I have plans for you." While we walked away from the table, I tried to act silly and giggly, resisting the urge to smack Nick upside the head.

Outside, I asked him what he thought about the encounter. "He said he wasn't available Sunday night. You suspect that he's going to attend the special auction?"

"I'd bet on it." Nick said. "We have two strikes against him now. He lied last weekend about there being no recent cruises to the Azores, and now he's booked for Sunday night."

"Wasn't that a risk? If you show up at that auction and he sees you, isn't he going to wonder why you're there?"

"Not necessarily. He'll assume I didn't want to tip my hand today any more than he did." Nick put an arm around my shoulders. "Don't worry, I won't show up at that auction unless I have enough backup to put everyone there out of business. All Parkington and the rest will be wondering about is how long they'll be in prison."

"You're counting on a lot happening between now and Sunday night," I said. "You don't even know the location yet, do you?"

"No. Buck's contact is withholding that until I've been vetted and approved. They have until an hour before it starts to confirm that I'm in. The emphasis on secrecy makes it sound even more felonious."

"They could be dealing in all kinds of illicit goods, up to and including human trafficking." My stomach knotted and my chest tightened. "Yet we still have nothing to convince Kass or the police down here to raid that auction."

"Seems that way. What we have so far would sound

worse than circumstantial. More like farfetched." Nick opened the car door for me. "Not to mention we don't know which law enforcement agency would be involved. The Bay Area includes a lot of different jurisdictions. Kass needs more, and we need to get busy."

"Then let's see if we can find something more concrete for him," I said. "It's still light out. Only seven o'clock."

"What do you have in mind?" Nick pulled onto the street.

"I'd like to go back to the dock where that man fell. Look around for a spent bullet."

Nick cocked an eyebrow. "Last weekend you weren't even sure his wound was caused by a gunshot. You still think it's worth the effort?"

"Why not? We're here. We have nothing better to do for the next hour or two."

Nick glanced at me. "I can think of something."

"Stop it. You're reminding me of that creep, Parkington."

"I'll bet I could grow a mustache, too. A big one just like his."

"Don't you dare." I swatted his arm.

Nick laughed out loud. "Okay…babe."

"Knock it off, Nick. Let's go look for a bullet."

"Not to throw a wet blanket on your idea, but even if we found a bullet proving he was shot, there's no guarantee the shooting has anything to do with Liliana's kidnappers."

"That man was arguing with someone on Carver's yacht just before he ran away and fell on the dock with a bloody head wound. That's enough to make me curious." I pointed to the marina entrance. "Here we are.

There's no one around. Any ideas how to get through the security gate?"

"I've acquired a handy utensil that should do the job."

I raised my eyebrows.

He grinned. "Don't ask."

TWENTY-SEVEN

THE DOCK WAS DESERTED, except for a few enterprising seagulls coasting overhead, seeking the usual food scraps dropped by messy humans. Evening fog rolled in over the Marin Headlands, bringing a moist chill to the air and making me glad we'd worn our Bay Wind jackets.

When we reached the location on the dock where I'd seen the man fall, a roly-poly harbor seal with impressive whiskers poked its head up from the basin's briny seawater. He gazed at us with round, curious brown eyes—another hungry resident hoping for a handout.

"Is this the spot?" Nick asked.

"It is." I pointed to the traces of bloodstain still visible on the planks of the dock. "He fell right there. That's where I took the blood sample."

He looked around. "How do you want to do this?"

"If it *was* a gunshot wound, the bullet must have grazed his head and kept going. If it had penetrated his skull, I'm pretty sure he wouldn't have vanished from the dock so quickly."

"Unless he fell over the side." Nick peered down into the dark water. "How do we know his body isn't in Davy Jones's locker?"

"We don't, but my guess is he would have floated by now. Someone would have spotted his body. Not to mention that I didn't hear a splash."

"They might have dragged him out of sight and

dumped him in the water later, you know. Or you didn't hear the splash because of the noise of the wind and the riggings. It's been a week. He could be in the Marin County Morgue as we speak."

I watched as the seal dropped out of sight in the murky water. "I know, but let's take it one step at a time. We didn't come here to search for a body. We came to see if we could find a bullet."

We spent half an hour pacing the dock, scrutinizing the pilings and checking the bows of nearby boats. To avoid looking suspicious, we pretended to admire the various yachts moored there, as if making up our minds what we might want for ourselves. I was just about to concede to Nick that our search was futile, when my cell buzzed. A text from Harry: God's Gift 2 owners Carver and Prine.

"Nick, look at this!" I held out my phone.

Nick read the text. "What gives?" He glanced toward the end of the dock where *God's Gift* was still moored. "I thought those two docs didn't get along."

"They got along okay until Paulo Ferrera turned up at TMC. When I asked Harry to check for other owners, I wasn't expecting this. I'd thought if there *was* a second owner, it might be someone from down here in the Bay Area. Maybe another Bay Wind Yacht Club member who has nothing to do with Timbergate Medical Center."

"How does this sit with those two overseeing Paulo Ferrera's medical care?"

"I don't like it." I brushed back a wisp of hair the breeze had skimmed across my face. "I'll have to run it by Cleo."

I texted my thanks back to Harry and asked if he'd

made any headway on Liliana's email account. He sent back a quick reply: Have an idea. Call me.

I called. He answered immediately. "We're not getting anywhere trying to guess how the Ferrera girl set up her hush-hush email account."

"I thought you had some sort of algorithm for that."

"There are so many variables, we can't count on it working in time."

That was awful news. I'd counted on Harry and his friends. "That girl's life is in terrible jeopardy, Harry. What else can we do? We need to fire up the police before Sunday night, or she may be gone forever."

"I'm still hoping we can sniff out that Francisco character, prove he was catfishing when he hooked up with her. We need to convince the police she was being targeted by a predator."

"If you can't get into her secret account, what do we do?"

"That's why I called. Tell me everything you recall Liliana's friend in the Azores saying about the online boyfriend."

"Not much. He spoke both Portuguese and English, and he was teaching Liliana some English."

"Can you be more specific?" Harry asked. "We need to know why Liliana hit it off with this Francisco. What did they have in common? Everything Liliana might have told her friend about the guy. We have to narrow this thing down."

"I don't… Wait. Mom asked Catia what it was about the boy that intrigued Liliana. She said it was a common interest in music. That's so typical of teens that I didn't give it a second thought."

"What kind of music do teen girls listen to in the Azores?" Harry said.

"Maybe Fado? I don't know what else, except kids all over the world seem to like American popular music."

"I remember Fado from last time I was there," Harry said. "Not sure what connection that would have for an American boy in California."

"Me, either, but Fado can be addictive, once you start listening to it."

"Do you know the names of any Fado singers?"

"Actually, I do. This last trip to the Azores got me hooked. I set up a Fado station on Pandora when we got home. I started it with Ana Moura. She's a Fado superstar. I can't think of any other vocalists' names."

"Whoa, here's something," he said.

"What? Are you doing a search right now?"

"Jackpot! Ana Moura has a connection to Mick Jagger and Prince."

"Really? Rolling Stones *and* the Purple One? Two American music icons! That would explain how a teen in the Azores and a teen in California might have music in common."

"Yep. This post implies that your Ana Moura is a protégée of Mick Jagger. Apparently, she might have dated him, but she also visited Prince in Minneapolis a few years ago."

"Sad, about his dying so young, but this sounds like tabloid stuff, Harry. Do you really think it'll help you identify Liliana's secret email?"

"Maybe," Harry said. "If Liliana and Francisco had music in common, this could be something to work with. I'll take it to my friendly hackers, but don't get your hopes up."

Hope was in short supply. "We don't have much time, Harry. By Sunday night, finding that email account will be the least of our worries. We have to do more."

"We will. You go ahead and talk to Kass. Maybe the police in Horta can jog Catia's memory. Maybe she still knows more than she's been telling. Another interview might produce something. Kass can expedite it with the police in Horta."

"Unless the prospect of being interrogated by the police again scares Catia speechless. She's easily intimidated."

"We'll have to trust that they know how to approach her." Harry paused. I heard a throat clearing that meant he was about to say something difficult. "Sis, are you and Nick keeping safe?"

Almost choking up, I swallowed hard and said, "We're fine, little brother, but we need your help. Stay in touch, okay?"

The sun had dropped behind the Marin Hills while I was on the phone, causing the light to fade and deepening the chill in the air. Nick had been strolling the dock while I talked to Harry. When he saw that I'd finished the call, he turned and walked back to me.

"Found something." He held his hand out to me, palm up. There it was. A spent bullet.

"Where was it?" I asked.

"Stuck in a piling." He raised his brows in a question. "Want to put it in that handy-dandy kit you carry around?"

"Yes, but not here. I know it looks like there's no one around, but I feel exposed and vulnerable. Let's go back to Buck's yacht. I'll fill you in on Harry's report on the way."

Down below, the ducted heating system in Buck's yacht kept us cozy as we sat in the main saloon, sipping wine in silence. The bullet was tucked away in my forensic kit.

I finally heard back from Kass, who called from Sacramento where he'd been tied up in court all day testifying in the Sawyer County change-of-venue case. I filled him in about the auction invitation and sent him the photo of Liliana.

"Have you forwarded this photo to anyone at TPD?" he asked.

"Not yet. Nick and I thought it would be best to run it by you first."

"I understand," Kass said. "I'll be back in Timbergate tomorrow morning. I'll get on this right away." He paused. "I'll also run it by the SFPD and the Marin County Sheriff's Office. See if they'll at least open a file. Keep in mind, she'd most likely be classified as a runaway, since she looks happy and unharmed."

"But there's no proof of when it was taken. Maybe her situation is different now. Her brother knew something that got him gravely wounded. I'm convinced it's all part of the same crime."

"I agree. This should help me justify putting more people on the Ferrera case. We'll get to work identifying who sent the auction invitation and the photo."

"There's more." I told him that Harry still hoped to get access to the Ferreras' laptop. "It's been at least a week since the Ferreras turned it over to your department."

"Why does your brother want it?"

"He has some friends with superior hacking skills who are willing to help out."

"Give me your brother's number. Tell him I'll be in touch."

I gave him Harry's cell number. Kass also agreed to contact the Horta police right away, but couldn't offer any assurance there. He implied that it would require a lot of tact on his part to convince them to question

Catia further about Liliana's social life without sounding critical of their methods. When I mentioned finding a bullet, and the likelihood that its target was a young man seen running from Prine and Carver's yacht, Kass was more responsive.

"I have a late meeting down here in Sac tonight, but I'll head back to Timbergate first thing tomorrow. For now, send a few photos of that bullet to my phone. Bring the actual bullet to me as soon as you're back in town. We'll compare it with the one taken from the missing girl's brother."

I assured him that was exactly what I had in mind and reminded him that we were still waiting to hear about what the security cameras on Carver's office building had recorded. Kass said he'd follow up on that, too, when he got back to Timbergate.

The evening wore on with Nick and me lost in thought. As each quarter hour passed, the ticking of the wall clock grew louder and more relentless. To break the silence, I opened my laptop and tuned to the Fado music station I had created on Pandora. Even without understanding the Portuguese lyrics, I found that the evocative voices of the female vocalists, combined with the soulful rhythms of Portuguese guitar, helped sooth my fraying nerves. I listened differently, proud of my Portuguese heritage, knowing that Fado was appreciated by music icons like Jagger and Prince.

Nick had hoped for an update from Buck about whether Nick's RSVP had been approved for the Sunday night auction, but as the hours slipped by, it seemed unlikely we'd hear anything before bedtime.

At eleven o'clock, Nick said, "What do you think? Shall we try to sleep?"

"Might as well."

SATURDAY MORNING, I woke to the harbor's usual salute to the senses: the crying of gulls, the pungent smell of seawater, and the bright morning sunlight striking my face through a porthole in the forward berth. The aroma of coffee confirmed that Nick had been up at least long enough to start a pot brewing.

"Do I hear signs of life?" he called.

"Think so," I mumbled.

"Peanut butter toast?"

"Sounds good."

After making a pit stop in the head, I brushed my teeth and ran a comb through my hair. Then I pulled on jeans and a long-sleeved polo shirt and joined Nick in the main saloon.

"Coffee smells good." I took the cup he offered. "Been up long?"

"Since six."

I glanced at the clock. "Seven now. What have you been doing?"

"Thinking about our day." He spread peanut butter and honey on toast and brought it to the table where I sat. "I didn't want to wake you."

"Thanks." I reached for a slice. "I'm anxious to hear your thoughts about the weekend."

Nick scooted next to me on the bench seat and placed a page of notes on the table. "These are in no particular order. I thought we'd use your left-brain approach to sort them out."

I scanned his list. It was long. And disheartening. There was so much we wanted to know. Was *Seashell* moored somewhere in the Bay Area? Was Liliana on the superyacht? If so, did she still believe she would be allowed to leave of her own free will? Had she tried to contact the person she thought was an online boyfriend named Francisco?

Gus Barba and Kiri D'Costa were on the list. Originally, Nick and I wanted to know if Paulo had come to California seeking Gus's help finding Liliana. Now we had to determine whether Gus was mixed up with whatever Carver and Prine were involved in. Was Kiri involved, too, and if not, was she in danger? Or were they both innocent? Just a young couple in a romantic relationship?

I pointed to where Nick had made a note about Liliana's secret email account. "I've pretty much given up hope on this. Think how long Harry's been trying."

"I have to agree. Harry's waited at least a week for the TPD to release the family's laptop." Nick looked at me with concern. "Even if he had it, there's no guarantee it would help."

"I know it's not likely. So far, that photo of Liliana modeling with the sculpture is the most concrete evidence we have."

"And we've been told it doesn't necessarily prove a crime," Nick said.

I shoved the rest of my toast aside. "But we do have Kass curious about the bullet you found. I think I've convinced him the shooter was on Carver's yacht. And he has evidence that Paulo was somewhere near Carver's office building close to the time of that shooting."

"The man definitely looks like a potential suspect." Nick underlined Carver's name.

"And now Kass is interested enough to want to compare the bullets. What we don't know is where Prine fits in." I went to the galley for a coffee refill.

"We have today and tomorrow to figure that out."

"We have to help Kass classify this as more than a

runaway teenage girl. Do you realize it's been a full month since she disappeared and three weeks since Paulo set out to find her?"

"But only two and a half weeks since he ended up at TMC." Nick held out his cup for a top-off. "Too bad we can't account for his five days in between."

"If only we could know what happened during that time." I sat next to Nick, wanting the comfort of being close. "Sometimes it seems all we have are loose ends and false leads."

Nick wrapped his arm around my shoulders, giving me a little shake. "Come on, you're the gal who never gives up. Where do you want to start?"

"Isn't today when Kass was going to do the DNA analysis on the blood I collected last weekend?"

"Right, but we still need a solid reason to think it's connected to the Ferrera case."

"That wounded man is connected to the yacht that Carver and Prine own. And so is Kiri D'Costa, who's connected to Gus Barba."

"I'll try to arrange to meet up with Gus today," Nick said.

"Are you going to ask Buck if he's arranged for us to attend that auction?"

"That's on my list, but it won't be both of us," Nick said. "If Buck manages to make it happen, it'll just me. I thought I'd made that clear."

"If that's how it is, I won't be far away."

"I'd like to argue that, but I know better," Nick said. "Kass told you he'd be back in Timbergate early today. Let's hope his people or Harry's will be able to determine where that auction flyer originated."

"I hate to be a wet blanket when we're trying to

stay positive, but I doubt TPD has access to the kind of cyber-forensic expertise that would require."

Nick nodded. "Probably not, but maybe Kass can enlist help. What about the FBI office in Sac?"

"He could try. The photos I took of the bullet you found, and the photo of Liliana modeling for the auction should give him some leverage, don't you think?"

"It should. The Horta police can confirm Liliana's identity. If I'm right, the fact that this incident might involve cybercrime could qualify it for an FBI investigation. But still, the knee-jerk reaction is going to be that Liliana is a runaway."

"I think Kass is beyond that now," I said. "Liliana's brother is close to dying from a gunshot wound in Kass's town, his jurisdiction."

Nick stood and picked up our breakfast plates. "It's up to Kass whether he contacts the FBI. You and I need to focus on what *we* can do." He put the plates in the sink and brought the coffee pot to the table. "What's the latest on the brother's medical status?"

"I'm about to find out." I checked the time. "Almost eight. Cleo's probably awake. I'm calling her now."

Cleo picked up after several rings. I asked her about Paulo Ferrera.

"We're losing him, Aimee."

TWENTY-EIGHT

CLEO'S VOICE WAS HOARSE, either from suppressed emotion, or because I woke her. "Prine is suggesting that the parents let Paulo go."

"That's terrible news." I glanced up at Nick, shook my head. "Has he asked for a second opinion?"

"Not that I've heard. Prine's going out of town again this weekend, but he doesn't want to leave Carver in charge. He's trying to persuade the Ferreras to take Paulo off the machines today. Wants it done before he leaves town this afternoon."

"How are the parents reacting? Have you talked to Mary Barton? Is there anything Social Services can do to help?"

"Mary Barton says they're so distraught, she's been unable to offer them much solace. Their sessions with the priest have been complicated by the language barrier and the need for an interpreter."

"Why is Prine leaving town now? Seems like he could postpone whatever he has going on."

"He's not about to tell me, of course." I heard Cleo yawn. She'd obviously been asleep when I called. "I asked Quinn if he knew where Prine was off to. He didn't. Just said Prine told him he'd be back early next week."

"And if the parents refuse to take Paulo off the machines today?" I asked.

"Then, until Prine returns, Carver will take over Paulo's case."

"Interesting, since Prine's been so adamant about keeping Carver out of it."

"Think of it this way…that young man is so close to dying, Prine must realize by now that Carver can't possibly make him any worse." Cleo sounded as down as I'd ever heard her. "This situation beats anything I've seen in my decade here."

"Then Jared Quinn *must* bring someone else in, other than Prine or Carver, to evaluate Paulo Ferrera's case."

"You're reading my mind, Aimee. I'll let you know what happens."

I ended the call and gave Nick the bad news, adding my concern that if Prine and Carver were in cahoots with regard to Liliana, neither of them would want to see Paulo emerge from his coma.

"What are the odds of having someone else step in?" Nick asked.

"That's what Cleo and I are hoping for, but it's up to Quinn."

"You'd think there'd be more than two neurosurgeons in Timbergate."

"I've heard there was a third, a few years before my time at TMC," I said. "Alcohol and drug abuse got him kicked off TMC's medical staff. Apparently, he entered an impaired physicians' program."

"Did it work?" Nick asked.

"I don't know."

"Shame, but we hear these stories all the time. That's why I like working for Buck. Any day we help shut down a drug trafficking operation is a good day."

"Next time I talk to Cleo, I'll find out if Quinn's

going to pull in a consulting neurosurgeon from Sacramento."

"Then let's get back to planning our day. Where were we?"

"The auction," I said. "We don't know if you're going to be admitted. Let's say you *are* vetted and invited to attend. When you arrive at the secret location, will you need some sort of prearranged password?"

"Probably," Nick said. "We'll see."

"Speaking of the location, I keep imagining it's going to take place on the superyacht from Horta. What do you think?"

Nick nodded. "It seems like the obvious venue. Someplace that can be here today, gone tomorrow."

"That's another thing. I'm almost convinced that the yacht Buck and Rella heard about in Florida—the one called *Seashell*—is the one we're looking for. I have to keep reminding myself I might be wrong."

"That question would be answered if Harry and friends ever manage to hack into Liliana's secret email account. She took a photo. You can be sure she sent it to Francisco, whoever he is."

I'd given up on that email account, but didn't say so. "One thing we can do is re-check the harbors down here where a yacht the size of *Seashell* could be moored."

"Anything else?" Nick asked.

"Just a call to Harry."

"While you do that, I'll see if I can set up something with Gus Barba. I'll ask him to drop by and give me a status report on the last hull cleaning and inspection he did for Buck." Nick went up topside with his phone.

I called Harry, who answered sounding out of breath, saying I'd caught him on a morning run with Rella. "What's up?"

I told him to expect a call from Detective Kass, who should be arriving back in Timbergate soon. "He's going to see about getting the Ferreras' laptop released."

"What about the photo of the girl modeling with the sculpture? Has Kass shown it to the parents to confirm that it's their missing daughter?"

"We've done all that. Kass says the photo isn't enough to prove a crime, since the girl looks happy and unharmed. He did say he'd pass it on to the Marin County Sheriff and the SFPD."

"I wouldn't expect too much to come of that," Harry said. "With no proof of a crime, they're probably not going to put out a lot of effort."

"Maybe not, but at least the police down here will have something on file to open a case, or whatever it is they do. Someone will be assigned to work with the TPD if it becomes necessary."

"Sounds about right," Harry said. "I'll be in touch if I get my hands on the laptop, and I'll try to sniff out the origin of that flyer Buck received. Just don't hold your breath."

I went up the hatch ladder and joined Nick, who sat in the captain's chair in the exterior cockpit. The crisp morning air and serene vista of a yacht-filled harbor lifted my spirits a couple of notches, reminding me there was still hope we would find a way to rescue Liliana before the Sunday night auction.

Nick nodded toward another chair. "How are you doing?"

I took a seat. "I'm having trouble keeping my hopes up."

Nick's phone buzzed. He checked the message. "Don't give up yet." He handed me the phone showing a text from Detective Kass.

Back in Timbergate. No luck w security cams. DNA profile in works maybe later today.

"It's only eight o'clock," I said. "Looks like he was serious about putting this case on the front burner."

"Let's hope the DNA gets a hit when he runs it through CODIS."

"If that doesn't work, there are lots of other databases out there now. People use them to check paternity and look up ancestry." I watched a pelican dip down, scoop its long, pouch-like beak into the bay, and fly away with breakfast. "Even if the DNA tells us who that bleeding man on the dock was, it may not tell us how he fits into this scenario, if at all."

Nick nodded. "We're counting on a lot of puzzle pieces fitting together this weekend."

"Speaking of puzzle pieces, did you get through to Gus Barba?"

"I did. He's meeting me here at ten thirty."

"How are you going to approach him?"

"Carefully. He's making a good living working on the vessels of a lot of rich, powerful people who depend on him to be discreet."

"Then what can you ask him that won't raise red flags? You can't ask about the yacht Prine and Carver own or about the superyacht *Seashell* without explaining why you're asking. You can't even question him about his relationship with Kiri."

"Not sure about that," Nick said. "I might have more luck there, as long as I use the right approach. Most guys don't mind hearing a compliment about a beautiful girlfriend." Nick flashed a smile that would have turned me on under different circumstances. "I know I don't."

I took a moment to think about Gus Barba. "You know,

something about Gus has been bugging me. Paulo's parents said he knew a man in the San Francisco area who might help him find Liliana. Someone called Ghost."

"I'm listening."

"Think about that name, Ghost. Remember how Senhora Ferrera pronounced it? It wasn't *Ghost*. What she said was, 'A ghosht.'"

"Wasn't that because of her accent?"

"Maybe, but my father had an uncle named Agostinho, and everyone called him Gus. I'd like to know what Gus's given name is."

"Go on," Nick said.

"Any chance we can find some paperwork about Gus on this yacht? Maybe filed away as an employment document?"

"Let's look."

We hurried down the hatch ladder. Nick headed to the chart table, lifted the lid, and flicked through a stack of papers. "Not here. Buck would know."

Nick pulled out his phone, tapped the screen. He listened and nodded to let me know Buck had answered. After giving Buck a quick explanation of what he needed, he listened for a moment, thanked him, and ended the call.

"You were right. Agostinho Barba. *A-ghosht.*"

My heart was beating double time. "What do we do, Nick?"

"We think this through," Nick said. "We have no guarantee Gus is the friend Paulo wanted to meet up with. When asked about Gus's references, Buck told us he was from Lisbon. That doesn't match up with the Ferreras saying Paulo met his friend when they worked on the docks together in Madalena."

"But it might. What if Gus left Lisbon and worked

for a while at the docks on Pico before moving on to California?"

"That's possible. And it might be a way I could approach him. Casually mention that I just got back from visiting the Azores. Maybe ask him if he's ever been there."

"And if he says he has? How will you decide whether to ask if he knows Paulo and Liliana Ferrera?"

"I'll take it one step at a time."

"I have a feeling I shouldn't be here when you meet with him." I glanced at the clock. "It's almost ten now. I'll take the car and re-check the harbors on this side of the bridge where superyachts could be moored. That should keep me busy until you finish with Gus."

"Wait," Nick said. "Are you carrying?"

"What?" It took me a second to grasp his meaning. "My gun? Again?"

"Yes, again." Nick took my gun and holster from my tote in the forward berth. He held them out to me. "Here you are, and please don't argue."

Much as I disliked the idea, I clipped the holster inside the waistband of my jeans and tucked the .38 inside. "You really think this is necessary?"

"Maybe not today, not right now, but I want you to make a habit of keeping it with you all weekend." He touched a finger to my waist. "You need to be aware that it's there."

"Then you're going to need to remind me." I tried a lighthearted smile. "It's not my favorite accessory."

Nick didn't smile back. "Maybe not, but it could be your most important one." He held my face in his hands and looked deep into my eyes. "Aimee, this is important. I know you're a good shot at the gun range. A dead-eye, really, but there the target isn't shooting back. Unfortunately, it doesn't prepare you for what might face us before this weekend is over."

I lifted his hands from my face and held them for a moment while I absorbed what he'd said. "You really think we'll be involved in a gun battle?"

"No. I think just the opposite. I don't expect either of us to come face to face with gunfire. With luck, that'll be handled by law enforcement…if it happens at all. Even so, I've told you that there are times when my work with Buck requires survival skills. I've spent a lot of time sharpening mine. I'm hardwired to be prepared, but you're not. If our plans go south, either this weekend or any other time, I want you ready, too."

I had mixed feelings. I appreciated his concern but also felt defensive. "I've been in tight spots a few times before, Nick. I even have a couple of scars to show for it."

"I know, but the stakes are higher here. The kind of criminals operating at this level won't hesitate to fire if they suspect we're trying to take them down."

I patted the slight bulge at my waistband. "Message received."

"Here's another piece of equipment you might need." Nick handed me a key. "It'll open the security gates to the harbors you want to visit."

"Is this what you used the other day to open the gate to Carver's marina?"

"Yep. Don't lose it. We may need it on Sunday night."

"I'm starting to feel like I'm in an 007 movie. Do you have any more tricks to show me?"

"All in good time," Nick said with a smile. "Have to be sure you've got the stuff to be a Bond girl."

"Oh, please." I glanced at the clock. "I'd respond to

that if we had time, but it's almost ten now. I'd better get going before Gus shows up."

"One last thing," Nick said. "Do you think there's a chance Gus would bring Kiri D'Costa with him?"

"I hadn't thought of that. Did he mention her being down for another weekend when you two set up your meeting?"

"No. I'm just thinking ahead, in case they're thick enough that she's coming down here every weekend. My meet with Gus wouldn't go well if she did happen to come along."

"Can you call him back? Maybe tell him I asked, since she and I know each other. If she's in town, coming along with him, I'll stay. If not, I'll go."

Nick called and confirmed that Gus was coming alone. I headed off in search of a behemoth of a yacht that only a few Marin County harbors could accommodate.

TWENTY-NINE

MOST OF THE marinas on our list were clustered near each other. None was more than thirty minutes away. My first stop was the one nearest to where Buck's yacht was moored—a short drive up Highway 101. I had decided it might save time to start there and work my way out.

With Buck's little car safely parked and locked, I made my way to the basin gate. The master key Nick had given me worked as advertised, allowing me easy access to the docks. Wearing deck shoes and carrying my small backpack, I hoped to blend in with the regulars.

I strolled along the docks, heading toward the areas farthest out where the superyachts would be moored. Along the way, I found myself checking for any boats bearing the Bay Wind Yacht Club burgee, although that was not the main object of my search.

A few people nodded politely as if I might be a new dock neighbor they had not yet met. A couple close to my age who were holding hands passed by. The mother carried a bright-eyed, curly-haired infant in a pouch strapped on her chest. Apparently, humans had taken a clue from the mother kangaroo. It looked like fun. A lot more fun than the little pouch clipped to my waistband. *Snub-nosed .38 or adorable baby?* I recalled James O'Brien at the play in Boston questioning me about starting a family. I pushed the thought away. This weekend wasn't about my future; it was about Liliana Ferrera's.

A thorough exploration of the first marina proved there was no superyacht moored there. After making my way north, repeating the process at the next three harbors with no superyacht in sight, I headed back down 101. Hungry from all the walking and fresh air, I called Nick to see if he'd eaten lunch.

"No, Gus just left. What are you thinking?"

"How about I stop and order takeout from that café we like in Sausalito?"

"Perfect. We can debrief while we eat."

"That won't take me long," I said. "How about you?"

"Some progress. We'll talk when you get here."

I ordered two turkey-bacon melts at the counter of the busy deli and waited at a table for two stocked with the usual condiments. The appetizing aromas in the café spiked my hunger. Curiosity about the superyacht made me even more impatient.

To pass the time, I took out my phone, thinking I'd call Cleo to ask about Paulo Ferrera. I had punched the first two numbers of her cell when I heard someone say my name.

"Aimee?"

I looked up, thinking my order had come. But it wasn't the waitress. Kiri D'Costa stood at my table, looking at me with a surprised expression. That answered the question Nick and I had considered earlier. Kiri's relationship with Gus had to be serious if she was coming to see him every weekend.

I put my phone away. "Kiri, what a surprise. You're down for the weekend again?"

"Yes, you too, I see." She looked at the empty chair across from me. "Mind?"

I nodded. "Of course not. Please sit. I'm waiting for an order to go."

She smiled. "Same here."

Okay, I thought, *where do I want to go with this?* Rather than bring up our common experience of saving Carver's behind by finding his missing CME credits, I decided on small talk. "Do you enjoy yachting, Kiri? Or do you come down here to get away from Timbergate's blistering summers?"

"Mostly the latter," she said. "I've always been a little nervous around water deep enough to drown in. I didn't learn to swim as a child."

"Oh, that's too bad. I grew up in Timbergate, where everyone heads for water in the summertime. Swimming lessons up there begin almost as soon as kids leave the womb."

"That makes good sense." Kiri went silent for a moment, looking around the busy café. "Will you let me pay for your lunch today? I'd like to do something to thank you for helping me the other day in Dr. Carver's office."

"That's not necessary, Kiri. It needed to be done." I felt myself blush, uncomfortable with her offer. I didn't want to insult her by refusing.

"I'm very happy that I came across you today," she said. "I have another favor to ask."

"Really?" She definitely had my attention. I waited while thoughts raced through my mind. Was she loyal to Carver? Were she and Gus mixed up with Carver and Prine? Or was she simply in love with Gus and wanting to talk about their relationship?

Before she could continue, the waitress brought both of our orders to the table. Kiri took my ticket, put it with hers, and handed cash to the waitress, telling her to keep the change.

"Thank you," I said. "If we have another occasion, it'll be my treat."

"I hope we will. I enjoy your company." She was making it harder and harder for me to suspect her of any ulterior motives or devious activities. The more I was around her, the more I liked her, but she was still a puzzle, and I was still curious.

"Kiri, you were interrupted a moment ago. You said you wanted to ask a favor."

"Yes, although I feel more than a little embarrassed." She ducked her head, avoiding direct eye contact and further piquing my curiosity.

"If there's something you need to ask me about, I'm happy to help. Does it concern your job? Or Dr. Carver?" The day we had worked together looking for the CME documents in Carver's office, I noticed the other staff members had looked at her with barely veiled disapproval. I recalled thinking Kiri hadn't seemed too knowledgeable about medical office procedures and protocols. Maybe the other women were resentful, assuming she'd been hired based solely on her stunning looks.

Kiri glanced up at me, seeming surprised at my question. "Oh, nothing to do with work. It's more personal. I was hoping to talk woman to woman about the man I've been seeing."

She wanted to talk about Gus? A slight chill traced up my arms. "Gus Barba? I'm not sure how I can help with that. I don't really know him, except as an employee of my boyfriend's boss."

"Perhaps you know more than you realize. I'd at least like your opinion." She scooted closer to the table, lean-

ing in toward me. "I've only been seeing Gus occasionally on weekends for a couple of months."

"How did you meet?"

"Dr. Carver invited his staff down to spend a long
weekend on the yacht. It was his way of thanking us
for working overtime without pay to help him move his
office to the new professional building above the river.
Without that first visit to Dr. Carver's boat, I wouldn't
have met Gus."

"You met him on Carver's yacht?" I asked.

"Yes. I was new to Dr. Carver's staff, and the other
women had all worked for him for a long time. They
were not…unfriendly…exactly, but I felt excluded from
their circle. Gus came aboard the first day we were
there. He talked to Dr. Carver about some detail of the
hull cleaning. I happened to be alone, sunning myself
on the bow. As Gus was leaving, he noticed me and
began a conversation."

"He's a very handsome man. I can see how you might
have been attracted."

"Attracted, yes, but not just physically. He and I realized almost immediately that we were both fluent in
Portuguese." She smiled. "It was pleasant, speaking the
language with him."

This was getting more interesting by the minute. I
tried to keep from telegraphing my eagerness to hear
more.

"That definitely gave you something in common," I
said. "I'm curious why you would need to ask me about
him. Has he done or said anything that concerns you?"

"No, he's been perfect—almost too good to be
true—even to holding off on any pressure about sleeping together."

That was a surprise. If she wasn't sleeping with him,

Nick and I were wrong about where she was spending nights on her weekends in the Bay Area. Maybe she *had* been sleeping on Carver's yacht.

"Kiri, I don't know how I can help you." *Unless Gus is mixed up in the kidnapping of Liliana and the shooting of her brother.*

"Gus doesn't volunteer much information about his past," Kiri said. "I try to prompt him to speak about his family, his home of origin, that sort of thing, but he manages to change the subject. It makes me wonder if he's hiding something. If your friend Nick is close to Gus, he might be able to put my mind at ease." She leaned back, brushed a lock of hair behind her ear. "I'm sorry to involve you, but I don't have anyone else to ask."

"I understand," I said. "I'll ask Nick. If he can offer anything helpful, I'll call you next week. We can get together for lunch."

Kiri frowned. "Oh, that's… I was hoping you might ask him this weekend. I'd rather not wait." She took a pen from her purse and wrote on a napkin. "You can reach me here."

I took the napkin, waiting for her to explain the urgency, but she didn't continue. Instead, she stood, picking up her takeout bag. She was obviously ready to leave. I stood, too, remembering I had takeout of my own. Nick would be hungry and curious about what took me so long.

Kiri and I walked together through the crowded dining space. Halfway to the door, a bustling waitress tripped over a patron's foot and knocked me into Kiri, causing us to grasp each other to keep from falling. As we tumbled into each other's arms, barely keeping a grip on our takeout bags, I felt my holstered revolver bump against a portion of Kiri's midsection that was unusually rigid. We pulled away from each other, righting ourselves. Our eyes met for a moment, but neither of us acknowledged what we had just discovered. *We both were carrying concealed weapons.*

THIRTY

Back at Buck's yacht, I found Nick down below and blurted out my news about Kiri.

"Nick, I'm telling you, it *can't* be a baby bump. It wasn't that kind of bulge."

"You sure? You said she's in a hurry to know more about Gus. If she's preg—"

"Arrrgh! Stop saying that. I'm *sure* it was a concealed weapon. After wearing mine all day, I know what it feels like." I'd already told him I'd struck out looking for a superyacht at the harbors I'd visited. The revelation about gun-toting Kiri was a more immediate concern. "We have to figure out how it fits with whatever you got from talking to Gus."

"We will, but right now, I'm starving." Nick was devouring the turkey-bacon melt. He didn't seem to mind that it had gone cold.

Food was the last thing on my mind. I stuffed my uneaten sandwich in the galley's little fridge.

"Kiri was so anxious to know more about Gus that when I suggested we get together next week back in Timbergate, she didn't want to wait. She wanted to know this weekend."

Nick swallowed a bite. "Sounds urgent, huh? I don't know. I'm still thinking pregnant."

I groaned. "Nick, she said she's not sleeping with him. Even if she was, they haven't been seeing each other that long. There's no way she'd already have a noticeable bump. Believe me, she was carrying a gun."

"Okay, I'll reserve judgment. How did you leave it with her?"

"She gave me this." I showed him the napkin where she'd written her number. "I told her you know Gus a lot better than I do. She's hoping I'll call her if you have anything more for us to tell her."

"We'll put that on hold for now. Although it might come in handy later to have that number." Nick held up the last quarter of his sandwich. "Almost finished."

"Eat fast," I said. "While you're doing that, I'll make a call."

I punched in Cleo's personal cell number, although I dreaded asking about Paulo's condition. Since she hadn't called me, I could at least hope he was still alive.

She answered on the first ring. "Hoped it was you. What's going on down there?"

I filled her in, finishing with my startling news about Kiri's concealed weapon.

"Whoa, what do you suppose that's about?" Cleo said. "She's never struck me as the pistol-packin' type."

"Me, either. I don't know what to make of it, but I wasn't about to question her, since I'm sure she now knows the same about me. We both feigned ignorance and kept moving."

Cleo sighed. "Good grief, Aimee. Whatever you and Nick are getting yourselves into down there, please be careful."

"We will," I said. "I hate to keep asking, but is there any change in Paulo's condition?"

"He's been unchanged for the last twenty-four hours. That doesn't mean a whole lot, but it's something. Carver's back on the case, at least for the rest of this weekend. Prine is due back on Monday."

"I thought Prine didn't want Carver anywhere near Paulo."

"He was overruled by Quinn and the chief of staff," Cleo said.

"Last I heard, Paulo's condition was grave. Any reason to hope he'll recover?"

"You know how it is with patient confidentiality. There's only so much I can infer from what his caregivers let slip." I heard voices in the background. "Just a sec, let me turn the TV down. Sig likes it loud." She came back. "That's better. Where was I?"

"Paulo's prognosis," I prompted. "You said no change."

"That's right. It's the weekend, so unless I come up with an excuse to go to the hospital, I won't hear anything before Monday. Let's assume no news is good news, since Quinn won't call me on my days off unless something unexpected happens."

"Unexpected, as in losing Paulo?"

"Sorry, but yes…probably."

"What about calling in an out-of-town neurosurgeon for a third opinion?"

"Quinn's still checking around. Damn shame we lost Parkington to substance abuse. He was sort of an ass, like Carver, but he did good work back in the day."

It took a moment for me to register the name she'd spoken. "Cleo, what did you just say?"

"Quinn's still checking around. I'll call you right away with any—"

"No, not that. What name did you just say?"

"Parkington? I've told you about him before. He was the third neurosurgeon on our staff."

"No. I mean, yes, you've told me there was a third, but you didn't mention his name." I nearly choked out my next words. "Is his first name Errol?"

"Yes. That's right." Impatience crept into her voice. "So I *did* tell you."

"Cleo, listen. I'm going to send you a photo. As soon as you get it, text me to confirm that it's the doctor you're talking about."

"Why? What's going on?"

"Just look at the photo and text me back. If it *is* the man you're talking about, I'll explain."

I ended my call just as Nick finished his last bite, washing it down with coffee. "Ah, that's better. Now you have my undivided attention."

"Good. Because Cleo just dropped a clue that might help anchor this case." I repeated what she had told me about a former neurosurgeon with the same name as that of the Bay Wind Yacht Club's cruising captain.

"Hmm. Interesting, but I'm not reacting as strongly as you are. A lot of wealthy doctors belong to yacht clubs. What are you reading into that?"

"A hunch, maybe? No. Stronger. Parkington knew both Carver and Prine back in Timbergate. And you're the one who suspects Parkington might be mixed up in the *Seashell* mystery. He told you he had another commitment and couldn't get together with you tomorrow night, when the auction is taking place."

"Go on." Nick picked up a pen and reached for the notes he'd started earlier. "I like where you're headed with this."

I took a moment to organize my thoughts, then continued, "Last weekend Parkington denied knowing of any recent Bay Wind Yacht Club vessels cruising to the Azores. He had to be lying. I know that doesn't prove anything, but it's very suspicious. On top of that, Parkington lost his license to practice medicine several years ago, but he still seems to be enjoying a lavish lifestyle. Where's his money coming from?"

"I'm with you."

"Good. Now where did you put that brochure?"

Nick stepped over to the chart table and brought back the Bay Wind brochure with Parkington's photo. "Here you go. Take your shot."

I clicked and sent the photo to Cleo. She texted back right away.

That's him. Why?

I showed her text to Nick, who smiled, folded the brochure, and stuffed it into his pocket. "Looks like we're on to something."

"Any doubt he'll be attending that auction?"

"I'd bet on it," Nick said. "Are you going to tell Cleo why you sent the photos?"

"Not everything. It would take too long to explain." I wrote that we'd met Parkington at the yacht club and there was something fishy about him that might involve Carver and Prine.

"All done?" Nick asked.

"Not quite." I dropped onto the settee next to Nick, crossing my legs yoga-style. "I want to know if Parkington got his medical license reinstated. If not, what's his source of income?" I added the question about his license and sent the text. "Done," I said. "Now it's your turn. Tell me what you learned from Gus…and be sure to include anything he said about Kiri."

"Let's start with that. He met her on Carver's yacht, *God's Gift*. That matches what Kiri told you. They've spent the last several weekends 'getting to know each other.' That's how Gus put it. He said Kiri's very private about herself."

"Huh, she says the same about him. Anything to support your theory that she could be pregnant?" I thought of the cute little baby I'd seen on the docks earlier, tried to imagine Kiri with one of those draped across her chest. Kiri with a baby on the way? It didn't make sense. But a gun, I believed.

"I didn't ask about Gus's sex life, and he didn't offer." Nick tilted his head, recalling the conversation. "The only other comment he made was that Kiri made it clear she wasn't interested in a serious relationship. More like the opposite. Made Gus wonder if she planned to return to India soon."

"That *is* interesting. I thought she was hoping to stay in America indefinitely."

"Let's get back to your theory about her packing a weapon." Nick leaned against the back of the settee, arms crossed. "If she is, and I'm not saying I'm convinced, do you have any guesses as to why a medical office assistant on a weekend getaway would be armed?"

"Only one. She might be in cahoots with Carver and Prine, and possibly Parkington, and whatever they have to do with that man who was shot running away from *God's Gift*."

Nick leaned forward, rotating his empty coffee cup for a moment. "If that's the case, Kiri'll be down here all weekend doing whatever it is that requires a weapon. If you run into her again, be prepared."

"What about you? If Kiri's involved, it wouldn't be a stretch to think she's pulled Gus in along with her. Right now, they might be doing exactly what we're doing."

"You think they're comparing notes?" Nick said. "Plotting against us?"

"Do I sound paranoid?"

"Unfortunately, no." He stood and stretched. "I haven't told you Gus's response when I brought up our recent trip to the Azores."

"That's right. You were going to slip that topic into your conversation. Any luck? Did he mention working in Madalena or knowing Paulo Ferrera?"

"As we guessed, Gus hop-scotched from Lisbon to the Azores before ending up here in Marin County. He and Paulo worked together in Madalena for several months. Gus said Paulo had texted him that he was coming to California and planned to look him up, but that was at least three weeks ago, and Gus never heard from him again."

"Then Gus *is* the ghost! *A-ghosht*. Paulo's mother was right all along. *Agostinho*. You believed Gus? Paulo never contacted him?"

"Not for certain." Nick pulled in a deep, conflicted breath and slowly released it. "I'm reserving judgment for now. Any other questions about Gus before we move on to another topic?"

"Yes. Did you get a chance to ask if he ever works as a hull diver on superyachts?"

"No. I couldn't slip that in without making him curious."

"So you picked up no reliable info on *Seashell*." I glanced at the clock. "Look, it's almost four o'clock. We have only the rest of today and all of tomorrow to stop that auction. We can't waste any time."

"Then let's concentrate." Nick tapped his sheet of notes. "We should hear from Kass anytime now. He said he'd arrange to have the DNA analysis on that blood

sample run today. He might even have some prelimi-
nary opinion on your photos of the bullet I pulled from
that piling."

"Hope so. If there's a chance it matches Paulo's bullet, we know the running man is part of this mystery."

Nick nodded. "And that would give Kass more jus-
tification to take the case forward."

"Speaking of Kass, he was going to arrange for
Harry to have access to the Ferreras' laptop today. We
should have heard something by now." I glanced at my
cellphone. "No new messages."

"That reminds me." Nick got up and walked to the
forward berth, coming back with his phone. "I turned it
off while Gus was here so we wouldn't be interrupted."
His eyebrows lifted. "Yes. Harry texted almost two
hours ago."

"What? Did he find anything?"

"He has the laptop. He and his IT friends are scour-
ing it for any hints that might help them identify Liliana's secret email account."

"I keep wondering why he thinks his friends can do
what the police in Horta and Timbergate couldn't do."

"Harry claims they're extremely skilled hackers who
enjoy a challenge," Nick said. "Remember those hackers in the news a while back who decrypted a terror-
ist's phone for the FBI?"

"I do. You're not suggesting *they're* friends of Harry's,
are you?"

Nick smiled at my startled response. "No, I'm saying there are bound to be other hackers out there who
can do what—to the rest of us—seems impossible."

"Like Harry's friends. So they've been at it for two
hours. Any newer messages from Harry?"

"Not yet."

THIRTY-ONE

FEELING STIFF FROM sitting cross-legged during our long conversation, I stood in the companionway and did some forward bends to loosen up. "We'll go crazy hanging around here waiting to hear from Harry or Kass," I said. "Let's head out and explore any other potential moorings for superyachts."

"You've covered the possibilities in Marin County, either by visiting them or by viewing their size accommodations online. Maybe we should be looking at San Francisco. I recall a lot of controversy back at the time of the 2013 America's Cup, about mega-yachts showing up and wanting to hang out with ringside seats for the race. Apparently, it would have been a problem if too many were moored along the San Francisco waterfront at the same time."

I opened my laptop. "Looks like something the size of the yacht we're searching for could be accommodated at two or three different piers near the Bay Bridge." Nick scooted next to me and studied the screen.

"Want to take a drive over there?"

"Might as well. At least we'd be doing something useful."

"It'll be time to eat when we get to the city. I'll buy dinner at the restaurant of your choice." Nick kissed the hollow of my neck, sending chills racing through my scalp and giving notice to other sensitive body parts.

"I'd love that, but can we have dessert first?"

Nick looked puzzled for a moment, then caught my meaning and smiled. "Oh, you mean right now?"

"The sooner, the better," I said.

"Happy to oblige."

He took my hand and led me to the forward berth. The moments we spent in each other's arms were a welcome antidote to the increasing stress we'd been under since arriving in Marin County.

An hour later, we crossed the Golden Gate, exiting on the San Francisco side. Nick stayed on Highway 101, passing Crissy Field and the Palace of Fine Arts Theatre. He left 101 at Lombard Street in the Russian Hill area, driving us down the hairpin turns that resulted in Lombard being dubbed the "Crookedest Street in the World." We proceeded from there to the famous Embarcadero, which skirted the many piers along San Francisco's waterfront. When we reached Fisherman's Wharf, Nick pulled into a parking lot.

"Now what?" I asked.

"Let's play tourist for a while. I promised you a nice dinner. How do you feel about dining al fresco on cracked crab and cocktail sauce?" He laughed when my stomach growled loud enough for him to hear. "Is that your answer?"

"Apparently." I looked up from searching on my phone. "We might as well eat now and then move on. The yacht we're looking for won't be at this pier. It accommodates boats up to a maximum of eighty-five feet."

"Are you finding any more likely locations?"

"Some. After we eat, let's take the Embarcadero to the piers closer to the Bay Bridge. I see one just south of the Ferry Building that looks promising."

We checked out the sidewalk food vendors, taking

in the mouthwatering aromas wafting from the wharf's seafood restaurants. At an outdoor crab stand, we ordered generous helpings of fresh crabmeat. With cocktail sauce and crusty French bread to complement the crab, we settled at an outdoor table. There we could watch tourists of every age, gender, and nationality pass by, speaking in myriad languages.

The sense of urgency behind our errand prompted us to finish our food more quickly than I would have liked. We weren't on a holiday, we were on a mission, and time was running out.

Nick gathered up our trash and walked to the nearest receptacle. I followed along, checking my phone again to confirm the location of the next pier we wanted to scout. We had just pulled out of the parking lot when my phone rang in my hand.

My heart quickened when I realized how many vital calls I was expecting. Was it Harry, saying he'd found Francisco? Cleo, with news about Paulo or an update about Errol Parkington's medical license? Or Kass, reporting on the DNA from the blood sample I'd collected or the bullet Nick had found?

"Nick, It's Harry. They've identified Liliana's secret account!" That news took my breath away. At last, we had a glimmer of hope.

"Excellent. What are they seeing?"

"Nothing yet. They're still working on the password. He says, stay tuned."

Nick kept his eyes on the broad, busy thoroughfare, slowing the car to avoid a jaywalking middle-aged couple laden with shopping bags. "If he gets into that email account, it won't be long before we hear more. How is your battery holding up? We don't want to miss any messages."

I glanced at my battery icon. "Shoot, it's low, but I'll squeeze off a text to Harry and tell him to send everything to both our phones. How's your battery?"

Sorry, it was low this morning, so I left my cell on the charger back on Buck's yacht. Didn't figure I'd need it for this quick recon trip. I did bring my camera, in case we spot the ship we're looking for."

We continued south on the Embarcadero, while the lowering sun to the west cast indigo skyscraper shadows across our path. As we passed the landmark Ferry Building, the Roman numerals of its iconic clock told us it was almost seven thirty.

"Nick, the pier we wanted to check first isn't too far from here. It's on the south side of the Bay Bridge."

"Are you back on your phone?" he asked.

"Just long enough to check the location. No new messages." I turned it off. "You know, if we were to spot *Seashell*, or another yacht of its size here, that raises a question."

"What's that?"

"It's about your invitation to the auction. If the people behind it are waiting until only an hour before it starts to give out the location, we'd be lucky to make it over here from Buck's yacht harbor in time. I wonder how many other potential bidders are in the same boat."

"None, would be my guess. I'm a special case because Buck and I are unknown bidders. I wouldn't be surprised if all the others have been preapproved. There can't be too many of them."

"That makes sense." I shuddered. "Makes sense in the creepiest of ways. I still don't get how you're going to pass their vetting process. You and Buck aren't exactly off the grid when it comes to checking your backgrounds."

"No, but we're also on a different grid. The dark web. That's where the vetting process for this event is going to happen."

"Fake identities? Is there no end to your surprises?"

"We've been using them for years."

"So who are you and Buck on the dark web?"

"I'm a drug pilot, of course. Buck is an entrepreneur of sorts, trafficking in any and all categories of contraband."

"Do the feds know about your dark-web identities?"

"Hope so," Nick laughed.

"That's not funny. I'm not crazy about associating with a black-market drug pilot, even if it is a ruse."

"Don't worry. Buck's got us covered."

"So, when Buck met these people in Florida, he gave them your criminal aliases so they could vet you?"

"Dead right. And that's exactly why we didn't ask for you to be invited. You have no alias. You wouldn't be found where they're looking. Not to mention this seems like a men-only event."

I broke out in something that felt like a premature hot flash. "Oh, man, this Bond stuff gets me in deeper with every question I ask."

Nick stopped for a red light. "Are you beginning to understand why I'm dead-set on your carrying a weapon?"

"Definitely, but please stop saying *dead*."

THIRTY-TWO

"Nick, we're almost there. You need to be in the left turn lane." We were still driving along the Embarcadero, nearing one of the piers south of the Bay Bridge that could accommodate a yacht the size of *Seashell*. I turned off my battery-challenged phone, hoping I wouldn't need it again.

"Got it." Nick executed a left turn into the parking area and pulled into an available space. "I don't see anyone around."

We began walking toward the pier, our vision already hampered by deepening twilight. A chill breeze whipped across the lot, making me glad I'd grabbed my windbreaker before leaving the car.

"We're losing light." I zipped my jacket. "Maybe we should have come sooner."

"I don't think so. For what we're doing, dark is on our side."

"Then let's hurry. I'd rather not have to explain to anyone why we're here."

Nick took a Giants ball cap out of his jacket pocket. He put it on, pulling the brim low, and handed another cap to me. "Here you go. We're sightseeing tourists in town for tomorrow's game, killing time by taking in the local color."

"Okay, so do we know who the Giants are playing?"

"Beats me, but I'm guessing you're about to look it up."

"Red Sox," I said, phone in hand.

"Don't forget, you're almost out of juice on that thing."

"I know." I started to turn it off, but noticed a text coming in. I stopped in my tracks. "Wait, Nick. I'm getting a message from Kass."

"At this hour on Saturday night? It must be important. Read it, but keep walking."

I read the text while trailing behind Nick.

"He says they got a hit on the blood. The DNA was in CODIS, and the name of the subject is...." I scrolled down. "Oh, my God, Nick. The subject's name is Francisco Santos. His address is in New York City. The Bronx."

That stopped Nick. "Son of a.... The Bronx?"

"I know. It's crazy, but look." I held out the phone to Nick. "Kass sent a mug shot. It looks just like the man I saw fall on the dock last weekend."

"You didn't gather that specimen immediately after he fell. Can you be sure it was his blood?"

"I took that sample only an hour later. I'm sure."

"What about the photo. You're certain it's the same guy?"

"Not a hundred percent." I searched my memory of the quick glimpse I'd caught the weekend before of the man's bloody face. "But it almost has to be the same man."

"Does Kass say what crime got the guy's DNA added to the CODIS database?"

"Graffiti."

"You're kidding. What's that about?"

I scrolled further. "He and some others were arrested a couple of months ago for marking up an empty storefront in the South Bronx."

"And that's the crime that put him in CODIS?"

"Looks like it. I know New York City has huge gang-related graffiti problems. The South Bronx probably has it worse than the other boroughs. I guess their graffiti laws are tough." I glanced at my battery icon. "I have to turn off my phone. My battery is being used up faster than I thought. It's about to die."

"First, see if you can forward that text to Harry."

"Wait. There's more." I scrolled to the bottom of the message. "Kass says the photos we sent of that bullet you found look like a match to the one that struck Paulo."

"He can tell from photos?"

"Forensic photo analysis can tell a lot. He says it's close enough that he has the Sawyer County DA convinced."

"Hope he's right." Nick started walking. "Let's get this done while we still have enough light to see where we're going."

I sent Kass's text to Harry and turned off my phone just as it died. In minutes, we reached the entrance to one of the docks and stood staring at the mist-shrouded sight of the largest yacht I'd ever seen. It dwarfed all the other crafts moored at an adjacent dock.

"That could be it," I whispered. "Can we get close enough to look for the name?"

"There are a lot of interior lights on inside," Nick said. "We'll have to be careful we aren't spotted."

"The bow is facing us. It's so dark I can't see a name displayed there. Do you see anything?"

"No. The name's more likely to be on the stern." Nick reached back and motioned with his hand. "Wait here and keep watch. I'll go ahead and see if I can spot anything on the aft end of the ship."

"I don't want you to take—"

"Don't worry. It's almost full dark, and the dock isn't lit. No one will notice me."

"I see light standards all along the dock. They could come on at any minute, Nick. It's too risky."

"Those lights are probably on a timer." He checked his watch. "I'll bet they're set to come on at nine sharp. That gives me five minutes. It'll take me three, max." He pulled a small digital camera from his jacket pocket.

"Then get going." I held my breath while I watched him move along the dock in a rapid crouch with the stealth of a cat burglar. He made it to the far end of the yacht, snapped a couple of photos, and started back toward me.

Nick had made it as far as the yacht's midsection when a man's voice shouted, "You there, stop!"

A spotlight caught Nick in its fierce glare. "Stop!" The voice boomed out again over a bullhorn.

Nick broke into a run, moving out of the spotlight's range and motioning me to hightail it back to our car. I took off, praying I wouldn't hear gunshots. Nick reached the car only seconds after me. We scrambled in and he peeled out of the parking lot and onto the Embarcadero. My heart knocked so fast, I couldn't catch my breath to speak. Nick recovered more quickly.

"It's *Seashell*," he said, "and I got the hull number."

The drive back through San Francisco to Marin County gave us time to recover. We were quiet most of the way, each considering what we'd learned and what we still needed to accomplish if we were going to rescue Liliana.

Back on Buck's yacht, I plugged my cell in to charge and opened my laptop.

"Looking for Francisco?" Nick asked.

"Might as well. Although the Bronx address has me baffled."

"You do realize that Francisco Santos is just *San Francisco* in reverse? Doesn't that seem a little fishy?"

"Not necessarily," I said. "Maybe his parents were partial to Saint Francis. He's known as the patron saint of animals and the natural environment, although that doesn't help us sort out this little Saint Francis knock-off."

"Any word back from Harry since you sent him Kass's text?"

"Not yet." I glanced at my phone, still charging.

"It's after eleven. You think he'll get back to you this late?"

"Maybe. He and his friends could easily lose track of time if they're zeroing in on that password."

"Okay, while you're prowling online for our Francisco, I'm going to hang out in the aft cabin and call Buck. I want to fill him in about *Seashell*. Maybe he'll have a progress report on getting me approved to attend that auction."

My search for Francisco Santos pulled up a South American politician and a baseball player from the Dominican Republic. There were lesser-known men of the same name on Facebook, but no one came close to matching the one I was searching for. He had told Liliana he was eighteen, but I couldn't even find a mention of a high school graduation.

"Any luck?" Nick came back into the main saloon just as I was finishing my search.

"No. He must have scoured all trace of himself off the Internet. I'm sure Catia said Liliana first met him on Facebook."

"He's not there now?" Nick sat next to me, looking at my laptop screen.

"Not in any way that I can find him. Harry and friends might know of some way to dig deeper, but I'm not savvy in the ways of hackers."

"Speaking of Harry, are you ready to give up on his contacting us tonight?"

"I guess so. We need to get some sleep."

"Okay. Now my turn. Buck heard back from the anonymous folks who sent him the invitation. I'm still being vetted. So is he, apparently. No way to know if they'll decide in our favor."

"How soon will you know?"

"That's not pinned down, but if I am approved, Buck will let me know right away. If I'm denied, Buck will be informed. All we know is the latest he'll hear either way is one hour before the start of the auction, and if it's a go, he'll be given the location. Apparently, it's easier to join the Secret Service than to become a member of this repugnant cabal."

"Meanwhile, those horrible people have poor Liliana. Nick, I can't stand this. We have to do something."

THIRTY-THREE

"ONE STEP AT a time, Aimee. Remember, if Kass has enough evidence to show probable cause to law enforcement at this end, they'll raid that yacht and recover Liliana without my going anywhere near it."

"If he can't show probable cause?"

Nick didn't look happy about my question. "Then I'll go in, buy Liliana, and get out."

"You make it sound so easy. What if they shut you out? Then what do we do?"

"Let's not get ahead of ourselves. And don't be including yourself in this rescue mission. I don't want you going anywhere near that yacht."

I didn't argue, but if it came down to desperate measures, I intended to be part of whatever it took to save that girl.

"I hope we're right about it taking place on *Seashell.*"

"There's not much doubt about that. Buck agrees."

"If you're not approved, will you and Buck end up on someone's hit list?"

"Hope not." Nick smiled, but his attempt at humor didn't reassure me.

We had just decided to shut down for the night when Nick got another call. He answered, looked at me. "It's Harry." He put the phone on speaker. "Talk to us."

"We're in. The last communication between Liliana and Francisco on the secret email account was the night of the party, before the superyacht left Horta. She sent him a photo of the craft and told him the name was *Seashell* and the destination was San Francisco. You can see the hull number in her photo."

"That's fantastic news." Nick grabbed his camera, compared the hull number to his photo and gave me a thumbs-up. "We've already located that yacht," I said. "Anything else?"

"Not much," Harry said. "He told her to keep in touch by phone and promised to meet up with her when she arrived."

"That's it?" Nick asked. "No more messages between them?"

"Not on this account. I'm guessing they were communicating by text from then on."

"We just heard from Kass about a Francisco Santos in the Bronx. His DNA matches someone Aimee saw on the dock down here last weekend. Any chance you can verify whether he's our guy?"

"The Francisco we have shows a residence address in Mill Valley, California."

"That's in Marin County," Nick said, "only a few miles north of the harbor where we're staying. Nothing to do with the Bronx."

"Must be some explanation. I'll dig around a little and let you know if I find anything to account for it." Harry read off the Mill Valley address and I wrote it down. He wished us luck before ending the call.

"Did you get that?" Nick asked.

"Yes." I pulled up a Mill Valley map on my laptop.

Nick scooted next to me and looked. "That'll be easy to find. Want to do a drive-by first thing tomorrow morning?"

"Definitely, but right now we need to get some sleep. It's almost midnight."

We locked the hatch and snuggled into our berth. Sleep had almost come when my phone rang. I groped, knocking it off the night table and onto the bed before I finally got a grip on it. Cleo was calling just after one o'clock in the morning. Galvanized, I sat straight up. A call at this hour didn't bode well for Paulo.

"What is it?" I asked. "Is it Paulo?"

"It's okay, Aimee. It's good news." Nick was awake now, leaning toward my ear.

"Wait until you hear this," Cleo said. "It was Carver who discovered what's been going on."

"Carver? What do you mean?"

"You know he's been back on Paulo's case since Prine left town this afternoon... I mean, not *this* afternoon.... It's Sunday now. I'm talking about yesterday, Saturday."

"I understand," I said. "Go on."

"Here's the thing," Cleo said. "As soon as Prine was gone, Carver ordered blood tests. Paulo's tests showed a drug in his system that can induce coma."

"Was it something Prine prescribed?"

"No. There was no order in the chart."

"That's why Paulo relapsed—medication error?"

"That's the mystery," Cleo said. "Paulo's ICU nurses swear they were giving only the appropriate drugs. They all know better than to administer the one that was in Paulo's system. They're all backing each other up, and Edna Roda is supporting them. She knows her ICU nurses, and she believes them."

Edna, TMC's chief nursing officer, was highly respected. If she vouched for her nurses, there was little chance one of them had been responsible.

"What does Quinn think?" I asked.

"He's leaning toward foul play, but he's having a hard time accepting the idea."

"Even after what you've told him about Prine and Carver?"

"I think he's almost convinced," Cleo said. "He's arranging for a third opinion. Strange as it seems, it's Carver who's insisting on it."

"That *is* strange. How soon will you be able to get someone in from out of town?"

"Dr. Sally Goldman is flying up from Sacramento Monday morning. We'll have her temporary privileges approved by the time she arrives. Meanwhile, Carver has asked that no one be allowed near Paulo—including himself—except for the ICU nurses and Dr. Poole. She's going to monitor Paulo's status until Goldman arrives."

"Good choice. I'd trust Poole with my own life."

"Kinda fitting," Cleo said, "since we already enlisted her help when Carver's CME credits came up short. He was a lot more cooperative getting that straightened out after she had a heart-to-heart with him." She paused for a moment. "I'm almost afraid to ask what's going on down there. Any new developments?"

I filled her in on everything that had happened since we last spoke: Kass identifying Francisco from the graffiti arrest, Harry pinpointing Francisco's address in Mill Valley, and Nick and I finding *Seashell*.

"What's next?" Cleo asked.

"Not sure. We need to get Kass on board about the auction, and then he's going to have to convince SFPD that there's probable cause to raid that yacht. It's in their jurisdiction."

"So you and Nick can step back? Stay out of harm's way?" Cleo sounded solemn.

"That's our plan." I had my fingers crossed.

"One last thing," Cleo said. "I requested info from the state board on Errol Parkington, the yacht club cruise captain you asked about. I won't have an answer about his medical license until tomorrow."

NICK AND I woke Sunday morning with a heavy sense of purpose. We couldn't help but acknowledge that this day would result in a new beginning for the Ferrera family or a terrible loss. We made a quick breakfast of toast and coffee, neither of us having much appetite. By eight o'clock we were on the road, heading up Highway 101 to Mill Valley with morning sunshine breaking through the coastal mist.

The GPS in Buck's car led us right to the address Harry had given. The neighborhood consisted of substantial homes on landscaped lots that spoke of affluence and community pride. Nick cruised past the house we were seeking, continuing until he reached a cross street. Slowing, he turned right, pulled to the curb, and cut the ignition.

"What do you think?"

"An upscale neighborhood," I said. "Hardly the breeding ground for a graffiti-spreading hoodlum in the Bronx."

"How about a pervert trying to lure young girls into harm's way? Let's try to flush him out."

I took out my phone. "I'll let Harry know it's time. He'll send Francisco a message from Liliana's secret email account, asking him to meet her."

"Go ahead. I'll pull back onto his street." Nick maneuvered the car into a spot with a clear view of the house. "This could take a while. Or it could be a waste of time."

I texted Harry. He responded five minutes later, saying that thanks to the *translate* function on his word processing program, he'd used a combination of English and Portuguese similar to the wording in Liliana's email messages. Francisco had taken the bait, sounding frantic because he hadn't heard from her in weeks and thought she had changed her mind about coming. When he replied, asking where Liliana was, Harry improvised, saying that she had taken a taxi to a motel in Mill Valley. She didn't have any way to pay for a room, so the desk clerk was letting her use a customer convenience computer in their lobby. I knew Harry was a quick thinker, but I had to admire his ability to morph into a runaway teenage girl at a moment's notice.

I relayed his comments to Nick.

"Excellent," he said. "Let's see who comes out of that house."

I kept my focus on the front door until a taffy-colored Cocker Spaniel pup distracted me, running up to our car barking.

"There!" Nick said. "He just came out. Is that the guy from the dock?"

I swiveled my head around just in time to catch a glimpse before our subject dropped into the blue Mustang parked in the driveway. "Yes! That's him."

Nick let the Mustang go a couple of blocks and then pulled out to follow it. It didn't take long before Francisco pulled up at the motel Harry had designated. Nick entered the lot, parking several cars away. We watched as Francisco hurried in the lobby entrance. Nick and I followed, keeping our distance.

Inside, we hung back, watching as the young man questioned the clerk, insisting that his girlfriend had just emailed him from a computer in the lobby. The clerk was perplexed, saying that was impossible. There were no computers in the lobby. Francisco stood there, shaking his head as if to clear it. He looked around. Spotting Nick and me, he approached, wild-eyed. A healing lesion on his forehead was partially covered by a thatch of dark hair. No doubt remained. He was the man I'd seen bleeding on the dock the previous weekend. A handsome boy in spite of his agitated state, tall and muscular, with the sort of teen-idol face Liliana might have fallen in love with.

"Did you see a girl in here a little while ago?" he implored. "She's eighteen, beautiful like a model, with long, shiny hair. She just emailed me from this lobby."

Eighteen? Liliana must have fudged her age by three years when she hooked up online with Francisco. I waited to see how Nick would handle the situation.

"Are you looking for Liliana?" he said. That took me by surprise, but I was sure Nick had a plan.

"Who are you?" Francisco looked as if he might bolt out of the lobby or start yelling for help. I pulled up the photo of Liliana on my phone and held it out for him to see.

"We're friends of the Ferreras. We want to help them find their daughter."

Francisco's eyes grew wide with fear. "I don't know where she is. Believe me." I thought the poor guy was going to break down and cry. I'd have bet big money he was nothing more sinister than a scared, eighteen-year-old kid.

"Let's go outside," Nick said. "We need to have a long talk."

THIRTY-FOUR

WE ADJOURNED TO the restaurant's sunny courtyard, where high-priced European sports cars cruised by on a street lined with boutiques and cafés. It took some convincing, but we managed to reassure Francisco we weren't kidnappers holding Liliana for ransom. It took a little longer to drag out everything Francisco knew about Liliana.

His story matched what my mother and I had been told by Catia when we were in Horta. He admitted to knowing she used a secret email account and the cell-phone he had provided. She told him it was because her parents were unjustly strict. When we told him she had only recently turned fifteen, he looked genuinely shocked.

"No, that can't be the same girl. She told me she turned eighteen a few weeks before I last heard from her. She said she was coming to California on a yacht."

"Francisco, look." I held out my phone again. "You see her photo, don't you? This *is* the same girl."

"Then I don't understand. Why hasn't Liliana been in touch with me? It's been a month, and now, today, when I got the email…I thought she was finally here."

"We're almost positive she *is* here," Nick said, "but if we're right, she's in grave danger. That's why we searched you out. You might help us identify the people who have her."

"Why me? I swear I didn't do anything—"

Nick turned to me. "You want to take this?"

"Are you saying you haven't even had a text from her since she left on the yacht?"

"That's right. Nothing. Something must have happened to her phone."

I didn't like thinking what that something might have been.

I pointed to the laceration on Francisco's forehead. "Tell us about last weekend. What you know about a yacht called *God's Gift*, and how you got that injury."

He reached up to touch the healing wound. "How do you know about that?"

"I was there. I saw you arguing on that boat. You ran, and you fell almost at my feet. Your head was bleeding. We're almost sure someone shot you."

"You? I saw someone hiding behind a boat. That was you?"

"Yes," I said. "Now we need to know what that was about. Please, Francisco, help us save Liliana. We're almost out of time."

"You won't tell my parents? They're prominent in this town. They would be furious if I caused a scandal."

I looked to Nick, who replied, "No promises, but we'll back you up any way we can. If I were you, I'd be more worried about several categories of law enforcement agencies than about your parents."

Francisco's eyes grew wide. Droplets of perspiration speckled his upper lip. "Okay, I'll tell you all I know."

Nick pulled out a small tape recorder and placed it on the table. "Francisco, I'm going to record what you tell us. Is that okay?"

"Will it help you find Liliana?"

"I hope so," Nick said.

"Then yes." Francisco leaned toward the recorder.

"Liliana texted me about a yacht called *Seashell*. She sent me a photo. She said she could catch a ride to California so we could meet in person. A man named Miguel was arranging for her passage."

I asked Francisco to send a copy of that photo to my phone, and he did. I encouraged him to go on with his story about Miguel.

"He was one of the Portuguese-speaking members of the crew," Francisco said. "He told Liliana she could pay for her trip by working as a maid on the voyage from the Azores back to San Francisco. They would even provide her uniforms."

"Did you get this Miguel's last name?" Nick asked.

"No. I'm sorry." Tears pooled in Francisco's eyes. Nick reached out, gripping the boy's shoulder for a moment. "Go on, you're doing fine."

"I was excited that Liliana was coming to me. She's so beautiful. I was…in love." He let a sob escape. "I thought we could run away and get married."

"You might still have your chance to meet her, Francisco. Please tell us about *God's Gift*," I urged. "Why were you there?"

"It was the man named Miguel." Francisco blinked, clearing his eyes. "I overheard him talking at a deli where my friends and I like to go. It's near the harbors. We stopped there for lunch after a bike ride."

Nick and I exchanged glances. How could it be the same Miguel who had coaxed Liliana onto the yacht? "This happened here, in Marin County, last weekend?" Nick asked.

"Yes. That man—I heard the other man call him Miguel—was speaking low at the next table, but I heard him making some sort of sales pitch. I thought he was a yacht salesman, so I tuned them out until I heard him mention a yacht called *Seashell*."

"Still no last name?" Nick kept his voice calm and encouraging.

"No, just Miguel. When he left the deli, I told my friends I had to leave. Miguel was on foot, so I followed him on my bike, taking my time so he wouldn't notice me. It wasn't difficult to gain access to the harbor where he had gone. I left my bike at the gate. I watched until he reached that yacht, *God's Gift*. I was excited, hoping he would be able to explain about Liliana. If he was the same Miguel from *Seashell*, Liliana might already be here. I didn't see him on the deck, so I went aboard to look for him."

"But I heard you arguing," I said. "What happened?"

"He came up from below decks, spotted me, and chewed me out because I boarded the yacht without asking permission."

"Did you get a chance to ask him about *Seashell*?" Nick asked.

Francisco hunched his shoulders. "I tried. I apologized about boarding the yacht and he calmed down some. When I asked about Liliana, he denied everything. He claimed he'd never heard of *Seashell*, didn't know any girl named Liliana, had never been to the Azores." Francisco stopped, out of breath.

"Okay, buddy," Nick said. "Take a break. I'll go inside and get us something to drink. Aimee will stay here with you."

While Nick was gone, I kept a close eye on the young man in case he decided to make a run for it. A few minutes had passed when his cellphone rang. He looked a question at me. Should he answer? I nodded. From his half of the conversation, I could tell it was his mother

calling. He assured her he'd be home soon. He said he'd
come to the deli to have breakfast with a friend. He
even asked her if he could bring something home for
her and his father. Not a bad effort, but I got the sense
that lying didn't come easily.

"Here we go." Nick came back with three takeout
cups. "Coffee all around." He emptied his pocket, dropping packets of sugar and creamer on the table. Francisco dumped three sugars and two creamers into his
cup, took a sip, and added another sugar.

"Ready to finish your story?" Nick asked.

"Miguel told me to get off the yacht and stay away
or I'd be sorry." Francisco squirmed in his chair, recalling, "When I refused, he pulled a gun. I thought he was
going to shoot me right there, but he smashed it against
my forehead and yelled, 'Go away if you want to live.'
I jumped to the dock and ran."

"Did you hear shooting?" I asked. I wanted to confirm that the bullet Nick found came from Miguel's gun.

"Yes, I slowed for a moment to look back. That's
when I heard at least one shot. He must have been shooting to warn me away. If he wanted to kill me, I'd be
dead."

"I expect that's true," Nick said, "but then Miguel
would have had some explaining to do."

"I'm puzzled about something," I said. "I saw you
trip on the rope and fall, then a moment later, you were
gone. How did you get away?"

"I slipped into the water," he said. "I've been on my
high school swim team all four years. It wasn't difficult
to slip into the water and hide under the dock." Francisco looked from me to Nick. "Can I go home now?
My parents are expecting me."

"We're almost finished," Nick said. "I'm curious how

you explained the head wound and the wet clothes to your parents."

"I told the truth," he said. "I slipped on the dock and into the water." He looked sheepish. "I only lied about my head. I said I banged it when I fell."

I looked at Nick. *What are we going to do with this boy?*

"All right, son. Get on home. Here's my cell number. Give us yours. If you think of anything else to tell us, text, don't call. Keep your phone on and charged. Do your parents ever check it?"

"No. They trust me. They don't check my phone or my email."

"Shame," Nick said. "If they had, everything we're dealing with here could have prevented."

BACK ON BUCK'S YACHT, Nick put in a call to Detective Kass to bring him up to date about our face-to-face meeting with Francisco. We sent Kass the matching photos of *Seashell*: the one Liliana had taken at the Horta Marina, and the ones Nick had taken the previous evening on the San Francisco waterfront. Finally, convinced that *Seashell* was the yacht Liliana was going to visit the night she disappeared, Kass agreed to contact the SFPD and request that a rescue operation be set in motion. He then ended the call abruptly, saying he had to make a lot happen very quickly, including a flight to San Francisco.

"He's sure he can get the Timbergate DA on board," Nick said, "but it won't be as easy to convince the San Francisco County DA to petition a judge for a search warrant."

"How soon will we know?"

"Kass is taking a charter flight, hoping for a face-to-face meeting in the San Francisco DA's office. He has to convince him there's probable cause, then they have to go to a judge."

"What can we do if he doesn't get the warrant?"

"Stay out of it. Kass said whatever we do, don't go aboard that yacht tonight."

THIRTY-FIVE

By four o'clock Sunday afternoon, Nick and I were going stir-crazy waiting around on Buck's yacht. We had called Harry and Cleo to report on our questioning of Francisco. Neither of them had new developments in Timbergate to share. We had heard nothing from Kass since he issued his direct order telling us to stay away from *Seashell*.

We were torn about whether to heed that warning. We'd spent countless hours over the last three weeks with one goal in mind: find Liliana. Now, when she was almost within shouting distance, we were told to stand down. Neither of us was taking it well.

"There must be something we can do, Nick. Should we head over to San Francisco?"

"I'm still not cleared to attend the auction. Let's wait to hear from Buck—and from Kass." Nick sat in the main saloon, watching me pace back and forth.

"So we sit around and do nothing? We don't even know if Kass is down here yet."

"If he is, he's bound to be busy. It might not be easy to convince the San Francisco County DA to petition a judge for a search warrant with so little evidence."

"You mean he might not get the warrant?" The thought made me physically ill. "If he doesn't, we'll *have* to do something ourselves."

Nick reached for my hand. "Come, sit. You're going

to wear a hole in the floor and fall into the engine room if you don't stop pacing."

I dropped next to Nick on the settee. "If Kass and the SFPD can't get a warrant, we have to go aboard that yacht."

"That would be impossible for you. Prine would recognize you, so don't even think about it. Parkington has met me, but he already suspects I'm a buyer, so that's not a problem." Nick rolled his shoulders, a sure sign of tension. "We have six hours. Kass could still pull it together by ten o'clock tonight."

"I know, but shouldn't we come up with an alternate plan…just in case?"

"Kass is right, Aimee. We should stay out of this." His words were saying one thing, his face another.

"We can at least brainstorm. It'll keep us from going crazy waiting to hear—"

I was interrupted by Nick's ringing cell. Finally, someone calling. I hoped it was Kass. Nick answered and his eyebrows shot up in surprise. He got up and walked to the hatch ladder, stepping up until he could look outside while he talked. I walked over, trying to hear his end of the conversation. He went up another couple of steps. I got the message. Wait until he finished the call. I guessed he had his reasons.

He came back down, looking at me with a resolute expression.

"What? Who was that?"

"It was Buck. I've been approved," Nick said, "and we were right about the location. The auction is taking place on *Seashell*. They even gave Buck directions to the pier."

"What about the time? Is it still set for ten o'clock?"

"Yes. That's confirmed."

"Six hours from now." I shook off a chill. "Then let's get back to brainstorming. I have a couple of thoughts I've been trying to sort out. Pieces that don't quite seem to fit."

"Run them by me." Nick was starting a fresh pot of coffee.

I sat at the table where he had been jotting and doodling on a notepad. "The most obvious is how Miguel, who lured Liliana onto that yacht in the Azores, could have turned up in Marin County two weeks before *Seashell* arrived in San Francisco."

"That crossed my mind," Nick said. "I did the math. Even if he left *Seashell* when it docked in Florida, which we know it did, Miguel wouldn't have been back in California in time to be the shooter who tracked Paulo to Timbergate."

"That's what's bothering me. The earliest he could have left the yacht was when it docked in Florida, but the timing isn't right. According to my research on cruising speed for that type of yacht, *Seashell* couldn't have arrived in Florida in time for Miguel to disembark, catch a flight to California, and chase Paulo all the way to Timbergate."

Nick stood up. His turn to pace. "If he's the man who shot Paulo, he was back in California in time to run interference when Paulo showed up down here looking for his sister."

"Where does that lead us? Are you suggesting someone else shot Paulo and we're wrong about Miguel?"

"Not if the bullets match, and Kass told you he was almost convinced they do."

"It doesn't seem likely there are two different Miguels in this slimy outfit."

"We're missing something." Nick gazed around the

cabin as if it held the answer. "What if he was never *on* the superyacht?"

I was stumped for a moment; then I caught his meaning. "Of course! He *wasn't* on the yacht. He stayed behind on the island when *Seashell* left."

"It's the best explanation. The parents said Paulo spent a week organizing searches for Liliana on Faial and on Pico."

"That would explain it. If Miguel was still in the Azores, he would have been tracking Paulo's attempts to discover what happened to Liliana."

Nick nodded. "And when Paulo arranged to fly to California—"

"Miguel was probably on that same flight," I finished for him.

"It's likely Paulo linked Liliana's disappearance to your Dr. Carver. Why else would he travel all the way to Timbergate and show up near Carver's office building?"

"You're thinking Miguel followed Paulo there, determined to silence him?"

"It looks that way. What we don't know is who gave the orders. Was it Carver?"

"That's the most obvious answer," I said. "But let's put that aside for a moment and take Miguel in another direction. Last weekend a man on *God's Gift* handed Kiri D'Costa an overnight bag. If that was Miguel, what does it tell us about Kiri?"

"Nothing good." Nick shook his head. "Either she's involved in this messy business, or she was two-timing Gus and doesn't have a clue about Miguel's criminal links."

"I hope she's just clueless and playing the field. Lots of women date more than one guy at a time. Doesn't mean she's twisted enough to be involved in human trafficking."

"You know, if she *is* involved, we can bet she's going to be on that yacht tonight. Didn't you say she told you she speaks Portuguese?"

I sucked in a breath. "Oh, you think she's going to be there to keep Liliana from suspecting what's really going on? A woman who Liliana thinks she can trust?"

"Hate to say it," Nick frowned, "but yes."

"That poor kid. They must have her convinced she's going to be *modeling* all the items that are up for auction. What better way to keep her compliant? She'll be having the time of her life until the truth hits."

"I imagine she'll be the last item of the evening." Nick slapped his palm on the tabletop. "I sure as hell hope Kass and the SFPD have this under control."

I looked at the time. Another two hours had slipped by and still we had not heard from Detective Kass. Where was he? My nerves were shot, and I couldn't wait any longer to speak my mind.

"Nick, we have to face facts. We've heard nothing from Kass and we're almost out of time. You'll have to go to that auction, but I'm coming with you. You'll bid on that girl, take her off that yacht, and I'll be waiting in the car to try to explain to her what's going on."

Nick shot up from where he'd been sitting. "Jesus, Aimee, even if I outbid everyone else, your being there is a crappy idea on so many levels. First, you don't speak Liliana's language. And second, there are so many ways that could go wrong, it could get all three of us killed. It's too risky."

"So we let Liliana go to the highest bidder? And how do we live with ourselves, wondering what her fate is going to be?" I pulled out my phone and brought up her photo. "Look at her, Nick. Barely fifteen. Are we going to tell her parents that we simply gave up?"

"Of course not," Nick said, "but we still have three hours. We could hear from Kass any minute."

"Then let's use the time to work out our own plan."

THIRTY-SIX

"Nick, it's almost eight o'clock. We have to decide."
We had waited so long to hear from Kass that the walls
seemed to close in on us. If we were going to show up
at that auction, it was time to get ready.

"I can't let you do it, Aimee. It's too dangerous. We'd
have to go in unarmed and without cellphones. Those
were the instructions Buck was given."

"We're not entirely unarmed," I said.

"How many times has Harry told his students not to
count on martial arts in a gunfight?"

"It's better than nothing. Besides, once you're in,
you'll outbid everyone, buy Liliana, and get her out
of there. I'll be waiting in the car with my Portuguese
dictionary and photos of her parents and Francisco. I'll
find a way to reassure her."

"All right, here's my offer," Nick ticked off his plan.
"We'll get ready, drive over to the city and find a place
to hang out and observe that pier. We'll have our phones,
so Kass can reach us as soon as he's put things together."

"You're still thinking he can pull off a raid?"

"He must be working on it. Even if he has the warrant, there's a lot of coordinating to do. We'd have heard
by now if he struck out."

"Maybe," I said, "but if he hasn't contacted us by ten
o'clock, what's our plan?"

"We'll put ourselves in place early to watch who arrives. If we don't hear from Kass in time, I'll go in. If

I don't succeed in buying her, I'll at least know who'll be leaving with the girl."

"And that's when we rescue her?" *Or die trying?* I tried to scrape that thought from my mind.

"By then," Nick continued, "if Kass is unsuccessful and he's on his own, I'm hoping he'll join up with us."

"I like that idea. Why don't you text him now? Ask for an update."

"Might as well." Nick did, and right away an answer came back. "Damn. He's got the DA on board, but they've been turned down by a dozen judges. Would you believe there are more than fifty judges in San Francisco County? No wonder this is taking so long. They're trying to contact one last judge—one of the few who doesn't own a yacht." Nick pocketed his phone. "Kass will be in touch either way, soon as she gives them an answer."

"Then let's drive over and start our stakeout, if that's cop talk for what we'll be doing."

"Close enough," Nick said. "Our phones are charged. We'll have them and our weapons with us, just in case. Kass can't object to our observing, as long as we don't get in the way."

It was close to nine when we reached the entrance to the pier. Nick drove into the unlit parking lot with our headlights out. He snugged our small, dark compact out of sight in a tight space between two large unoccupied panel trucks parked nose-in against a chain-link fence. The logos on their doors appeared to advertise a catering service. Of course—elaborate refreshments for the auction attendees. We slumped down in our seats, hoping to avoid notice.

"Do you see anyone standing guard?" I asked.

"Not yet." Nick cracked our front windows half an

inch. "I expect they'll post someone pretty soon. Eyes and ears open."

He was right. At nine thirty, a man with the build and walk of a bar bouncer advanced toward the parking area from the direction of the dock. He stood alert, watching as a set of headlights shot an arc across the lot. A limousine turned in. The first arrival. It pulled up close to the dock entrance, allowing three men to unload. They were stopped by the guard, who took a moment to look at something one of the men handed him. They were patted down then allowed to proceed to the yacht.

The limo backed up, giving us a good view of its lighted license plate number before it drove away.

"I got the plate number," I said.

"Good. It might be helpful. Probably a livery service from the airport. Apparently, most of the bidders are from out of town. This location makes sense, now that I think of it. A quick, straight shot to and from SFO. They arrive, do their business, and leave on a chartered flight with whatever they've bought."

"No commercial airline security checks or hassles, and no one's the wiser. Disgusting."

"But clever."

A few minutes passed, and another limo pulled in. Same routine, only with one passenger. By quarter to ten, we had counted a dozen people arriving. All of them were men, mostly late middle-aged, dressed in business suits.

Just before ten, one more vehicle arrived. When the limo stopped, a slender woman in dark slacks and a blazer stepped out. Even in the faint illumination provided by the adjacent dock lights, I recognized Kiri D'Costa. The man who stepped out behind her was much younger than the others we'd seen. He wore a dark suit.

"Nick, is that Gus Barba?" I whispered.

"No. I'm thinking it's her other boyfriend, Miguel." Nick turned to me. "She's definitely mixed up in this."

"That means you can't go in, either," I said, suddenly deflated. "She'll recognize you."

We sat in the dark for half an hour watching the posted guard, whose shadowy movements were back-lit by the dock lights. He alternated between puffing on cigarettes and checking his phone. We were on his list of bidders. Was he waiting for us to show up? Despite Nick's attendance being preapproved, we were shut out. Kiri had seen to that. Even worse, she might have guessed that we were on to her. I suspected that guard was not waiting to greet us as last-minute arrivals. He was waiting to take us out.

Nick suddenly sat up and pulled out his phone. "A text." He read quickly. "Kass says they got the warrant."

"We don't have to leave, do we? Not until we're sure Liliana is safe."

"Kass doesn't know we're here. He said to stay away. Now that we know SFPD is on the case, we can't interfere. They'll want the element of surprise when they arrive. No one knows what's on that yacht. They're bound to be heavily armed. If we pull out now, we'll alert that guard."

Nick and I sat in tense silence. "They'd better hurry," I said. "Who knows how much longer this auction will last?"

"Long enough," Nick said. "Look, SFPD is here."

A convoy begin creeping into the parking area, lights out. Two bulky SWAT vehicles entered, followed by half a dozen SFPD cruisers. The thrumming of a helicopter grew in volume as it came closer. The smoking guard's head jerked up. Pivoting, he started to run toward *Seashell*'s gangway and had almost made it when a K-9 leapt on his back, sending him sprawling face down.

Nick and I slid down in the front seat of our car, hoping we wouldn't be noticed between the two large delivery vans.

The next moment, we were assaulted by an explosion of sound. The deafening, relentless *thump-thump* percussion of the helicopter's blades drummed the air over our heads, sending shockwaves throughout my body. Its spotlight turned night into day as it trapped *Seashell* in its glare.

The back doors of the panel trucks on either side of us crashed open, spewing at least two dozen uniformed officers wearing tactical vests and helmets. I saw lettering on the back of one officer's vest as he ran toward the dock. What I expected was the SWAT logo. What I saw emblazoned there was "DEA."

"Nick," I whispered, "what's going on? Did Kass say he'd contacted DEA?"

"No. I had no idea."

"Cripes! We've been sitting right here between them for almost an hour, but they didn't chase us off."

"They couldn't, not without giving themselves away."

We witnessed the combined forces of SFPD officers, their SWAT team, and the DEA enforcement personnel swarming the yacht, holding deadly weapons at the ready and barking commands. The thundering of the helicopter muffled every other sound, but the sense of urgency came through. None of it gave us a clue about Liliana's fate.

"Nick, look on the dock. Is that Kiri coming this way? She's dragging someone along with her." The area where we were parked had been deserted by the troops, who were still aboard the yacht. "There's no one out here to stop her. Does she have Liliana?"

Kiri came directly toward where we were parked. We slumped down, hoping she wouldn't spot us. I heard her open the door of one of the DEA's phony delivery trucks.

"Nick," I whispered, "we can't let her get away. We have to do something."

"Get your weapon ready." He opened his door, whispering, "Go."

We had surprise on our side and were able to come at Kiri from behind as she was trying to hoist the limp body of a woman into the passenger side of the truck.

"Stop!" Nick shouted. His gun was pointed at Kiri's head. "Put her down. Gently."

My gun was aimed at Kiri's midsection, but I was sickened at the thought of sending a bullet into her vital organs. Her reply to Nick took a moment for me to comprehend.

"Thank God!" She gently lowered the young woman to the ground. "Aimee, this girl's been drugged. Can you get her to the UCSF Med Center at Mission Bay?" I looked at the face of the girl lying on the ground between us. *Finally, Liliana.*

"What?" I said. "How did you...?"

Kiri read the confusion on my face. "I'm DEA," she said. "Please do this. They're expecting her. She's stable for now, but we don't know what drugs are in her system."

"Of course." I looked at Nick. "We'll do it."

"Good," Kiri said. "Take the Embarcadero south to King Street, then go left on Fourth. It's only minutes away. You can't miss it. I'll explain later. I have to go back. There's another girl in there."

"Want some help?" Nick asked. "I have some previous experience with your agency."

Kiri nodded. "I'll take your word for it, but it's bad in there. A couple of officers are down."

Nick lifted Liliana into the backseat of Buck's car and put the keys in my hand. "I'll meet you at the hospital as soon as I can." He turned to Kiri. "Let's go."

I set the GPS for backup, and then pulled out of the parking lot, intent on following Kiri's directions. I adjusted my rearview mirror to keep a visual check on Liliana. She remained limp and unconscious.

The first stoplight I came to turned red as I approached. Tension strained my patience. A dark SUV pulled up next to me in the lane to my right. The man behind the wheel looked like the same man who had arrived at the yacht with Kiri.

Miguel.

Was *he* DEA as well? Or had Kiri been cozying up to him undercover to get the goods on *Seashell*? His next move was my answer. He pointed a handgun at my head. Red light or not, I shot through the intersection. He followed.

THIRTY-SEVEN

GREAT. A SAN FRANCISCO car chase. I was caught up in a movie cliché. I couldn't imagine myself rocketing through city traffic at midnight with Miguel dead-set on taking both Liliana and me out of the witness pool. No way did I want to risk my life or Liliana's, not to mention the lives of innocent bystanders. The trouble was, I had no other choice.

I drove the little compact as fast as I dared, jockeying around other vehicles, maneuvering to put a few of them between myself and Miguel. He bullied his way around them, nearly driving one or two off the road. The engine in my car was no match for the power of his. I readjusted the rearview mirror, hoping to see him falling behind, but instead he was gaining.

"Ajuda! Where I am?" A bewildered voice with a heavy Portuguese accent rose from the backseat. The worst timing ever. Liliana was waking up. *"Onde estou?"* I heard rustling, angled the rearview mirror again and saw her struggling to sit upright.

"Down!" I shouted. She blinked, looked around, dazed. "Get down," I said again, cursing my lack of her language. I heard a loud crack and realized a bullet had punched through the back window. A look in the rearview mirror confirmed it. A spider web of cracks with a hole in the center spread across the window. I prayed Liliana wasn't hit, but she was out of sight. Crouching on the floor, or struck by that bullet?

We'd gone several blocks when I looked in the rear-view again, calling out to Liliana. Too late, I faced forward, approaching an intersection where a homeless man shuffled along directly in my path, pushing a shopping cart piled with his meager belongings. I slammed on my brakes, barely missing him and sending my little compact spinning donuts in the center of the intersection. By the time I came to a stop, I realized Miguel had swerved to avoid me and ended up squished against the nose of a heavy-duty garbage truck coming from the opposite direction. The burly truck driver stood peering into Miguel's window.

I shouted, "Is he alive?"

"Yeah," he yelled back, "but he's pretty messed up. I'm calling the cops." He held up his phone, waving it at me.

"I have a sick girl with me," I shouted. "We're on our way to the hospital." I got out to check on Liliana. She was on the floor in the backseat, no longer conscious. I examined her and found no blood, no sign she'd been hit by Miguel's bullet.

I called out to the truck driver, "I can't stay. I'll be glad to testify once I get my girl to the hospital. You can take a photo of my driver's license, but hurry!"

I pulled out my phone and clicked a few hurried shots of the scene while he jogged over, his torso straining the fabric of a blue T-shirt emblazoned with the late Merle Haggard's whiskered face. He pointed his phone at my license and clicked.

I put my license away and tossed my purse in the front seat. "That man was trying to kill me," I said. "Don't let him get away."

"You got it, lady. I saw his weapon." He gave me a thumbs-up.

I started to get back in the car, when the homeless man shuffled over with his hand out. I set my phone down on the front seat while I leaned in to grab my purse. I handed him thirty dollars. All the bills in my wallet. The least I could do, after I'd nearly killed him. He nodded his thanks and slowly made his way to the sidewalk.

Back in the car, I prayed it would start. It did. The confused GPS was recalculating, but I'd made it to the intersection of King and Fourth Streets. From there, I knew the way. As I drove off, the homeless man waved at me, beaming with a toothless smile.

THIRTY-EIGHT

IN THE WEE hours of Monday morning, I sat at Liliana's bedside in the Emergency Room watching her eyelids and fingertips, praying for any sign of movement. Blood had been drawn and she had been given Narcan, a drug commonly used to reverse overdoses. The ER doctor seemed confident Liliana would pull through, but waiting was taking its toll. The thought of both Ferrera children in comas was almost more than I could bear. But that was only half my misery. I'd had no word from Nick.

Kiri had reached the hospital not long after I did, escaping unscathed from the firefight at the yacht. She had managed to rescue the other drugged, abducted girl, and both of them arrived via helicopter. In a vigil similar to mine, Kiri sat at the second girl's bedside in an ER cubicle next to Liliana's.

Kiri had told me the battle was over and her fellow agents were sorting out the damages on both sides. All the bidders who had attended the auction were in custody, along with the auction's organizers and armed enforcers—at least those who weren't in the hospital or the morgue. Bodies were in the process of being identified. No word so far about Dr. Prine or Errol Parkington, except that both had been at the auction.

No word about Nick, either. I closed my eyes, refusing to consider the prospect of life without him.

"Aimee?" I heard Kiri's soft voice. I opened my eyes. "Want some company?"

"Sure. How's your girl doing?" I asked.

"She's coming out of it. Her name's Sarita, by the way. It means 'little princess.' How about your girl?"

"Not yet. I've been watching. Hoping." Kiri's somber face prompted me to ask about her fellow officers.

"Keeping my fingers crossed. We have two in surgery."

"Mind if I ask another question?"

Kiri managed a weak smile. "Go ahead. I owe you some answers."

"Are you really Sanjay's cousin?"

Kiri laughed softly. "Yes, but not his first cousin from India. I'm second-generation American...from Illinois. Sanjay and I are distant relatives, but we had never met until I needed the undercover job in Dr. Carver's office."

"Does Sanjay know you're DEA?"

"He does now. I spoke to him a little while ago. He said Quinn's arranged to have Liliana's parents flown down. Nick's co-pilot will fly them here in one of Buck Sawyer's planes."

I hoped Harry would come along with Rella and the Ferreras. I needed my brother in case of bad news about Nick.

"How soon will they arrive?"

"Another hour or so," Kiri said.

I glanced at Liliana. "I hope she'll be awake when her parents get here. They've spent enough time at her brother's bedside in TMC."

"How's he doing? Any word?"

"I'm told he's emerging from his coma, but we've been through this before. The last time it happened, he relapsed."

"Paulo?"

"Yes. That's his name. You must know it was his gunshot wound that prompted Nick and me to get involved in this case."

"I do, Aimee." Kiri smiled. "But it wasn't me who just spoke his name." She nodded toward the bed where Liliana lay. "It was her."

I drew a quick breath and grabbed the nurse's call button.

"*Onde estou?*" The girl stared at me. "*Onde é o Francisco?*"

I looked at Kiri. "What is she saying?"

"She's asking where she is. And she's asking for someone named Francisco. Do you know who she means?"

Puzzled, I said, "You mean you don't?"

"No. We haven't run across that name in our investigation. It was only recently that we became aware that the two girls were on the yacht. We've been tracking this operation for quite some time, but our focus was drugs and other contraband. We weren't aware of human trafficking." Kiri glanced toward Liliana. "What shall I tell her?"

"Please tell her that her parents will be here soon. It's probably best we don't mention Francisco."

Kiri spoke in Portuguese to Liliana, who seemed confused, but simply nodded and closed her eyes.

Eric, the nurse who'd been checking on Liliana, came by to take her vitals. As he spoke to her, Kiri interpreted. Liliana managed to open her eyes and murmur responses.

Eric said he would alert the doctor. Arrangements were being made for the hospital's medical interpreter to come in. He left, asking us to use the call button if we noticed any changes.

"I should get back to my charge," Kiri said. "We're still trying to figure out where she's from. All we have so far is her name."

"She wasn't taken from the Azores?" I asked.

"Not as far as I can tell. We're thinking runaway from the Miami area. We're thinking she's Cuban American. I'm pretty sure she's bilingual—Spanish and English—but she's still pretty incoherent."

"Are you as disgusted by this as I am?"

Kiri's lips twisted. "I am. Just when I'm convinced human beings can't think of anything worse to do to each other, someone comes up with another creative way to prove me wrong."

"We're not all like that," I said.

"Of course not." She stood, looked down at Liliana. "That's why we keep doing what we do and hoping we're tilting the odds in favor of decency and humanity." She blushed. "Listen to me. I sound like a self-righteous hypocrite."

"Why do you say that?"

"Because that scum Miguel is in critical condition, and I don't have a forgiving bone in my body where he's concerned. I honestly don't care if he survives. It was his idea to auction those girls. I just wish I'd known what he was up to before he drugged them."

"The doctors have determined that neither girl has been attacked or molested. That's something to be grateful for."

"That's because they were tricked into feeling safe until the night of the auction. And because they were being advertised as virgins. Miguel and the *Seashell* crew members had been warned to keep their hands off the merchandise."

"You know, Miguel's in critical condition because of me. I caused his accident."

Kiri nodded. "I heard about that."

"Have you heard the odds of him surviving?"

"So-so. If he does, he'll have one of the ugliest faces on death row. Does that bother you?"

"Not so much," I said. She snickered, I giggled. Clearly inappropriate considering the setting and circumstances, but the tension of the night had caught up with us. We had to release it somehow.

Kiri went back to check on Sarita. I was glad we at least knew her name. She deserved an identity more fitting than *Jane Doe*.

Both girls were soon admitted to the ICU. Because neither girl had family available, Kiri was permitted to stay with Sarita. I was allowed to sit with Liliana.

On our way up to the ICU, I asked Kiri if she'd heard any news about Nick.

"No. I'm only hearing about the people in my task force," she said. "Nick hasn't called you?"

"I don't know. I've lost track of my phone. I used it to take photos of the accident. When I got here, I couldn't find it."

Then it dawned on me. *The homeless man.* No wonder he was smiling so happily as he waved goodbye. Oh, well. I *had* almost killed him.

"I'll see what I can find out," Kiri said.

She went back to sit with Sarita. I settled into the bedside chair in Liliana's ICU cubicle. It was soft and comfy, made more so when her nurse brought me a blanket and a pillow. Although it was past two in the morning and Liliana was progressing well, I wouldn't give in to sleep. Not until I knew if Nick was safe.

"Aimee." A familiar voice called my name from the depths of a dream. I was walking on a pier with a curly-haired, sleepy baby riding in a carrier strapped to my chest. The baby's eyes were the same stunning shade of turquoise as the pristine seawater ringing the beaches of the Azores Islands. The same shade of turquoise as Nick's. The baby had just drifted off to sleep against my chest when I heard the voice again.

"Aimee?"

"*Shhh*, you'll wake her," I mumbled.

"It's okay, sweetheart. She's awake."

"Nick?" My eyes slowly opened, tugging me out of the dream. "Are you really here?" I was clutching a pillow to my chest.

He set the pillow aside and raised me up into his arms. "I'm here."

I sobbed, unable to stop myself. "I was so afraid."

Liliana's parents were sitting on either side of her bed, holding her hands. "When did they arrive? How long have I been sleeping?"

"A few hours," Nick said. "The Ferreras have been here awhile. I thought we'd give them some time alone with Liliana. Feel like walking down the corridor to the waiting room?"

Several familiar faces looked up when Nick and I walked in. Harry and Rella were there. So was Buck. The fourth face I'd seen only twice before. It was a remorseful-looking Francisco Santos, sitting next to a middle-aged couple who had to be his parents. After introductions, we asked about Francisco's graffiti arrest.

The Santos family had been visiting relatives in the

Bronx, when two of Francisco's older male cousins decided to initiate him into city life. An hour of fun with a few cans of spray paint had resulted in Francisco's DNA turning up in CODIS.

THIRTY-NINE

Faial, The Azores

PETER'S CAFÉ SPORT in Horta bustled with the usual yachting clientele on the bright, breezy afternoon that our group of happy tourists dropped in. A month had passed since the raid on *Seashell*.

Fado music streamed from speakers high on the walls, accompanying the lively conversations going on around the room. Mouthwatering aromas redolent of Portuguese cuisine shifted our appetites into high gear. Our party started with Nick and me and two couples: Harry and Rella and Kiri D'Costa and Gus Barba. Gus wasn't exactly a tourist, having lived there for a time before moving on to Marin County. Then there was Buck Sawyer, on his own since his wife had taken a pass in favor of renting a villa in Belize with a few of her friends. It was heartwarming to see Paulo Ferrera well enough to join us. He was still using a walker, but he was healing, and his brain function had not been impaired by the drug-induced coma.

We found a convenient table and ordered beers and *pão de alho*, Pete's famous garlic bread.

The Ferrera family had remained in Timbergate until Paulo was well enough to be flown home in one of Buck's planes. By the time they were ready to return to the Azores, the rest of us had decided to make another attempt at a vacation. This time, with no mystery to solve.

All the law enforcement agencies involved, including the DEA, had determined that Errol Parkington, BWYC Cruising Captain and former TMC neurosurgeon, was enmeshed in the trafficking ring, as was Dr. Oliver Prine. To my surprise and Cleo's, Dr. Godfrey Carver was completely ignorant of their illegal activities, even though Carver and Prine co-owned not only *God's Gift* but also the new medical building in Timbergate.

Everyone had been wondering how Paulo fit in. We were finally hearing his story.

Paulo knew that some of the marina dock workers were more honest than others. In the week before he flew to California, he found the worker who had been bribed by Miguel to refuel *Seashell* without documenting the superyacht's presence at the marina. Paulo didn't get the yacht's name, but he elicited enough information to point to Marin County and the Bay Wind Yacht Club. His informant begged Paulo not to tell the police about the bribe. He had a family to feed and couldn't afford to lose his job, but that was only part of the problem. Miguel had threatened the dock worker's family. That detail had convinced Paulo to keep the bribe from the police.

Paulo interrupted his narrative to sip his beer, clearly uncomfortable with all the attention. Kiri spoke to him in Portuguese, and Gus added a few words, apparently reassuring him enough to continue.

After he arrived in Marin County to look for Gus, he had made a crucial mistake. He spotted Miguel on *God's Gift* and heard him speaking Portuguese. Paulo hadn't been able to find Gus, so he questioned Miguel about BWYC, telling him that he was looking for a superyacht and the people who had abducted his sister. He revealed that information without first asking for a name, which gave Miguel a chance to lie about this identity.

In Paulo's defense, although he had heard Catia's story about a man who had lured them onto the yacht, he assumed that man was still somewhere in the Atlantic Ocean, not in Marin County.

We learned that Miguel had contacted Oliver Prine for instructions. Prine's orders were to get Paulo to Timbergate. There were many isolated areas in Sawyer County where, if it came to that, his body would never be found. But first, Miguel must convince Paulo to go along willingly without getting suspicious. Miguel drove Paulo to Timbergate in the guise of helping him locate his sister. He timed the drive so they would arrive at Prine's office before dawn.

Miguel stopped at Carver and Prine's new building, left Paulo in the car, and went inside to find Dr. Prine. By this time, Paulo was having serious doubts about Miguel, who seemed more nervous and jumpy with each passing minute. While waiting for Miguel, Paulo searched the car for anything that might explain the man's shifty behavior. He found registration papers in the glove box made out in Miguel's name and immediately left the car. He had gone only a few feet when Miguel exited the building, caught sight of him and called him back.

Paulo ran off, veering around behind the building and ducking down the embankment toward the river. He heard gunshots and ran for cover under the bridge, unaware that he'd been hit until his legs buckled and he fell on the rocky beach in full view of the homeless people camped there. Fortunately for Paulo, one of those people happened to be Tango Bueller, CI for the Timbergate Police Department. We all knew the rest of the story.

Miguel had survived and been detained, along with the other thugs working for the traffickers. Charges against them, and the jurisdictions, were being sorted out. Other leads might still lead to additional arrests. Prine and Parkington remained in custody.

Dr. Godfrey Carver's innocence didn't excuse his being a pain in the rear, but it did leave TMC with one highly qualified neurosurgeon. Jared Quinn was busy trying to recruit a couple more.

FORTY

THE FOOD OUR group had ordered arrived, along with another round of beers. Paulo stood, holding up his drink and speaking in Portuguese.

Kiri interpreted for him. "He says that he and his sister thank us. Their parents cannot begin to express the gratitude they feel for what we've done to make their family whole again."

I choked up as I looked around and realized that it had taken all of us, along with the DEA, Detective Kass, the SFPD and its SWAT team to pull off the raid.

I asked Kiri if she had heard anything more about Francisco Santos. "Is he being charged with any crime?"

"No. But his parents are keeping him on a short leash." She grinned. "From what I hear, he's a decent kid. Almost too innocent for his own good. That's how he and Liliana got themselves caught in the middle of our mission."

"What about Liliana?" I asked. "Do you think she's learned her lesson?"

"Probably." Kiri smiled. "Her parents have threatened to send her to a convent school on the Portuguese mainland if she steps out of line again."

"That should do it," I said. "Considering how much she cares about fashion and designer clothing, the thought of wearing a convent uniform for the next three years would scare her straight faster than the threat of another abduction."

"What about the other girl?" I asked. "Did you find her parents?"

"Unfortunately, no," Kiri said. "It turns out she was orphaned and homeless. The good news is we were able to place her with a Cuban-American foster family in Miami. I hear she and Liliana promised to stay in touch."

"Here's to happy endings." Nick raised his beer. We all joined in the toast.

With evening coming on, the members of our party broke up to head their separate ways. Nick and I had decided to get an early start the next morning, taking the ferry to Madalena. We were finally going to have our chance to hike to the summit of Mt. Pico.

Outside Pete's Café, Nick took my hand. "Want to walk the marina before we go back to your parents' house?"

"Sure."

Holding hands and walking with Nick had never seemed as special as it did that evening.

The air was comfortably cool, with the sun riding low in the west, about to dip into the sea. As we walked along, enjoying the tinkling music of riggings moving in the breeze, I noticed a young couple strolling toward us. The woman wore a baby carrier on her chest like the one I'd seen on the mother back in Marin County.

Their lively child was obviously a little girl, decked out in a pink fleece jacket and a matching knit beanie with a fluffy pom-pom on top. As the family came near, the baby's joyful, bubbling laugh set dimples dancing on her rosy cheeks.

After they passed by, I flashed back to the evening in Boston when James O'Brien had asked if I was thinking of starting a family. I had told him Nick and I were taking our time. Then I recalled how delighted Nick was several months ago when his nephew was born and he was asked to be the baby's godfather. I wondered then how he would react to having a child of his own.

Back to the present, I turned toward Nick. "Did you see the dimples on that baby?"

"What baby?" he said.

"With the couple who just passed by."

We both turned, glancing behind us. The little family had disappeared from sight.

"I guess I missed it," Nick said.

Why had I taken such notice of that little family? And of the other couple I'd seen walking the dock back in Marin County with their baby? And why the dream about carrying a child of my own? Was it because of James O'Brien's offhand comment back in Boston? Sooner or later, Nick and I would have to talk.

I thought about his dangerous work, and about the risks he and I had faced in the past, not just during Liliana's rescue. Nick's recent revelations about the intrigue and danger involved in his work for Buck Sawyer cast the idea of raising a family in a stark and troublesome light. Considering the trouble we had been getting ourselves into, what kind of parents would we make?

Nick's next comment interrupted my thoughts. "There are no babies in sight now. Are you sure about what you saw?"

"Of course. They passed by just a few minutes ago." I turned in a full circle but still saw no sign of the family.

He stopped my spinning, put an arm around my shoulder, and kissed my forehead. "Aimee, you seem a little worked up. Is something bothering you?"

"Maybe, but I don't know if we're ready to talk about it."

A light dawned in Nick's eyes. "Ah, babies. That's it, isn't it? Your clock is ticking."

"Come on, my clock will still be ticking ten years from now, but remember your reaction when I told you about Kiri's concealed weapon? Right away, you thought she was pregnant. Somehow that must have stuck in my mind. It got me thinking about whether people who go around carrying concealed weapons are parent material. Maybe that's why I've been seeing babies everywhere. I even dreamed…."

Nick took my hand and led me to one of the marina's concrete benches. "Let's sit. I'm thinking this could take a while." I let him pull me toward the bench and a conversation that might scuttle our second attempt at a romantic island vacation.

The sun had dipped into the sea, cloaking us in azure shadows deepening toward indigo. Light fixtures placed low at intervals along the marina cast muted pools of illumination along the walkway. In the tranquil semi-darkness, water licked against the hulls of nearby yachts moored in their slips, while their riggings danced to the rhythm of the tide.

Nick took my hand and broke the silence between us. "Ready to tell me what's on your mind?"

"I might as well, since you've already put the subject on the table." A waft of chilly air passed over me, causing an involuntary shudder.

"Hey," Nick chuckled, "was that your gut reaction to the idea of motherhood?"

"No, but you have to admit the topic of having children seems to be the elephant in the room."

"Or in our case, maybe the whale on the dock," Nick said. "We're in the middle of an ocean, so we might as well go with seafaring metaphors."

That earned him a laugh and lightened the moment. "Okay," I said, "but to extend the metaphor, we need to decide whether that whale could turn out to be Moby Dick."

"Wait. You're worrying that a talk about kids could sink us?"

"That's just it. We've never discussed our future, and now that I know what your job entails—the dangers and intrigues—it's started me thinking. Maybe you don't see yourself in the role of family man." I shivered again, this time from the emotion of the moment.

"Let's put that aside for a moment." Nick snuggled closer and put his arm around my shoulder. "Better?" I nodded. "Then tell me, if you had kids, what kind of parents would you want them to have?"

"I'd want them to have parents like my own. Loving, kind, honest, courageous. Parents who have the special kind of love and courage it takes to marry as an inter-racial couple."

"We have that covered," Nick said. "What else?"

"I'd want us to teach them to look beyond their own egos and desires and find ways to improve the lives of others."

"You work in a hospital; I work for a foundation that battles the illegal drug trade. I think we've got that covered, too."

"We have it all covered, Nick, except for the whale on the dock." I took his arm from my shoulders, turned toward him and linked my hands with his. "I want my kids to grow up with two parents who are alive and safe and well. How do we guarantee them that?"

Nick pulled me into an embrace. "How can any parents guarantee that?" He kissed my forehead. "And speaking of your parents, last month when I went sailing with your dad, he quoted his favorite saying about sailing. Want to hear it?"

"I know the one you mean. *A ship is safe in harbor, but that's not what ships are for.*"

"There you go," Nick said. "No guarantees. If having a family *is* in our future, I expect that there will still be occasions when either or both of us will have to leave the harbor. That's the best I can offer." He didn't say take it or leave it, and I didn't want him to.

"You're right, of course. I know there are no guarantees. Anyone who works in a hospital realizes that."

"So are we okay for now?" Nick said. "Is our ship still afloat?"

"We're okay." I leaned into his physical warmth, treasuring it. "I'm glad we talked."

"So am I, but we need to get off this metaphorical ship and onto dry land. We have a big day tomorrow on Pico. What do you say we turn in a little early?"

"We might as well," I said. "We do have that mountain to climb."

* * * * *